The Blood Moon Feeds on N
A Noir Urban Fantasy N

This is a work of fiction. Names, characters, organizations, places, events, and incidents are either products of the author's imagination or are used fictitiously. Any resemblance to actual persons, living or dead, or actual events is purely coincidental.

Copyright © 2023 by Douglas Lumsden
All rights reserved.
ISBN: 9798396874329

No part of this book may be reproduced, or stored in a retrieval system, or transmitted in any form or by any means, electronic, mechanical, photocopying, recording, or otherwise, without express written permission of the publisher.

Cover design and art by Arash Jahani (www.arashjahani.com)

The Blood Moon Feeds on My Dreams:
A Noir Urban Fantasy Novel

By

Douglas Lumsden

To Rita. Always.

Books in this Series

Alexander Southerland, P.I.

Book One: *A Troll Walks into a Bar*

Book Two: *A Witch Steps into My Office*

Book Three: *A Hag Rises from the Abyss*

Book Four: *A Night Owl Slips into a Diner*

(Standalone Novella): The Demon's Dagger

Book Five: *A Nymph Returns to the Sea*

Book Six: *The Blood Moon Feeds on My Dreams*

Table of Contents

Chapter One 1
Chapter Two 11
Chapter Three 23
Chapter Four 33
Chapter Five 43
Chapter Six 51
Chapter Seven 61
Chapter Eight 71
Chapter Nine 79
Chapter Ten 87
Chapter Eleven 97
Chapter Twelve 107
Chapter Thirteen 119
Chapter Fourteen 127
Chapter Fifteen 135
Chapter Sixteen 145
Chapter Seventeen 153
Chapter Eighteen 163
Chapter Nineteen 173
Chapter Twenty 181
Chapter Twenty-One 193
Chapter Twenty-Two 203
Chapter Twenty-Three 211
Chapter Twenty-Four 219
Chapter Twenty-Five 229
Chapter Twenty-Six 239

Chapter Twenty-Seven 249
Chapter Twenty-Eight 257
Chapter Twenty-Nine 263
Chapter Thirty 269
Chapter Thirty-One 277
Chapter Thirty-Two 287
Chapter Thirty-Three 295
Chapter Thirty-Four 303
Chapter Thirty-Five 311
Chapter Thirty-Six 321
Epilogue 329

Chapter One

    I tipped the scales that morning at two hundred fourteen point nine pounds and decided to celebrate with a bottle of beer and a shot of rye. The beer was my reward for losing fifteen pounds over the past three months, and the shot was for dropping that extra point one.
    I was feeling good about myself, having just finished a ten-mile run through the city in time to watch the sun rise over the building containing my downstairs office and upstairs apartment. After a shower, I toasted a waffle and covered it with peanut butter and sliced bananas. No maple syrup, though. I still needed to lose another five pounds to meet the goal I'd set for myself. No, not five, I reminded myself, but four point nine. Well, maybe just a bit of syrup then. I'd earned it.
    With breakfast out of the way, I checked my cellphone for messages. The P.I. racket has its peaks and valleys, especially a two-bit one-man operation like mine, and I hadn't worked a case in four weeks. All the dough I'd received from that one had gone toward keeping a roof over my head, frozen pizzas and beer in the fridge, and the Dragon Lord's government off my back. My annual tax payment to the Realm of Tolanica had strangled my bank account and left it on life support, and I needed to drum up some business before the August rent came due. Either that or I'd have to cut back on booze. I considered my options and made a mental note to call Lubank later in the day to see if he had any work for me.
    As it turned out, I didn't need to.
    When it came to modern communications technology, I had to admit I was something of a dinosaur. Somehow, I'd managed to run my one-man investigation agency for nearly a decade without much of an internet presence beyond a phone listing, relying instead on word of mouth and repeat business from a few established clients, especially Robinson Lubank, attorney at law. A few days earlier, however, my friend Walks in Cloud, a computer wizard with few peers, had set me up with a brand-new holy shit professional website on the internet. I'd been reluctant to change my way of operating, but she'd told me I was too young to be acting as if I'd been born in the Stone Age. I might look like a fuckin' cave man, she'd said, but it was time for me to accept the fact

that I worked in a modern world, a world that existed as much in electromagnetic radio waves as in trees and mud. The thing with Walks in Cloud is that she was both intelligent *and* persistent. With more than a little reluctance, I let her teach me how to use the new tool she'd given me out of the goodness of her heart.

I'd just picked up my phone to call Lubank, when it buzzed to alert me that someone was trying to contact me on my new internet site. I clicked on the link and found a message from a Mrs. Clara Novita:

> Dear mister Sutherland. I hope you can help me. My son Jalen has been disappearing at night and he wont tell me jack shit about what he is doing. I called the police but they wont do nothing about it. Help me please he is 16 and a good boy and not in a gang. He has never run off anywhere without telling me before. What he is doing now is not rite. Please call me riteaway. I will be home because I cannot bare to go to work because I am worried sick. Thank you.

A phone number had been typed into the box provided on the electronic form.

I had to admit I was impressed. It had all worked just the way Walks had told me it would. Someone had found my website, filled in the online form, and my phone had notified me that a potential client was waiting to hear from me. It seemed like science fiction to me, like I'd been asleep and awakened in the world of the future. Was this the way my competitors worked? Maybe Walks was right. Maybe I really *had* been living in a cave.

Still fearing the whole thing could be a prank, or a mistake, I reread the message, considering what I might learn from it. The language in the note wasn't refined, but Mrs. Novita was literate enough. With my eleventh-grade working-class education, I certainly had no room to be judgmental about anyone's spelling, punctuation, or grammar. I could even forgive her for leaving the 'o' out of Southerland. People made that mistake all the time. Mrs. Novita had a job and went "to work" rather than to "the office," which told me she probably wasn't well heeled. She had a son, Jalen, who was old enough to get a driver's license, quit school, and make babies. But her son was a "good boy." He lived at home with his mother, and he wasn't in a gang. Boys his age were prone to displaying a lot of angst-induced rebellion, but, according to Mrs. Novita, her son hadn't been in the habit of running off somewhere on a whim, not until recently at least. But now he was disappearing at night and keeping his activities secret from his mother. Mrs. Novita had been worried enough to call the police, not that they were likely to be of any help. They'd assume the boy was out having some fun that he didn't want to tell his old lady about. I wondered if the boy had a father. Mrs. Novita hadn't mentioned one, but that might not mean anything. The message box had a character limit and wasn't meant to include more than a brief summary of the problem. I reread the message one more time and considered it.

My gut instinct told me the message was from a genuine potential client, and that Walks in Cloud hadn't left it herself as a dry run to show me how the website worked. For one thing, Walks would have dreamed up a more enticing case, something involving a long-lost heir, stolen jewels, or a cheating wife. Something that would pique my curiosity. This case sounded too routine to be anything but legitimate. Mrs. Novita had somehow found my site that morning, probably through a routine internet search, and was reaching out to me, hoping I'd drop everything and call her right back. I debated whether to ignore it. The cops had the right idea: young Jalen was most likely sneaking out to get drunk with his buddies and maybe sow some wild oats. That's what *I'd* been doing when I was his age. It didn't strike me as anything to fret about. Mrs. Novita sounded like an overly protective mother with a son who was ready to chew through his leash. Still, a case was a case, and potential clients hadn't exactly been kicking my door in as of late. I wondered if this potential client was in the process of leaving messages with every P.I. in town. According to Walks in Cloud, most of them had put up websites before I'd dropped out of school to join the army.

I picked up my phone and called Mrs. Clara Novita, wondering if I was already too late.

An anxious woman's voice answered my call after the first ring. "Hello?"

"Mrs. Novita?"

"Speaking."

"I'm Alexander Southerland. You left some information for me on my website."

"You're a detective?"

"A private investigator, yes. I'm assuming you've contacted a few?"

"Yes, but you're the first to get back to me. I didn't know if anyone would. The police don't think I got nothing to worry about. But they're wrong, mister. Will you help me?"

"I can't say yet. I'd like to meet with you to go over the details, and then we'll see if there's anything I can do."

After a brief pause, Mrs. Novita asked, "Do I have to pay for a meeting with you? I mean, even if you don't do nothin'?"

"No, ma'am. The consultation is free. I'll go over the terms when I see you, but I won't charge you anything unless I agree to take the case."

"Fair enough. I don't want to go to your office, though. Jalen will be in school until three. Can you come to my house right now? There are some things here you need to see."

"All right. Will the boy's father be available?"

Mrs. Novita hesitated a beat before answering. "No."

"You're a single parent?"

"No. Sonoma and me are both Jalen's parents."

"Sonoma?"

"She's my wife."

I hesitated, giving myself time to get the lay of the land. "That's fine, Mrs. Novita," I said. "Give me your address and I'll be right over."

***

Mrs. Novita's "house" turned out to be a top-floor unit in a seedy six-story apartment complex called Tulan Heights, located in the gritty Tanielu District between Downtown and South Market. It was a grand name for a building that had seen better days. Tulan Heights loomed over the busy street like a concrete fortress. All of the windows in the complex were barred, even on the upper floors, and the apartments could only be entered from inside the structure. The lock on the graffiti-covered building entrance had been broken long ago, probably for the convenience of the street walkers and bootleg drug dealers who rubbed shoulders with the street campers and juiceheads on the sidewalks of the Tanielu. A rusty chain was draped across the open elevator inside the building, and I was forced to climb the six flights of stairs to the apartment Mrs. Novita had directed me to. Before knocking on the door to the unit, I paused to catch my breath. I'd been working on my conditioning the past couple of months, but I still had a ways to go.

The woman who answered my knock wouldn't have topped five feet if she'd been sporting three-inch heels rather than the worn leather slippers covering her feet. She was neatly dressed in a pale blouse with matching slacks. She peered up at me with a plain round flat-nosed face capped by closely cropped dark hair that fit her head like a helmet. She wore no makeup except a bit of concealer that failed to erase the bags under her eyes. A tiny pearl hung from a silver chain around her neck, and she wore a thin silver band around the ring finger on her left hand. She was otherwise unencumbered by jewelry. The woman squared her shoulders and asked, "Mr. Southerland? Excuse me for asking, but do you have some kind of identification?"

I pulled my P.I. buzzer from my wallet, and she snatched it from my hand with calloused fingers. She made a point of comparing my picture to my face. I removed my hat to make it easier for her.

She frowned. "You were a little younger when they took this picture."

"I was twenty-two. That was nine years ago. I'll have to renew my license in another year."

She stared up at me, lips pursed. "You look like the picture on your website, though."

"That one's more recent."

She stared for another moment before handing back my identification card. "All right, you can come in. You can't be too careful in this neighborhood."

"I understand. I live over in the Porter District." That got me an approving grunt and a hint of a smile, one working-class hero saluting another.

Mrs. Novita's apartment was cramped, but tidy. Framed photographs and art prints fought for hanging space on the walls, and I guessed that none of the room's furnishings had been moved in years, if not decades. Mrs. Novita directed me to an overstuffed easy chair that threatened to swallow me whole.

"Would you like coffee?" she asked. "I put on a pot while you were on your way."

"Sure, if you don't mind."

She stepped toward her kitchen. "Cream? Sugar?"

"Black for me, thanks."

"I like sugar in mine. Two lumps."

I liked a splash of rye in mine, but I didn't ask for it. This was a professional call.

A minute later, we were seated on opposite sides of a round glass-topped coffee table. I took a short sip from a porcelain cup shaped like a flower that nearly disappeared into my hand and looked as if it might shatter if I stared at it too hard. "All right, Mrs. Novita. Tell me about your son."

In response, Mrs. Novita reached for a framed photo sitting on a nearby end table. "This is Jalen," she said, pointing at a thin teenaged boy standing on a sidewalk between Mrs. Novita and a taller woman.

I pointed at the other woman. "Is that Sonoma?"

"Yes. She's the big one in the family." She was indeed. Tall and angular, with broad shoulders, bulky arms, and a thin waist, Sonoma dominated the shot. She wore a man's button-down shirt and a pair of working-man's khakis. She had a tattoo on her right upper arm that I couldn't quite make out, and a band of silver, noticeably wider than the one worn by Mrs. Novita, on the ring finger of her left hand.

I studied the photo. Jalen's dark brown uncombed hair hung over his forehead and loosely over his ears. He was simply dressed in a navy blue sweatshirt and a nondescript pair of casual slacks. His mouth was open and spread in a toothy smile that told me he was saying "cheese" without much enthusiasm. He could have been any child in any high school in the city.

"When was this picture taken?" I asked.

"About a year ago. Jalen looks about the same now, except his hair is longer. He still wears that stupid sweatshirt. It makes him look like gutter trash, but I can't get him into decent clothes. He's got nice shirts and jackets in his closet, but he won't touch them. Teenagers don't listen to their parents anymore, and Sonoma spoils him. I have some more pictures of him on my phone if you need them."

"Maybe later. He's in school?"

"He's a sophomore at Tennison's." Walker Tennison was the local public high school.

"That's not far from here, is it?"

"Just a few blocks away. Jalen walks there every morning, rain or shine. It's good for a boy to be outdoors and get plenty of exercise. You don't want them growing up soft." Mrs. Novita leaned a few inches closer to me across the coffee table, where her cup sat untouched. "He walks home every day at three when school lets out, and he's almost always here when I get home, doing his homework. When he's not, he leaves me a note. A written note, not a text message. I insist on that. I want to know that he's at least made it home before he runs off with his friends."

"When do *you* get home?"

"About five-thirty give or take. Depends on the traffic."

"And Sonoma?"

"A little later, usually around six. She's a bus driver for the city."

"She's at work now?"

"That's right."

I took a sip of my coffee. "What about you, Mrs. Novita? What do you do?"

"I'm a kitchen aide at Howard Michaelson's."

"The prep school?"

"Yes. And let me tell you. Jalen is as bright as any pampered son of a trophy wife in that school. Works harder, too. He's a real whiz at math. Jalen wants to go to college when he's done with high school and completes his government service, and Michaelson's is one of the most reputable private schools in the realm. If he graduated from there, he could have his pick of colleges. I'd get him in if I could, but the tuition is way out of reach for a working-class bitch like me. They won't give me no employee's discount, neither. They won't even give me a fuckin' student loan for my boy. They'll let me work in their kitchen, but Lord forbid they'd let me put my kid into their high and mighty institution, no matter how smart he is." She huffed out a breath. "So, he goes to Tennison, where he's surrounded by the children of drug addicts, common thieves, and pimps."

Mrs. Novita still wasn't drinking her coffee, so I resisted taking another sip of my own. I pushed myself to the edge of the chair. "You say your son has been leaving the house at night. How long has this been going on?"

"I'm not sure. And the worst part is, I don't even know how he's getting out."

"What do you mean?"

"I mean that something strange is going on with him." She glanced toward the back of the apartment. "I first noticed something was wrong about three weeks ago. It was getting harder and harder to get Jalen out of bed in the morning to get ready for school. He was looking tired, and he was quieter than usual. Not just in the morning, but in the evenings, too. I could see something was on his mind, but that's the way it is with young boys. Anyway, I thought maybe he had his mind on a girl. He's about reached that age, you know."

A few years *past* reaching that age, I thought, but I kept it to myself.

Mrs. Novita continued. "After putting up with this for a few days I asked him what was going on. He said he was fine and wouldn't talk about it. But I knew there was something he wasn't telling me." She looked across the table at me. "You got kids, Mr. Southerland?"

I shook my head. "No. Never had the pleasure."

"That's a shame. Kids make life worth living. But they ain't always such a pleasure, believe me. Especially when they get to be fuckin' teenagers. When they're children, they depend on you for everything. When they reach their teens they start thinking they're finding out about things that you don't know nothing about, and that you don't got all the answers anymore. They think they know more than you do about fuckin' everything. But you can't try to tell them otherwise. If you do, they fight back, and that's when you lose them. That's what Sonoma keeps telling me, and she's right, but she goes too far the other way. She lets Jalen run her life. Like I say, she spoils the boy." Mrs. Novita sighed, and some tension drained from her face. "Well, maybe between us, we get it right. We both mean well, anyway."

"Maybe you'd better start from the beginning," I suggested.

Mrs. Novita's lips spread into a terse smile. "You're right. Sometimes I get to yappin' and you can't shut me up." She folded her hands in her lap and prepared to launch into her story. "It was last Thursday morning, so a week ago today exactly." She pointed toward a hallway. "The bedrooms are back there down the hall. Sonoma and me got the one at the end, and the nearest one is Jalen's. About four or five in the morning, something like that, I had to get up to go to the toilet. I'm on my way back to bed, crossing in front of Jalen's room, when I hear something. A kind of *whoomph*, like... I don't know... like a gust of wind, and it rattles his door. He keeps it closed, of course, and I don't disturb the boy's privacy." She lowered her head a little and looked across at me under her brow, a sly smile on her lips. "You open up a door to a sixteen-year-old boy's room and who knows what you're going to see, right?"

I took a sip of my coffee, and she continued. "I knocked on his door, soft, 'cause I don't want to wake up Sonoma. 'Jalen!' I say. 'You all right in there?' He don't answer. Like I say, I don't want to invade the boy's privacy, but he's got school in the morning, and I want to make sure he's not up playing his video games. So I open the door a crack and peek in. And there he is, sitting in his chair in front of his computer. I get a little pissed because now I think he *is* playing one of those fuckin' games of his instead of sleeping, and I've told him time and again he can't do that on a school night. But then I notice he's not in his pajamas. He's not only fully dressed, including his shoes and socks, but he's wearing his coat, like he just come in from the cold. I say to him, 'You been outside?' He says, 'No, Mother.' I'm Mother, and Sonoma is Momma. I say, 'Then what you got your fuckin' coat on for? It ain't cold in here. You goin' somewhere?' Well, he don't have no good answer to that, and I tell him to get his butt in bed 'cause he's got to get his sleep before he gets up for school."

"You think he snuck out for the night?"

Mrs. Novita gestured toward the front door. "You see that door? It's got three locks on it. One in the door handle and two deadbolts. I set them locks every night, and you need three different keys to unlock the door from the outside. Jalen's got keys, of course. He needs to be able to get in when he comes home from school. But those locks ain't quiet. You heard me unlock them when I answered the door for you, didn't you?"

I remembered the clank of the locks and bolts as they slid into place. "I did."

"And that's a heavy door, made of real thick wood. You're a big man. You look like you've been in a few scraps. You're probably pretty tough, being a private dick and all that. You've got that look about you, the look of a fighter. But I doubt that even you could kick that door in. It's real solid, most solid thing in this room. But even through that thick wood, you heard me unlocking the door. On this side of the door? Those locks are even noisier."

I met her eyes but didn't say anything.

"Point is, Mr. Southerland, whether you unlock that door from the inside or from the outside, it makes a racket. Now I'm a light sleeper, and this neighborhood isn't the safest in the city. If I hear something that's off, it wakes me the fuck up. My point is that Jalen can't sneak out that door or sneak back in without me hearing him. And he didn't climb out of no window, neither. Those bars over them have been set in place for years."

"But he does have a window in his room, right? And it still opens?"

"Sure it opens. The boy's gotta get himself some air, doesn't he? But I couldn't squeeze myself between those bars. Jalen might not be the biggest boy on the block, but he's bigger than me. And none of those bars are loose. You can test them yourself if you want."

I nodded to assure her that I was listening. "So you're saying he had his coat on, but he never left the apartment."

"No, Mr. Southerland. That ain't what I'm saying. He left the apartment all right. He went out and he came back in. And he's done it a few times that I know of and most certainly a few times that I don't know of. He just doesn't use the door or the window."

I blinked. "Then how does he do it?"

Mrs. Novita finally picked up her coffee cup and held it to her lips. "If I knew the answer to *that*, Mr. Southerland, I wouldn't need no private detective." She fixed her eyes on mine and sipped her coffee.

Chapter Two

The first thing I did after Mrs. Novita led me into Jalen's room was examine the bars on the window. As she'd told me, the bars were solid, secure, and too close together for a human older than a toddler to slip through.

"You say he's been out of the apartment more than once?" I asked.

"At least twice that I know of since I caught him sitting in here with his coat on last Thursday."

I gave the bedroom a quick once over, using more than my eyes. It wasn't exactly what I was expecting. The single bed was carefully made, covers laid in place with no wrinkles, the bedspread forming a perfect crease at the pillow line. My own bed hadn't been that well made since I left the army. A desk was pushed against one wall, schoolbooks and video games neatly stacked next to the computer on the desktop. A wooden chair was tucked against it. A low chest of drawers with an attached mirror sat against another wall. A closet revealed shirts, pants, sweatshirts.... Some of them looked as if they'd never been worn. It was a typical boy's room, except that it was neat as a pin. No clothes on the floor, no used candy bar wrappers lying around, no empty soda bottles, everything neatly stacked and put away. I shrugged. Takes all kinds, I thought, thinking about the state I tended to leave *my* room in when I was Jalen's age.

"Do you make his bed for him?" I asked.

"Fuck no. That's the boy's job."

"You taught him well," I said.

"I run a tight ship. He might not've grown up in luxury, but that don't mean he has to be sloppy. The time to teach someone good personal habits is when they're still a child. And like I told you before, he's a good boy."

I picked a video game disk off the top of the stack on his desk. I didn't play video games myself. Couldn't see the point. But I knew they'd become increasingly sophisticated over the years. The one I was looking at was called The Battle of the Isthmus, and the cover showed soldiers shooting at each other and dying amidst broad-leafed jungle trees I'd never seen in that part of the world, while rain poured down on them from a dark cloudy sky. I wondered which of the numerous battles fought in the Isthmus this game was based on. I'd fought in one of them, and I couldn't fathom why anyone would ever want to recreate that nightmare in a game.

I replaced the disk on the stack and turned to Mrs. Novita. "Tell me about those other two times he was out during the night."

Mrs. Novita was examining her son's bed with pursed lips and an arched eyebrow. She reached down to smooth an invisible wrinkle in the bed cover before turning to face me. "Nothing happened over the weekend. Then on Monday night, sometime after midnight, something woke me up. I don't know what it was, but suddenly I was wide awake. I was kind of suspicious after that other time, you know, so I was specially tuned in to anything out of the ordinary. Anyway, I get up and open the door to Jalen's bedroom. He was gone."

"You checked around to see if he wasn't somewhere in the apartment?"

"Of course I did. I looked in the kitchen, the living room, the bathroom—I even looked in that fuckin' closet and under his bed. He was just *gone*."

"You're sure it wasn't the sound of the front door being opened and closed that woke you up?"

"I'm positive, mister. I'd've known if it was."

I nodded. "Go on."

The stern little woman straightened herself, trying to be as tall as possible. "I can see you don't fuckin' believe me, and maybe I wouldn't believe me neither if I was in your shoes. But I made sure of it. Before I went to bed, I put a table with a lamp on it in front of the door so that if anyone tried to sneak in that way while I was sleeping, the door would bang into the table and maybe knock the lamp off onto the floor. That would wake me up for sure. It would even wake Sonoma up, and she's a heavier sleeper than me by a damn sight."

I grunted to acknowledge her precautions. "All right. What did you do then?"

"I didn't know what to do. Tell Sonoma? Call the police? Go out and look for him myself? I just didn't know. I was exhausted! And while I was trying to decide, I must have just drifted off. I was dreaming about something I don't remember, but it woke me up with a start. I went to check on Jalen, and there he was, sound asleep in his bed, just like nothing had happened. The table and lamp were right where I'd left them, completely undisturbed. And it was harder than ever to get him up in time for school, too. Wherever he'd been, he hadn't got himself any sleep, I can tell you that. I thought I was going to have to dump a glass of cold water over his head!"

"I see. And the next time?"

"It was the next day. Tuesday. I stayed up this time, reading. So I was wide awake when I heard that whoomphing noise coming from his room. I got right up and went to check on him." Mrs. Novita spread her arms out wide in an elaborate shrug. "Gone again, just like before. And this time I remembered to do something I hadn't done the other time. I checked to see if his coat was hanging in his closet. It wasn't. Wherever he'd gone, he'd put his coat on before he went. This is July, and the weather's been nice lately. The only time he needs his coat is at night."

"I get the picture. Go on."

She sighed. "I tried to stay awake, but I couldn't. I made myself some coffee, and I sat up for a bit in that chair." She indicated the chair at her son's desk. "But after a couple of hours I got where I couldn't keep my eyes open no more. So I went to bed, thinking I might hear him when he got back. But it didn't work. I fell asleep and didn't wake up until Sonoma woke me up. By the time I dragged myself out of bed, Jalen was already getting ready for school."

"Did you ask him where he'd been?"

Mrs. Novita shook her head. "No, not then. I wanted to, but we were already running late, and I decided it would keep until that afternoon. But I told Sonoma all about how I'd woke up in the night and found him gone. That was yesterday."

"How'd she take it?"

She grimaced. "Hmmph. A little too well, if you ask me. She didn't seem concerned at all. 'He's growing up, Clara,' she says. 'He's flexing his muscles a little. Don't worry about it,' she says. Like *that* was gonna happen. Then she tells me that he's just rebelling against my 'strict regimen,' or some shit like that. Like I've got too many rules. I tell her to try to remember who the parents are and who's the child. She just says she'll have a talk with him. I'm still waiting."

I met the smaller woman's eyes. "Teenagers have been known to be a little rebellious at times."

She glared back at me. "There's nothing wrong with a little discipline. I don't know how you were raised, and I don't care. I get the feeling you were a little son of a bitch, and that's okay. But in this household, we do things the right way. We're a civilized family, and me and Sonoma teach our son manners. When he breaks the rules, we have to discipline him." She pointed a finger at me. "No hitting. That's not what I'm saying. We don't do that in this family. But if he's been slacking, we give him extra chores, or, if it's bad enough, we might send him to his room without dinner." Her face softened, and she lowered her finger. "But, like I say, he's a good boy. He doesn't give us a lot of trouble. And he didn't go out last night. I checked on him at about three in the morning, and he was in bed, sleeping." She made a scoffing noise. "Wish *I* could have slept. I was up the whole fuckin' night!"

"Did you talk to him about it?"

"I tried last night before he went to bed," she said. "Sonoma went to bed early. She was in a mood for some reason. I told him that I knew he'd been out, and I asked him if he was seeing someone. You know, a girl." Her lips pursed into a tight smile. "I would have been okay with that. Or a boy, for that matter. Coming from a household like ours… well, we're obviously open about sexual orientation. He just got all sulky and told me it was nothing I needed to worry about and he didn't want to talk about it. 'Don't worry,' he says. Well, what am I supposed to do with *that*?" She buried her face in her hand. "Everyone always tells me not to worry. When does that ever work?"

"But you don't think he's going out at night to see someone."

She lowered her hand from her face and let out a long breath. "I don't think so. Not like you're saying. He wouldn't have any reason to hide something like that from us. Or to sneak out of the house in the middle of the night to do it. Lord Alkwat's balls, I've been encouraging him to loosen up a little. To have a little fun. He's an intense boy, and he studies hard. Lately he's always got his nose buried in that math book of his, even when I tell him he's studied enough and it's okay for him to go see his friends. I told you he wants to go to college. His grades mean a lot to him. I tell him to relax a little. He's a bright kid. He doesn't have to spend *all* his time with his schoolwork. But, no, I don't think he's covering up some kind of secret romance. It doesn't feel like that."

"What does it feel like?" I asked.

Mrs. Novita's face fell. "It feels like drugs, Mr. Southerland. Maybe bootleg meth. Lord knows it's a big problem at his school."

I considered that. "Does he act like he's on something?"

She frowned. "Well, here's the thing. Not so's I can tell. I've seen people when they're high. I mean, you can't miss that kind of thing around here. Sonoma and me don't do junk, but we know plenty of people who do. Jalen's eyes have been redder than usual, but that would just be from not sleeping, wouldn't it?"

"Have you seen any changes in his behavior since this has been going on?"

"He's testier than usual. Quieter. He won't talk to me or Sonoma about much of anything. He's obviously hiding something from us. Maybe all that's just him being sixteen but, I don't know. I've gotta think drugs might be involved. Me and Sonoma have both talked to him about it. We like to think we're open-minded. We've told him he should stay off the junk, and not just because he's underaged. Narcotics are bad for the brain, regardless of how old you are. And the bootleg junk that they peddle around here, it's a huge risk for anyone, no matter how old they are. I mean, who knows what you're getting. But if he's gonna experiment we want him to be honest with us about it. We've told him we won't punish him for it, but we want him to know what that shit does to a person, and we want him to know we don't approve. We tell him that if he's gonna insist on doing it, we'll get him the legal stuff. At least it's tested. He nods and says, 'All right, Mother,' and he don't show no interest. I mean, he don't even smoke tobacco. None of us do. Sonoma used to, but not since she's been with me. But, you know, it's all around him, and you never know when he might get curious about it."

I nodded. "Drugs are always a possibility. But it doesn't explain how he's getting in and out at night. That sounds like magic to me."

"That cop I talked to on the phone said the same thing."

"You mentioned that you'd talked to them. When was that?"

"Tuesday, during my lunch break. They weren't no help, but the cop I talked to said if he wasn't coming in or out through the door or window, it must be magic. But the son of a bitch couldn't be bothered to check into it himself. He told me to find a witch or a private dick. Detective, I mean. Pardon me. Sometimes I get a little loose with my language. It's a bad habit but a hard one for me to shake. Anyway, me and Sonoma talked about it last night. Bringing in a detective, I mean. She was against it, and I don't like the idea of someone spying into my boy's affairs, either. But this whole thing ain't right. And we can't get Jalen to tell us what's going on with him. He's disappearing at night! And he won't tell me how he's doing it! I don't know why Sonoma ain't taking it seriously. She coddles the boy too much. I mean, I'm willing to give the boy his space and let him live his own life to a point, but this is too much. This could be fuckin' dangerous. Don't you think?"

"It's unusual," I said, not willing to commit myself just yet.

She let her shoulders slump. "Anyway, I couldn't go to work this morning. I'm worried sick. I thought about it all night." She grimaced.

"Jalen didn't go out last night, far as I know, but I was still worried after he got off to school. And he still won't tell me nothing." She squared her shoulders again. "So, I made a decision. I got on the internet and found some detectives. You're the only one so far who's responded." She peered up at me. "What do you say? You think you can find out what my Jalen is up to? Will you help me?"

I looked into her tired hazel eyes on her concerned face and nodded. "I'll try. Let's go into the other room and discuss my rates."

When we were once again seated in the living room, I took a contract from my briefcase and quoted Mrs. Novita my standard fee, by which I mean the reasonable one I offered to working-class clients from a two-income family. She considered my offer and told me it seemed a little steep, but that she wouldn't trust me if my price was too low. I handed her a pen, but before she could sign I gave her one last chance to back out.

"Mrs. Novita, you need to be aware that during the course of my investigation I may discover some things about your son that you don't necessarily want to know about."

Mrs. Novita looked up from the contract. "What do you mean?"

"You say your son is a good boy, and that he's stayed out of gangs. But kids can sometimes fool their parents. Let's say I discover that Jalen has fallen in with a new set of friends that he knows you wouldn't approve of. Further, let's say that in association with these friends he's been engaging in criminal activity. You say you're afraid he might be using drugs. But what if I were to find out he wasn't *using* drugs, but *selling* them. Would you want me to tell you about it? Or would you rather I handled it a different way."

She frowned. "A different way? Like what?"

"Like extricating him from the situation. By force, if necessary."

Mrs. Novita's jaw set. "I don't want you hurting my boy, Mr. Southerland."

"Sometimes a slap in the mouth is the best way to get a young man's attention."

Mrs. Novita put the pen down on the table. "Perhaps, Mr. Southerland, you aren't the right man for this job. I told you, we don't hit children in this household, and I'm not going to let any outsider get physical with him, either."

"I'm just establishing terms, Mrs. Novita. If you don't want me to touch the boy, I won't. I'm just offering it up as a possibility. But I can do the job with kid gloves, too, if that's the way you prefer it."

Mrs. Novita forced me to endure her glare for a few moments before speaking. "Here's how it's going to be. No matter what you find out about Jalen, you tell me. Tell it to me straight up and proper. I'm no delicate flower. And I can assure you that I don't treat my son with kid gloves. I don't need to. I've taught my boy the difference between right and wrong, and he's a fast learner. He may be going through a phase right now, a little bump in the road, maybe, like all kids do, but I can handle anything you find out about my son. And if Jalen requires discipline, me and Sonoma will give it to him. Not you. And not the cops, neither. You keep the cops away from him. Is that clear?"

"Perfectly."

"I'm paying you good dough, Mr. Southerland, and I want my money's worth. That means you find out where he's going and what he's doing. But you don't let him know you're watching. You get me? Whatever he's up to, it might be perfectly innocent. And if that's the case then I don't want him to know that I hired someone to watch him."

I frowned. "I was planning on talking to Jalen when he got home from school. Maybe we can sort this whole thing out with a simple conversation."

Mrs. Novita shook her head. "Absolutely not! I want you to be invisible. Jalen doesn't need to know that his mother hired a private snoop to check up on him. I feel bad enough about this as it is. If he doesn't have to know, then I think it would be best if he doesn't."

I shrugged. "You're the boss, Mrs. Novita. It might be a little harder this way, but I'll play it the way you want me to play it."

Mrs. Novita picked up the pen and held it over the blank requiring her signature. "This isn't an easy thing for me, Mr. Southerland. A mother hiring a man to spy on her own son. It's not something I ever dreamed I would do. It feels like I'm failing as a parent, and that's not something I want to admit to. But I'm at my wit's end. Whatever is going on with Jalen, I need to know. And another thing. You're dealing with me. I don't want you saying nothing to Sonoma. She doesn't know I've gone ahead and done this, and I don't know yet whether I'm gonna tell her. I guess that depends on what you find out. Is that jake with you?"

"Like I said: you're the boss."

After holding my eyes for another moment, Mrs. Novita signed the contract. "I hope I ain't gonna regret this," she muttered.

***

Mrs. Novita didn't want me to talk to her son, but she agreed to let me search his bedroom to see if I might be able to figure out how he was getting in and out.

"I'll stay out here," she said. "Call me if you have a question, or if you want to show me something, but I don't want to be a bother while you're working." She frowned as she gave me a quick once-over. I towered over the little woman by more than a foot and was more than twice her weight. I had a face that was charitably described as rugged, and eyes that have never been described as warm. The look on her face suggested she was having second thoughts about allowing a semi-tame ape into her only child's bedroom. "I'd appreciate it if you didn't fuck anything up," she told me. "I don't want Jalen to know that I've had anyone in his things."

Mrs. Novita needn't have worried. I was reasonably certain I wouldn't have to look hard to find what I was looking for.

Searching is something I do pretty well, thanks to some talents and skills I've picked up along the way. For one thing, my awareness had been enhanced by an elf, a creature that wasn't supposed to exist since their failed rebellion against the Dragon Lords. As a result, I didn't need eyes in order to "see" or ears in order to "hear." Also, I had recently been adopted more or less by a spirit called Cougar, who had assumed the role as my spirit guide. Afterward, I'd discovered that my awareness had extended into the realm of the supernatural. Among other things, I could sense the presence of magic and, to a limited degree, determine something of its nature. I had a strong suspicion that Jalen had been using magical means to leave and return to his room in the early hours of the morning, and when I'd been in the room earlier I'd caught a glimpse of magical energy, like a faint vibration I could feel in my back teeth, somewhere on his desktop.

Jalen's computer seemed to be a logical place to start. I honed in on the screen and the keyboard, but nothing resonated from either. Not the computer, then. I turned my attention to the neatly stacked video game disks, taking each one from the pile and examining it. They were all commercially produced: no bootlegs, nothing that appeared to be unusual in any way. None of them gave off any magical vibes, either. So not the disks.

That left the books, but they all appeared to be standard school texts. Mrs. Novita had described her son as studious and motivated, and the textbooks seemed to confirm it. Literature, alchemy, history, algebra... I shuddered when I looked at the imposing pile of academic instruction I'd done everything in my power to avoid during my own days in school. I certainly never brought books home. I had better things to do with my time than homework, like hanging out on street corners with my delinquent pals and bouncing beer bottles off the sides of passing cars. It was only when I was in the army that I began to take my studies seriously, and that was because the military instructors did a better job of motivating me than the public school teachers ever could. Not that I blame the teachers. They tried everything they knew how to do, but their beatings, electroshock treatments, and waterboarding only fueled my recalcitrance. The military instructors had ways of breaking down my resistance that I'm not able to discuss thanks to posthypnotic suggestions and psychological manipulations that leave me shaking in irrational fear whenever I try. Let's just leave it at that.

The algebra textbook was on top of the stack. I picked it up and immediately felt the tell-tale buzzing in my back teeth and lower jaws that signified magic. "He's a real whiz at math," Mrs. Novita had told me. Right.

I opened the book and flipped through the pages. I didn't find anything out of the usual until I was about a third of the way through. The instruction on page one hundred sixteen didn't appear to be a typical lesson in math. Instead, I found an incantation disguised as a traditional word problem:

> A train leaves the station at Ixquic traveling at sixty-six miles per hour. We offer our praise to Ixquic. A train leaves the station at Ixquic traveling with sixty-six passengers. We offer our light to Ixquic. A train leaves the station at Ixquic traveling in the wind and rain. We offer our thanks to Ixquic. A train leaves the station at Ixquic singing a song of travel. We offer our allegiance to Ixquic. A train leaves the station at Ixquic on tracks fixed in the rock. We offer our blood to Ixquic. A train leaves the station at Ixquic. A train leaves the station at Ixquic. A train leaves the station at Ixquic. The train remembers the way to Ixquic.

Magic flowed through the words but reading them aloud produced no magical effect that I could discern. Still, I believed that I had found at least part of the method Jalen had been using to leave and re-enter his room. The name "Ixquic" sounded vaguely familiar to me, but I couldn't place it. When I got back to my office, I'd have to do some research to determine whether the name had any significance. For the time being, I took a picture of the passage with my cellphone and waited to make sure it stuck. You never knew with magical incantations. I checked through the other books on the desk, too, but they seemed to contain nothing out of the ordinary. The only enchantments on those pages appeared to be spells with the power to bore me senseless.

I made a cursory check of the rest of Jalen's bedroom, but my only discoveries of interest were a pack of peppermint candies in his desk drawer and the fact that his bottle of spray-on cologne was filled with something other than your basic commercial fragrance. When I sprayed a sample of the mist into the air, I recognized the neutral scent of a bootleg masking agent popular among teenagers. I knew what it was used for, too: removing the smell of tobacco from clothing. Jalen was keeping more than one secret from his mothers. I smiled and left everything in place. I didn't smoke myself, except for the occasional cigar. Cigarettes were a vice I'd avoided. But I hadn't been hired to find out whether Jalen was sneaking smokes in the boys' room at his school. As far as I was concerned, it was a secret the kid could keep.

After some time, Mrs. Novita called to me from the living room. "You about done in there? I don't want Jalen or Sonoma coming home early and finding you here."

"Yes," I answered. "I think I've got enough to go on for now."

Mrs. Novita was standing with a slight crouch, her eyes wide and questioning, when I joined her in the living room. "Did you find something?"

"Maybe. Maybe not. I need to do a little research before I come to any conclusions."

"Oh." A look of disappointment settled across her face. "So you don't know how he's pulling off his vanishing act?"

"Not yet. Let me look into a few things and get back to you."

"When?"

"I beg your pardon?"

"When will you know something for sure?" Mrs. Novita's hands were clenched together in front of her waist.

"Hard to say."

"Well, is there anything I can do?" She glanced down at her hands and forced them apart.

"Yes. Keep an eye on your son for the next few nights. If you discover that he's taken a powder, call me, no matter what time it is." I handed her one of my plain black-and-white business cards, the one that shows nothing except "Alexander Southerland" and a phone number centered on one side. I produced the cards myself on the cheap at a copy shop in the Porter within walking distance of my home and office. I couldn't see the point in spending a lot of dough for anything fancy, like borders or a logo, when the only purpose of the card was to let people know who I was and how to reach me.

"Don't confront Jalen," I continued. "Try not to let him know you're checking on him, and don't try to stop him. Just call me if he disappears. Agreed?"

Mrs. Novita took the card and examined both sides before glancing back at me with a dull expression, as if she were having second thoughts about contacting me.

"Don't worry," I said. "I'll call you if I learn anything new. By the way, have you ever heard of something called Ixquic?"

"Ish-kick?" Mrs. Novita pronounced the syllables carefully and frowned. "No, I don't think so. Why do you ask?"

"Just wondering. It's probably nothing."

"Should I ask Jalen about it?"

"No, ma'am. Definitely not," I said, watching her face to make sure she was listening. "If it's anything, and I doubt that it is, I don't want you to let Jalen know you've ever heard of it until I have a chance to check some things out. This is important, all right?"

Mrs. Novita pursed her lips. "All right, if you say so."

I put on my best disarming smile. "I'm a professional, Mrs. Novita, and I know my business. I'll get in touch with you tonight if I find anything of value. If not, you'll hear from me no later than tomorrow afternoon."

Chapter Three

    I didn't get in touch with Mrs. Novita that night. I meant to, but things got complicated.
    When I'd returned to my office, I'd gone straight upstairs to my apartment for a mid-afternoon pick-me-up. I smeared a liberal blob of peanut butter over a slice of wheat toast, added banana chips, plopped a scoop of vanilla ice cream on top of it all, and doused the whole concoction with maple syrup. I ate it at the kitchen counter and washed it down with a cup of joe flavored with a shot of rye. When I was finished, I felt like a new and better man: refreshed, fit, and ready to lick the world.
    Back downstairs, I printed out the incantation I'd found in Jalen's algebra book and re-read it several times. I turned the word "Ixquic" over in my mind, tasting it and trying to remember where I'd heard it before. Did it represent a point from which one traveled and returned? Did it represent an otherworldly spirit who required praise, blood, and uncompromising loyalty? The more I thought about it, the more I was convinced that Ixquic was both the name of a place and the ruler of that place. That was the only way the incantation made any sense to me, insofar as incantations ever made any sense at all. I poured myself a cup of coffee and settled in for some serious online research.
    Three more cups of coffee and more than an hour of fruitless digging later, I gave up. Whatever or whoever Ixquic was, it had no presence on the internet. Frustrated, I jumped out of my chair and began pacing the floor of my office to stretch my legs. What was it about that name? The spelling of the word conjured up memories of the Borderland, the disputed territory between Tolanica and Qusco that Lord Ketz-Alkwat and Lord Manqu had been fighting over for decades. I'd spent two long years there in the service of the Tolanican Army and had been suppressing my memories of the place ever since. Ixquic... Ixquic.... What was it? The name of someone I'd met in the Borderland? A story I'd heard while I was stationed there? A village? A town? A lake? A River? A Hill?
    Alkwat's flaming pecker! I needed a drink.
    Suddenly, the image of a shanty-town bar in the shadow of an ancient kapok tree rose from the murky depths of my memories. In my mind's eye I saw the name painted on a sign over a door, a pale red moon

painted above the letters. The Ixquic Bar and Grill, described by the service personnel stationed in the region as a place "where the beer is warm and the women are cold." Yes, now I remembered the Ixquic. There were times when it had been the only port in the storm. But no trains ran to or from the joint. Just soldiers and Borderlanders looking for a break from the tropical heat after another day of drudgery. It wasn't one of the popular hangouts, and it didn't surprise me in the least that the internet had nothing on it. I still didn't know who or what Ixquic was, but I had a region of the world to focus on for more information. A bar in the Borderland was named after somebody or something called Ixquic. Perhaps it was nothing more than the bar owner's name, but I hoped it was something more significant, a reference to a part of the broader culture of the Borderland, a person or place in Borderland lore.

Whatever it was, it was outside my experience. I needed to consult with an expert. Fortunately, I knew one. Dr. Kai Kalama, a history professor at Yerba City University who headed up an archeological dig in Azteca outside Teotihuacan, had advised me on Borderland culture in the past. I'd met him through his wife, Laurel, a homicide detective with the YCPD. The detective and I had worked together on a couple of cases, and she'd had me out to her home to meet her husband and daughter, Nalani, over barbecued steaks and drinks. The Kalamas were real professionals on the job and good people off it, and I guess that's about the best anyone can say about anybody. I took out my phone and prepared to call Professor Kai.

Before I could punch in the number, I checked the time and was shocked to discover that the afternoon was fast approaching evening. Rather than risk interrupting the Kalamas at dinnertime, I decided to put off calling Kai until morning.

I was about to get up to make a fresh pot of coffee when my eyes began blinking rapidly. Gates in my head were closing, while other rust-locked gates were swinging open. My eyes ceased to function, though I was aware of taking a pen from my desk drawer and scribbling away with it furiously. My heart was pattering like a drum roll on a snare, and blood was rushing through my temples. The word 'seizure' came, went, came again, and stayed. I found myself gasping for breath. Darkness fell.

I awoke from a dreamless sleep slumped in a chair and feeling like an empty bottle of booze. With a groan, I sat up and used my elf-enhanced awareness to examine my surroundings. I was in my own desk chair in my own office, just where I'd been before my... episode? A quick check of the clock on my computer revealed that more than an hour had passed. Nothing seemed to have changed, except for two things. I had a splitting headache, and on my desk, on a sheet of copier paper, was a picture of a woman's face drawn with the pen that was still in my hand.

A year earlier, a godlike spirit called Thunderbird, manifested in this world as a ten-year-old troll with severe speech apraxia, had begun communicating with me from a distance through a process experts in supernatural phenomena refer to as "automatic writing." To put it simply, Thunderbird would "possess" my hand and use it to scratch down a message in his own words and handwriting. I'd been through the experience with Thunderbird on several occasions, and it was always disconcerting. For me, I mean. For Thunderbird I'm sure it was all very copacetic.

The picture of the woman on my desk had not been drawn by Thunderbird. What I'd just gone through had been a completely new experience for me. Disconcerting? This had felt more like a near-death experience. While Thunderbird merely took over control of my hand, whoever had caused me to draw this woman had seized my entire self, body and mind, forcing my internal organs to behave in ways they never had before. I had no doubt that a longer episode would have drained the life from me for keeps.

I was, nevertheless, impressed with the results. Unlike Thunderbird's torturous scrawls, this picture was beautifully rendered. My own ability to draw was limited to stick figures and sloppy geometric shapes, but the dame I was looking at had been portrayed in exquisite detail. I would recognize her if I saw her walking past me on the city sidewalks, and not simply because of her large pair of pointed troll-like ears, her birdlike beak of a nose, and the pointed teeth behind her snarling lips. Though the black ink of my pen revealed no color, it was clear to me from the drawing that the woman had white or silver hair, pale gray eyes, dark lips, and a face the color of ivory. My blood grew cold as I stared at her image.

Centered beneath the drawing in bold block capital letters was a name: IXQUIC. Centered beneath that was a message: SHE HUNGERS.

I'd needed to consult with an expert. It seemed that an expert had decided to come to me. Unfortunately, my expert had failed to leave a calling card. The only thing I knew for sure was that he was certainly *not* Professor Kai Kalama. I had no way of knowing who it was that had contacted me—violated the core of my being, actually—and I had no way of returning this expert's call.

I scanned the picture of Ixquic and attempted to find a match of the image on the internet, but no dice. It was a longshot, but I had to try. Despite my big lunch, I was hungry (like Ixquic herself, apparently). I broke for dinner: a whole microwaved frozen pizza and a couple of cold brewskis. I wondered what Ixquic hungered for, but I didn't spend too much time speculating. With those pointed teeth, it was reasonable to assume she wasn't a vegetarian.

I didn't have a lot to report to my client, but I'd promised to touch base with Clara Novita that evening. I decided to phone her and give her what I had. I remained convinced that I could clear up the entire matter after a simple conversation with Jalen, and I wanted to take one more shot at convincing Mrs. Novita to allow me to talk to her boy. I rehearsed a few arguments and reached to pick up my phone.

Before I could place the call, I detected footsteps on the walkway leading up to my front door. The door opened and a tall, broad-shouldered woman stepped into my office. A large purse with an extended strap hung from a man-sized shoulder. A colorful tattoo covered the upper part of her right arm, and I recognized the beautiful blue and purple flower of the passionfruit that bloomed for only a day or two in the Borderland during the summertime. The frail flower seemed incongruous on the virile woman's jacked triceps.

"Mr. Alexander Southerland?" Her voice was as muscular as her arms.

I stood. "Yes."

"My name is Sonoma Deerling. I think you know who I am."

"I do. Come in." I indicated a seat across the desk from me. "Would you like some coffee? It's been on the hotplate since lunchtime, I'm afraid. It's probably mud by now, but I can put on a fresh pot."

"That won't be necessary, Mr. Southerland. I don't plan to stay long."

Long enough to take the seat, though. After I'd parked myself into my own chair, grunting a little with the effort, I asked, "What can I do for you, Mrs. Deerling?"

"First, call me Sonoma. Second, I want you to discontinue your investigation of my son."

"I see. Does Mrs. Novita know you're here?"

"She does not."

I let out a disapproving "hmmm" before adding, "Well that's a problem, Sonoma. I'm working for Mrs. Novita, and only she has the authority to terminate my services on her behalf."

Sonoma frowned and glowered at me beneath her brow. "You may be correct, legally speaking," she said, "but, then again, you may not be. Jalen is as much my son as he is Clara's, and I'm asking you as his parent to cease your investigation. I believe I have that moral right, if not necessarily a legal one, although I may have a legal one, too. Do I need to consult an attorney, or will you do the moral and reasonable thing and let this case go?"

I made a show of thinking about it. "Sonoma, your wife is quite concerned about Jalen, and I have some reason to believe he may be in danger. Wouldn't you like me to find out? It seems that would satisfy your moral concerns."

Sonoma folded her hands on her lap, fingers interlocked and thumbs pressed together. "I am aware—more aware than Clara—of what Jalen has been doing during the night. For reasons that don't concern you, it is important that Clara remain unaware of Jalen's current activities. I can assure you, however, that my son is in no danger. He is merely pursuing a path that I approve of, while Clara, if she knew about it, would not."

I pushed back my chair and crossed my legs at the ankles. "I'm going to need more than that, Sonoma. Why don't I call Mrs. Novita. Since she's my client, I need her input on this matter."

"Please don't, Mr. Southerland. She's sleeping. I've become aware that she's been keeping herself up all night in an attempt to monitor Jalen's nocturnal visits. She's worried herself sick. Unnecessarily, I might add."

"I think, under the circumstances, she'll understand if I wake her up," I insisted.

Sonoma reached a hand across my desk, as if threatening to take the phone away from me if I picked it up. "No. She won't answer. I... I gave her a mild sedative to help her rest before I came to see you. Jalen is with her, so she's fine. She needs her sleep. She's already missed a day of work, and she can't afford to miss another. Fourteen years she's worked for that damned prep school, since she was still a teenager, but that doesn't make her irreplaceable. Do you understand?" She lowered her hand. "Look, Mr. Southerland. I'll tell you what. I'll talk to Clara myself in the morning and explain that I've advised you not to pursue this investigation of our son. Then she can call you herself and confirm that she has no further need of your services. In the meantime, please leave my son alone and stop with your inquiries, at least until you hear from Clara. Is that satisfactory?"

I met Sonoma's eyes and said nothing.

"If it's a matter of your fee," she began.

"It's not," I said, cutting her off. "It's a matter of doing the job I was hired to do. I understand your concern, but I've got concerns of my own. Concerns about a spouse who drugs her partner and goes behind her back to stop a job she has hired me to do. No offense, Sonoma, but your part in this matter is striking me as more than a little suspicious."

Sonoma's eyes flashed, and her face hardened. It was a boxy, masculine face. Her dark hair was cut short, well above her broad shoulders. Tall and bony, with those iron arms and a flat midsection, she looked as if she could deck the average pug with a single sweeping roundhouse from deep left field, and, moreover, she had the self-confident air of someone who had done so a time or two.

I stared into those flashing eyes for a few moments, and her face softened by a degree. "You know, Mr. Southerland, I might want that coffee after all. You don't have to make a fresh pot, though. Just warm up what you have. I like my coffee muddy."

"So do I," I said. "A cup of mud, coming right up."

***

After we'd both slurped a few sips of strong hot brew without speaking, Sonoma set her cup down on the desk and leaned back in her seat. "Yes, Mr. Southerland, I can see why you might have your doubts about me. Would it help if I told you that I have only my son's best interests at heart? Perhaps not. It's true, though. You see, Clara has ideas about Jalen's future. She wants him to get into college after his three-year mandatory and study to become a doctor, or a lawyer, or some other high-class professional. But Jalen is no scholar, and he doesn't want to be. He has other paths he wishes to follow. Paths more in line with my side of the family."

I swallowed more sludge. "What do you mean by that?"

"My family's roots are deep. They go back to nations that existed in this part of the world before Lord Ketz and Lord Manqu arrived here with their hordes of trolls and dwarves, and humans from western Huaxia. My family managed to hang on to certain traditions banned by the Dragon Lord's government. I don't think the Dragon Lords really mind all that much. We don't threaten them anymore, and I accept that. Still, my family felt strongly about the old ways. I do, too."

"Your family's not around anymore?"

Sonoma's eyes narrowed. "What do you mean?"

"You talk about them in the past tense."

Keeping her eyes on me, Sonoma picked up her coffee cup but stopped short of drinking any. After a few moments, she said, "I think you know something of what I'm talking about. You have a spirit guide, don't you." It wasn't a question. "Mind telling me who it is?"

"Can you guess?"

"One of the wild ones. Not Wolf, though. Something feline. Something local. Something large? Jaguar? Cougar."

I was impressed. "I'd call that a lucky guess, if I thought you were guessing."

"A deduction based on observations. My own spirit guide is special. Are you familiar with Cizin?"

I shook my head, slowly. "Kissin? No."

"He used to be a highly respected spirit in my homeland," she said. "He was the chief lord of the dead. He's weaker now, practically a different spirit altogether. But he still guides the dead to an afterlife."

"An afterlife? There's more than one?"

"It's complicated," Sonoma explained. "There is only one, known by my people as Xibalba, but it was fragmented when its lords were conquered by Ketz-Alkwat and Manqu."

"Sheeba...."

"She-BALL-ba."

I nodded. "Right. So tell me about... Cizin?"

"He is one of the *wayob*, the spirits who feed on dreams. It is said that Cizin was once one of the most powerful spirits of all, the ruler of the dead. He was a cruel spirit, and greatly feared. According to the old stories of our people, he appeared before the dying as a monstrous skeleton smoking a cigarette and reeking like a week-old corpse. But after the victory of the Dragon Lords, he was reduced and humbled. He resolved to help those he had once terrified and tortured, to guide them past the dangers and traps of the underworld. The Cizin I know is a kind and caring spirit. The shape he takes now is of a wolf with gentle eyes."

"Okay."

"My people refer to his chosen ones as ghost dancers."

"And you are one of his chosen ones."

"Yes, Mr. Southerland."

"Which means you..."

"Communicate with the spirits of the dead."

"I see."

"You don't, but that's okay. My point is that Jalen doesn't want to go to college. That's Clara's dream for him, but one he doesn't share. He'd rather find his own destiny, and I support him in this quest."

"Are you saying that his disappearances have something to do with this... quest?"

"That's exactly what I'm saying, Mr. Southerland. Jalen has been called by a spirit guide."

"Cizin?"

Sonoma's face tightened with a slight twitch. "No. But I don't know which one. Not yet, anyway. But he's been called, and that's why he's been disappearing at night."

"Does Jalen know who is calling him?"

"If he does, he's not saying. Perhaps the spirit has not identified themself yet. I think that Jalen is still being judged."

"But he's in no danger?"

Sonoma hesitated. "There is always a risk when you're dealing with the spirits. Many of the spirits are tricksters who delight in tormenting their chosen ones, even while enlightening them."

"I know what you mean," I said. "Cougar hardly ever has a straight answer for me. I'm told that spirit guides are mostly good for filling our heads with riddles and then laughing at us while we try to figure them out."

A quick smile flashed across Sonoma's lips but didn't linger. "The spirits guide in their own ways, and, almost always, the process is enlightening, at least eventually, if you pay attention. But it takes patience, especially in the beginning stages, and the most critical stage is the feeling-out process when the spirit is deciding whether or not to adopt an initiate. It is vital during this stage that no outsiders interfere. The initiate, my son in this case, walks the edge of a knife. Your intervention is almost certain to be more harmful than helpful. That's why it is important for you to stay out of it."

"What's the worst-case scenario here? Are you saying that if I continue my investigation I could bring about your son's death?"

"No, Mr. Southerland. The worst-case scenario is that your disruptions could rip away Jalen's sanity and turn him into a raving madman for the rest of his life." She raised a single eyebrow and took a delicate sip from the cup she'd been holding. Her hand was steady as a rock.

After a few moments, I nodded. "All right. I'll give it until tomorrow. But if I don't hear from Mrs. Novita by one o'clock, I'll call her to see what's up."

Sonoma set her cup on my desk. "Fair enough. I'd like—wait!" Her eyes widened, and she turned her head to gape past me at the door leading to my back hallway. "Something's coming!" She shot to her feet.

I stood as well, aware that something was indeed advancing toward the door at the back of my office from the hall. "Don't make eye contact with it," I warned, just as the door flew open to reveal a creature the size and shape of a bearded goat with thick curved horns. It walked through the door upright on its hind legs.

"Chupacabra!" Sonoma shouted. Her body stiffened as she stared straight into the creature's glowing red eyes and squared herself into a fighting stance.

"Chivo," I said, keeping my voice somewhere between calm and firm. "This is a guest. I'm in no danger."

The Huay Chivo lowered himself to all fours, the eyes in his goat's face focused on Sonoma's. The spikes trailing down his spine stiffened to attention, and his hairless rat-like tail extended straight behind him like a spear. He bared his teeth and began to growl.

The first thing I noticed was that Sonoma was not overcome by a sudden bout of nausea. I'd never known anyone who was entirely immune to the Huay Chivo's stare. It even affected me to some degree, although I could resist it after an initial moment of queasiness. "It's not a chupacabra," I told Sonoma. "Don't make any sudden moves, and we'll all be fine." Stepping between Chivo and Sonoma, I extended a hand toward the beast. "Are you hungry, Chivo? Let's go back to your room and I'll get you some yonak. Okay, buddy?"

Chivo's growl grew louder as he tried to peer past me toward Sonoma.

I turned on my old sergeant's voice, the one I used on new grunts in the Borderland. "Chivo! Back off. Go back to your room and I'll feed you. Now." Keeping my eyes on Chivo, I half-turned toward Sonoma. "Make your way slowly to the front door. I'll keep Chivo under control."

Sonoma didn't move. "Did you call that thing Chivo? Is that...? Can it be...? The Huay Chivo?"

Inwardly, I groaned. "Maybe we should go with chupacabra after all. A relatively tame and intelligent one."

"Don't bullshit me, Mr. Southerland. That's the Huay Chivo!" Sonoma reached into her purse and pulled out a blade the size of a machete.

Chapter Four

"Wait--stop!" I shouted, holding out a restraining arm. But Sonoma brushed past me and advanced on the Huay Chivo, machete at the ready. Before I could stop her, she knelt before the growling Chivo and slashed the edge of the machete lightly over the palm of her left hand. Letting the blade fall to the floor, Sonoma squeezed blood from her palm and offered it up to the creature in front of her. Chivo rose to his back legs. His upper lip curled, exposing his bared teeth.

I watched, frozen in place, as Chivo sniffed Sonoma's bloody palm, nose twitching and snuffling. As Sonoma knelt, head bowed, eyes cast to the floor, Chivo began to lap the blood from her palm with his long, thin tongue. He didn't stop until no trace of blood was left on Sonoma's hand.

"Alkwat's flaming balls," I muttered under my breath.

After maybe half a minute, the spikes along Chivo's spine flattened, and he lowered himself to all fours. Sonoma, still on her knees, raised her head and stared straight into Chivo's eyes, a dreamy smile on her face. The creature's head nodded once. He turned on his heels and stepped through the door into the hall. A few moments later, I became aware of the door leading into the alley behind my building opening and shutting as Chivo disappeared into the night.

I looked down at the kneeling Sonoma, who was staring at the palm of her hand, free of blood and showing no sign of a wound.

"You want to tell me what just happened?" I asked.

Sonoma stood, smiling like a child. "Thank you for the coffee," she murmured. "I've got to go now."

"Wait, what's your hurry?"

She turned and moved toward the front door.

I took a step in her direction. "Wait a minute. You can't just leave. What did you do to Chivo?"

Sonoma didn't turn.

"Hold on a second. Tell me about Ixquic."

Sonoma whirled. "What did you say?"

I reached into my desk drawer and pulled out the drawing. "Ixquic. I think this is who your son has been going out to see."

Sonoma hurried back across the room and stared at the drawing. Looking up, she asked, "Where did you get this?"

"Never mind that," I said. "Do you know who she is?"

"This is.... Who gave this to you?"

"That's not important."

"On the contrary, Mr. Southerland, it is extremely important. You should not have this picture. Whoever gave this to you does not have your best interests at heart. My advice to you is to burn this drawing and forget you ever heard the name Ixquic."

I put the drawing back in the drawer. "You're going to have to explain that to me more carefully."

Sonoma's jaw set, and I could almost hear her grinding her teeth. "Stay away from my son, Mr. Southerland. Your interference in his quest will not only be dangerous for him, but for you, too, if you continue to stick your nose where it doesn't belong."

That sounded like a threat to me. "The deal is I stay out of it until I hear from Mrs. Novita."

"You'll hear from her tomorrow morning. I can assure you of that." With that, she turned and walked out of my office without looking back.

**

That night, I dreamed I was back in the Borderland. I stood in a clearing lit by the dull light of a waning moon the color of blood. Stars dotted the night sky like the dust of diamonds, and I heard the wind rustling the leaves of trees I could barely make out in the darkness beyond the clearing. The air was thick with humidity. I tasted the salt from the sweat dripping from my upper lip, and my sleeveless cotton shirt stuck to my back. Mosquitoes feasted on my exposed skin, and I slapped at my arms to drive them away. The world around me seemed flat and dull, and it occurred to me that my senses were no longer augmented by elf magic. The thought made me shiver despite the tropical heat.

The deafening growl of a howler monkey echoed through the forest. I searched for it and saw it peering down at me from the end of a branch high up in a nearby tree. My eyes were drawn past the monkey to the nearly full moon, which pulsed and shimmered as I fixed my gaze upon it. The heat intensified, and I realized it wasn't coming from the tropical air, but from somewhere inside me. The sweat evaporated from my skin, leaving it bone dry as I burned with fever. My legs grew weak, and I sank to my knees in the tall grass. All the while, my eyes never left the pulsing blood-red moon. The scarlet moon grew brighter as my skin grew warmer. I struggled to wake myself from sleep, but the world around me was too real to be a dream. Hot blood burned through my veins, and I strained to breathe through my collapsing lungs.

A shadow passed in front of me, and I was able to tear my eyes away from the moon. I dropped to all fours. When I looked up, a brown hunting owl with round orange eyes was perched in front of me, framed by the red glow of the moon. The bird's head tilted as he studied me.

Old parchment lined my throat. "Water," I croaked.

The owl's head straightened, and he blinked at me with one eye. His beak opened, and words poured into my head. "My boy, wouldn't you rather have whiskey?" The owl's wings spread, blotting out the last of the moonlight.

I woke in my own bed, the sheets soaked with sweat, feeling no trace of a fever. A glance at the clock next to my bed revealed that it was just a few ticks past twelve-thirty. I knew where I needed to go, but I would have to hurry to get there on time.

***

It was ten till two when I walked through the doors of The Night Owl in my best and only suit and tracked down the maître d'. He gave me a look that suggested I'd made a wrong turn on my way to whatever working-class neighborhood watering hole I'd been heading for and asked, "Is there something I can do for you?"

"I'm here to see Mr. Clearwater."

The maître d' sniffed as he gave me the once over. "And you are...?"

"Alexander Southerland."

That got me a raised eyebrow and the slightest of disapproving scowls. "Yes, he's expecting you. If you'll come with me?"

I followed the maître d' down a hall to a closed door in the back of the club, where the sounds of big-band jazz and the buzz and clatter of the night's revelers were bottled up and blended into an indistinct murmur. The maître d' knocked once on the door before opening it. "Mr. Southerland, sir," he announced. He walked back the way we'd come without looking at me. I got the feeling I'd ruined the perfection of his evening by not wearing a proper tux, gloves, and top hat.

The distinguished sharper sitting at his desk inside the office was sporting the tux and gloves, and the hat was perched on a mannequin's head on a table next to his private bar. A thin ivory-handled cane hung from the side of the table. Armine Clearwater appeared to be a short, rotund man with candy-apple cheeks and a monocle over one of his large liquid brown eyes. I knew he was much more than a man, and I wasn't fooled by the twinkle in his eyes or his ready smile. I stepped into the room with more than a little trepidation.

He rose as I entered. "Mr. Southerland. Would you like a drink? Yours is avalonian, right?"

"When I can get it," I said, extending my awareness into every corner of the office.

He gestured toward the bar. "Help yourself, my dear boy. It's on the top shelf. Would you mind being a pal and pouring one for me, as well? There's a good man." He resumed sitting.

"How much danger was I in tonight?" I asked as I poured some golden liquid into two crystal glasses. "Did you save my life?"

Clearwater waved my concerns away. "Not at all, my boy. The Blood Moon is treacherous, but she doesn't kill indiscriminately. I merely saved you some discomfort. And some pain. Definitely some pain. But you're a resourceful chap with a healthy degree of grit. I'm sure you would have made it through in one piece without my help. Still, I did spare you some temporary damage, and it appeals to me to have you somewhat in my debt. Please, have a seat."

I sat in an elegant deep-red leather smoking chair and sipped at the avalonian, feeling its pleasant burn in my throat.

Clearwater flipped the lid of a box on his desk. "Cigar? They're Qubaoan."

Of course they were, with leaves soaked in rum, no doubt. I waved them off. "Thanks, but no."

"Suit yourself." He took one for himself, trimmed it neatly with his thumbnail, and lit it with a lighter I guessed was made of pure gold.

After he'd puffed the Qubaoan to life, Clearwater chuckled through the smoke and shook his head. "Ah, Mr. Southerland. What am I going to do with you? You attract trouble like a chorus girl attracts stage-door johnnies. Do you have any idea what you're getting yourself mixed up with? Or did you stumble into it like a blind man falling into a pit of serpents?"

I shrugged and took another sip of the avalonian. Say what you will about Clearwater, he not only ran one of Yerba City's classiest night spots, but he had excellent taste in liquor.

Clearwater grunted. "So, it's as I thought. How much *do* you know about the mess you're in?"

"Not much. I ran across a name while working on a case and was looking into it."

"Care to tell me the name?"

"Ixquic."

Clearwater's eyes told me I'd given him the answer he'd expected. "And what do you know of her?"

"I'm told she's hungry."

The cigar nearly fell from his lips as Clearwater let out a short burst of laughter. "Oh, she's that, all right. She is most certainly that. And now that she's had a taste of you, you can be sure that she's only begun to feed."

"Who is she?"

"The Waning Blood Moon."

"You mentioned that earlier. Is it supposed to mean something to me?"

The tip of Clearwater's cigar glowed red, and he blew smoke out of the corner of his mouth. "She's the daughter of a ruler of the dead."

"Cizin?" I asked.

A small smile appeared on Clearwater's face. "You've heard of him. Good. It's difficult to explain the properties of spirits and our relationships to each other to mortal humans. In a way, Ixquic *is* Cizin, but less than him, although you'd hardly know it by the way she acts. And Cizin is less than he used to be." He started to say something more, but stopped and shook his head. "You humans require years of learning and enlightenment to gain some insight into who we spirits really are and how we operate."

"Are you really all that complicated? Look at you, for example. You transform into an oversized bird, and you control other smaller birds. You rip your talons into anyone who gets in your way."

Clearwater waved his cigar in dismissal. "Please. You make me sound like some kind of common human shapeshifter."

"Your ambitions are human enough."

He opened his mouth to object, thought about it, and shrugged. "Some of them are."

"Like running this nightclub?"

"It's a means to an end."

"What end?"

"Why, my pleasure, of course." He drew in a puff from his cigar, held it, and breathed it out slowly.

"Pleasure is a very human goal," I pointed out.

"My *eternal* pleasure, my boy." His satisfied expression implied that he had settled the matter for good. Maybe he had.

The faint sound of jazz reached a climax, and muffled cheers and applause echoed through the hallway and into Clearwater's office. "What can you tell me about Xibalba?" I asked.

Clearwater placed his cigar over the edge of an ashtray. "Xibalba is one name for the realm of the dead, a name recognized by peoples living in the southern reaches of Tolanica and the northern regions of Qusco, including the disputed area you call the Borderland. The lords of Xibalba have many names, including Cizin, but, in reality, they are different moods of one spirit."

"Moods?"

"Moods, aspects, functions, personalities.... As I said, it's difficult to explain to humans."

The beginnings of a bluesy ballad drifted through the closed door of the office. After a short intro, a husky female voice cut through the horns and moaned indistinct words about desire and pain. I shut my eyes and sipped at my avalonian, losing myself in the song. If anyone asked me how I'd spent my evening, I was going to tell them that I'd enjoyed a show at The Night Owl, Yerba City's hottest new nightclub, comped in by the owner himself and drinking his whiskey. "How was it?" they would ask me. "Not bad," I'd say. "The band was good, but I was too far from the stage."

After a few moments, I opened my eyes. "Earlier tonight I met a woman who claims that Cizin is her spirit guide."

Clearwater took a quick puff of his cigar. "Indeed? Is that where you heard the name?" He returned his cigar to his ashtray and leaned back in his seat. "It is certainly possible, although the spirit she refers to as 'Cizin' is most likely nothing more than a pale shadow of one of the lords who once ruled the realm of Xibalba." He frowned. "Still, it is telling that you met this woman on the same night you were contacted by the sleeping Ixquic."

"The moon I saw was bloody enough, but it didn't look like it was sleeping."

Clearwater let out a short laugh. "My boy, I fear I am dropping too much enlightenment on you in too short a time."

"The woman I mentioned told me that Cizin is a *wayob*. Is Ixquic a *wayob*?"

That earned me a pair of raised eyebrows. "Very good, my boy. Perhaps I've underestimated you." He chuckled. "But it wouldn't be the first time, would it. I must remember to be on my guard when it comes to dealing with you. Yes, you are correct. Ixquic is a *wayob*, a word used by some for the dream travelers. But don't ask me to explain exactly what that means, except to say that, among other things, they are prone to wander through the dreams of humans, in which case your dreams become something more than dreams. The *wayobs* enter the minds of the dreamers to manipulate and influence them."

"I'm told they feed on dreams."

Clearwater nodded. "Dreams are fueled by your life energy. The dream travelers enter your dream and draw nourishment from the energy you use to create your dream. Sometimes one gets excited and latches on to the flow of energy fueling the dream, forcing an increase in the flow. Turning up the faucet, so to speak. If you've ever had an especially vivid dream, one that seemed more real than the waking world, it might have been because a *wayob* got greedy and drew more dream-creating energy from you than you are accustomed to expending. That's why you wake up from these dreams feeling drained."

"So they're parasites?"

Clearwater chuckled. "Yes. Yes, they are."

I looked up. "Can they kill you in your sleep?"

Clearwater's lips pursed. "Hmph. It's frowned upon."

"That doesn't give me a lot of comfort."

A fog was settling into my mind, dampening my thoughts. I downed the last of my drink, letting the liquid fire unclog the blood vessels leading into my brain. "Why did you send for me, Clearwater?"

"Hmm? Why? Perhaps it was just a whim, Mr. Southerland. Sometimes I don't know why I do what I do. Sometimes life in your world gets a bit routine, and the urge comes upon me to shake things up a bit. And sometimes I know things that I don't wish to share."

I let out a breath. "Fine, don't tell me. Thanks for the whiskey." I gathered myself to rise from the chair.

Clearwater chuckled. "Oh, come now, Mr. Southerland." He lifted his cigar from the ashtray and sucked it to life. "Don't be cross with me. You humans are so lacking in patience. I was listening to the sweet sounds of a superb collection of musicians and savoring a fine brandy. I drifted into places you wouldn't comprehend, and I awoke to find myself soaring through the forest of your dream. I observed your peril. It amused me to come to your aid. And, I must confess, seeing you at Ixquic's mercy reminded me how very weary I've become of that arrogant self-entitled bitch. I decided then and there that if she wanted you, she couldn't have you."

I settled back into my seat.

Smoke streamed from Clearwater's nostrils. "That's more like it, my dear boy. Needless to say, as of tonight I no longer serve the Blood Moon, and I'm grateful to you for giving me the opportunity to take my leave of her. I brought you here so that I may answer a question. You've asked me several, but not the one you need to ask."

"What question do I need to ask?"

Clearwater smiled. "Clever boy. But that, too, is the wrong question. You get one more try. Think carefully before asking. If you ask me the wrong question now, you will lose your opportunity to receive the answer you are looking for. And you must ask me now. I'll give you one minute." He sank back into his seat, waiting.

Spirits and their riddles, I thought to myself. The man who called himself Armine Clearwater was, in fact, Night Owl, an ancient and powerful force of nature, and I knew he was playing with me for his own amusement. It was a habit with him, playing with his prey before swooping in for the kill. This wasn't our first encounter, and he had every reason to hate me still. But spirits couldn't be counted on to operate according to human principles. Witches made bargains with spirits, or they played them against each other to compel their cooperation. I was no witch, but I had the sense that Night Owl, for reasons of his own, or perhaps under the compulsion of another, was prepared to do me a favor. So, what question could I ask the owl spirit? What question was he in a position to answer? I had to get it right.

No. I was taking the wrong approach. Forget that it was Night Owl I was asking. How had he put it? "The answer you are looking for." What was the question I truly wanted to know the answer to?

It came to me in a flash. "The boy, Jalen. Is he in danger tonight?"

Clearwater's lips spread into a grin that crinkled the edges of his eyes, which gleamed with an odd light. "Yes, my dear sir. Indeed he is. And if you do not act quickly and decisively, before the rising of the sun the boy will die a most horrible death."

I stood from my chair, ready to bolt for the door.

"Wait," Clearwater commanded. As my feet rooted themselves to the floor, the distinguished old man pulled open a drawer and began rummaging through it. He shut that one and opened another, muttering to himself.

After opening a third drawer, Clearwater's face broke into a satisfied smile. "Ahh, here they are." He placed a small walnut case on his desk and opened it. Several hooked items were piled in the box like scattered jewelry. He picked one up, and I saw that it was a small talon, about a half an inch long. "This one will do."

Clearwater stepped around his desk and held up the talon for me to take. I extended a hand, but he ignored it. Moving too quickly for me to react, he shoved the talon into the center of my forehead.

"Hey!" I shouted.

"Now, now, don't fret, my boy. It's just a small enchantment, a little extra protection for you in the nearly certain event that you'll be needing it."

I reached up to wipe away blood and was surprised to discover there wasn't any.

"Right," said Clearwater. "Let's get you on your way."

Chapter Five

Clearwater had been gracious enough to open an interspatial portal that would take me from his office to where he said I needed to go. He was perverse enough to make sure that when I emerged from the portal after a single step, I would fall from a height of a dozen feet into an open trash dumpster. It could have been worse: the dumpster hadn't been emptied in a week, and most of the garbage had been stuffed into plastic bags. After giving myself the once-over, I found no injuries more serious than the wound to my dignity.

I climbed out of the bin and into an unlit alley, trying to figure out my next move. Clearwater had promised to put me in a place where I could prevent Jalen's death, but I didn't know exactly where that might be. Somewhere in the city, I assumed. I used my magical awareness to "look" up and down the alley, "feeling" the wind for impressions and "listening" for echoes. My awareness didn't exactly work through my senses, but it was easier for me to understand what the elf had done to me by thinking about it in sensory terms. What I discovered was that, apart from a couple of stray cats, I was alone. But something about the alley nagged at me. I could half hear sounds I couldn't identify and almost see shapes that weren't quite there. To my eyes and ears, the alley seemed empty, but my senses told me I was a step away from a busy thoroughfare.

The dumpster I'd fallen into sat behind a complex of small shops topped by residential apartments. The smell of cooked meat and grease competed with exhaust fumes and the fainter odor of cat piss. I made my way down the alley toward the sound of light traffic.

When I reached the street, I discovered that I was in the Tanielu District only a few blocks from the Tulan Heights where I'd visited Mrs. Novita some sixteen hours earlier. Jalen's nocturnal excursions apparently hadn't taken him all that far from home.

I walked to the main street in front of the shops and encountered a row of lean-tos and makeshift tents fashioned from blankets and sheets and propped up with metal poles and scrap wood. A dozen or so homeless street campers lay snoring on the sidewalk or sat shivering against the walls of the shops and peered with empty eyes into the night.

I stepped past them, watching the few cars that drove by and keeping an eye out for Jalen.

I sensed him coming toward me from behind, as if he'd popped into the same alley I'd just left. That made sense, I guess. I don't know much about interspatial portals other than the fact that most powerful spirits seem to be able to create them, but they probably followed rules. Maybe this alley was a nexus point for portals. That would explain the odd sense of nearby activity I'd picked up earlier. If I had stayed where I was, I probably would have been there when Jalen arrived.

I stopped walking and turned to intercept him. He saw me turn, and slowed, staring at me with caution, if not suspicion.

"Jalen?" I said. "Your mother sent me to find you."

Jalen's eyes narrowed as he looked me up and down. "That right? Which one?"

"Clara," I said.

"That bitch! She'll ruin everything!"

"That's no way to talk about your mother, kid."

He glared at me. "You don't know fuck all about nothin', shitlicker!"

"And that's no way to talk to me."

"Fuck you!"

Despite his bravado, I could see that the little punk was thinking about running. "Look, Jalen. I'm here to help you," I told him. "It's not safe for you here."

He was sixteen, and not big for his age. I figured I had him by a good sixty pounds. Maybe seventy. I wasn't as trim as I'd been when I'd turned thirty more than a year before. "Don't run, kid," I said. "I'm not going to hurt you, and you couldn't stop me if I was."

He considered it, and decided to stand his ground, although he was clearly ready to shout for help. Not that anyone in that neighborhood would play the hero for him. More likely they'd wait for him to get worked over and then search his body for anything his attacker left behind.

"You've come to see Ixquic, right Jalen? The Blood Moon?"

His eyes widened at the name.

"Tonight's not a good night," I said. "Let's go back home and talk about this with your mothers. Both of them."

Jalen forced a slight grin. "Who are you?"

"My name's Alex. Like I said, I'm here to help you. I've received a warning. Your life is in danger. I need to get you away from this place and back home. It's not far. We can walk and I'll explain everything on the way." Moving slowly and deliberately, I pulled my phone from my pocket. "I'm going to call Mrs. Novita now and let her know we're on our way."

Jalen's grin widened. "No, I don't think you will," he said.

I became aware of a hulking figure looming behind me before something stung me in the back of my neck. I whirled....

**

My head was killing me. Had I been drinking all night? I had a vague recollection of a cool jazz band and an appreciative crowd, and of golden fire in my throat. I'd been trying to cut back on the alcohol lately, and I thought I'd been doing a good job of it, but my hangover was telling me a different story. I couldn't even remember making a night of it. Where had I been? I'm not normally a blackout drunk, especially since the elf's gift of enhanced awareness came with some quick healing mojo that usually prevented me from falling into such a sorry state. I only hoped it would kick in before I had to move from... from wherever I was.

I couldn't open my eyes. I hoped I wasn't in a drunk tank. My head was filled with a dull droning. I tried to reach out with my magical awareness, but the elf's gift let me down. A wave of dread washed over me, but it failed to kick the jolt of much-needed adrenaline into my bloodstream. I wanted to groan out loud, but it required more effort than I could muster. I couldn't move at all. Was I paralyzed? Was I blind?

What had I been drinking? The good avalonian I'd started with wouldn't do this to me—would it? Had I been drugged? Possibly. I had a vague recollection of something like an insect bite in my neck.

The droning was making my head throb. Low and steady, never ceasing, like the rolling of a river. I leaned into it, let the sound surround me, tried to drown myself in it. It was voices, I realized suddenly. An undercurrent of background voices laying down a foundation and one distinctly female voice rising above the others, speaking rhythmically, endlessly. I could hear words with no meaning, spoken in a language I didn't know. A long, dull speech.... No! Not a speech—an incantation! An entreaty to a spirit, the weaving of a spell....

I was desperate to wake up. I fought against the current of rolling words. My head was shattering. Fine, I thought. Let it. Maybe the pain would escape through the cracks in my skull. I focused all my energy and all my strength on a single task: open my eyes. And if opening both was too much to ask, I'd settle for one of them. My left one, I decided. Open my left eye. Open it! Just enough to let in some light....

The lids of my left eye separated the barest fraction of an inch, and a dull glow rushed through the slit into my brain. It was enough. The pressure of the light forced my left eye open, and my right eye followed suit. My head still ached, but it no longer felt as if it were on the verge of exploding. I became aware of my surroundings.

I was lying flat on my back on a thick wooden surface, a rectangular tabletop, wearing nothing but a thin rag draped over my privates, my wrists and ankles restrained by metal clamps. A figure in a hooded cloak loomed over me, face turned to the ceiling of an enclosed space the size of a three-car garage. The incantation was coming from the figure, a woman, the volume and pitch of her voice now rising, slowly, but perceptibly.

A little behind her stood a burly fellow in a cloak similar to the woman's. Unlike the woman, the man's hood was rolled back, revealing a weathered face almost buried beneath a mane of bristly chestnut-colored hair that merged with an impressively full beard. He stood with a slight stoop, giving the impression of age, though I saw no gray in his hair. I'd only had the briefest of impressions of the man who had drygulched me on the street, but I knew I was looking at him now. He turned toward me, and his eyes fell as they met mine. Was he regretting what he'd done to me? Too late for that, I thought. I let my head roll a few degrees and saw a dozen or so other figures turned in my direction. They were all down on a knee, faces peering out from the depths of oversized hoods, chanting a name over and over again: Ixquic.

Last time I'd seen anything like this, the poor slob on the tabletop was about to get a dagger plunged into his heart. My first thought was relief. I hadn't been on a bender after all. I hadn't drunk myself into oblivion. I wasn't suffering from the worst hangover I'd ever endured in my life. No, I was merely going to have my heart cut out of my chest. Soon. I figured I had until that voice finished building to a crescendo, and it was getting noticeably louder every second.

It was time to upset the applecart. I sent out a call and hoped the cavalry would arrive on time.

As far as I know, no one has ever discovered why some people are born with the ability to summon elementals, or why some people can summon one type of elemental but not another. I had no idea why I couldn't call on earth, water, or fire elementals, but I'd been summoning and commanding air spirits since I could talk. Small ones, nothing too powerful. I had limits. But in the past couple of years, I'd developed abilities to do some things that elementalists couldn't typically do. For example, the elf's gift of magical awareness had freed me from the necessity of drawing or scratching out summoning sigils. The restraints on my wrists would have prevented most elementalists from producing the necessary glyphs to attract an elemental. I, however, could call on elementals by picturing the appropriate sigil in my mind. Also, your typical elementalist needed to use voice commands to control the nature spirits once they arrived. But after Cougar had elected to become my spirit guide, I developed the ability to command elementals by "thinking" my desires at them. These were handy skills, especially when you were bound to a sacrificial altar and you didn't want to alert anyone as to your intentions.

Within seconds, tiny puffs of whirling air began to find their way through cracks, creases, and vents into the room. Not that these little spirits were going to be of much use to me, but the distress call I'd sent out had been a blanket appeal. These small fries had simply been the closest at hand. The bigger gun I really wanted was still on its way.

For most of my life, the elementals at my beck and call were mostly good for jobs requiring subtlety and low visibility. They were good at things like observation and recording, which made them valuable resources for someone in my line of work. But after my encounter with the elf, I discovered that he'd given me a different kind of tool, an elemental with the power of a small, compact tornado. The spirit I'd named Badass couldn't level a town, but he could overturn a small car. And disrupt a ritual sacrifice. Or so I hoped.

He'd have to reach me in time first, though. And when the last words of the incantation ceased echoing throughout the room, and a dead silence hung heavy in the air, I knew that my time had run out.

The woman standing over me, face buried deep within her hood, was not holding a blade, but the supernatural energy surrounding her was making the hairs on my body stand on end as if I had wandered too close to an electromagnetic generator. She lifted her arms until the palms of her hands were hovering a few inches over my outstretched torso, looking for all the world as if she were preparing to catch my heart as it flew from my chest.

A chill fell over me, freezing me to the bone. My bare feet turned into blocks of ice. A million frozen needles stabbed at my fingers, sending pain shooting like an electric current into my palms and up my arms. An icy sludge pulsed through my temples, filled my head, and pounded at my eardrums. Searing white-hot wires pierced the back of my skull and pushed through my brain into my eyeballs. Heat left my body in waves, rising from the center of my chest and from the right side of my abdomen. The world around me shrunk until I was straining to peer through an ever-narrowing tunnel. The tunnel darkened, and I slipped into its depths.

The pain slicing through my head suddenly ceased, as if the wires firing electricity into my brain had been disconnected. Something warm and pleasant formed in my forehead where Clearwater had inserted the enchanted talon, and, as the warmth spread to the back of my skull, I stopped sliding into oblivion. Forming sigils in my mind, I screamed a mental command to the elementals in the room.

Six tiny puffs of whirling fury streaked inside the woman's hood, forcing it back off her head and yanking the neckline of her cloak into her throat. Startled, she reached up to keep the cloak from choking her. The burly hairball was at her side in a flash. The sharp pain in my side lessened to a dull ache, and the pressure in my chest relaxed, though my heart continued to pound. Hot sweat leaped from my pores, drenching me as if I'd been pushed into a shower. A pleasant warmth saturated my body, and the stabbing pain in my fingers, hands, and arms vanished without a trace. I turned my head to the now exposed face of the cloaked figure and recognized the features someone had compelled me to draw hours before. My first thought was that Ixquic looked much angrier in person.

The air spirits were no real threat to her, and once she realized what was happening, the elementals vanished. I don't know what Ixquic did. Maybe she just wished them away. But the little spirits had bought me a few moments of time, and, as it turned out, those moments were all I needed.

Ixquic's head jerked toward a shaded window just as it burst inwards, sending shattered glass, plastic blinds, and torn wooden framing into the room with the force of an explosion. The hooded figures in the room screamed and scattered, making way for a six-foot cone of whirling wrath drawing the shards from the window into its midst.

Winds swept through the room, blowing the hoods off the heads of several of the people inside. I was shocked to realize they were all just kids, teenagers. I locked eyes with the one kid I recognized. Jalen quickly looked away and pulled the hood back over his head. He raced out of the room through an open door along with the others. "That's right, kiddos." I thought to myself. "Show's over."

I smiled at the whirling funnel. I didn't have to say it out loud, but I wanted to. "Badass!" I pointed at Ixquic with my chin. "Attack!"

Badass swept past me and plowed into Ixquic like a twister targeting a single-wide in a trailer park. The spirit of the Blood Moon, along with her hairy bodyguard, disappeared inside the black winds and slashing glass. My satisfaction at the sight was tempered with the realization that I was still clamped to the top of a thick wooden table. Also, the rag covering my privates was nowhere to be seen, but that was the least of my worries. I hoped Badass would find a key in the bloody remains of the moon spirit when he was done with her.

If only it had been that simple.

Any human facing that devastating onslaught of concentrated gale-force blasts and jagged glass would have been battered, broken, and shredded. Even a troll would have been incapacitated, at the very least. But spirits are neither human nor troll, even when they take a corporeal form. As I watched, the ferocity of Badass's attack began to noticeably wane. Its wind velocity diminished, and the darkness of the funnel grew more and more translucent until I could clearly see the outlines of Ixquic and her assistant standing within the whirlwind and bearing the brunt of Badass's attack. As the winds slowed, the shards of glass fell from the funnel and crashed to the floor. In another moment, Badass had been reduced to a throbbing sphere of air, like a giant soap bubble drifting in the breeze. From within the bubble, Ixquic turned her head until she was staring directly into my eyes. She raised her arms from her sides and drew in a long, long breath, pulling Badass into her open mouth until the winds of the elemental disappeared.

I reached out, sending a mental summons to Badass. I felt no connection and got no response. I reinforced the image of his unique sigil in my mind and extended my reach as far as I could. Nothing but blackness. I changed tactics and focused on Ixquic, hoping to find a sign of the elemental somewhere within her. Again, nothing. No trace of the air spirit remained anywhere. I sensed only emptiness. Badass was gone.

Elementals are more than air, earth, water, or fire: they are sentient spirits of nature. They are alive, but they aren't exactly creatures, or animals, and they certainly aren't human. Elementalists often give names to frequently used elementals, but usually only as a convenience to make them easier to summon, instruct, and command. Budding elementalists are taught since they are schoolchildren to think of elementals as tools, and they are discouraged from personifying them, or from thinking of them as pets. Most experts in the alchemy of elementals will tell you that these natural forces have only a rudimentary sense of self-awareness, and that they have no more personality than a screwdriver or a gun.

I knew better. I knew that elementals were capable of independent thought, that they could show emotion, that they even had a sense of humor. I knew that elementals could develop attachments to those who summoned them. Badass was more than an elaborate tool, more than a talking bag of swirling air. The air spirit was a larger and more powerful elemental than I should have been able to summon and control, and I knew that it had originally answered my call because it had been assigned by the elf to serve and protect me in times of need. But I also knew that Badass, in its own way, had come to enjoy working with me. I'd become aware that the air spirit no longer served me at the behest of the elf. Over the past few years, I'd grown accustomed to a connection with the elemental that had become ever-present. Badass was always nearby, always there when I reached out with my mind. Even though I lacked the power to compel it, after a time it had started serving me by its own choice, of its own free will.

I was a loner by nature with few real friends. I think it wasn't until that moment, the moment when my intimate connection to the elemental had been replaced with an empty hole in my heart, that I realized Badass had become one of them.

Could the air spirit be dead? What did that even mean for something that was made of air and had been alive since the beginning of the world? Can wind die? Or is it simply stilled until it blows again. I didn't know the answer to those questions. All I knew was a sense of something lost.

I pulled at my restraints until the metal cut into my skin. "What did you do with Badass, you bitch?!" I shouted.

Ixquic answered me with an expression of contempt and loathing that spoke more clearly than words. I strained without success to tear the clamps from the wood. I was going to go down, and I wouldn't be swinging. With no other weapons at my disposal, I spit in her direction. Even that act of futility fell short. I opened my mouth and let out one last frustrated roar of blind, blind rage.

Chapter Six

"Control yourself," came the low, melodious voice from within me. "Breathe and be calm."

I was aware of a faint feline scent, and I knew Cougar was with me. I took a deep breath and let it out slowly. I closed my eyes and withdrew into my mind, tuning out my surroundings and opening my mind to my spirit guide. Once I was relaxed, my throat expanded and my jaws tingled as Cougar began to speak through my mouth.

"Blood Moon hungered. Blood Moon desired to feed. Blood Moon wished to make an offering to Itzamna, to seek the blessing of the ancient spirit of the day, the sun, the sky, and the moon, the toothless one who brings nothing but good. Blood Moon captured a son of the Cougar and bound him. Blood Moon sought to feast on the heart and liver of the youngest son of Cougar. But a devil of the wind set itself upon Blood Moon, seeking to protect the son of Cougar. Blood Moon prevailed against the attack of the devil wind and consumed it. Now, Blood Moon's hunger is sated. Blood Moon no longer desires to feed upon the heart and liver of the son of Cougar."

A soundless ripple passed through the room, and a wave of dizziness pulsed through my head.

Ixquic listened to Cougar's reality-altering story in silence, her hairy associate standing mute and wide-eyed at her side. When Cougar was finished, she answered: *"Blood Moon hungered. Blood Moon desired to feed. Blood Moon wished to make an offering to the ancient spirit of the day, the sun, the sky, and the moon, the toothless one who brings nothing but good. Blood Moon needed the blessing of mighty Itzamna, because the two sons of Blood Moon are threatened. Blood Moon hungered for strength to oppose the enemies of her children. Blood Moon consumed the devil wind and remained unsatisfied, for the wind does not make a meal. Blood Moon yet desires to feed."*

The dizziness struck again, just for an instant. Something about the room seemed changed, but I neither saw nor sensed anything different.

Cougar appeared from nowhere. He sat on his haunches and spoke to Ixquic: *"Blood Moon prepared a sacrifice to Itzamna, the ancient spirit of the day, the sun, the sky, and the moon. Blood Moon wished to receive the blessing of the toothless one who brings nothing but good. The devil wind blew, and the followers of Blood Moon scattered. Blood Moon was weakened. Blood Moon was filled with the devil wind, and her bloated belly caused her to be ill. Blood Moon was too ill to offer a sacrifice that would please Itzamna, the ancient ruler of the heavens. Blood Moon withdrew into the night to recover her strength. Blood Moon withdrew into the night to await the day in which her sacrifice would be pleasing to the toothless spirit of the day, the sun, the sky, and the moon."*

A soundless rumble filled the room. Though the floor hadn't moved, I lost my bearings for a moment and was saved from falling by the shackles on my wrists.

Cougar lifted his eyes to peer into the face of Ixquic, and she stared back at him. "I will sacrifice to Itzamna when I have recovered my strength," she said. "I will await the day when I am strong enough to make a sacrifice that is worthy of the toothless spirit of the day, the sun, the sky, and the moon. On that day, I will make my sacrifice. And on that day, you will not interfere."

Cougar bowed his head. "That is acceptable. It will be as you wish."

Both spirits nodded once. Ixquic, her hairy assistant, and Cougar grew transparent. They faded from view, and I was alone in the room.

I was also still clamped to the table. Alkwat's balls! My wrists and ankles burned with pain, and the cold air chilled me to the bone. I turned my head this way and that to examine my surroundings with both my eyes and my magical awareness. I was in the bare room of an apartment over a shop or store of some kind—a beauty parlor, I guessed after picking up the scent of dyes and chemicals—closed for the night. The sky outside the shattered window was dark, and no stars were visible through the low-hanging clouds. Only the occasional car or truck rolled by on the city street, and I heard only the snores of the street campers and a few isolated pedestrians shuffling down the sidewalk. I guessed it was maybe four or five in the morning. The chances of anyone coming to my aid were as slim as a slice of meat at a cut-rate sandwich shop.

I considered my options. An elemental wasn't going to get me out of those clamps. I tried to call on Cougar, but to no avail. Spirits. He'd promised to cease interfering with Ixquic, and I guess he figured he'd done me enough solids for one day by convincing Ixquic to delay her sacrifice. At least my heart and liver were still where I wanted them to be: safely inside my skin. I owed Cougar for that, but it didn't appear that

I was going to receive any further help from him for the time being. "Other options?" I asked myself. "Sorry," I answered. "Fresh out." I resolved to stay where I was (as if I had a choice) until the shops opened downstairs. And then I would shout for help and hope for the best.

As I lay on the tabletop altar, helpless, I heard a clear whistle from somewhere nearby. It rose in both pitch and volume before descending and fading. The whistle, long and piercing, was repeated several times. I turned my head this way and that, trying to find the source of the whistling. Was a bird perched in the window? I couldn't see one anywhere, even though my augmented awareness told me that the source of the whistling had to be practically on top of me. The cognitive dissonance was making my head spin, and I was on the verge of losing consciousness when the whistling came to a sudden stop.

"What the fuck!" I shouted. No one answered.

The wait seemed interminable, but at least there was no reoccurrence of the strange whistling. After about an hour, I heard cars pulling up outside, doors opening and closing, and footsteps hustling up the stairs to the apartment. Someone knocked, and a voice shouted, "Police! Open up!" After a short pause, I heard a crash, followed by the heavy footfalls of cops bursting through the door. I heard the cry of "Clear!" A familiar voice said, "Check the back room." The door to my room opened, and a cop entered, his heater pointed in my direction. After sizing up the situation, the cop lowered his heater and peered back over his shoulder. "He's in here, detective."

Detective Laurel Kalama stepped through the door and crossed the room until she was standing over me. Her eyes traveled the length of my body, from head to toes, and then halfway back to my head. She sighed and shook her head. "I gotta tell you, gumshoe," she said sadly, "I was expecting more."

***

One of the officers with Kalama found a key to the clamps hanging from a hook on the wall, and another officer brought me my clothes and other possessions, all intact. As I was tying my shoes, I asked the detective how she had found me.

Kalama sent the other officers out of the room before answering me. When we were alone, and the door was shut, she asked, "Are you familiar with the name Clara Novita?"

Something about the way Kalama asked the question made me uneasy. Maybe it was because she worked homicide, and she had led a team of officers to find me at an hour when she would still have been in bed if she weren't working. "Yes," I answered, rubbing at my wrists. "Why?"

"She was found dead in her apartment earlier this morning."

"Alkwat's balls. Murdered?" I stood and leaned against the makeshift altar I'd been clamped to for most of the morning.

"Jury's still out, but it's a strong possibility. She was messed up pretty badly."

"How badly?"

"Sliced. Diced. She's missing a large chunk of her neck and chest, along with an unusual amount of blood, which is odd because not that much of it was found at the crime scene. The heart and liver were removed. Torn out of her body with claws, it looks like."

"Lord's balls! Th'fuck, man. She seemed like a nice lady." I shook my head and suppressed a shudder.

Kalama's head tilted by a degree. "Was she a client?"

"Yes. A new one. We just met earlier today. Well, yesterday now, I guess. Any idea what got her?"

"I have a few thoughts."

I looked up to find the detective staring at me with a hard expression.

"Like what?" I asked.

"Last time I saw a stiff in that kind of condition was on the floor in your office. It had been attacked by a deadly animal living in your laundry room. One you said you had under control."

"Chivo? Not a chance, detective. This is way out of his territory. You think he's going to roam all the way to the Tanielu to target a skinny dame in her own apartment?"

"He might if you asked him to. If, let's say, she had something to do with the situation I just found you in."

Blood rushed to my temples. "Come on, detective. You know me better than that."

"I know you have a tendency to get yourself in over your head and use whatever it takes to dig your way out."

"You think I turned a monster loose on a sweet little lady half my size? And then what, walked a few blocks up the road so I could strap myself to an altar to be sacrificed?"

54

Kalama glanced at the tabletop. "Is that what was happening here?"

"Ah, this is crazy, detective. You can't seriously believe Chivo killed Mrs. Novita."

The detective's eyebrows raised. "Why not? We both know what that creature is capable of. We know you had a connection to the victim. We know that connection landed you in hot water. And speaking of connections, can you talk to that monster of yours the same way you do elementals? Over long distances with your mind?"

"No."

"But I bet you could send one of your elementals to fetch him."

"You're barking up the wrong tree, detective. It doesn't work that way. Chivo isn't at my beck and call. He wouldn't cross the room to me if I called him unless I was holding his food dish."

"I thought you told me you controlled him?"

"I don't control him like a puppet. I just meant I could keep him from attacking innocent people who happened to be visiting me in my home."

Kalama's eyes narrowed. "Could he have followed you to her apartment?"

"Not a chance. The last time I saw Chivo was in my office well after I'd left Mrs. Novita's home, and I haven't been there since. As far as I know, he didn't know who Mrs. Novita was or where she lived."

"Could he have tracked you to the Tanielu without you knowing about it?"

I let out a chuckle. "Not by the road that got me here."

"You want to explain that?"

"Not until you tell me how you knew where to find me. You still haven't told me."

Kalama's face softened a bit, and she let out a breath. "All right, gumshoe. I'm a little on edge. This is a messy one. The place... it was tidy, immaculate even. Yet the décor, the furnishings, the framed photos of happy people.... The place was pleasant. A home. And the butchered body in the middle of it all. The smell of the blood, and the guts, and the feces. I've seen a lot of stiffs, and a lot of them were in bad condition. But this... This was horrible. Whatever... *thing*... did this is a monster, flat out. And when we found your business card in her apartment, my first thought was how similar she looked to that body I found in your office last year. The one mauled by your pet demon."

"Chivo's not my pet, and he isn't a demon. He's an ancient brain-damaged sorcerer who was transformed into a goat... thing."

"A goat?"

"Kind of. A goatish creature who can stun his victims and make them violently ill by staring into their eyes."

"And then tear out their throats and drink their blood."

"Well... yeah. I guess so," I admitted.

"And rip out their hearts and livers for a snack?"

I shrugged. "Lots of creatures can do that."

Kalama glared at me. "But I only know one whose roommate was working for the victim."

"We aren't roommates. Chivo is more like a boarder."

"You know I'm going to have to bring him in."

I softened my voice. "Don't do it, Laurel. Once Animal Control knows you've got him, the Dragon Lord's agents will snatch him up and haul him off to a secret government facility. He fought against Ketz and Manqu. Lord Ketz still considers him an enemy of the realm."

The detective shook her head. "I can't keep quiet about him anymore. Not after this. You should have seen what was left of your client."

"He didn't do it."

"You don't know that."

Didn't I? I thought about it for a moment. "Wait a minute. The last time I saw Chivo was last night. Mrs. Novita's wife, Sonoma, came to my office. Have you spoken to her?"

Kalama stared at me for a few moments, and I could see that she was considering what to tell me. Finally, she took a deep breath and blinked. "You and me go back a ways, gumshoe, and I think I can trust you. To a degree, at least. Look me in the eyes and tell me you had nothing to do with Clara Novita's death."

I met her eyes. "I had nothing to do with her death. At least not directly, and not knowingly. She hired me to find out how her son, Jalen, was disappearing from his room at night and returning without passing through the doors or windows of their apartment. I discovered that he was involved in some way with a nasty nature spirit called Ixquic, or the Waning Blood Moon, from a region in or near the Borderland. Armine Clearwater—Night Owl—somehow put himself into the picture. He told me that Jalen's life was in danger and sent me here from his club through a portal that opens up in the alley behind this building. I ran into Jalen out on the street but got ambushed and snatched by Ixquic, or, more likely, by her big hairy servant. That's when the lights went out. When I came to, I was clamped to this table. Some kind of ceremony was going on. Jalen was here for the party. So was Ixquic and the hairy lug. I think he's a bodyguard or something. Miss Blood Moon was about to separate my heart from my chest when Badass arrived."

I broke eye contact. "Badass chased away the crowd, but Ixquic...." My voice caught on something, and I waited until it found a passage. "I don't think Badass made it."

Kalama's eyes widened. "Shit. Elementals die?"

My jaws tightened. "I don't know. I've never known it to happen, but I guess there's no reason why not. But... I don't know." I finished lamely.

Kalama didn't say anything, and after a while I continued. "Cougar showed up then. He and Ixquic did that spirit thing where they tell stories and bend reality. They came to some sort of arrangement, and everybody vanished."

"What do you mean, 'everybody'?"

"Cougar, the hairy lug, and Ixquic. But I don't think she's done with me."

"Lord's balls, Alex. How powerful is this Blood Moon?"

I shrugged. "She's a spirit. A daughter of death, I'm told. She was powerful enough to take out Badass."

"That's not good. I hate spirits, natural or otherworldly. What the fuck have you got yourself mixed up with?"

My lips stretched in an involuntary grin. "Nothing I was expecting when I walked into Mrs. Novita's apartment, that's for sure."

The detective let out a breath. "Spirits. What is it with you and spirits? First there was that dog spirit."

"Xolotl."

"Right. He nearly killed us both. Then there was the Sihuanaba."

"You buried a knife in her," I pointed out.

"Didn't kill her, though."

"True."

Kalama sighed. "Is it me, or are we running into more of these spirits every day?"

"I guess they've always been around. The oldest stories we know talk about them."

Kalama grunted. "Kai says elves invented the spirits when they were explaining the world to the first humans."

I glanced at her. "Come again?"

"He says that spirits came into being when elves began teaching humans how to speak and how to live in the world they'd been born into. It's all over my head, but the point is that spirits are only as old as the stories that talk about them."

I thought about that. "Hunh. So what are you saying?"

Kalama shrugged. "I don't know. Maybe the more we talk about them, the more likely it is we're going to keep running into them."

I thought about it for a second. "So let's talk about something else. Quick."

A smile flashed across Kalama's face. "Tell me about this bodyguard you saw."

"Not much to tell. Big burly guy. Old looking face, but lots of dark brown hair, so he might be younger than he looks. Impressive beard."

"You didn't happen to catch his name, did you?"

"He never tossed it."

Kalama nodded. "All right. You say Clara Novita's son, Jalen, was here? How long ago was it that you last saw him?"

I nodded toward the broken window. "He scattered with the rest of them when Badass crashed the party. A little more than an hour and a half ago now, I guess. Maybe two hours."

"All right, that fits. He got home and found his mother's body. His other mother, Mrs. Deerling, wasn't home. He called the police."

I looked up. "He found the body? How's he doing?"

Kalama's eyes dropped. "Not well. We managed to get some information from him. After we found your card, he told us where you were and that you might be needing some assistance. We had to push him for it a bit."

I snorted. "Nice of him. He didn't seem to think much of me in the little time we had getting acquainted."

The detective shot me a half smile. "Imagine that."

I held out my arms. "So now what?"

Kalama's lips pursed. "Your monster isn't off the hook. I want to find him. I've never been comfortable with the idea that I allowed you to keep a dangerous beast in your home without telling anyone about it."

"But—"

The detective held up a hand to cut me off. "I'll give a description and tell my officers to keep a look out. I won't tell them he lives with you. It's on public record that he's been seen in the Porter District, and I'll be sure to mention that in my briefing. I'll offer him up as a possibility, but not a priority. Like you say, there's a lot of creatures out there that could have left a corpse in that condition. And her son is involved with a major spirit with a taste for blood and internal organs. And then there's the other mother, Mrs. Deerling. I don't like it that she wasn't there when the kid found the body. Finding her is our highest priority."

"Fair enough. You're done with me then?"

Kalama gave me her detective's stare. "I'll need a full statement from you."

"I've been up for twenty-four hours, detective."

She made a scoffing sound. "I've seen you stay awake for longer. With that elf mojo in you I'm surprised you need to sleep at all. You want some breakfast? I had to leave the house without it, and there's a diner not far from here. You can talk to me over eggs and coffee."

I sighed. "All right. Anything else before we go?"

"You've given me an outline. Anything important you want to add?"

I hesitated for just an instant, but Kalama picked up on it. "Southerland?"

I ran my hands through my hair and smeared the sweat on my trousers. "Sonoma Deerling's spirit guide is some kind of lord of death. She's got some mojo of her own. Chivo came into my office while she was there, and she was immune to his death stare. She recognized him as the Huay Chivo. She cut her palm with a machete and let Chivo lick the blood. That's when Chivo took a powder. She left after that, too, but only after I told her that her son had been going out at night to see the spirit of the Blood Moon. She didn't seem happy about that. She told me to drop the case and stay away from her son, or else."

Detective Kalama stared at me for several long moments. When she spoke, her voice was hard. "The diner's called The Good Egg. When you go out the front door, turn to the left and go half a block past the first light. Give me another half hour to finish up here. Make sure I've got a cup of coffee waiting for me. Now get out of here. I've got work to do."

I got as far as the door before Kalama stopped me.

"One other thing, gumshoe."

I turned.

"Try not to lose your pants on the way there."

Chapter Seven

When I was finished telling Detective Kalama everything I knew about Clara Novita, Sonoma Deerling, Jalen Deerling-Novita (or maybe it was Jalen Novita-Deerling), Ixquic, Night Owl, and the last time I saw the Huay Chivo, I asked, "So what do you think?"

Kalama set her coffee cup on the table. "I think the eggs are overcooked, the potatoes are undercooked, the sausage is too greasy, and the coffee is too weak."

"I don't disagree," I said. "Also, the service is slow. Good thing you're buying."

Kalama snorted. "What makes you think I'm paying for your breakfast?"

"I'm here against my will. Besides, this is business. You're taking my formal statement. Charge it to your department."

"You think cops get expense accounts?"

I shrugged. "Flash your badge at the cashier. They won't charge an officer of the law."

Kalama pushed her half-finished plate away from her. "You've got a dim view of cops."

"Most of them," I agreed. "You done with that?"

Kalama gave me a look of disbelief. "Seriously?"

I scraped the remains of her meal onto my empty plate. "Sacrificial ceremonies make me hungry, especially when I'm the star of the show. Anyway, I've had worse."

"And you still expect me to pick up the tab?"

"My client died before she could pay me."

The detective shook her head. "Next time make sure they give you a retainer. Cash up front and under the table. Isn't that how most of you private dicks operate?"

"You have a dim view of independent operators."

"Most of them." She picked up her coffee cup, grimaced, and set it down again without drinking. "This case stinks, Southerland. From what you tell me about Mrs. Novita, her only crime was hiring a peeper to snoop into her son's affairs. Who does that?" She paused for a beat. "No offense."

I swallowed a mouthful of undercooked potatoes. "None taken."

"I get that she cared about her son and was worried about him, but, if you ask me, hiring an investigator doesn't say much about her parenting skills. Still, her death was ugly. She didn't deserve that."

Our waitress breezed by our table, ignoring my almost empty coffee cup. Good thing I wasn't paying, because she'd just blown her chance for a tip. I turned back to Kalama. "What do you think happened? And don't try to pin it on Chivo. That's a bum rap."

"Maybe it is, and maybe it isn't. You got any better suggestions?" Kalama stirred an extra sugar cube into her coffee and took a cautious sip before setting it back on the table with a grimace.

"You say the son found the body. Maybe *he* did it."

Kalama's lip curled at the suggestion. "You think the kid cut his mother up and bit a chunk out of her neck?"

"Maybe not. But Mrs. Novita's description of her son doesn't fit what I've seen of him. According to her, he's a bright student who's working hard to get good grades so he can go to college. She said she tried to get him to relax a little and have a social life, but he was too wrapped up in his schoolwork. She said he always had his nose in his algebra book."

"The book with the incantation in it?"

I nodded. "Yep. I guess we know what he was really studying when he was supposed to be doing his math. I'd like to look at that book again more carefully, see what else might be in it."

"That book is evidence now. We'll make sure the right people go over it with a fine-toothed comb."

"By right people, I assume you mean your witches?" I knew the YCPD employed several magic users.

The detective gave me half a smile. "If there's anything there, they'll find it. Tell me more about the kid."

"Sonoma—Mrs. Deerling—told me the boy isn't interested in college."

"You mentioned that. She told you he was on a spirit quest, right? Looks like each parent had their own ideas about Jalen's future. Question is, which way was the boy really leaning?"

"Toward Sonoma, I think. Especially if he was studying spells instead of numbers. When I met him on the street, he didn't strike me as someone who was there against his will."

"How *did* he strike you?"

"Sullen. A troublemaker. Kind of an asshole."

"So, a typical teenager?"

"Hmph. I suppose so. Kind of reminded me a little of myself at his age."

"He reminds me a little of you now." Our waitress came by to refill our cups. Kalama put a hand over hers and shook her head. I accepted mine with a mumbled "Thanks," but let it sit. The waitress dropped the check next to my plate.

"Jalen watched Ixquic's henchman ambush me," I continued. "He didn't have a problem with it. When I saw him at the ceremony, he was ready and willing to watch Blood Moon remove a couple of my essential internal organs. I mean, at least the heart is essential. The liver has probably seen better days." I lifted my eyes to Kalama's. "Neither of us knows what that kid is capable of."

Kalama pushed a strand of hair off her cheek. "I'm not buying it, gumshoe. He was pretty shook up about what happened to his mother. If he was faking those tears then he should be in pictures. I've been at this for a while, and let me tell you something: it's harder to fake shock than most people think it is, at least in front of someone who knows better. That kid was in the kind of shock that grabs you by the throat and makes you wonder if it will ever let go."

I slurped some scorched coffee. "All right. Then what about the mother? The other mother, I mean. Mrs. Deerling. That's a spooky broad. What she did with Chivo.... I've never seen anything like it."

The detective frowned. "I'm still not clear about what happened there."

"To tell you the truth, I'm not all that clear about it myself. It looked to me like she was offering her loyalty to Chivo, like he was some kind of lord. She laid a machete at his feet and gave him some of her blood, which he accepted."

"Hmm, creepy. What kind of person offers herself up to a monster like that?"

"She called herself a ghost dancer. I don't know exactly what that means, but I think she's some kind of necromancer."

Kalama looked thoughtful. "You think she called up a zombie to kill Mrs. Novita?"

I shrugged. "It's worth considering."

"But why would she kill her wife? Were they having trouble?"

I thought about my conversations with the two mothers. "I don't know. Other than some disagreements about their son, they seemed okay. But they are two very different kinds of people. Mrs. Novita was small, but feisty and a little rough around the edges. She ran a strict household. I got the feeling she was very much in charge of the place. Mrs. Deerling is a big lady. Probably packs a mean punch. She drives a city bus. You'd expect her to be rougher around the gills than a prim little lady like Mrs. Novita, but it was just the opposite. Mrs. Deerling's speech was more polished, or at least less profane, and she was more composed. And there's the whole supernatural element at work here. I didn't see any of that in Mrs. Novita. I'm guessing she didn't have a lot of respect for that sort of thing."

"Did you dig up anything on their backgrounds?"

"I never got the chance."

Kalama wiped her lips with her napkin. "Any other pearls of wisdom you want to pass on to me before we wrap this up?"

I shrugged. "You know. Be observant. Be thorough. Go where the evidence takes you. Should be a walk in the park for a professionally trained flatfoot like you."

Kalama gave me a smirk and began to slide out of the booth. "Let's hope so. Because it's in our hands now. You're a person of interest in this case and a potential witness. That means it's hands off for you. I know you're going to be tempted to look into the death of your former client, but you need to leave this one to us. That means no contact with the family, no contact with the kid's friends or his school, no background checks, and no looking for this Blood Moon spirit. If she contacts you again, you call the cops. Get it?"

"Got it."

"Good."

I pushed the check across the table toward Kalama, and she picked it up.

***

Kalama was right. As a person of interest in the death of Clara Novita, it was my legal obligation to pull away from the case and leave all investigations into the matter to the YCPD. Any further involvement on my part would probably do more harm than good and leave me open to charges of interfering with the course of justice. The best thing for me to do was to let the police do their job.

I had a couple of problems with that idea. First, I was certain that Ixquic wasn't finished with me. Cougar had bought me some time, but it sounded to me like she intended to complete her ceremony, probably sooner rather than later. Second, Ixquic had done something to Badass.

Try as I might, I couldn't sense any trace of the elemental that had never been more than a few minutes from my side since it had first come to my aid nearly three years earlier. I didn't want to believe that Badass was dead, or dispersed, or whatever happens to elementals. I wanted to believe that the elemental was still out there, somewhere, fighting its way back to me. Sure, I was in denial, but I didn't care. If I had any say at all in the matter, Ixquic was going to pay for what she had done. At the very least, I was going to have a chat with my spirit guide. I had every intention of learning as much about Ixquic as I could. If the Blood Moon spirit had a weakness, I was going to find out what it was.

After making my way back to my apartment, I plopped myself down on my sofa, closed my eyes, and called up a memory of a place I'd discovered by accident during a routine patrol in the Borderland. In moments, I was transported into a clearing in a tropical rainforest where a narrow stream poured about twenty feet down to the base of a rocky incline into a small dark pool before continuing on its way into the brush. It was my own personal place of tranquility, a vision an army doctor had trained me to recall during times of stress, a vision so vivid that it might as well have been real. It was a place where I could sometimes find Cougar, provided he was in the mood to communicate with me directly. After ten minutes of meditative peace, I concluded that this was not going to be one of those times. That's the problem with spirit guides: they have their own schedules and their own ideas about guidance. Either that, or they just suck at their jobs.

When I opened my eyes, I was, of course, back in my apartment, since physically I'd never actually left. I was disappointed at being stiffed by my spirit guide, but I quickly realized my mental journey had not been without benefit: although it had been more than twenty-four hours since I'd last slept, I felt remarkably refreshed and invigorated. Maybe Cougar had given me something after all.

Nevertheless, I still needed information about Ixquic. I kicked myself for not calling Kai the previous evening. Asking him for help at this point was no longer an option, since his wife had pretty much ordered me to steer clear of the matter.

I considered another possibility. I was certain that Madame Cuapa, the most powerful witch in western Tolanica, if not the entire realm, would know everything there was to know about Ixquic. The bruja had hired me a couple of years earlier to find out who had compelled her to cast a spectacularly fatal spell on someone. I'd been successful in finding the culprit, but the resolution of the case hadn't left us the best of friends. I was reluctant to call on her because... well... quite frankly because she scared the crap out of me. When I'd first met the bruja, she'd told me she could bring about events that could eliminate life on earth, and I'd seen enough evidence to convince me she was telling the truth. She'd also come very close to ending my life, sending me to the very gates of the land of the dead before using her powers to pull me back to our world. Madame Cuapa wasn't someone I wanted to bother unnecessarily. Still, she'd helped me out a time or two, and I got along well enough with Cody, her personal assistant.

What was she going to do if I called—turn me into a toad? I mean... she could. But would she? I shook off my fears and punched the bruja's number into my phone, knowing that the Madame had an aversion to telephones and that Cody would be the one who would answer. At least, I hoped so.

In the end, it didn't matter. My call went unanswered, and it didn't kick over to voicemail. I wasn't even sure Madame Cuapa *had* voicemail. I gave it ten rings before giving up.

I needed another approach. I let my mind drift over the past twenty-four hours. Clara Novita's death had me shook. I hadn't seen it coming, and I wondered if I'd missed something that would have warned me she was in danger. Her wife, Sonoma, was an odd duck, but she'd given no indication that she might be motivated to harm Mrs. Novita in any way. I wondered where she'd been when Mrs. Novita had met her end, and where she was now.

Thinking about Sonoma reminded me of her encounter with Chivo, and *that* reminded me that the YCPD was hunting for him. I made my way to the laundry room to see if he was there. He wasn't, and the bowl of yonak I'd left for him hadn't been touched. My nose wrinkled in protest at the odor rising from the mixture of rancid meat, blood, and unidentifiable spices added by the butcher at the corner store where I bought the stuff.

The smell of the yonak competed with Chivo's lingering scent to make my laundry room an unpleasant environment for decent people. It didn't help that I also used the room as a makeshift gym, where I occasionally messed around with some old barbells and pummeled a homemade heavy bag I'd hung from the ceiling. Fortunately, an elemental I'd named Siphon was happy to spend twenty-four hours every day drawing the malodorous air out through the room's window and replacing it with fresh air from outside. Between the yonak, the repulsively gamey Chivo, and the smell of my own sweat, Siphon had a monumental task. The spirit didn't mind, though. I'd released it from its service, but it had formed some sort of bond with the room and didn't want to leave. It said it was happy to continue working, too, and who was I to interfere with an elemental's life choices?

I stared at the uneaten yonak. Chivo's normal routine was to sleep the day away in the dog bed I'd bought for him, eat his yonak sometime in the late evening, and then disappear into the night before returning around sunrise. I asked Siphon if Chivo had been in the room since the previous evening, and the spirit indicated that he hadn't. It bothered me that Chivo hadn't touched the yonak. I established a mental connection with Siphon and instructed the elemental to find me wherever I was and alert me the moment Chivo came back.

Frustrated and restless, I grabbed my hat and went out for a walk to clear my head.

It was a warm, cloudless summer day in Yerba City. In the evening, I knew the wind would kick up and the temperature would drop, but for the time being I was comfortable in shirtsleeves. I walked south through the Porter District, trying to think of anything except lying on a cold tabletop waiting for the spirit of the Blood Moon to yank out my life energy while the mutilated body of Clara Novita lay bleeding on her apartment floor a few blocks away. Naturally, as I ambled past the hundred-year-old multi-story apartment buildings crowded side-by-side along the tree-lined streets, I couldn't think of anything else.

I was walking past a graffiti-covered office building housing an insurance office, a shoe-repair shop, and a massage parlor when I heard a series of long, clear whistles, one after the other, each one rising and fading, a repeat of the whistling I'd heard while clamped to the makeshift altar. They sounded like bird calls, or the cries of a small animal of some kind. Despite the warmth of the day, a cold shiver ran up my spine as I realized that, as before, I could hear the whistling from somewhere near at hand, but I couldn't sense the presence of who or whatever was doing the whistling. I stopped in my tracks and focused my awareness on the source of the whistling, searching for passing birds and scanning for some other animal. The calls were coming from somewhere behind me, back the way I'd come. They were also getting louder and closer, but I could neither see nor otherwise sense anything or anyone approaching. The effort to reconcile the disparity between my inability to see what my ears were telling me had to be there was causing my head to float. I shut my eyes in order to keep from keeling over onto the sidewalk.

Keeping my peepers closed, I felt for the buzz of the supernatural, but sensed nothing except the mundane. The whistling continued to grow louder, as the whistler drew nearer. My eyes popped open of their own accord, and I fully expected to see something right on top of me. I saw nothing. Dizziness swept through my brain, and the taste of greasy half-digested sausages from my morning's breakfast filled my mouth. I had to lean against the wall of the massage parlor in order to keep from falling. Unable to stand it, I slid down the wall until I was sitting on cement.

The whistling stopped. The dizziness subsided, and my stomach settled. I sat on the sidewalk, braced against the wall until the blood stopped pounding through my temples and my breathing returned to normal.

What the fuck had just happened?

The whistling had been so clear. The sound of it was still in my head. I pursed my lips and re-created the whistle. A warning? I didn't think so. It seemed more like a lure. A mating call? Maybe, but my gut was telling me something different. I couldn't hear it in my own whistling, but I could feel it in my memory of the whistling I'd just heard. I don't know how, but I sensed... hunger. Hunger borne of starvation. The hunger of an animal desperate to feed and calling for its prey.

When I got back to my place, my office was a shambles. Files and papers pulled from my file cabinets littered the floor, and the cabinets themselves had been toppled. My office chairs had been slashed. The desk drawers had been yanked out of their tracks and emptied. My water cooler was a wreck and the glass container shattered. Fortunately, it had been nearly empty. The screen of my computer had been smashed, and my keyboard had been broken in two. Worse, my coffeemaker had been demolished.

I ran upstairs to my apartment. It was intact. It seems that whoever had ransacked my office had not bothered with my living quarters. I returned to the ground floor and opened the door to my laundry room. It had met the same fate as my office. My heavy bag had been pulled from the ceiling and slashed, spilling sand over the floor. The washer and dryer appeared to have been bashed with a club. Chivo's food dish had been emptied on the floor and tossed across the room. His bed had been shredded. I sensed a familiar presence and looked up into a corner of the ceiling where Siphon was whirling fiercely, as if it were attempting to drill a hole through the wall.

"Siphon. What happened? Who did this?"

Siphon darted around the room like a caged swallow.

"Siphon! Stop!" I visualized the elemental's sigil and fought to connect with it, but it was like trying to grab a speeding bullet with a pair of tongs. I stepped in the elemental's path and mentally shouted a command: "STOP!"

The two-foot funnel of wind swirled around my face, lifting my hat off my head. "Slow down," I commanded out loud, putting all of my will into it. "Elemental! I order you to slow down!"

My temples throbbed with the effort, but Siphon's whirling slowed until the elemental drifted in front of me like a fat bubble.

"That's better." I had a connection, and I seized on it so that it wouldn't slip. "Tell me what happened here."

Siphons's voice emerged, sounding as if it were coming from the tube of a trumpet. "The room. They hurt the room."

"They? Who, Siphon? Who hurt the room?"

"The room. The room is wounded." Siphon's voice wailed.

"Who were they, Siphon? Who did this? Listen to what I am asking you. Who hurt your room? Were they humans?"

"Human, and not human." At the best of times, Siphon's communication skills were little better than that of a child's, and the disruption to the room it had bonded with had left the elemental rattled.

"One human and one not human?" I asked.

"Shape was human. Siphon sees human and not human."

I tried to puzzle that out. I knew from experience that air elementals didn't actually see, but perceived the world differently than the truly sentient species did. They could register shapes, but their primary sensory input consisted of patterns of temperature. I concluded that Siphon had perceived shapes that suggested human, but the heat patterns marked the shapes as something different. A shapeshifter, perhaps?

Unable to get a clear answer from the shaken air spirit, I tried a different tact. Siphon might not communicate ideas well, but the elemental was an excellent mimic.

"What did they say, Siphon?" I asked.

"They were loud," Siphon said. A deafening roar emerged from the bubble of air, and I clapped my hands over my ears.

"Stop!" I said. The screeching ceased. "Did you hear any words?"

"Huay Chivo," Siphon said in its own voice. "They wanted to find Huay Chivo. They are angered because Huay Chivo not here. They hurt the room."

Siphon abruptly broke its connection with me and darted to the window, where it settled into its chosen function, siphoning air out of the room and drawing fresh air in from outside. I tried to reestablish contact, but Siphon repulsed my attempts. If the elemental had been human, I would have thought it was suffering from shock. With a sigh, I walked out of the room and left it in peace.

Chapter Eight

The front door had been locked when I'd returned to my office, and I saw no signs of a break-in. I went through the place and checked all the windows, confirming that they were all locked from the inside. The back door to the alley was also locked, and the deadbolt was in place. I filed the information away for later.

I didn't call the police. The last thing I wanted was a herd of YCPD bulls stomping through the wreckage of my office. I called my lawyer, instead.

A cheerful woman's voice soaked in nicotine answered after two rings. "Robinson Lubank's office. How can I help you?"

"You could find me a housekeeper who doesn't mind a challenge."

"I'll play house with you, sugar, but I doubt you'd be much of a challenge."

"House*keeper*, Gracie, not…. Never mind."

Gracie giggled. "Like I said, not much of a challenge."

"What am I going to do with you, Gracie."

"Oh, honey. I keep waiting to find out."

"We'll need to get rid of that husband of yours."

"Get rid of Robbie? Don't be silly, baby. We'll need him to bail us out of all the trouble we'd get into."

"Yeah, well, speaking of trouble…."

I heard Gracie breathe a cloud of smoke out the side of her mouth. "Oh, Alex. What have you done now?"

"Me? Nothing. But someone did a number on my office. Trashed the whole place. They even smashed my washing machine and my dryer. My computer, too."

"Lord's balls, Alex! Did you call the police?"

"I thought I would talk to Rob first."

"Smart move. The cops might find whatever it is you're trying to hide."

"I'm not hiding anything."

"Then why did someone ransack your office?"

"Hell if I know. Maybe they were looking for the bottle of good avalonian I hid under the floorboards."

"They didn't find it, did they? That would be a real shame."

"I think I might have polished it off myself a few weeks ago."

"Not by yourself, I hope. I keep telling you, sugar, you need to get out more. You ain't gettin' any younger, you know."

"Gee, thanks, doll. I'm working on it."

"Sure you are. I've got another call coming in, so I'm going to have to transfer you to Robbie. Hang on, sugar...."

A minute later, my lawyer's voice blasted out of my phone receiver. "Southerland! I'm glad you called. I've got some work for you. I need you to bring down a scumbag huckster who's suing my client for defamation. I'm thinking of getting a joy girl to lure the huckster into a hotel room, and when things get hot, you'll be there to kick in the door and snap some pictures. It'll be fun!"

"Who's your client?"

"Evita Diamond."

"The gossip columnist? The one they call the 'Queen of Slander'?"

"Hey, watch it! She's a legit investigative reporter."

"She's a sleaze peddler."

"Wrong. She's a *rich* sleaze peddler."

"Don't you have anything else?"

"You're so busy you can pick and choose?"

I sighed. "I had a client. Unfortunately, she was murdered. Some monster ran off with her heart and liver."

"Th'fuck, Southerland! At least tell me she paid you before she was knocked off."

"A poor woman is butchered—and all you can think of is money?"

"Money makes the world go round, Southerland. If you weren't such a low-rent dick, you'd know that. So did you collect your dough or what?"

"No. She was torn apart before she could pay me."

"Why didn't you collect up front, you knucklehead? Lord's balls, Southerland! There's no profit in dying poor."

"Anyway, that's not why I called. Someone ransacked my office."

"Did they get whatever you were hiding?"

"I wasn't hiding anything."

"Lord's balls! Then why did they take your office apart?"

"It might have something to do with the murder of my client."

"Do you know who did her in?"

"No. I was shackled to a tabletop when it happened. A spirit was trying to sacrifice me to another spirit. I got away, but I think the murder and the attempted sacrifice are connected. I think whoever tore my office apart is part of it, too. He might be the same mug who killed my client."

"Th'fuck, Southerland! And you're telling me all this because…?"

"Because something's going on, and I don't know what it is or where it's headed. I may need some legal assistance before it's all done. Also, I wanted to get some input from a mind more devious than my own."

Lubank paused for a few moments. "Okay. You know a place called Muvo's? A bar and grill on Gaunt Street?"

"No, but I can find it."

"Good. I'll meet you there in an hour."

He disconnected the call.

***

I walked up the block to Giovanni's Auto Repair to pick up my ridiculous beast of a car. As a private investigator, the last thing I wanted to be was noticed, and the beastmobile stood out in traffic like a shark in a school of sardines. It wasn't a proper car for a professional peeper, but I couldn't bring myself to let it go. I'd acquired it almost by accident, and I'd kept it because I liked how I felt when I was sitting behind the wheel watching other cars scramble to give me room. It had power to burn, and Gio and his son, Antonio, kept it running like a top. Plus, I could sleep fully stretched out in the damned thing if I needed to, something I'd proved more than once.

When I got to his shop, I found Gio gazing at the engine of a twenty-year-old cherry red rag top like a man in love. Hearing me coming, Gio turned his gaze my way and smiled.

He nodded at the convertible. "Back when I was single, I would have given my left nut to own a chick magnet like this. Couldn't afford it then. If I bought one now my wife would think I was fuckin' cheating on her. Or trying to." He shook his head. "After I replace the oil pan gasket, I'm going to take it downtown for a test drive. Cruise the boulevard on a Saturday night, just like the old days."

"Having a midlife crisis, Gio?" I asked.

He looked back at the object of his desire. "Nah. That's still a couple of years off. Maybe when Antonio gets out of school. I still can't believe he's going to be a senior this year. Then it's off to his three-year mandatory. I told you he wants to work on jet engines, right?"

I nodded. "He should have a good shot. He's a good mechanic."

Gio wiped sweat off his forehead with a greasy rag. "On cars, sure. I told him he should apply to a motor pool. But you know kids. They're never satisfied."

"Could be worse," I said. "If he didn't know how to fix engines, the realm might want to make a soldier out of him."

Gio grimaced. "That would be tough on his mother, that's for sure."

"Not you?"

Gio forced a smile on his face. "You and me both got through it all right. But I ain't gonna lie, I'd be a lot happier if the kid never saw combat." He snapped his fingers. "That reminds me. Antonio downloaded a government application for training on jet engines, and he needs a couple of references. Would you be willing to write a letter for him? It doesn't have to be nothing fancy, just a note saying he's done a crackerjack job working on your car."

"I'd be happy to. When do you need it?"

"He doesn't need to send in his application until the beginning of September. And thanks, pal. I'll owe you a beer."

"I'll get it to you as soon as I can. If I haven't given it to you by sometime next week, you have my permission to nag me about it until I do."

"I'll hold you to that. You been busy? You missed poker last night."

"Yeah, sorry. I had a case. Unfortunately, it ended early."

"What happened?"

I took a deep breath. "Well, among other things, the client died."

"Holy shit, man!"

"Yeah. Also, someone broke into my office this morning and trashed it."

"Alkwat's fuckin' balls! You call the police?"

"I'm holding off on that for now."

Gio stared at me for a few moments before slowly shaking his head. "Fuck, Alex. How much trouble are you in?"

"Hopefully no more than I can handle. The office is a mess. I gotta see my lawyer right now, but I've got some cleaning up to do when I get back."

"You need a hand? I'll get Antonio to help you. It's the least he can do for your recommendation."

I waved away his offer. "No need. I'm sure he's got better things to do with his time during his summer break."

74

"Are you kidding? The lazy fucker hardly comes out of his room anymore. When you bring your car back, I'll send him over to see you."

I considered the idea. "I guess I could use the help, but only if he's willing. And I'll pay him for his time."

"All right, but don't pay him too much. He'll just waste it on cigarettes and fuckin' video games. Those games are sucking his brains out. He's hardly come up for air since school let out. It's all I can do to get him to help out at the shop from time to time. And now he wants to work on fuckin' jets? It's like cars ain't good enough for him no more." He sniffed and spat on the asphalt. "Anyway, work his ass off. A little hard work'll do the boy some good."

***

Lubank was perched atop an elevated stool when I stepped into Muvo's Bar & Grill, his feet dangling high over the floor. The gnome's obvious hairpiece was pushed a bit too far toward one large, rounded ear, and the overexposed gnome ear bulging up from the other side of his face gave his head an unbalanced look. His expensive miniature green and red striped suit and emerald tie were out of place in the B & G, but his air of supreme confidence combined with the always angry gleam in his eyes was sufficient to turn away potential troublemakers, even ones twice his size.

"You're late," he admonished when I pulled myself onto the stool next to his. "My billable hour started six and a half minutes ago."

"You should have suggested a place closer to mine."

"Why the fuck would I do that? Anyway, I'd've charged you for the drive over. You want a beer?" He snapped his fingers in the direction of a waitress, who veered away from the table she'd been heading for and hurried our way.

For the next forty-five minutes, over beers and deep-fried calamari, I gave Lubank the skinny on my previous day's activities, finishing with a detailed account of the state of my office. He mostly let me talk, asking only a few questions along the way to clarify some points here and there. When I mentioned the strange whistling that had disoriented me during my walk, Lubank stopped me. "And it was the same whistling you heard while you were strapped to the tabletop?"

"Far as I can tell," I said. "Why? Do you know something about it?"

"Maybe. It reminds me of a story I heard a few years back. I was at a cocktail party with some other prominent members of the legal profession. A certain judge whose name I won't mention was getting very chatty with me, especially after I'd slipped a little something in his drink to loosen him up. I was recording him with my phone, hoping he'd reveal some dirt about his past that I could use as leverage against him some day. No luck in that department as it turned out, but I remember this story he said his mother used to tell him about a demon they called the Whistler. According to the story, a boy lived in poverty with his mother and his no-good drunken papa. One day, when the boy and his papa were out hunting, the boy killed the papa and cut him up. He brought the liver and heart back home to his mother and told her to cook them for dinner. He said they came from a pig. But the mother got suspicious and cursed the son to wander for all eternity. Oh yeah, the mother was a witch or something. I forgot to mention that part."

I shrugged. "So what does this have to do with a whistle?"

"Hold your horses, peeper. I'm getting to it." Lubank knocked back some of his beer and let out a quiet belch. "So, anyway, the son wanders the earth, hunting for food. Part of the curse his mother laid on him was that he was always hungry. I forgot to tell you that earlier. Anyway, to attract game, he whistles, which is why they call him the Whistler. And when you hear the whistle, it means something bad's about to go down. Like someone's gonna die or some shit like that. I can't remember the details. But here's where it gets interesting. This is the part that reminds me of what you were talking about. When you hear the whistling up close, it means that the Whistler is far away, and everything's copacetic. But when the whistle sounds like it's far away, what that actually means is that the Whistler is right on top of you, and he's about to fuck you up." Lubank growled and held his hands up, his fingers bent like claws.

"Right." I said. "So when I heard the whistling up close, it meant the 'Whistler' wasn't anywhere near me. And that's why my senses were sending me the wrong signals."

Lubank smiled. "So you're safe as long as you can hear the whistle from nearby."

"And if it seems to be coming from far away..."

"Then..." Lubank made a cutting gesture across his throat with his thumb.

"Cute story."

"Hey! Disregard it at your peril." Lubank finished off his glass and signaled the waitress to bring another round.

Once we had fresh glasses, Lubank asked, "Do you think Kalama's right? Did your whatchacallit, your pet monster... do you think he hacked up your client, followed you home, and went berserk in your office?"

I didn't want to answer. Finally, I said, "I don't think so. I mean, sure, he's capable. But I don't think it's in his nature."

"You don't think it's in his nature? Th'fuck, Southerland! It's a wild animal. I don't let Gracie come anywhere near the Porter District since we heard you were hiding that insane man-eating creature in your fuckin' laundry room. You're lucky I haven't called Animal Control—they've been after that thing for years!"

"Okay, Chivo is insane. I'll grant you that. But deep down inside, he's human."

Lubank barked out a single chuckle. "Oh, he's *human*! Like all you humans aren't a little crazy."

I lifted my eyes at him. "You're married to a human."

"Gracie? You're making my point for me, Southerland. She's crazy as a loon! That's what I love about her."

I sipped the foam off my beer and bit off a chunk of calamari. "Possums and raccoons aren't safe from Chivo. Maybe he's a danger to stray dogs and cats, too. And it's been a while since I've seen any coyotes in my alley at night. But going out of his way to hunt down one of my clients? That doesn't jive with what I know about him."

Lubank gave me a sidelong glance. "Oh? And how much is that? How long have you owned him?"

"I don't own him. I just keep him well fed and give him a place to sleep. He's been coming by for a little more than a year, and in all the time he's been with me he hasn't hurt anyone who wasn't either trying to kill me or breaking into my house. As far as I know, at least." The last part came out in a mumble, and I bit off some more calamari.

Lubank gulped some beer and frowned. "What about that thing with the other lady, Sonoma Deerling. You say she was pledging her loyalty to your monster?"

"That's what it looked like to me."

"I've been thinking about that. What if you're wrong?"

I stopped chewing. "What do you mean?"

"Blood is a powerful substance, and it can be used in a lot of different ways. You wouldn't believe some of the things I've run across in my time. I could tell you stories that would make your fuckin' hair curl. You say this Deerling dame follows a spirit of death?"

"Cizin."

"Right. And you say she recognized your monster and was immune to its stare. She's got some fuckin' mojo, right? Do you know how much?"

"Well.... No," I admitted. "Not exactly. It might be a lot."

"What I'm wondering is if maybe she didn't offer up her blood to seal a bond of loyalty, at least not in the way you're thinking. What if she gave him her blood in order to control him? Blood can be used that way, you know. It could be that she's in charge of your monster now."

"She's in control of Chivo?"

"It's a possibility. And if I'm right...." He bit off some calamari and washed it down with the remainder of his beer. "If I'm right, then maybe she was pissed enough at her wife to feed her to that fuckin' thing."

Chapter Nine

Antonio's eyes popped when he saw the wreckage in my office. "Dad told me someone broke into your place, but this is fucked up!"

"This is nothing. Come on." I led him through the back door of my office and down the hall to the laundry room.

"Alkwat's balls! Look what they did to your washing machine. And where'd all that sand come from?"

But my attention was drawn to the corner of the ceiling, where Siphon was drifting quietly, a bubble of translucent air about the size and shape of a basketball. I called up his sigil and tried to make contact, but the elemental wasn't receiving.

"Mr. Southerland? You okay?"

I turned back to Antonio. "Yeah, no problem." I held out a plastic garbage bag. "Scoop up the sand and bag it. There's a shovel and a broom in that closet."

"What are you going to do about your washing machine and dryer?"

Good question. "I don't know yet. They're probably beyond repair. I guess I'll have to dump them."

Antonio stared at the appliances. "Did someone smash them with a sledgehammer or something?"

I studied the machines. "Your guess is as good as mine. I don't think it was any kind of hammer, though."

"Why not?"

I pointed at the dryer. "See how long and narrow this dent is? A hammer would have made something more round." I placed my arm over the impression.

"Ketz!" Antonio exclaimed. "It looks like you did it yourself!"

I snorted. "Not me. I'm not *that* strong."

Antonio thought about it. "Hmm. You think a troll did this?"

"I don't think so. The indentation would be wider. It's not even as wide as my arm. Maybe someone used a bar of some kind."

"Like a tire iron?"

"Maybe." I studied the dent more carefully. "Or maybe not. I don't think anything metal did this unless it was covered with cloth. Notice how the enamel isn't scratched?"

Antonio shook his head. "I don't know, Mr. Southerland. You're the private eye. Why would anyone do this? You think they'll come back?"

"Beats me, kid. I sure hope not." I gave the side of the dryer a slap. "Well, let's get to it."

After an hour of scooping sand and picking up debris, I was surprised by the amount of progress we'd made. We hauled the washer and dryer out to the alley, and I told Antonio it was time for a break.

"You want a beer?" I asked him. "You've earned it."

"Sure!"

"Wait here, I'll get you one."

When I returned to the alley, Antonio was leaning against the wall with a cigarette in his lips. I handed him a bottle and took a drink from my own. "Your dad says you want to work on jet engines."

The kid's eyes lit up. "Sure do! I think that'd be crazy!"

"You don't want to work on cars anymore?"

He tipped his bottle to his lips and gulped down some cold brew. "Don't get me wrong, I love working on cars. Especially the beastmobile! I'll be happy to take it off your hands whenever you say." He smiled, showing me his teeth, and took another sip from the bottle. "But I've been working on cars since I learned to walk. I want to do something different with my mandatory service. The realm might give me an opportunity to do something new. Something bigger. You know?"

"I hear you," I said, sipping at my brew.

"And, who knows, if I'm working on jets, maybe I'll stay in the service and keep on working on them."

"Three years won't be enough for you? You wanna be a lifer?"

"Not for just any ol' thing," Antonio said. "But I think I could stand working for the realm for a long time if it meant working on jets."

I studied the boy as I nursed my beer. He'd been a gawky fourteen-year-old when I'd first met him. He was still skinny, but he'd grown half a foot since then, and the scruff on his face was more than peach fuzz. I guessed he was shaving at least every other day now. "What'll you do if the realm decides it doesn't want you working on jets?"

He frowned and dropped his eyes. "I guess I could work in a motor pool. But... I don't know...." He looked up. "It would be the same ol' thing, you know? They say mandatories are supposed to give you an opportunity to improve yourself. To challenge yourself, you know? I can already fix cars. Fuck, I can fix any car that's ever been driven. I'm as good at it as my old man." He smiled. No teeth this time, though. "I'd say better, but no one's better with cars than Dad."

"That's true. He's been at it a long time."

Antonio's smile disappeared. "Yeah."

"You know he'll make you a partner after you've finished your three-year stint."

The kid's face hardened. "I know. But that's just it, you know? I mean, I don't want to spend my whole fuckin' life doing something I already know I can do without fuckin' knowing whether I could have done something else that might have been... I don't know... been better? Or... something? I mean.... Does that make sense?"

I gulped down a swallow of beer, feeling old.

Antonio nodded at me. "Did you always want to be a private investigator? I mean, when you were my age?"

I chuckled. "When I was your age all I wanted to do was bum around on street corners. I thought private eyes only existed in movies and TV shows."

"How did you get to be a P.I.?"

"I finished up my service in the military police. I bummed around a little after that and just kind of eased into it. It wasn't much of a stretch, though, after my time as an MP."

Antonio pointed at me with his cigarette stub. "See what I'm sayin'? If it hadn't been for the service, where would you have ended up?"

I finished off the last swallow from my bottle. Jail, probably, I thought to myself. Out loud I said, "I have no idea."

Antonio smiled, like he knew.

"Your dad says you'd like a letter of recommendation from me."

He blew a stream of cigarette smoke out of the corner of his mouth. "Sure, if you're willing."

"I'll give it my best shot. You better get one from someone respectable, though, too. Maybe a teacher?"

Antonio's toothy smile returned. "Don't worry. I've got that covered. I actually did pretty well in my alchemy class last year, especially after my little sister started helping me with my homework."

"Gemma?"

"Yeah. Once they found out she had the talent, she really got into studying up on formulas and potions. It's a real advantage having a witch helping you out with your alchemy. She's crazy good with that shit!"

I flipped my bottle into an open garbage can and stretched, working the kinks out of my shoulder and knowing I was going to be sore in the morning. "You ready to get back at it? It shouldn't take the two of us long to finish off the laundry room. We've finished with the worst of it."

"What about your office?"

I suppressed a smile. The teenager's energy was boundless. "I think I can take care of it myself," I said. "Thanks for helping out with the washer and dryer."

"No problem. Thanks for the beer." The kid took one last gulp and let out a belch that echoed down the length of the alley.

***

I gave Antonio some pocket change when we were done and told him to use the dough to take some nice girl on a date.

"Can I pick her up in the beastmobile?" he asked, smiling broadly.

"Sorry, kid. No father in his right mind is going to let you take his daughter out in that motel on wheels. Besides, I may be needing it myself tonight."

Antonio's smile grew even broader. "Oh yeah?"

"For business," I said.

"Whatever you say." He gave me a thumbs up.

***

The physical labor and lack of sleep caught up to me after Antonio left, and I fell into bed, exhausted, for what I hoped would be a short nap. My eyes closed, and my thoughts faded into oblivion.

I stood at the end of the Old Placid Point Pier, the tide rolling gently beneath me through the pilings. The structure was new and intact; the heavy damage Badass had inflicted upon the railings was not evident. As I gazed at the reflection of the bright moonlight rippling on the water, I became aware of the old elf standing next to me, his head covered by the hood of his cloak.

"It is a time for hope, my friend." As always, the elf's mesmerizing voice captured my whole attention. "The hope I invested in you has proven to be fertile, and a great harvest is at hand. The work on the stem cells you recovered for me has borne fruit, thanks to the reifying formula you retrieved. Ketz-Alkwat's attempt to give birth to a new dragon has been stalled. Thunderbird, whom you aided in his time of need, grows and blossoms. We have achieved much in a short period of time. Our pace has been... remarkable."

"You're going to do it then? You're going to destroy the Dragon Lords?"

From within the hood, I could see a yellow gleam in the elf's eyes as they reflected the light of the moon. "Mmm, who can say? It has been several thousand years since the dragons all but eradicated the elves, and for several thousand years I have been plotting against our conquerors. I see an end, but it is still far off. Many generations of humans will rise before my hopes are fulfilled, if fulfilled they ever will be. And yet, it is because of the brief lives of humans, lives that flare brightly for a moment and pass in an instant, that my plans have progressed as they have."

The elf took a long breath. "I was wrong to have avoided humans for so long. When humans turned on elves and chose to fight for the Dragon Lords, I let myself be blinded by resentment. I have only recently come to realize what strength lies in the short lives of humans. How the very fact of the brevity of human life inspires creative thought and motivation to act."

The elf turned his head, revealing a small, sad smile on his hooded face. "Elves will delay putting plans into action for a thousand years in order to wait for the time to be ripe. Why not? Death does not press us, and we have no reason to hurry. But humans, who live in the imminence of death, must act quickly, and they must quickly find ways to make the time suitable for action. The problem, of course, is obvious."

"What do you mean?"

"Strengths carry their own weaknesses, my friend. Humans burn briefly, but with the light of a star. And they reproduce so rapidly. That much energy, if unrestrained by the other sentient species, would destroy the earth and several other nearby realms of existence besides. But I don't have to tell you that."

I had no idea what he was talking about, but I was paralyzed by the sound of his voice.

The elf reached up with both hands and pulled back his hood, exposing an ancient weather-worn face framed by large, pointed ears. His smile broadened, and I was swept into the lime-green pools of his wide, almond-shaped eyes. "Since I made the decision to reconcile with humans, a newly found energy flows within me. I spend less time plotting and more time accomplishing. I have a renewed hope." He raised a finger. "But hope can ever be thwarted."

The elf slowly lowered his finger until it was pointed at me. "You must preserve our hope. You must act quickly and decisively, as only a human can. You must discover who has brought about the death of Clara Novita. You must do so quickly, before those forces that seek to snuff out the brief flare of your existence succeed in doing so. Indeed, finding the murderer is the key to preserving your own life."

I made myself speak. "Forces? You mean Ixquic?" My voice sounded like the braying of a crow after the elf's melodious tones.

The elf lowered his hand. "Yes. She hungers."

"She.... Wait." Realization dawned on me. "It was you! You were the one who made me draw that picture of her."

"Of course." He frowned. "I thought you knew that. Didn't I make it clear to you?"

"No, you didn't."

A puzzled look crossed the elf's face. "Hmmm. Apparently, I overestimated your powers of comprehension. I still have much to learn about human perception and intelligence." He shrugged. "No matter. You are aware now that I was the source of that communication, correct?"

"Sure, now that you've told me."

He smiled. "Very well, then. You must not let the Waning Blood Moon deprive you of your life's energy until you have completed your task. It is vital that she not succeed in convincing Cizin to provide his support in her quest to appeal to Itzamna. The Waning Blood Moon would grow in strength, and, of course, her increased strength would increase the strength of Ketz-Alkwat and Manqu, in turn."

I frowned. "It would do what now?"

The elf turned to stare at me. "Surely you can see that." I noticed that the old elf had become transparent. I looked through him to the rolling swells of the ocean. The light reflecting off the water was tinged with scarlet.

"Uhh..."

"Hush. You have much to do. I will endeavor to speak with you again when you have finished your task."

Questions darted through my head, but before I could ask them, the elf faded from view, along with the pier and the rolling red ocean.

It was just getting dark when I climbed out of the bed and into a hot shower.

***

Clean, but feeling as if I hadn't slept at all, I went downstairs to see if Chivo had returned while I was in bed. I knew my dreamlike conversation with the elf had not, in fact, been a dream, which meant I'd been conscious through it all. I wondered if the elf drew upon the life energy in dreams the way Clearwater told me the dream-traveling *wayobs* did. If I'd slept afterward, it had been dreamless and unsatisfying. My mind lagged behind, floating in a sea of mud, as my body dragged itself down the stairs and into the laundry room.

Chivo's bowl of yonak was untouched, and the creature was nowhere to be seen. Neither was Siphon. I tried to contact the elemental, but it was no use. I tried to contact Badass, too, with the same result. I clamped down on the pit of ice that was opening in my chest and midsection and forced myself to think about something other than loss. Like the letter I was going to write for Antonio. Good kid, Antonio. I hoped they'd let him work on jet engines. Seemed like a good career for the young man.

Back upstairs in my living room, I checked my phone for messages. I had several, most of them from scam artists trying to steal my identity, but only one of importance: a voice message from a number I didn't recognize. I assumed it was another scammer until I heard the message.

"Mr. Southerland, this is Sonoma Deerling. We need to talk. Call me, please, and I'd appreciate it if you kept the police out of it for now. I'll explain."

I tapped the call button, and Sonoma's voice came on the line. "Mr. Southerland? Are you alone?"

"I'm alone," I said. "Where are you?"

"Avoiding the cops. Jalen is with me."

"Jalen? I thought he was with the police. Is he all right?"

"He's fine. I didn't kidnap him, if that's what you're thinking. He's with me by choice."

"Can I talk to him?"

After a brief pause, I heard a sullen male voice. "I'm fine. Um, this is Jalen. I'm with Momma. The police think she killed Mother, but they're full of shit."

I heard Sonoma tell Jalen to give her back the phone, and she came back on the line. "Jalen's a little upset, but he's right. The police think I had something to do with Clara's death. I'm afraid I lost my patience with them, and I... took Jalen and myself away from them. I'll explain all this later. If I tell you where I am, will you promise to come alone?"

"Maybe. Do you know how Mrs. Novita died?"

Sonoma didn't answer right away, and I heard her sigh. "I... I might. And if I'm right, then Jalen's life might be in danger, too. And mine. Will you help us?"

"Why me? What do you think I can do for you?"

"That's something we can discuss when you get here."

The air in my apartment was beginning to grow stifling, and I was nearly overcome by a need to be outside. "I don't know, Mrs. Deerling."

"Sonoma, please."

"How do I know you aren't going to play me for a sap, Mrs. Deerling? Running from the police was a bad idea. I think you should call them and tell them you made a mistake."

"I can't do that, Mr. Southerland. Cops are lazy. When someone is murdered, their first thought is that the domestic partner did it. If they can pin it on the wife or husband, they don't bother to investigate any further. But this time, they're wrong. I'm innocent."

"Then turn yourself in."

"They won't believe me. They'll blame me for Clara's death."

"Look, Mrs. Deerling—Sonoma—I know the homicide detective working your case. She's a good cop, the best I know. If you're innocent, you don't have anything to be afraid of. But she'll need you to answer some questions so that she can find out who did it."

"I'm not going to argue with you, Mr. Southerland." Sonoma sounded exasperated. "She might be a great cop. She might be the greatest cop in the world."

"So talk to her."

"*I can't!*"

"Why not?"

She sighed. "Because I might be the reason Clara was killed."

I didn't say anything, but I didn't disconnect the call, either. I listened to the slow, steady thumping of my heartbeat until Sonoma said, "I didn't kill her, Mr. Southerland. But it's possible that I might be responsible for her death. The things I'm involved in, things I've set in motion.... Please. It's been a horrible night, and I've barely slept. I need to see you. Alone. I'll tell you everything I know, and then you can decide what to do with it."

I took in a breath and held it for a beat before letting it out. "All right, Sonoma. Tell me where you are."

Chapter Ten

The address Sonoma gave me was a tiny basement studio apartment beneath a secondhand clothing store called Mandy's Closet in the Tanielu only a few blocks from her home. The apartment consisted of a single low-ceilinged room with basic kitchen appliances against one wall, a few items of furniture, and a small walled-off toilet in one of the corners. A trapdoor in the ceiling presumably opened into the clothing store above. The room was lit with a single candle whose light didn't penetrate the darkness to the street outside. My elf-enhanced awareness worked in the dark, and I knew Sonoma and Jalen were the only people inside the place.

"The owners of the store are friends of mine," Sonoma explained after guiding me to a chair and sitting on a sofa across from me. "They know I'm here and that Jalen is with me."

"How long do you think you can stay here before the cops find you?"

"A long time, I think. But I don't want to test it. I'm only planning to stay the night, and then we'll be on our way. My time in Yerba City has been good, but I'm afraid it's no longer a safe haven for Jalen and me. We will be leaving as soon as we can. I've got some friends who'll help us."

I turned to look toward the back of the room where Jalen sat on the floor in darkness, glaring at me with surly eyes through the glow of the candlelight.

I nodded in his direction. "You okay, kid?"

He let his mother answer for him. "He's upset about his mother. We both are."

"Tell me what happened."

She leaned forward, her hands folded at her knees. "Ixquic, the Blood Moon, came to me in a dream several weeks ago. As I told you, I am a chosen of Cizin. Ixquic and Cizin have been estranged for a long time, since the coming of Ketz-Alkwat and Manqu. She wishes to settle the grudge between them. Cizin will not speak with Ixquic, but he has agreed to allow a greater spirit, Itzamna, to arbitrate their differences if he is willing to do so. But he will not contact Itzamna himself. Cizin says that it is Ixquic who must convince Itzamna to settle their differences."

"Itzamna is the 'toothless one who brings nothing but good'?"

Sonoma nodded. "Yes. But do not refer to him as the 'toothless one.' He is the high spirit of the heavens. He is more properly addressed as the spirit of the day, the sun, the sky, and the moon."

"I thought Ixquic was the spirit of the moon."

"She is the Waning Blood Moon." Sonoma sighed. "The spirits are not humans. It is useless to try to understand them as if they were. The labels we use for them are for our convenience, not theirs. Ixquic is the moon in one of its... its..."

"Moods?"

Sonoma shot me a surprised glance. "Yes, that's right. One of its moods. But Itzamna is the moon in its totality."

"Along with the day and the sun."

"And the sky. As I say, Itzamna is the high spirit, the greatest of all spirits, and a spirit of goodness. But he is, and has always been, a passive spirit. He allows others, who are lesser, more capricious and less kind versions of himself, to act according to their own desires."

I was getting restless, and I squirmed in my seat, trying to get comfortable. "I'll take your word for it. Get to the part where I don't call the police."

Sonoma studied her folded hands for a few moments, gathering her thoughts. She looked up and said, "For reasons too complicated to get into at this time, I decided to help Ixquic. The rift between Cizin and Ixquic must be healed. It is not right that they are in opposition. It upsets a precarious balance. To petition Itzamna, Ixquic needs to accumulate certain energies. To gather these energies, she needs followers. I asked her to choose Jalen and be his spirit guide, and she agreed. In return, Jalen would gather followers. I am hoping that my efforts will lead to the opening of a fruitful communication between Cizin and Ixquic."

"You told me that Jalen was seeking a spirit guide. You didn't tell me that Ixquic had already chosen him."

Sonoma dropped her eyes. "I'm sorry. I wasn't entirely honest with you. I felt it best if you didn't know... certain things."

I didn't like being lied to, and something stirred inside me, sending a wave of unpleasantness up from my stomach and into my head. I clamped down on it. "Uh-huh. So your son got some of his buddies to be Ixquic's batteries?"

"Well... crudely put, but something like that. And, yes, they all came willingly. I explained the situation to Jalen, and he was eager to help. There is... reward in it for him. And for the others that he contacted.

Ixquic is a potent entity. A goddess, for all intents and purposes. Near enough, anyway."

"I see. It all sounds perfectly dandy. Except for the part where Ixquic clamped me to an altar so she could rip my heart out."

Sonoma's face tightened. "Yes. And I apologize for that. Let me assure you, it wasn't planned. You shouldn't have been there. You should never have been involved at all. Clara... well, I guess that was partly my fault. I wasn't honest with her, either. But if she had known what was going on...." Sonoma's eyes moistened, and her hand flew up to pinch the bridge of her nose.

That's when the anger and frustration that had been growing inside me since the night before decided to break free. Maybe I could have controlled it better if I'd been better rested, if it hadn't been more than a day and a half since I'd had any proper shuteye. As it was, I spoke without restraint: "You mean she might still be in possession of her heart and liver?"

Sonoma jerked her head to glare into my eyes. "How dare you! I was protecting her! You have no idea."

I couldn't hold back. "You were protecting her?" I asked, scorn in my voice. "Sure you were. How'd that work out for her?"

Sonoma shot out of her seat. "You have no right! Who the fuck do you think you are?" Behind her, Jalen was staring at the two of us with alarm.

I remained seated, but my whole body was shaking. "Sit down, Mrs. Deerling. You're right. I was out of line, and I apologize. I'm sorry you lost your wife. She seemed like a caring and decent woman. But you brought danger on your household when you started fucking around with nature spirits and so-called goddesses that were too big for you to handle. The least you could have done was let your wife know what kind of trouble you were setting her up for. Her and her son."

"Her son? Yes, Jalen is her son. But only for half his life. I'm the one who gave birth to him. And I'm the one who brought him here. Clara was good to Jalen. She loved Jalen, and Jalen loved her. But Jalen comes from *my* people, not from Clara's. He was born into my culture and my traditions. The spirits of my people have been watching him since he was born."

The anger drained from Sonoma, like water from a wet towel hanging on the line, and she lowered herself to the sofa. When she spoke again, her voice was quieter, but no less firm. "Clara didn't understand. She wanted to separate him from his culture. She tried to deprive him of his identity. We may have moved north, but our hearts are still with the family we were forced to leave behind. I didn't bring the spirits down upon our household. The spirits have been with us both for our entire lives. They are a part of who we are."

I pressed her. I couldn't help myself. Something ugly had pushed its way past restraints weakened by lack of sleep. My blood was running hot, and I wanted her to hurt. "Sure, Mrs. Deerling. They're a part of who you are. And they're a part of who your son is." My voice raised. I couldn't stop it. "But they aren't a part of who Clara was. Was she in their way?"

Sonoma made a choking sound and put her head in her hands. "Maybe. Maybe." Tears streamed from her eyes. "You think I don't know what I brought into her life? Fuck. Fuck. Oh, fuck, Mr. Southerland. What if I'm the one who killed Clara after all? What if it's all my fault?" She began to cry out loud, emitting one great wrenching sob after another, each one erupting from deep in her chest.

This wasn't the reaction I'd been expecting. With each sob, a little of my anger dissipated into the thick air of the tiny basement room, until I sat slumped in my seat, sticky with sweat and feeling like a heel.

Jalen rose from the floor and went to his mother. He put an arm around her shoulder and glared at me, flickering candlelight shining from his eyes. "This is bullshit. Momma didn't kill Mother. She wasn't even there. Tell him, Momma."

Sonoma wiped away her tears with her sleeve and turned to me. "After I returned from your office last night, I argued with Clara over the direction we wanted for our son. Jalen was out. She was awake, but drowsy from the sedative I had given her. I told her everything about Ixquic and Cizin, and what Jalan and I were doing to bring the two spirits together. Clara was furious. She wanted nothing to do with any of it, and she didn't want Jalen to be a part of it. It was the biggest fight we'd ever had, and I ended up stomping out of the house. But she was alive when I left, even though no one is going to be able to prove it."

"Where did you go?"

"I went to see the Children of Cizin." Seeing the quizzical look in my face, she continued. "We're a community of people who have been chosen by the Lord of Death. There are thirteen of us here in Yerba City. We meet at a temple." She smiled with half her mouth. "Really just a small loft over in the Humback near Bunker Park."

That seemed appropriate. The Humback District was located in the center of town and was celebrated as a free-spirited haven for fringe groups of all types, whether it be political, artistic, sexual, or occult.

"What time did you leave your apartment?" I asked.

"A little after three in the morning."

"Odd time for a meeting."

"Special circumstances. I called it because of the Huay Chivo."

I sat up in my chair. "What about him?"

Sonoma sighed. "I grew up on the Cutzyetelkeh Peninsula, Mr. Southerland. Technically, it's part of Tolanica, but we're right up against the Borderland, and fighting from the war there spilled into our fields and villages. My family was very poor. We never had much, and we lost a lot to the fighting, but we hung on to our traditions. The man who became the Huay Chivo used to rule a kingdom that stretched over most of Cutzyetelkeh, and my family and neighbors were descended from his subjects. Most people have forgotten that man's name, but it is preserved among my people: Lord Cadmael. Cadmael was not only a warrior, he was a great sorcerer. When Lord Ketz-Alkwat came, Cadmael put up a heavy resistance, but, after nearly thirty years of fighting, Cadmael was not only overcome, he was driven mad. Ketz-Alkwat captured Cadmael and punished him by locking him into the monster's form Cadmael had adopted at the end of his reign. Ketz-Alkwat kept him as a pet for a time, but Cadmael—now the Huay Chivo—escaped."

I repositioned myself in my seat. "This is all very interesting, and I'd love to know more about Chivo, but…"

Sonoma cut me off. "Bear with me, Mr. Southerland. This affects you, too. How long has the Huay Chivo been with you?"

"Couple of years. He pretty much goes his own way, mostly at night, but I keep him fed in order to protect the neighborhood pets, and I give him a place to sleep during the day."

Sonoma and Jalen both stared at me, eyes wide. Finally, Sonoma shook her head. "Remarkable. All this time….." She turned to me again. "When Jalen was six years old, my husband left me. Believe me when I say that I don't miss him. He was a lousy drunkard, a cruel man who was abusive to both me and Jalen. He fed us rats and scorpions when he was with us, and he left us with nothing but bare cupboards. Soon after he disappeared, Cizin came to me in a dream. He had chosen me when I was still a child, but he hadn't spoken to me in years. He told me to take my son and go north. When I asked him why, he said he wanted me to find the Huay Chivo and cure him of his madness. He said it was time."

I stared into the candle, mesmerized by the flickering glow. "Are you sure it was really him? I mean, why would he send you after the Huay Chivo?"

Sonoma smiled. "Why *not* me, Mr. Southerland? I found him, didn't I?"

I held up a hand. "Point taken. I meant no offense."

She raised an eyebrow and continued. "Yes, well, I must admit I asked him that very same question. Why me? He said he'd chosen me, and he assured me that I had the qualities he was looking for. What those qualities were, he wouldn't say. He also told me that he had chosen Lord Cadmael for himself back when he was a much more powerful spirit than the one he'd become. He'd suffered with the coming of Ketz-Alkwat, too, and he'd lost much of his power. He also lost his connection with Cadmael, now the Huay Chivo. I was to find the Huay Chivo, cure him, and reunite him with Cizin. Together, when the time was right, they would once again join the fight against Lord Ketz-Alkwat."

I leaned back in my chair, my mind racing. I'd heard stories about Chivo—the Huay Chivo--but never one as detailed as this. And, to be honest, I had never taken the stories I'd heard all that seriously. Chivo, a bad-smelling goat-faced monster with mangy fur and a stare that made people puke.... Chivo, who slept in a dog bed in my laundry room and slurped rancid troll food from a bowl I set out for him every day.... Chivo had really been a legendary ruler who'd fought against the Dragon Lord and held him at bay for years?

My skepticism must have shown on my face, because Sonoma said, "You don't believe me, do you."

"Chivo is a dangerous critter, and I know there's a human sorcerer somewhere in there, but it's hard to imagine that he's the same mug as some legendary warrior-king who stood toe-to-toe with Lord Ketz some six thousand years ago."

"Not six thousand years ago, Mr. Southerland. The Dragon Lords have been lying about that. Ketz-Alkwat and Manqu came across the ocean and conquered this part of the world no more than about five hundred years ago."

What was this? I began wondering whether Sonoma was as sane as she'd seemed. She might as well have told me that the sun first popped into the sky last Thursday.

Sonoma gave me a thin smile. "It's true, Mr. Southerland. It was only five centuries ago that Ketz-Alkwat and Manqu came to the West with their hordes of trolls, dwarves, and humans from the western

Huaxian Empire and conquered the ruling spirits and their human allies on this side of the world."

I shook my head. "You've lost me, Sonoma. I mean, the Dragon Lords came out of Hell six thousand years ago and created the Seven Realms. That's common knowledge."

Sonoma scoffed. "Common knowledge. Among you northerners, maybe. Don't you know that those who control the present shape the past to their own desires? What you call common knowledge is simply the knowledge the Dragon Lords allow you to possess."

"But you said that Lord Ketz and Lord Manqu came out of the Huaxian Empire, right? That's Ao Qin's realm."

"Right. Ao Qin and the other four Dragon Lords *did* come out of Hell six thousand years ago. They convinced the humans to betray the elves, and they conquered all of the lands of the East. But they never came to the West. The East was all they could handle. Five hundred years ago, more or less, Ketz-Alkwat and Manqu were brought out of Hell. They served Ao Qin at first. The Huaxian Empire is huge, and Ketz and Manqu helped him keep the western part of the Empire under control for a short time. But they wanted lands of their own, and eventually Ao Qin either gave them permission to go to the West, or they turned on him and did it against his will."

"And once they established their realms, they just lied and said they'd been in this world as long as the other Dragon Lords?"

"Yes, and that they'd been part of the original conquest. They wanted the same status and credibility as the other Dragon Lords, so they lied. And by controlling the output of information, they turned the lie into truth after just a few generations. They encouraged, and even forced, intermarriage between the Huaxian migrants and the people of the West in order to create a cultural mix. Only a few small close-knit communities have been able to hang on to the real history of their people, and most of them live in or near the Borderland. The wars there between Ketz-Alkwat and Manqu have made it difficult for them to suppress the traditions carried on by the people of that region."

My head was spinning, but I found myself believing Sonoma. In truth, I'd heard hints from people I trusted that Lord Ketz had lied about his past. Ralph, a nirumbee from a tribal community in the Baahpuuo Mountains in the Province of Lakota had once said something to me along these lines, but I'd had other things on my mind at the time and hadn't given it a second thought. Kai had said something to me a while back about some odd discoveries he was making at his architectural digs that cast doubt about the accepted history of the Great Migration of humans from western Huaxia, discoveries he said the government would never allow to see the light of day. But this was the first time anyone had ever flat out told me that Lord Ketz had rewritten history. I thought about the amount of control the Dragon Lords exerted over the dissemination of information in the media and in schools. Was it so hard to believe that we only knew what Lord Ketz wanted us to know?

"Manqu went along with this?" I asked once my thoughts had settled.

"Yes. Manqu and Ketz-Alkwat weren't always at each other's throats. My people have always believed that the two Dragon Lords are brothers. They were brought out of Hell at the same time."

"Brought out? By who? Ao Qin?"

Sonoma shook her head. "No, Mr. Southerland. By Ixquic. The Waning Blood Moon brought Ketz-Alkwat and Manqu to this world against the wishes of her father, Cizin, to be her children."

"You're telling me that Ixquic brought Lord Ketz and Manqu out of Hell?"

"And she encouraged them to come to the West to set up realms of their own. That's why Cizin hates his daughter Ixquic to this day. She is responsible for his fall from power."

"And now she wants to make up with him?"

"Not exactly. She wishes to bring her father to her side. She wants him to aid the Dragon Lords."

I blinked, trying to keep up. "Why would Cizin want to help the Dragon Lords?"

"I don't think he does. I think he just wants to know what Ixquic is up to. But it isn't always easy to know what he's thinking." Sonoma leaned toward me. Light from the candle cast shadows on her face, distorting her features in a way that made me believe she was a child of death. "Mr. Southerland," she said, lowering her voice as if she feared to be overheard. "There are forces at work trying to overthrow the Dragon Lords. Forces that would be greatly aided by the spirit of death reunited with a cured and restored Cadmael. That's why I want to summon the Huay Chivo and cure him. The Children of Cizin are going to do it tonight. And we need you to help us do it. May the Lord Itzamna help me, I think... I'm afraid it was the Huay Chivo who killed my wife. You have to help me stop him before he kills anyone else."

Jalen stood over his mother, who was slumped on the sofa, and tried to comfort her. Sonoma looked up at me, her face covered in shadow. "When I saw the Huay Chivo in your office, I couldn't believe it. I've been searching for him for so long, and there he was. I couldn't let him wander off without establishing a connection."

"That's why you gave him your blood."

She nodded. "Yes. Just a touch, but enough to establish a link between us. I needed to act fast. I had to get the Children of Cizin together right away to prepare for a proper summoning. But... I'm afraid I may have been reckless. I came home, and I think the Huay Chivo followed me, using the link that I'd established. I think he got into the apartment after I left, and... and...." She buried her face in her hands, unable to continue.

"You don't know that, Sonoma," I said.

Her head jerked up, eyes angry now. "No? You think it's all just one big coincidence?"

"I'm just saying we shouldn't jump to conclusions. Chivo's been with me long enough that I think I know him a little. I've never seen him attack anyone that wasn't threatening him, or me, in some way. And I don't believe for a minute that he would have considered Mrs. Novita to be a threat to either of us."

The anger left Sonoma's eyes, and I could feel her grasping at my words as if they were a lifeboat. "Do you really think so?"

"Let's keep an open mind until all the facts are in," I said. "What I'd really like to do is find Chivo before the authorities do. You said something about summoning him?"

Sonoma sat up. "Yes. We have a ritual, and we're going to use it tonight. It's all set. But I need you to be a part of it. You're an air elementalist, aren't you?"

"Yes, and I'm wondering how you know that."

"It's hard to hide much from Cizin, and he spoke to me this morning while I was sleeping. The ritual requires the presence of all four spirits of nature: air, earth, water, and fire. One of the Children can call up an earth elemental, and an adaro friend of mine has agreed to help out. She'll call up the water elemental."

"An adaro?"

"Yes. She's a licensed prostitute, so she's allowed out of the settlement. We don't have an air elementalist, though, but that's where you come in. Maybe that's why the Huay Chivo came to you in the first place. Some higher spirit must have arranged it. Maybe Cizin himself."

"You said Cizin lost his connection with Chivo—Lord Cadmael, that is—after Ketz-Alkwat trounced him. That's why he sent you to find him."

Sonoma scowled. "The link between them was broken, but maybe it wasn't completely severed. He might have still been able to influence the Huay Chivo in some way. Sometimes the spirits operate in ways that are a mystery to us."

"Uh-huh. What about fire?"

Sonoma's face sagged a little. "Fire elementalists are hard to find, so we have to improvise a little. But we've got it covered. I think. I hope."

That didn't sound too encouraging to me, but I agreed to help out. I very badly wanted to see Chivo, and only partly because I was used to having him around. Kalama and Sonoma had both fingered Chivo for killing Mrs. Novita. That didn't sit well with me. If they were right, then maybe Chivo had been playing me for a sucker these past couple of years. I wanted to be able to look him in his glowing red eyes and find the truth for myself.

Chapter Eleven

Jalen leaned away from his mother. "Do I have to go to the temple tonight?"

Sonoma frowned up at him. "Yes, you have to go. You're blood of my blood. You have to be there. It's important."

Jalen scowled and looked at his feet. His face was shrouded in darkness as he turned away from his mother.

Once again, unrestrained heat rose to my face. "What's the matter, Jalen? I thought you liked rituals. You liked the one where your girlfriend had me laid out on an altar."

The kid's head jerked my way, and he tried to scorch me with the fire in his eyes.

Sonoma put a protective hand on her son's arm and glared at me. "That's not fair. Jalen had nothing to do with that."

"No? Maybe not. But he wasn't having a problem with it, either."

Jalen rose to his full height. "You should be honored to have been chosen by the Blood Moon! Anyway, she wasn't going to hurt you. She was just sending some of your energy to the father spirit. You would have been fine. She's done it to a bunch of us. And it was supposed to be *my* turn! I was the one who was supposed to be honored. You butted in and ruined everything. The Blood Moon was going to channel some of *my* energy to the father spirit, to introduce me to him. It was *my* time! And you ruined it. First, she took you instead of me, and then you went and summoned that fucking demon. Me and the others were lucky to get out of there alive!"

I remembered what Clearwater had told me, that Jalen would die a horrible death if I didn't do something about it. "You got it wrong, kid. Ixquic was hungry. She wasn't looking for an appetizer. The lady was going for a full meal."

Jalen rolled his eyes at me. "Wrong. It was all set up. She even had a portal ready to take me home when we were done, same as she always did with the others."

I sighed and pushed back on my rage. "I don't know, kid. Maybe she'd've gone easy on you, but she was sucking the life out of me. If it hadn't been for my elemental, you would have been a witness to a murder."

"You're full of shit!"

Sonoma's head jerked toward her son. "Jalen!"

Her son didn't take his eyes off me. "He can't talk about Ixquic like that!"

"Sure I can, kid. She doesn't have me strapped down to a table at the moment."

Jalen shook his head and fixed me with the kind of snotty knowing look that no adult ever wants to see from a punk half their age.

This was getting me nowhere, and the last thing I wanted to do was get into a debate with a starry-eyed adolescent. I held up a hand. "All right, I'm not going to fight you. Maybe she was going to leave me a stiff and maybe she wasn't. That's neither here nor there. But I have a couple of questions for you, and I want you to answer them honestly. You think you can do that?"

Jalen lowered his eyes but didn't say anything.

"Who was that palooka with Ixquic? The one with all the hair."

Jalen looked up. "Hunbatz? He's just a servant."

"Hunbatz. Right. I think he's more than that."

"Yeah? Well, you don't know shit."

Sonoma yanked at her son's elbow, and he glowered at her for a moment before turning back to me. "He helps Ixquic out with stuff. Helps set up the chairs. Passes out the robes. Shit like that." He shot his mother a quick glance, and she rolled her eyes.

Shit like knocking out people in the street and strapping them down to be sacrificed, I thought to myself. Out loud, I said, "All right. Where did you go after you left the ceremony? Did you go straight home?"

"Yeah."

"Did you go through a portal?"

"No. Ixquic opens the portals for us, but she was kind of busy this time, so I had to walk." He struck me with an accusing glare.

"Did you see anything on the way?"

Jalen shrugged. "Like what?"

"Like the Huay Chivo?"

He lowered his eyes. "No."

"All right. You got home. Was the door open or locked?"

Jalen hesitated. "I don't know. Locked, I guess. I don't remember."

"You don't remember?"

He shrugged.

"But you have a key?"

"Yeah."

"Did you use it? Think!"

Jalen glared at me. "I don't know! I mean, I guess so. Mother always keeps the door locked." He faltered. "Kept it locked.... Wait a minute! Yes, I remember now. The door was definitely locked."

"You're sure?"

"Yes. The door has three locks, and a different key for each one. I was still upset about what happened at the ceremony, and I was fumbling around with my keys and in a hurry to get inside. My mind wasn't on what I was doing, you know? Anyway, I was unlocking the door, and I didn't get the top deadbolt unlocked all the way. I almost broke my fuckin' nose when I banged into the door. Then I got it unlocked and went in."

"Okay." I paused for a beat and gentled up my voice. "And when you walked in, what did you see?"

The kid's eyes gleamed in the candlelight. Sonoma turned to face me. "Why are you interrogating my son? He's already been through all this with the police."

I met her eyes across the darkness. "He doesn't have to answer me if he doesn't want to, Mrs. Deerling. But Mrs. Novita struck me as a good woman. I only just met her, and I didn't know her. But I liked her. She was strong. No nonsense. And sweet in her own way. She loved her family. She wanted what she thought was best for her son. I'd like to find out what happened to her." I nodded at Jalen. "He might be able to help me, if he's up to it."

Jalen spoke before his mother could. "She was on the living room floor, over near the couch. I saw her as soon as I walked through the door. I... can't remember what I did next. I... I kind of blanked out for a second, I think. I just remember being down there on the floor, next to her. She... there was blood everywhere. I got it on my hands. I think I tried... I tried to revive her. You know. CPR. And mouth-to-mouth. But...." He turned his head away from me, his eyes squeezed shut.

"And then you called the police?" I asked.

Jalen nodded. "I knew she was dead." He forced the words through a throat that didn't want to let them through. "I didn't know what else to do. So I called the cops. Then... then I sat next to her... holding her... and waited."

"And you didn't see or hear anybody in the house?"

Jalen shook his head. "No. Nobody. Momma wasn't there. Just me." The glow of the candlelight reflected off the tears on his cheeks. "That's all I know."

***

I agreed to meet Sonoma at her "temple" at midnight, which was still a couple of hours off. In the meantime, a hole the size of the moon was growing in my stomach, and I remembered I hadn't eaten since my early breakfast with Kalama, unless you counted the squid I'd munched during my meeting with Lubank. I had a rule about that: bar food doesn't count as a proper meal. My stomach was begging for something solid.

I didn't know any good restaurants in the Tanielu, but the Humback was filled with nice eateries if you could find your way past the vegetarian houses and the trendy exotic spots that had popped up in recent years. The latter tended to serve microscopic portions of mysterious foreign cuisine for prices that qualified as grand larceny. Just off the main street running through the center of the district was an older diner called The Hungry Hodag that served a decent steak sandwich with mushrooms and grilled onions and left you with enough dough to pay your rent, provided you had a steady job. My job wasn't all that steady, but I was hungry enough to risk it. Maybe Sonoma would pay me to find out what happened to Mrs. Novita if Chivo hadn't done it. It was a possibility.

As I made my way to the Humback in the beastmobile, I went over Sonoma's story. I have to admit I'd been surprised to hear that Jalen was her biological son. Mrs. Novita had seemed more... motherly. Sonoma was nearly as big as I was and almost as masculine. I shook off the thought. Drawing conclusions based on stereotypes was lazy, unprofessional thinking, and it led to a lot of false assumptions. Knowing that Jalen had come north with his birth mother from a village near the Borderland gave me insight into the kid that I'd lacked when all I had to go on was Mrs. Novita's description of a dedicated student trying to get into college. It struck me that Jalen was in a precarious position. His momma was a chosen of Cizin, who had fought against the Dragon Lords and still opposed them. Jalen, on the other hand, was being recruited by Ixquic, who, if Sonoma's story was true, had brought Lords Ketz-Alkwat and Manqu into our world and regarded them as her children. Sonoma was attempting to bring the two spirits together, but, at least for the time being, Jalen's momma's spirit guide and the spirit guide he was seeking for himself were still feuding. If it came down to a test of loyalty, I wondered which side the kid would choose.

The steak sandwich at The Hungry Hodag was as good as I remembered, and I tore into it with gusto. When I was done the waitress asked me if I wanted to try the Hungry Hodag's specialty dessert, an unsweetened chocolate cake baked with a liberal dose of cannabis and spiked with rum, but I settled for a cup of strong black coffee instead. I didn't know what to expect from the Children of Cizin's summoning ritual, and I wanted to be clearheaded when I walked into it.

When I left the diner, I still had more than an hour to kill before I needed to be at the temple. It was only a six-block walk, and I decided to hoof it, partly to walk off the sandwich and partly because the evening was clear, calm, and more crisp than cold. Nights like that were the exception in Yerba City, where the weather after sundown leaned toward foggy and windy, even in the summertime.

I pulled my hat low on my forehead and buried my hands in my coat pockets as I turned onto Bunker Street, the Humback's main drag, and strolled down the sidewalk in the direction of the temple, weaving through the heavy Friday-night foot traffic. Bunker Street was a popular weekend bar crawl, not only for out-of-town jaspers looking for big-city dolls in a more authentic part of the city than the touristy downtown area, but for college students and young privileged locals from upscale neighborhoods looking to rub shoulders with the would-be avant-garde artists, outspoken political radicals, and tribes of junkies who flocked to the streets of Yerba City's most notorious district. Runaways from all over Tolanica migrated to the Humback in search of romantic notions of social freedom and counter-cultural lifestyles, only to find they'd traded traditional authorities, like parents, teachers, and elected political officials, for new ones, like pimps, dealers, and cult leaders. That's the way of things: wherever you go, someone is going to want to be in charge.

I was enjoying the walk past the old clubs and bars, gazing into the night at the lights of the passing cars and listening to the music spilling into the street, where it harmonized with the buzz of the neon signs, the squeal of tires on asphalt, and the blare of honking horns, when I came upon a crowd of people, most of them young suburbanites pretending to be street punks, their faces locked into expressions of sincere concern. They were listening to a one-armed firebrand in a weathered army jacket, who was standing on a wooden crate and giving an impassioned speech about the war in the Borderland. Opposition to the seemingly endless conflict, which had been raging on and off for nearly a century, had been flaring up lately due to a recent escalation in hostilities, and the Humback had always been a hotbed of political dissidence originating in dimly lit living rooms and bars and occasionally breaking out into the streets. Realm officials usually clamped down on the rabblerousers before they could get out of hand and stir up too much trouble. They were well-practiced in the art of stifling dissent. The Dragon Lord's government had learned long ago that when dealing with serious popular protests, a deft hand was more effective than a heavy one. Law enforcement agencies would monitor the protests carefully, infiltrate the most problematic groups, and either buy off the leaders or make them disappear, leaving the rabble to dissipate.

Protests against the Borderland Wars tended to be especially divisive, and they attracted radicals for and against the conflicts like shit attracts both beetles and flies. I wasn't interested in hearing about it. After fighting in the Borderland for two years and serving another year in the region with the military police, I wanted to spend the rest of my life forgetting the place existed. But the onlookers at this impromptu rally had spilled into the street, where they were blocking a lane of traffic, and I was having difficulty pushing through the tightly packed throng of impassioned onlookers. I brushed against a jasper in radical chic a little more forcefully than I'd intended, and he gave me a shove in return. I tried to excuse myself, but he wasn't having it. He steeled his scrubbed face and glared at me through pupils the size of pin pricks. I detected a faint chemical odor beneath the smell of the whiskey on his breath.

"Watch the fuck where you're going, bull!"

Bull? Did this mid-peninsula hophead really think I was a cop? I held up my hands in surrender. "Sorry. I'm just passing by."

"Fuck you, bull! You think I don't recognize Leea when I see it?"

Great. In this juiced-up dipshit's fantasy, I was an agent for the LIA, the Lord's Investigation Agency.

"I'm not Leea," I told him. "I'm not a cop, either." I nodded toward the speaker. "And you're missing the best part of the man's speech."

I tried to slip by with no further trouble, but it wasn't going to be that kind of night. The dipshit jasper lunged at me as I went by, and my reflexes, born in the alleyways of my old neighborhood, heightened and honed by army training, and reinforced in numerous scrapes after I was discharged, kicked in. Before he could touch me, the dipshit was down on his knees, and I was standing over him forcing his arm up his back. I planted a foot on his faux-thug ass and pushed until the kid was sprawled on the sidewalk. The crowd around us surged back in all directions, giving me room to beat a hasty exit.

Unfortunately, the jasper wasn't going to let me off easy. "Bull!" he shouted for all to hear. "Fuckin' Leea tool of the oppressors!"

That caught the attention of the speaker, who stopped his rant and pointed in my direction. "There's your enemy, friends. There's the representative of the ruling class pitting you against your Qusco brothers and sisters, forcing you to fight for *real estate* for Lord Ketz. It's the black-suited gray-faced LIA, coming for you in the dead of night. The enemies of the Truth. Hey, gray man! Do you have a gun? Did you come here to silence me? Are you going to make me vanish? Where are you going, gray man? You going to report to your superiors? Are you calling in your army of Leea dogs to chase us off our streets? Why are you so afraid of us, gray man?"

Bodies pushed in on me from all sides, too many of them for me to deal with without hurting somebody bad. I ducked grasping hands and struggled to keep my feet. I threw an elbow and saw a double stream of scarlet flow from someone's unblemished nose. A bottle broke over the top of my head, and, although my hat absorbed some of the blow, I staggered as the right side of my body momentarily ceased to function. I recovered quickly, but strong arms encircled me and tried to pull me off my feet. I put a thumb into something soft, and the arms fell away, but that only allowed room for fists and feet. A weight came down upon me from behind, driving me to my knees. A steel-toed boot to my midsection forced the air from my lungs as I struggled to regain my feet. I didn't get there. I ate pavement and was buried beneath the crush.

The weight lifted off my back, and a powerful hand pulled me off the sidewalk. Before I could register what was happening, I was thrust through the door of a long black sedan and pushed across the seat away from the steering wheel. A huge bulky body followed me inside and pulled the door shut. Rubber squealed as the car leapt away from the mob. I heard their muffled cries recede swiftly, replaced by the discordant blasts of horns as the sedan sped past a yellow light and through an intersection.

I looked up at the driver, a mammoth figure whose hairless head brushed against the car's ceiling. His oversized pointed ears and loose gray skin confirmed that my rescuer was a troll, an ancient one by the looks of him. He turned his wrinkled head and smiled at me, his glowing red eyes shining through the lenses of a pair of sporty shaded glasses. He grunted, and said, "I see you're as popular as ever, Southerland."

My jaw must have dropped a foot. "Stormclaw?" I said. "What the fuck are *you* doing here?"

"Pulling your sorry ass out of trouble."

"Thanks, but that doesn't answer my question."

"Nope." He pulled a flask from inside his coat. "You look like you could use a pick-me-up."

I stared at the flask. "Is that trollshine?"

"Yep. It'll curl your chest hair."

"It'll make my head explode! Thanks for the offer, but I'd rather live through the night."

Stormclaw put the flask away. "Suit yourself. Got somewhere you need to be?"

"Yep. It's just a few blocks from here, over near Bunker Park. Make a left at the light."

"Good. I've got to get myself back to that party before things get hot." Using one hand, he effortlessly steered the sedan into a narrow gap in the left lane before easing to a stop at the light.

I glanced his way. "Last time I saw you, you were driving cars and busting heads for Fulton." Lawrence Fulton had been the head of security and chief fixer for Mayor Darnell Teague before Teague was dragged by a dead woman into an otherworldly portal.

"Yep."

"I expected you would go with him to New Helvetia."

"He asked me to. I told him I was comfortable here in Yerba City."

"Settling down?"

The old troll gave me a quick glance. "I'm coming up on two hundred twenty years old, young man. That's old even for a troll. My globetrotting days are behind me. And I like Yerba City. I like that it's close to the ocean. I like that the days are breezy and cool. I even like the fog. It suits me. I want to spend my golden years here." He lurched ahead quickly before the light had finished turning green, shooting the sedan through the left turn before the oncoming traffic could get off the mark.

"I don't get the feeling you've retired," I said.

"Nah. With Teague gone, I got a job working with the new mayor's chief of security."

I sat up. "Wait. You're working for Anton Benning?"

"Yep."

"Benning works for the Hatfields." The Hatfield Syndicate was Yerba City's most notorious crime family. Not only did they rule the city's underworld, but, through Benning's influence, they also had an iron grip on the mayor's office. "Fulton hated Benning."

"Fulton don't sign my checks no more."

"Working for the Hatfields doesn't bother you?"

"Got nothing against the Hatfields. I reckon their money spends as good as anyone's. And Mayor Harvey pays his people a lot better than Teague ever did. He was a cheap son of a bitch."

"Teague didn't have the Hatfields backing him."

"Nope, he sure didn't."

I gazed sightlessly at the brake lights flaring up in the jalopy ahead of us as Stormclaw slowed his town car to a smooth stop. "You never answered my question," I said after half a minute.

"What question was that, young man?"

"What were you doing back there when I got jumped by that mob? Uhh, go straight for another three blocks."

"I was keeping an eye on that one-armed speechmaker back there. Colton Randolph. That young man can sure stir up a mob. My job is to make sure he gets away when the cops show up. Or the LIA. Imagine my surprise when I saw your familiar face getting rearranged. I couldn't stop myself from giving you a hand. My mama always said I had a soft heart."

I tossed a glance Stormclaw's way. "You were there to protect the agitator? Then he's...?"

"Yep. He's with the Hatfields."

I pushed my hat to the back of my head and wiped sweat off my forehead. "Why do the Hatfields have a two-bit street preacher stirring up spoiled rich kids slumming in the Humback?"

Stormclaw shrugged. "Beats me."

I readjusted my hat. "Five will get you twenty the weekend punks who roughed me up were juiced on some of the syndicate's designer drugs. I wonder if the Hatfields bought themselves a few shills and planted them in that crowd to give their demagog some credibility."

"Wouldn't surprise me. But I don't ask questions. I just do what Mr. Benning tells me to do. And he's got me transporting that crazy young troublemaker around the city so he can do his speechmaking, and then yanking him out of there before the law can close in and get their mitts on him. It's a sweet gig for an old fellow like me. I gotta get back, though. Can't leave him alone too long. Mind if I drop you off at the corner?"

"No problem. I've only got a couple blocks to go from here."

After the barest of glances into his rearview mirror, the old motorman whipped the luxury sedan across the right lane and into a bus stop. "Okey dokey. You all have a pleasant evening, Mr. Southerland. It's been nice getting reacquainted."

I'd barely shut the door when the sedan sped away into the night.

Chapter Twelve

When I reached the block where Sonoma had told me I would find the temple for the Children of Cizin, I spotted a half-dozen men and women lugging suitcase-sized cages up a stairway on the outside of a closed used bookstore. As I drew closer, the sound of clucking told me what was inside the cages. The chicken-bearers disappeared through a door at the top of the staircase into what I assumed must be the "temple." I followed them upstairs.

I emerged into an unfurnished open loft. Black curtains blanketed the windows, and the only light in the room came from two rows of dim overhead track lights. The buzz of electric current flowing through the fluorescent tubes echoed throughout the wide-open space. The six people I'd followed joined four others standing next to cages containing chickens, two or three in each enclosure. Jalen sat on the floor next to a closed door in a back corner of the loft, looking glum. Maybe he was thinking about his mother. Maybe he was just bored.

The door next to Jalen opened, and Sonoma, wearing a white robe, emerged with a man and two women. She spotted me and waved me over. I met them in the center of the room.

"This is Mr. Southerland, our air elementalist," she told the others. Indicating one of the women, she said, "This is Manaia. Water elementalist, obviously."

Obviously. Manaia was the adaro Sonoma had told me about earlier. The amphibious adaros were all born with the natural ability to summon and command water elementals. Manaia's dark blue hair concealed the gills on either side of her neck, and she gazed at me with large eyes the color of the ocean in the afternoon sun. She nodded but didn't say anything.

Sonoma directed me to the other man in our group. "This is Tlalli. He's our earth elementalist."

Tlalli smiled and held out a large, calloused hand. "Pleased to meet you." A little under five and a half feet tall, Tlalli was shorter than the three women next to him, but everything else about him was solid and thick. He gave my hand just enough of a squeeze to let me know he could crush it if he felt like it.

"And this," said Sonoma, turning to the last member of the group, "is Tayanna. She's not actually an elementalist, but she's a good substitute."

Her long, gray hair and the creases in Tayanna's weatherworn face suggested a woman in her sixties, at least, but she appeared to be trim and fit and had a bearing I would have described as distinguished, even stately. She studied me with clear eyes and a sly smile. "Sonoma says the Huay Chivo has been living in your house. Is this true?"

"He's been sleeping in my laundry room for a little more than a year."

Her head tilted by a degree, as if she were examining an interesting new species of fauna, possibly a lizard. "Were you aware of who he was?"

"I knew Animal Control considered him to be a dangerous creature."

"You didn't alert them?"

"I called them. I didn't like the agents they sent to my place to capture him. They were rude."

"Fascinating," she said, her voice soft. "If we'd only known. I have so many questions for you, Mr. Southerland." The glow of the fluorescent lights caught her eye, and for a moment it reflected a flicker of orange, like a flame.

"I'm afraid they'll have to wait," Sonoma said. "We need to get in our places. Tayanna, you're behind me. You'll be in front of me, Mr. Southerland. Tlalli will be over there." She pointed to my right. "And Manaia, you'll be on the other side. I'm going to need room, so all of you need to be right up against the walls. When you're in position, summon your elemental."

Back in her basement hideout, Sonoma had told me in broad terms how the summoning ritual was going to work, and she'd explained my role in it. After Stormclaw had dropped me off, I'd sent out a summons for my most reliable elemental. The two-inch air spirit I'd named Smokey was already hovering near the ceiling of the room, unnoticed by anyone but me. As I moved to my appointed spot, I sent out a mental call, and Smokey lowered itself to my shoulder.

Smokey was my favorite elemental, and, for my type of work, the most useful. The little fellow wasn't a powerhouse, like Badass, but it was the most intelligent funnel of wind I'd ever worked with, and the most well-trained. I'd encountered and named the elemental some three years earlier, and since then I'd used it often, mostly for surveillance, both visual and audio. Elementals tend to understand commands in literal, mechanical fashion, but the more I worked with Smokey, the better it seemed to understand what I needed. I'd been taught from childhood that elementals were natural forces with no more individual persona than a rock or a cloud, but I knew this was bullshit. Smokey was a unique character who could reason, learn, and respond to the world with emotion and even humor.

At the moment, what I was sensing from the elemental was agitation, if not outright fear.

"Are you ready for this, Smokey?" I asked.

A hissing voice emerged from the tiny funnel of wind. "The winds are strange."

"What do you mean?"

The elemental whirled silently on my shoulder for a few moments before whispering, "The winds don't blow straight."

"Listen, Smokey," I said. "If something threatens you, if you think anything at all is a danger to you, you get out of here fast. You go back to the Minotaur Lounge and hang out in the cigarette smoke and the beer fumes. You understand?"

"Smokey understands."

"Good." I'd lost one elemental. If I lost Smokey, I'd never forgive myself.

The funnel of air pushed itself inside the collar of my shirt and nestled against the side of my neck, where it threatened to bore a hole into my shoulder.

"Hey, slow it down, little guy. Everything should be all right."

The whirling slowed to a gentle breeze.

While I'd been talking with Smokey, the ten chicken-bearers had taken white robes matching Sonoma's from hooks on the back wall and pulled them on over their clothes. They'd each grabbed a cage full of chickens and were forming a circle in the center of the room. When they were set, they each reached inside their cages, pulled out a chicken, and held it securely against their midsections. I looked to my right, where a small layer of sand was now stretched out at Tlalli's feet. To my left, I saw Manaia standing in a puddle of water that had soaked up through the floor. Across from me, behind Sonoma, Tayanna was gazing at nothing, an odd smile on her face.

Sonoma stood in the center of the circle, her eyes closed. The room was silent except for the gentle clucking of the chickens and the buzzing of the fluorescent lights. No one moved, and the air around me grew thick with tension. Smokey sat on my shoulder, no longer spinning at all, a bubble of unmoving air.

After what seemed an hour, but was probably no more than a few seconds, Sonoma pulled her robe open and let it drop to the floor. She stood wearing only a white cloth over her lower abdomen, naked from the waist up. A thin sheen of sweat already covered her body, and her bared breasts gleamed in the reflected light of the flickering fluorescent bulbs. My eyes were drawn to the jet-black ink that covered her torso from beneath her breasts to just above her navel, a near life-sized tattoo of a skull with a cigarette dangling from its teeth: an image of Cizin, the ancient lord of death.

Soon I became aware that Sonoma was muttering to herself under her breath, chanting words in a language unknown to me, or perhaps making quiet meaningless noises. The robed figures holding the chickens swayed from side to side in no discernable pattern. After a time, Sonoma began to rock back and forth, almost imperceptibly. Her muttering, or chanting, grew louder, and her movements more pronounced. As a neon buzz crackled through the overhead fluorescent lamps, the robed figures around Sonoma began humming their own unique series of notes, producing a harsh cacophony that reminded me of an orchestra warming up their instruments before the opening overture of a concert. Sonoma thrust out an arm, and then her other arm. She lifted a foot off the floor and stepped to one side, knee bent at a right angle. She did the same with her other foot and stood with her loin cloth plunging from her lower abdomen halfway to the floor. The skull-faced image of Cizin, lord of death, regarded the assembly from Sonoma's exposed belly, smoke seeming to rise from the tip of his cigarette. Sonoma stepped forward without straightening her legs, first with one foot, then the other, bending her arms at the elbows and pointing them into the air one after the other, like stop-motion animation. She stepped back the same way, keeping her elbows and knees spread wide apart. Her steps fell into a rhythm, and she broke into a dance that grew progressively less robotic and wilder and freer with each step. The volume of the humming increased, and I began to discern a complex syncopated counterrhythm emerging from the chaos of sound. Sonoma felt it, too. She dipped and spun to the primitive beat. She leaped from foot to foot, her arms writhing like snakes. Her eyes closed as her face contorted into an expression of unbridled ecstasy. On her belly, Cizin's bony mouth stretched into an amused grin.

Out of the corner of my eye, I saw Jalen rise to his feet and dance with the same abandon as his mother. Soon, everyone in the room was caught up in the frenzied dancing. Smokey gyrated and thrashed against my neck. Ripples and waves appeared in the puddle of water at Manaia's feet and in the sand in front of Tlalli. No two dancers moved in the same pattern, but as I let my gaze sweep across the room I realized that everyone was caught up in some sort of complex choreography, with each individual part contributing to a unified whole I could almost, but not quite comprehend.

Except for Tayanna. She was dancing, but it was to her own beat. Her movements were jarring and out of synch with the rest of the room.

I was the only one in the room who wasn't dancing. I wanted to. A magical energy pulsated throughout the loft, and a compulsion to let go and join the others rose inside me. But it was against my nature. It wasn't that I disliked people, or that I avoided them, but I wasn't much of a joiner. When the magically infectious rhythm of the dance pulled at me with its siren call, I resisted. Whatever was happening, I determined that I was going to keep a clear head and an eye on the exit.

When Sonoma's dance sent her leaping into the air, Tayanna turned her face toward the ceiling and a five-foot jet of flame shot from her open mouth. As if this were a cue, the robed figures stopped dancing. They all grasped their chickens by the neck and spun them violently until the chicken bodies, wrenched from their heads, flew into the air. The headless chickens fell at Sonoma's feet, where they righted themselves and began racing frantically around her in all directions, blood spurting from their necks onto her bare legs and over the floor. Her discarded robe was soon soaked with it. The chickens continued to scurry until, one by one, they each stumbled to the floor in a heap, released their bowels, and bled out.

I almost sent Smokey away at that point. When Sonoma had described the summoning ritual she intended to perform, she had failed to mention a few details. She had not, for example, told me anything about chickens, not to mention a mass sacrifice of the screeching fowl. I shouldn't have been surprised, though. I knew that this sort of magic almost always involved a little blood, and a ritual to summon a creature like the Huay Chivo was bound to require a lot of it. The stench of blood, chickenshit, and chicken feathers was overwhelming, but, perceiving no direct danger to either Smokey or myself, I swallowed back the queasiness building in my gut and refrained from commanding Smokey to beat a hasty retreat. The summoning spell required the presence of an air elemental, and Sonoma had assured me the ritual would be safe. I decided to see it through. After all, if I couldn't trust the acolyte of a lord of death, who could I trust?

Tayanna breathed another stream of fire into the air, and once again the robed chicken handlers reached into their cages. Ten more headless chicken torsos were sent scrambling through the circle and spilling their blood for the summoning ritual. Sonoma continued her frenetic dancing amidst the headless carcasses until no chickens remained in the cages. When the last chicken ceased to move, the dancing came to a stop.

The lights dimmed as a red mist rose from the circle to the ceiling and swirled in the shifting breeze. Smokey was right. All the doors and windows in the room were shut tight, but a languorous breeze drifted throughout the room, carrying with it the barnyard odor of the slaughtered chickens. A palpable tension filled the air, and the room seemed too small to contain it. As I reached up to wipe the dampness from my forehead, I became aware of how hot and humid the atmosphere in the room had become, saturated by the sweat from a dozen ritual dancers and the blood from three dozen sacrificial chickens.

Sonoma stood in the center of the mist, head thrown back and arms extended into the air. Her chanting grew louder, and the robed figures hummed tunelessly, creating a background buzz that sounded like a nest of hornets. The mist in front of Sonoma darkened. The hornets' buzzing became frantic. Sonoma shouted unfamiliar words at the form taking shape before her. A few seconds later, I recognized the figure of the Huay Chivo, covered in blackened chicken blood.

Sonoma stopped shouting. The robed figures and the other three elementalists slumped, exhausted by the tension and the dance. Chivo—the Huay Chivo—shook himself like a soaked dog and rose on his hind legs. Sonoma produced a blade from her robe. As she had done in my office, she sliced the palm of her hand and offered her blood to Chivo, who lapped at it eagerly.

One by one, the Children of Cizin cut their palms and squeezed out their blood for Chivo while Sonoma presided over the offerings, chanting under her breath. The robed figures went first, followed by Tayanna and Tlalli. Manaia, not a certified member of the group, hung back. She was sitting cross-legged in her water elemental, letting the ocean water restore her energy.

When Tlalli was finished giving his offering to Chivo, Sonoma waved her son toward the center of the room. Jalen made his way to her with obvious reluctance, his eyes looking everywhere except at the creature standing with her. Sonoma gave him a nod of reassurance. When Jalen reached his mother, he slowly raised his hand, palm up, and Sonoma drew the blade across it. Jalen, eyes glued to the floor in front of him, turned slowly and offered his bloody hand to Chivo.

Chivo stared hard at Jalen, who slowly lifted his head, but wouldn't meet the creature's glowing red eyes. A low growl emerged from Chivo, and Jalen jerked his hand away.

Sonoma put an arm on her son's shoulder. "Go ahead, Jalen. It's okay. Your blood will help cure him. We're reversing the Dragon Lord's spell and helping the man emerge from the beast."

With an effort, Jalen raised his hand. Chivo's growl grew louder.

A puzzled look crept over Sonoma's face. "What's the matter, Lord Cadmael? He's the blood of my blood. He wants to help you."

Jalen looked up and met Chivo's gaze. He let out a groan and fell to his hands and knees, coughing and retching. Chivo raised a clawed hand and prepared to rip Jalen's throat.

"Chivo!" I shouted. "No!"

Chivo turned toward the sound of my voice and curled his lips, exposing a mouthful of pointed teeth stained with blood. He let out a bellow and caught my eyes with his red glare. I was struck by a wave of intense nausea, but I steeled myself and fought it with the force of my will. I glared back at Chivo as if I possessed his own power to sicken. We stared each other down for an eternity, and I wavered in the face of his gaze. Sweat poured down my cheeks and needles of pain pierced my midsection.

A whirling gust of wind brushed against my ear. Jaws set and teeth clenched, unable to speak out loud, I sent out instructions with my mind.

Smokey shot to the floor and scooped up a pool of chicken blood. In an instant, the elemental rose and sent a thin stream of blood into the Huay Chivo's eyes.

Chivo's concentration broke, and the sudden release of pressure almost caused me to fall on my face. With a strangled bleat, Chivo shot his gaze around the room. When he cast his eyes on me again, I saw confusion there. And something else, too: fear. He let out an anguished bellow, dropped to all fours, and bolted for the door. Before I could stop him, Chivo lowered his ram-like horns, butted the door off its hinges, and leaped over the balcony railing into the street.

***

The Children of Cizin scooped the dead chickens off the floor and put them in their cages. From what I gathered, they would be plucked, refrigerated, and served up at a barbecue that the Children would hold the next day in Bunker Park.

Manaia, Tlalli, and Tayanna were gathered near Sonoma, who, having donned a fresh robe, was slumped against a wall looking defeated. Manaia ran her fingers through Sonoma's hair, comforting her. Jalen stood next to his mother, his expression unreadable. I approached the group and asked, "What now?"

Sonoma looked up at me. "We keep trying to bring the Huay Chivo in. Tonight's effort wasn't a complete failure. We made some progress. But we're not done. We can't stop now. We have to finish the job of curing him so that he can take his place beside the Lord of Death."

Jalen's head jerked toward his mother, his eyes flashing with anger. "Why? Mother is dead, and all you care about is that fucking monster!"

Sonoma pushed herself off the wall and glared down at her son. "Don't you take that tone with me, boy! You think I don't care about my wife? You think I'm not sick about it?"

Jalen refused to back down. "Then why don't you show it! That... that *thing* tore Mother to pieces! Why are you trying to help the monster that killed her!"

"He's not a monster. He's a great man who was punished by the Dragon Lord with a curse. We can cure him. That's why Lord Cizin sent us here. It's our mission. It's been our mission since we left Cutzyetelkeh."

Jalen leaned in until his face was only inches from Sonoma's. "It's *your* mission—not mine! Nobody ever asked me what I wanted. I don't give a *fuck* about that piece of shit!"

Sonoma's hand was a blur as she slapped Jalen across the mouth hard enough to send him thudding against the wall. Before anyone could move, she grabbed her son by the collar and yanked him back toward her. "Don't you *ever* speak to me like that again," she hissed, spraying Jalen's face with spittle. The kid took one look at the deadly expression in his mother's face and wilted. Sonoma pushed him away, but not with any force. "I know you're upset about your Mother. Of course you are. I'm upset, too. I loved Clara, and the way she died was horrible. I'll grieve when I can, and soon. But I can't think about it right now. I've got a job to do, and so do you. Cizin chose me and gave me a purpose. After all these years, I came close to fulfilling that purpose tonight, but something went wrong." She lifted a finger and pointed it at Jalen. "Something that had to do with you."

Jalen shook his head. "I didn't do anything."

"Not on purpose, maybe. But everything was going perfectly until it was time for you to make your offering. Something about you, or something you did, spooked him, and I need to find out what happened."

"I don't know what I did," Jalen whined. "The mons—, uh... he didn't like me for some reason. I don't know why."

Sonoma let out a breath. "All right. We'll talk about it later. Go wait for me by the door." Jalen slunk away. When he reached the broken doorway, he leaned against the wall next to it.

"Sonoma?"

Sonoma turned to Manaia, who continued. "If you don't need me anymore, I'll be going. The bars are closing soon, and I need to get some business in. But if you want to... *talk* later, give me a call."

Sonoma put a hand on the adaro's shoulder. "Of course, Manaia. And thanks for coming. If we have to do this again, I'll call you."

Manaia's lips parted in a wry grin. "You'll have to find more chickens first."

Sonoma returned her smile with a sad one of her own. "That may take a while. We pretty much cleaned out our stock." The two gave each other a hug that lingered a bit. After they parted, Sonoma turned to wave goodbye to several of the other Children who were carrying cages of headless chicken corpses to the door.

Tlalli leaned in to get Sonoma's attention. "I'm heading out, too, Sonoma. Bad luck tonight." He turned to me. "Nice meeting you, Southerland. That was a clever thing you did with your air spirit, even if it chased the Huay Chivo away. Thanks for that. Once he went crazy like that, he might have—" He cut himself off and glanced at Sonoma. "I mean, a lot of us might have been hurt." He reached out to shake my hand, and this time he dialed back on the pressure.

Manaia walked out after him, but not without pausing to give me an appraising look, as if she were picking out vegetables at the grocery store. Apparently, she didn't sense the vibe she was hoping for, and, with a brief sigh, she turned and walked out the door.

"Will the two of you excuse me?" Sonoma took Tayanna and me in with a glance. "I need to give the others a hand."

"Go ahead," I said. "I'd like to have a quick word with Tayanna." I looked her way. "If that's okay with you, that is."

The older woman shrugged. "Sure. I'm in no hurry."

I waited a moment as Sonoma left us to ourselves. "The thing with the fire...," I began.

Tayanna let out a chuckle. "Don't worry, I'm not a dragon. You understand that we were all chosen by Cizin, right? Except for you and Manaia, I mean."

"And Jalen," I pointed out.

"Right, and Jalen. Anyway, that means we're ghost dancers. Are you familiar with that term?"

"Sonoma mentioned it to me. Something to do with communicating with the dead?"

Tayanna nodded. "With what remains of their life energy, yes. It's... hard to explain. Anyhoo, one of the dead I have contact with was a fire elementalist when he was alive."

"And he..., what, possesses you?"

"Not exactly. I channel his talent."

"You're not a fire elementalist yourself?"

"No. They're rare, but I guess I'm not telling you anything you don't already know. As far as I can tell, there isn't a single fire elementalist in the city."

I shrugged. "You never know. The government tends to recruit them when they're still children, and then they disappear into their service. There might be a few tucked away in the local offices of the LIA."

Tayanna nodded. "Could be. The one I channel was in a special unit of Lord Ketz-Alkwat's army. They used him for strategic strikes in the war in the Borderland."

"When was this?"

"About two hundred years ago."

I was stunned. "Two hundred years ago? But the Dragon Lords have only been fighting over that land for a hundred years."

Tayanna shrugged. "Maurice—that's his name—lived a century earlier than that. I guess Ketz and Manqu have been at each other's throats on and off for longer than they care to admit, at least publicly."

I processed that information and stored it away for the moment. "When you channel this Maurice character..."

"I can call up fire."

"From a fire elemental?"

"Yes, well.... It's a little more complicated than that. I can't summon the elemental myself. Maurice summons it for me. But the elemental isn't here in our world. It's in Xibalba."

"The land of the dead."

A smile accentuated the deep lines in Tayanna's face. "Right! My fire comes straight from the land of the dead. I channel it the same way I channel Maurice's energies."

I studied Tayanna, and my respect for her must have shown.

"It's no big deal," she said, though her pride showed in her eyes. "Maurice's energies have been with me all my life. When I was a child, he was my secret friend. Too bad I can't manifest him bodily." A sly expression crept over her face. "We might have had a swell life together."

I returned the stately old woman's smile but decided not to pursue the subject of intimate relationships with long dead elementalists. "What do you think happened with the Huay Chivo?" I asked. "Why do you think he reacted that way to Jalen?"

Tayanna shrugged. "You know him better than I do. I would have thought he would have welcomed Jalen's blood."

"Why's that?"

Tayanna gave me a quizzical look. "Didn't Sonoma tell you? She's a direct descendant of Lord Cadmael, which means Jalen is, too."

"That's not what she told me. She said she was descended from one of Cadmael's subjects."

Tayanna shrugged. "Oops. Maybe I've said too much." Her sly smile indicated she wasn't concerned about letting the secret slip.

I turned to look at Jalen, who was staring at the floor with dull eyes and a blank expression. "Does the kid know this?"

Tayanna glanced at Jalen and shrugged. "Sure. He doesn't look much like the heir to a man who held his own against the Dragon Lords for nearly three decades, though, does he. Looks like the bloodline has thinned some over the years."

Chapter Thirteen

The Blood Moon invaded my dreams again that night. The memory of the headless chickens running about the room, along with the expression of confusion and fear on Chivo's face before he'd burst out of the temple, kept me tossing and turning long after I'd turned in. When sleep finally found me, those memories followed. In my dream, however, an amorphous crimson light beamed down from the ceiling over the Children of Cizin as they performed their ritual. The light throbbed and pulsed before resolving itself into the image of a red waning moon. I was suddenly alone in the Children's temple with the light of the moon shining down on me. Then the moon was gone, and the pale figure of Ixquic stood before me, mouth parted to reveal pointed teeth.

"Your sacrifice is not complete." Her lips didn't move, but her words pounded inside my head.

"Let's keep it that way," I said. I wanted to move away from her, but my feet were riveted to the floor.

"I hunger."

"Not my problem."

"I have claimed your life for Itzamna, the toothless one who brings nothing but good. I will give him your life in return for his blessing."

"I'd rather you didn't."

Ixquic raised a hand, and a sudden lethargy swept through me.

"Hold on," I said. "You made an agreement with Cougar."

"I have honored my agreement. I postponed the sacrifice for a day." A chill descended on my head, and I slipped into the edge of darkness.

"Wait," I said without speaking. "Why me?"

She narrowed her eyes and glared into mine. "You are the guardian of the Huay Chivo."

"I wouldn't put it that way." The darkness was almost complete. A groan leaped unbidden from my throat. "Don't do this," I croaked.

Pressure built up inside me, and I thought I was going to explode. I tried to rip my feet from the floor, but I could no longer feel them. All sensation had left me from the neck down. I tried to force open my eyes, but they stayed shut tight. I tried to inhale, but the air seemed to have disappeared from the room. I heard a strangled whine and realized it was coming from me. Heat rose from my body, and I struggled to hold it in.

The pressure building under my skin stopped suddenly. I heard Ixquic's voice from far away, asking, "Do you wish to keep your life?"

"If at all possible," I said with my thoughts.

"Give the Huay Chivo to me and you will live."

"He's not mine to give." I tried once again to pull away from the spirit, but my feet still weren't moving.

"The Huay Chivo will come to you. Kill him and cut out his heart and liver. Bring them to me, and you will live."

"I won't do it."

"In the next rising of the full moon, I will come for the Huay Chivo's heart and liver. If you do not bring them to me, I will take your life, instead."

Warmth poured into my body. My head lay on a damp pillow, and sheets soaked in sweat covered my body. Exhausted, I took a full breath and slowly let it out. I pushed the sheet away from me, turned, and stared straight into the eyes of the Huay Chivo.

"Lord's balls!" I shouted, jerking myself away from the bloodstained whiskered goat's face and the curved ram's horns.

"Baaahhh!" Chivo bleated.

I rolled away from Chivo and fell out of the bed to the floor in a heap. Scrambling to my knees, I peered over the bed at the creature, who stared back at me, stone-faced.

"Th'fuck you doing!" I blurted.

Chivo's lips curled over his thin beard, and his mouth opened. "Baaaalleck," he bleated.

I stared at him, stunned. After several tries, I managed to choke out a few words. "Did you…? Can you…?" I swallowed something dry down a parched throat.

"Baaalleck. Aiiiiarrriiikhh…" Chivo's eyes glowed red, and he slammed his human-like forepaw on my bed.

I rose to my feet and stared openmouthed at Chivo. "Are you trying to speak?"

The creature dropped his eyes. He let out an almost inaudible growl: "Baalleckk."

Alex. He was trying to say my name. "That's okay, Chivo. I've got you. Are you hungry? Do you want some yonak?"

Chivo looked up at me and nodded.

I led Chivo down the stairs, past the mess in my office, and into the laundry room, where Siphon hovered at the window. Chivo waited patiently for me to scoop some yonak into his bowl before lowering himself to all fours and lapping the troll food up as if he hadn't eaten for days. I watched him until he had licked the bowl clean.

"You want more."

Chivo snorted and crossed the room to his bed. He crawled in, curled up, and was asleep almost immediately. I watched his chest expand and contract as he breathed, taking note of the right side of his body where the liver rested beneath his leathery skin. It was Saturday morning. On Wednesday evening, the moon would be full. I stared at Chivo's exposed right flank for several seconds before leaving the room and closing the door gently behind me.

***

Over a hearty breakfast of toasted waffles, peanut butter, chocolate ice cream, and spiked coffee, I thought about how I was going to keep Chivo hidden from the cops and Animal Control. Kalama had assured me that she wouldn't let anyone know the Huay Chivo had been staying with me, but it was well known that Chivo had last been spotted in the alleys of the Porter District. That had been more than a year ago, but now that they suspected Chivo of killing Mrs. Novita, my neighborhood would be a logical place for the authorities to search. I had no idea how Chivo had made it back to my place from the temple in the Humback, or how he had stayed out of sight, but he was clearly exhausted. He'd need my help to stay free.

Should he be free? Had he followed Sonoma back to her apartment and attacked Mrs. Novita? I didn't want to believe it, and my instincts told me it wasn't true. Chivo had gobbled down that yonak as if he'd been starving. Typically, a big meal would last him for a couple of days, and Mrs. Novita had been attacked and partially eaten only a little more than twenty-four hours ago. Chivo wouldn't be that hungry again so soon... unless.... Unless the summoning ritual had somehow drained him.

But what about the blood he'd taken from Sonoma and the other twelve Children of Cizin just a few hours earlier? Surely that should have amounted to the equivalent of a full meal. But, in that case, why was he so hungry this morning? As I recalled the scene in the loft, I realized that Chivo hadn't exactly feasted on the Children. He'd probably only lapped up a smear of blood from each of them. Nothing more than a light liquid snack, I supposed. A shot or two of whiskey, at most.

These thoughts were getting me nowhere. Truth was I didn't know nearly as much about Chivo as I should have. I'd been giving him yonak, which he liked all right, but I didn't know that much about his natural feeding habits or what made him tick. I needed to talk to someone who did. I was going to have to get back in touch with Sonoma as soon as possible, sometime before the cops came calling.

Before I could pick up my phone, however, I sensed a familiar presence approaching. Detective Kalama was dropping by for a surprise visit. And she wasn't alone.

When the door buzzer sounded, I scooped up the last bite of waffle, peanut butter, and melted ice cream with a serving spoon and let it slide into my mouth. The buzzer went off again as I washed it all down with the last of my coffee, savoring the burn of the rye whiskey I'd used to strengthen the brew. I hoped Kalama would take the hint and come back another time, preferably on some other day.

Kalama was too stubborn for that. A fist pounded on my door, and Kalama shouted, "Southerland, if you don't open this door in five seconds, I'm going to knock it down."

With a groan, I pushed myself away from the table and headed for the stairs. "Hold your horses, detective," I shouted. "I'm coming."

The pounding on my door continued until I opened it a crack and slipped out onto the porch.

Kalama stepped back to give me room and greeted me with a smile. "Hello, gumshoe. Mind if we come in?"

I glanced at the pug standing a half step behind and slightly to one side of Kalama. He was a couple of inches shorter than Kalama and about a half foot shorter than me, but I doubt that I outweighed him. He looked like he could stop a tank in its tracks and crush it with his bare hands. The pug had the long, droopy face of a bulldog, with heavy jowls dragging the corners of his mouth so severely downward that I doubted he had the ability to smile. He had the lined and leathery skin of a man who had been born outdoors and took shelter only with the greatest reluctance. I took a quick glance at the forty-five automatic he carried openly in a holster that hung low on his right hip.

Kalama pointed her chin back toward the pug. "This is my partner, Detective Blu. Blu, this is Alexander Southerland."

Detective Blu extended a meaty paw in my direction. "Suddalund." He gave my hand a squeeze that traveled all the way up my forearm and down to my shoes. I did my best not to let the pain show in my face.

"I didn't know you had a partner," I said, once Blu allowed me to retrieve my crushed hand.

"The brass didn't want me flying solo anymore. You got the coffee on?"

I didn't move. "Are you inviting yourself in?"

"Not if you're hiding anything from the cops. You aren't hiding anything from the cops, are you, gumshoe?"

"No, but I'm in the middle of remodeling my office."

"We don't mind." Kalama turned slightly toward her partner without quite facing him. "Do we Detective Blu?"

Blu's face remained blank as he stared at me without speaking.

I let out a breath. "Okay, but don't say I didn't warn you. And no coffee, I'm afraid." I opened the door and led the two detectives inside. Gesturing to indicate the condition of my office, I added, "No chairs, either."

Kalama sighed. "Lord's balls, Southerland. When were you going to report that someone broke into your place again?"

"I didn't see the point," I said. "Nothing was taken."

"So this was, what, someone you pissed off?"

"I'm not sure. Maybe."

Kalama nodded toward the shattered glass on one side of the room. "They broke your water cooler. And your coffeepot."

"They broke my computer, too."

"I don't see a stiff on your floor this time. Did you already dispose of him?"

"Very funny. Now that you've seen the mess, should we have our conversation outside?"

Kalama's eyebrows raised. "Where the neighbors can listen in? Nah, we're fine. Right detective?"

I glanced at Blu, whose hangdog expression never changed. He gave no impression that he'd heard Kalama speak. I wanted to pass my hand in front of his vacant eyes to see if they would move. I might have, but I was afraid he might snap my wrist if I did.

I turned back to Kalama. "What do you need, detective?"

"Hmm? Oh, we were in the neighborhood and thought we'd drop by. A bunch of us are out looking for the Huay Chivo. You don't happen to have seen him recently, have you?"

"Face and body of a mangy goat? Big curved horns like a ram? Spikes down his spine? Hairless rat's tail? Hands and feet like a human's? Nah, haven't seen hide nor hair of him."

"Uh-huh." Kalama shifted her weight from one foot to the other. "Well, you should keep an eye out. Animal Control is convinced that he has a lair somewhere in the Porter. Who knows what a dangerous creature like that could do if he broke into someone's house. Or office. He might mess it up pretty good."

"Thanks, detective. I'll be sure to watch out for him."

"Right…. Say, gumshoe, Blu and I really could use some coffee. You wouldn't happen to have any upstairs, would you?" She drew in a long breath through her nose. "I'm pretty sure I can smell some brewing. Maybe we could all go up and take a load off. If that's jake with you, of course. I mean, I don't want to interrupt anything if you've got company. You got any company up there, gumshoe?" She gave me a hard stare.

I sighed. "No, it's just me this morning. Come on up if you'd like. I'm sure I've got some cups."

The detectives followed me upstairs to my apartment. When we were inside, Kalama swept her eyes over my living room and kitchen. "Nice place, gumshoe." I realized that while Kalama had been to my office on several occasions, I'd never had any reason to bring her to my apartment. "Doesn't look like your intruder came up the stairs."

"Nope."

Kalama turned to me. "Were you here when he hit your place?"

"Nope. It happened yesterday morning. I was out walking. When I got back, the office was trashed. Things came up, and I didn't get a chance to clean it up. I was going to start on it today after I had my breakfast, but a couple of cops showed up on my doorstep looking for coffee, so…." I shrugged.

Kalama nodded. "I see. Speaking of which…."

"Have a seat at the table." I cleared away my breakfast dishes and carried them to the kitchen sink. "How do you like your coffee, Detective Blu?"

"Cream."

I'd known the pug for nearly ten minutes now, and this was the second word I'd heard him speak. I got the distinct impression he wasn't going to turn out to be chatty.

When we were sitting around my kitchen table, I turned to the burly detective. "How long have you been in homicide, Detective Blu?"

The detective slurped coffee and said nothing.

A smile appeared on Kalama's face. "Detective Blu isn't much for small talk, gumshoe. He listens like no one's business, though. Where were you last night?"

"In my bed. Sleeping." I picked my coffee cup off the table.

Kalama grunted. "You don't talk much more than my partner, do you. What time did you get in?"

"Late."

"Where were you before you went to bed?"

"Out."

Kalama nodded. "We know that. I wanted to see if you were going to lie and tell me you were home all night."

I sighed. "What's this about, detective? If there's something you want to know, tell me. I'm not hiding anything."

"No? Then who broke into your office?"

"I'll let you know when I find out."

"It wasn't the Huay Chivo?"

"No."

"You're sure about that?"

"Positive."

Kalama held my eyes as I took a sip of coffee. Finally, she nodded. "Okay, gumshoe. But I want to know if you see him. Maybe he killed your client, and maybe he didn't, but he's still a danger to the people of this city."

"Is that what you came here to tell me?"

The detective took a drink from her cup. "This is good. Four sugar cubes, just the way I like it. Sure a lot better than that dishwater they serve at The Good Egg."

"It's the Ghanaian stuff that Walks in Cloud likes."

"She's got good taste. In coffee, anyway." She set the cup on the table. "No, I came to ask you a few questions about Sonoma Deerling. How well do you know her?"

"Not well." I glanced at Blu, who had added a quarter cup of cream to his half-empty coffee cup and was slurping it like he was in another part of the world.

"Have you run into her since the last time we talked?"

I sighed, knowing Kalama wouldn't have asked the question if she didn't already know the answer. "I might have seen her last night."

Kalama nodded. "Where?"

I studied Kalama, wondering how much she knew. "She's part of a group called the Children of Cizin. They have a temple of sorts in the

125

Humback. Just a loft over a used bookstore, really, but they meet there to plan their social events and hold ceremonies."

"And you attended one of these 'meetings' last night?"

I wondered how she'd found out. "Yes."

"And Deerling was there?"

"Yes."

Kalama leaned a little closer toward me. "Know where she went afterward?"

I didn't answer, and Kalama sighed. "Did she hire you to find her wife's killer?"

She hadn't, and I kicked myself for not asking her to. Keeping my face straight, I said, "You know where I stand regarding client confidentiality."

"She's wanted for questioning in a possible murder case, Southerland."

"She knows. Look, if I run into her again, I'll talk her into coming in to see you, all right?"

"Make it quick, gumshoe. And be persuasive. Bring her in yourself if you have to. She can't hide from us for long, and it will be all the worse for her if we have to haul her in ourselves."

"You don't think she killed her wife, do you?"

"What the police think is the business of the police. I can't have you protecting someone who may be a material witness at the very least. There are people at HQ who take a dim view of private dicks interfering in homicide investigations. And you're about due to have your license extended, aren't you?"

I nodded. "I get the picture."

"Good." She took a healthy sip from her cup and returned it to the table. "Thanks for the coffee, gumshoe. Ghanaian? Blu loved it. You can tell by the ecstatic expression on his ugly mug. I'll have to bring some home for Kai." She rose from her chair, and, without changing his expression or saying a word, Detective Blu followed suit.

Chapter Fourteen

I had a lot of things I wanted to do after the detectives left, and putting my office in order wasn't one of them. I needed to find a way to protect myself against Ixquic before the rising of the next full moon on Wednesday evening. That was only five moonrises away. But I didn't have any good ideas at the moment, and the office wasn't going to clean itself, so I rolled up my sleeves and dove in.

A couple of hours later, things were almost back to normal. I'd need a new water cooler and coffeemaker, and my computer was a wreck. The monitor was a lost cause, and the keyboard was in two pieces. The tower was dented, but otherwise intact, and I wondered if the guts of the computer were still operational. I decided to box up all the pieces and bring them to Walks in Cloud to see what she could do with them.

I called Walks to tell her what had happened and to make sure she was going to be available for a visit.

"A customer just left," she told me. "Next one's not coming in till two-thirty. I think I can squeeze you in. Bring some Huaxian take out, would you? Braised shrimp and rice. And a dozen egg rolls."

"A dozen?"

"I'm on a diet."

Forty-five minutes later, I pulled the beastmobile into a parking garage in Nihhonese Heights. The heat from the afternoon sun was tempered by a cool ocean breeze as I walked past the unmarked van where a pair of agents from the LIA were conducting their surveillance of Walks in Cloud's technical consulting and computer repair shop. The shop, half a block up the street from the van, had no sign, no windows, and no marked address, nothing to indicate that the city's preeminent computer wizard could be found inside. I waved at the LIA agents through the van's windows as I walked by, and they waved back. It had been three months since Leea had stopped pretending they weren't keeping a round-the-clock watch on Walks, and their presence on the street no longer bothered her.

"It's not like I'm hiding anything from them," she'd said.

"Aren't you?" I'd responded.

"Well, okay," she'd admitted. "I'm hiding quite a lot of things, actually. But they'll never be able to find any of it. That's why I get the big dough."

Walks and I assumed the LIA was hoping to discover whether she possessed the formula for Reifying Agent Alpha, an alchemical substance that could provide the means for Lord Ketz-Alkwat to produce an offspring. In fact, she *did* have a copy of the formula stored in an ethereal space guarded by the Cloud Spirit. What the Lord's Investigation Agency didn't know was that three months earlier we'd given a copy of the RAA formula to the elf. What the elf was doing with the formula was anyone's guess, but he'd seemed pleased to have it when he'd appeared to me in my sleep the previous evening.

That hadn't been the first time the elf had walked into my dreams, but thus far his visits had been rare. I hoped he wasn't thinking about making a habit of it. Between him and the Blood Moon, I was getting seriously shorted on my forty winks lately. Thinking about it made me realize how tired I was.

I found Walks where I expected to, behind a computer screen tapping away on her keyboard with a nonstop stream of clicks that sounded like a driving rain on a tin roof. A cigarette dangled from her lips, and the front of her shapeless dress was stained gray by the ash that had dropped from its tip. She glanced up when I entered and nodded at her empty coffee cup. I put the boxes of Huaxian on the worktable she used as a desk and took the cup to the far side of her office, where half a pot of coffee sat on a heating plate.

It wasn't until I'd returned with two steaming cups of black brew that she pushed her wheelchair away from her keyboard and smiled in my direction.

"About time you got here, Jack. That cup's been dry for a half hour."

"You could've got your own," I pointed out.

"Too busy. The eye-tee guys at a big law firm think they've been hacked, and they can't figure out how anyone could have got past their security. I just finished typing up my report."

I pushed a carton of braised shrimp across the desktop. "Were they hacked?"

"Yep. Their security is shit. Fuckin' amateurs. I drew up a proposal to fix it, and now we'll see if they're willing to cough up the dough." She unfolded two napkins and spread them over her ample lap.

I yawned. "Sounds like a fun way to spend a Saturday."

Her eyes gleamed. "You scoff, Jack, but that's because you have no appreciation for the beauty of security analysis."

I opened a carton of mushroom beef and mixed in some jasmine rice. "Right. They write poems about it, don't they?'

"In hexadecimal iambic pentameter."

"Is that a thing?"

"It should be. Pass me the soy sauce."

After a minute of focused food consumption, Walks nodded toward the file box I'd placed on the floor next to me. "That the computer?"

"What's left of it. Whoever broke in did a number on it. Looks like he used a hammer."

Walks talked around a mouthful of shrimp and rice. "Is the motherboard intact?"

"Maybe. What is it and what does it look like?"

"It looks like a motherfucking motherboard. What do you *think* it looks like?"

I put an innocent expression on my face. "I don't know. Does it wear a dress?"

That got me half a grin. "Don't be a pig. Have you forgotten I keep a shotgun in my desk?"

"Well, I don't know a motherboard from a fatherboard. You'll have to check it out and let me know whether it can be saved. You going to eat all those egg rolls?"

"I thought I'd give half of them to the Leea lugs."

"What for?"

"As long as they're there, and as long as everyone in the neighborhood knows it, no one is likely to break in here and do me like they did you."

"So they're your building security now?"

"Sure, why not? They don't seem to be going anywhere, so I might as well take advantage of the situation. Be a lamb and run six of those egg rolls out to them while I crack open your computer chassis." She wheeled herself to the file box.

I rose from my seat. "I'll get that for you."

"Don't be a sap. I've got it." She bent down and lifted the box to her lap and swung it onto her worktable without straining. Looking up at me, she said, "Get those egg rolls out there before they get cold. Tell them a representative from the city auditors is coming in at two-thirty, and that I'd appreciate it if they didn't spook him. The city is my best customer."

When I returned after completing my task, I found Walks working on a fresh cigarette and frowning over a circuit board she'd pulled from my computer tower.

"Problem?" I asked.

In response, she pulled an electronic doodad from the board and held it up for me to look at.

"What does this look like to you?" she asked.

I barely glanced at it before shrugging. "I dunno. A widget? A gizmo?"

She blew a puff of smoke into the air above my head. "Look at it more closely."

I leaned over the worktable and studied it. "Huh. If I didn't know better, I'd say it was a microphone."

"Give the man a cigar. Although microphone is a bit simplistic. In the biz, we refer to it as an audio transmission device. Sort of a microphone and radio transmitter all in one."

I gave the doodad another look. "Wait—really? It's tiny."

"Hang on a sec. Let me take off this shielding." Walks used a miniature screwdriver on some miniature screws and removed a miniature section of metal from the doodad. "Just as I thought. You feel that?"

A faint shrill squeal, like the buzzing of a microscopic drill, vibrated the fillings in my back teeth. "Magic," I said. "It's enchanted."

"Yep. Someone loaded a very sophisticated little bug onto your motherboard. An expert job, too." She pulled on her cigarette and filled the area over her worktable with a gray cloud.

A jolt of adrenaline shot through my veins. "I've been under surveillance?"

"You sure have, ya big lug. I'm guessing the enchantment is for boosting the transmission while keeping it hidden from detection devices. My bug finders didn't detect it, and that's unusual. If I hadn't removed the motherboard and taken a good look at it, I wouldn't have known it was there." She let out a smoke-filled breath. "This thing is fucking beautiful!"

"Alkwat's balls!" I could feel my face burning.

"Calm down before you pop an artery. You should be flattered. Someone spent a shitload of dough to keep tabs on you. To tell you the truth, I'm a little jealous. This dingus is worth more than they pay those two poor mugs out in that van in a year. Maybe two."

I took the device from Walks and held it up in the light to study it. It was no bigger than a grain of rice. "What does this thing do exactly?"

Walks raised her eyebrows. "It's a microphone and a transmitter. It broadcasts sound over distance."

"Thanks, Miss Computer Wizard. I hope you're not gonna charge me for that bit of wisdom."

"You already owe me for finding it, and my time is valuable." She looked up at me and smiled. "That means you owe me a favor of my choosing."

"I already delivered egg rolls to your boyfriends in the van. What more do you want?"

A sly look settled on her face. "Don't worry, Jack. I'll think of something."

Walks held out her hand, and I returned the device to her. She put it under a magnifier and her expression turned thoughtful as she examined it. "This is an interesting piece of hardware. The miniaturization, the enchantment...." She looked up. "Someone went to a lot of trouble to make sure they could keep tabs on you. And we aren't talking about just anybody. I'm thinking government. And not just any government agency, either. A well-funded one."

"LIA," I said.

"That would be my first guess. But the LIA is a huge megalith with a lot of different parts. Some of those parts are more well-funded than others, and the parts closest to the Dragon Lord are the most well-funded of all. I think we're looking at something pretty high up the chain." She took a final puff from her cigarette and crushed it into an ashtray.

"You think this might have something to do with RAA? I can't think of any other reason why the highest levels of Leea would be interested in me."

Walks looked up from the device. "Really? You stopped a South Nihhonese spirit from burying the city under the ocean a few months ago and helped a busload of adaro refugees escape back into the sea in the process. You think they might not have taken notice of that?"

"How would they know I had anything to do with that?"

Walks snorted. "Not much gets past the LIA, Jack."

I had to concede the point. Something else occurred to me. "Can you tell how long that bug has been in my computer?"

The computer wizard picked up the circuit board and placed it under her magnifier. "All I can tell you right now is that it wasn't a rushed job. Someone took their time. Give me a chance to study it with the Cloud Spirit and I should be able to tell you more. Leave all this with me and I'll work on it tonight. I'll call you and let you know what I find out."

I reached for my unfinished carton of mushroom beef. "All right. By the way, is that thing still broadcasting?"

Walks grinned. "It's trying to. But the Cloud Spirit has this place locked tight. No signal gets out of here, even if it's enchanted."

"You're sure about that?"

She nodded. "Absolutely. Speaking of which, let me see your cellphone."

She held out her hand and I passed my phone to her. Within seconds, she had the inner workings of the phone laid bare under her magnifier. After a few moments, she looked up. "It's clean. They either couldn't get to it or they didn't need to."

"That's a relief. I guess."

Walks frowned. "And while we're on the subject. There's something I've been thinking about. You remember that air elemental you scared out of my shop a few months ago? Back during the freak rainstorm?"

"The one that was spying on you? Sure. It hasn't come back, has it?"

"No, but here's the thing. I was never satisfied with the idea that something had gotten past the Cloud Spirit and penetrated my other security. And I could never figure out what anyone could have expected an elemental to discover in here even if it did. But what if that little elemental hadn't been spying on me at all? What if it had been following you all along?"

"Me! Why would...." My voice faltered as I considered what Walks was saying.

"Someone put an expensive and very sophisticated bug in your computer. But they didn't touch your phone, maybe because they couldn't get to it. But also, like I was saying, maybe because they didn't need to. Maybe they already had a way to track you when you were away from your computer."

"An air elemental? I'd have seen it."

"Would you? You only spotted it here when you were looking for it."

I started to object, but clamped down on it. That elemental had been a tiny thing, the size of a teardrop. If I wasn't looking for something that small, would I ever see it? And if I did, would I suspect it was tailing me and listening in on my conversations?

Walks raised her eyebrows. "Kind of makes sense, doesn't it."

I nodded slowly. "Yeah, it does."

"It won't be able to get back in here again," Walks said. "The Cloud Spirit will make sure of that. But once you're outside...."

"Right." I'd have to search the air around me with a fine-toothed comb, and even then it was possible that an air spirit that small could lose itself in the mists and breezes.

Walks nodded at my naked phone, "I see you've removed almost everything that would allow anyone to track you with your cell. You can't do much with this old thing except take pictures and access the internet. For a so-called 'smart' phone, it's pretty stupid."

"I can also use it to make telephone calls. That's smart enough for me."

"Despite your best efforts, though, this phone can still be tracked by people who have the right equipment and know what they're doing. It doesn't even have to be on."

"Can you track me?"

Walks smiled. "What makes you think I don't, ya big lug?" She winked and blew me a kiss.

Alkwat's balls! I'd always thought of myself as a solitary type, a lone figure gliding unseen through the darkness. Now I was a big clumsy snail in a goldfish bowl. Was there anywhere I could go without someone tracking my every move?

Walks took another look at my phone through her magnifier. "As long as I've got it here, why don't you let me tinker with it a little. I could add some magical doodads that would alert you if someone was trying to trace your phone."

"Thanks, but I'll pass. My phone's already a mystery to me. Besides, magical doodads can be traced by magical doodad tracers."

Walks looked up from the magnifier. "Not *my* doodads. They're specially blessed by the Cloud Spirit."

"Could you design something that would get past the Cloud Spirit's blessing?"

Walks thought about it. "It's theoretically possible. But I'd need the Cloud Spirit's assistance in order to make it."

I shrugged. "Who's to say the Cloud Spirit wouldn't help someone break through your doodads to track my phone? Just because you're on her good side doesn't mean I am."

Walks rolled her eyes and threw a small screwdriver at me. "Lord's balls, Southerland. Now you're just being silly."

I shrugged. "I don't trust magic. I barely trust electronics."

"One of these days you're going to have to crawl out of that cave you live in."

Walks quickly reassembled my phone and handed it back to me, free of esoteric doodads, magical or otherwise. As far as I could tell, at least.

The good news was that my motherboard was salvageable, thanks to Walks in Cloud's computer wizardry, and that I hadn't lost any of my data. Walks told me to leave the board with her, and she'd have a new working computer for me by Monday at the latest. If I needed to send emails or get on the internet before then, I'd have to use my cellphone.

"For your purposes, your phone is just as good as a computer," she told me.

"Maybe. But those little keyboards weren't made with my fat fingers in mind."

Walks took out her phone and began tapping at it. My own phone buzzed, and I found she had texted me a message: "Most people use their thumbs and get by just fine." The message was followed by a smiley-face emoticon.

Hardy-har-har.

Chapter Fifteen

Once back in my apartment, I peeked into my laundry room and found Chivo still fast asleep in his bed. Satisfied, I went upstairs to my apartment, sat back on my sofa, and prepared my mind to reach out for Cougar. I needed to find a way to protect myself from Ixquic before Wednesday evening, and I hoped Cougar would have some ideas. After all, what good is a spirit guide if you can't use him to fight off another spirit, right? When my mind was properly attuned, I visualized the jungle clearing where I'd first met Cougar and found him waiting for me at the base of the waterfall.

As soon as I was settled, Cougar got down to brass tacks. "You seek aid against Blood Moon," he said, his words sounding in my mind. "I can give little. I have her assurance that you will be spared if you give her the Huay Chivo's heart and liver as an offering. She has also promised not to take your life's energy before the full moon rises."

"She came for me last time I settled down for some shuteye," I said, speaking out loud.

Cougar answered in kind, his mouth moving in ways that an earthly beast would not be able to duplicate. "You were in no danger. She was making a point. You are safe from her for now, although she may still come to you with threats and torments. She has been prohibited from doing you lasting harm, however."

"Prohibited? Who's stopping her?"

"Itzamna."

"Isn't that the mug Ixquic wants to sacrifice me to?"

"That is correct."

"Why is he helping me?"

Cougar lowered himself to the ground so that his head was level with mine. "Itzamna follows his own counsel for reasons he does not reveal."

Well, wasn't that dandy. "Is there some way I can appeal to him directly?" I asked.

"He will not hear you."

"What if I sacrificed a chicken or something?"

"Then you will have a dead chicken."

Great. I spent a few moments listening to the rush of the waterfall as it plunged into the deep pool at its base. Did the actual fall still exist where I had stumbled onto it in the Borderland all those years ago? Or did it now exist only in my mind. The world of nature seemed so firm and solid, but, in reality, it was subject to both the vicissitudes of a changing climate and the destructive designs of sentient animals bent on war and industrial development. The waterfall I'd seen had probably only existed because a heavy rain had been falling for days before I'd found it. How soon after the cessation of the rains did the streams feeding the falls dry up and disappear? Perhaps battling armies had destroyed the landscape with bombs and shells. Or maybe the area had been cleared for the construction of an airfield or a military camp. Did it matter? I decided it did. As real as this place of tranquility was in my memory, I would have been disappointed to discover it had vanished from the physical world.

I shook off my thoughts and turned to the patiently waiting Cougar. "I have no intention of letting that bitch get anywhere near Chivo's liver. And I don't want her claws on me, either. You're my spirit guide. Give me another option. At least tell me if Ixquic has a weakness I can use against her."

"I am prohibited from giving you further direct aid against Blood Moon."

"Let me guess. By Itzamna?"

"That is correct. When I convinced Ixquic to spare you before, I agreed not to further interfere in her plans. Itzamna has chosen to hold me at my word. He has imposed limits on my involvement in his business with Blood Moon, and I am bound by his injunctions."

I filled my lungs with moist jungle air and let it out with a groan. "You spirits have a lot of rules."

Cougar lowered his head to his paws. "It is complicated."

"I'll say."

Cougar's eyes raised. "Others have the ability to help you."

"Oh? Who?"

"I am prohibited from saying more."

"Terrific. Can you do something for me?"

Cougar raised his head. "That depends. What do you wish?"

"I want you to deliver a message to Itzamna."

"That may be possible. What is the message?"

"Tell him to fuck off."

***

Cougar refused to carry my message, suggesting that Itzamna was already aware of my feelings and regarded them as inconsequential.

I was back in my apartment and, other than knowing I was more or less safe from Ixquic until Wednesday's moonrise, no better off than I'd been before my visit with my spirit animal. According to Cougar, others had the ability to help me. I thought about who these others might be.

The obvious answer was Madame Cuapa, but the thought of her didn't fill me with much enthusiasm. She had provided me with help in the past, but it was usually unexpected and offered to further the bruja's own schemes. My earlier call had gone unanswered. The Madame had an antique phone with no caller identification, but I knew she didn't need it. I wouldn't have been surprised if, for obscure reasons of her own, she had ordered Cody to ignore the call.

Nonetheless, I tried again, and, as before, my call went unanswered. I thought about driving to the bruja's home but quickly discarded the idea. If she didn't want to see me, she'd likely turn the beastmobile into a pumpkin and me into a mealworm. I'd never actually seen or heard of her doing anything like that, but that didn't mean I was keen to chance it.

With a resigned sigh, I accessed the internet on my phone and searched for information on Ixquic. I gave up an hour later, having uncovered nothing more than I'd found in my previous searches. Deciding to try something different, I entered Hunbatz into a search engine and discovered that Hunbatz was a family surname, if not necessarily a common one, in the Borderland and in northern Qusco. I found no information on its origins, however.

On a whim, I searched the online phone directories to see if there was a listing for Hunbatz in the Yerba City area. Almost immediately, I found one for a Cozumel Hunbatz. I stared at the screen on my phone, feeling like an idiot. Was it really going to be that simple? I shook my head and used my thumb to tap on the number. Somehow, I missed it, and nothing happened. I carefully tapped at the number with the tip of my forefinger and got the desired result. Thanks a lot, Walks. Thumbs indeed. Not with these meat hooks I called hands. Not on a phone that could fit in my shirt pocket.

The woman who answered the phone confirmed that she was Cozumel Hunbatz and wanted to know who was asking.

"My name is Alexander Southerland. I'm a private investigator. I'm looking for a man named Hunbatz who is currently in Yerba City. You're the only Hunbatz listed in the Yerba City phone directory, and I was hoping you might know the man I'm looking for."

The woman paused for a beat before responding. "What do you want him for?"

I had a number of responses I used in situations like this, depending on the circumstances. Sometimes I said I was working for an estate attorney, and that the person I was looking for had inherited a lot of dough. Sometimes I said I was working for a noted celebrity looking for a child she had given up for adoption. Money and celebrity were big motivators when I was working on someone who was reluctant to cooperate. Cozumel Hunbatz sounded to me like she knew something and that she might be ready to tell me, so I played it straight. "I'm going to be honest with you, Mrs. Hunbatz."

"It's Miss Hunbatz."

"Miss Hunbatz. The man I'm looking for is involved in a cult venerating a dangerous nature spirit. One that practices blood sacrifices. Their meeting place was raided by the cops, but the members of the cult dispersed before the cops got there. They'll come together again somewhere, and I'm trying to find out where."

Miss Hunbatz didn't respond right away, and I waited for her to process what I'd told her. When she finally spoke, I thought her voice sounded tight, as if her throat had constricted. "Do you have an office, Mister... Southerland, was it?"

"I do. It suffered some damage recently, and I'm a little short on furniture, but we can meet here if that suits you."

I gave her my address, and she told me she'd be there in an hour.

My old office chairs were in the alley behind my building waiting to be hauled away, so I lugged a couple of my dining room chairs down the stairs for my meeting with Miss Hunbatz. I also brought down a coffeepot and a couple of cups from my kitchen and set them on my desk, which was damaged but still standing. After making sure Chivo was still sawing logs in the laundry room, I straightened my tie and settled in to wait for my guest.

I left the door open for Miss Hunbatz, but she knocked at it anyway before stepping inside. She stopped short, and I quickly sized her up: about my age, trim, medium height, sweet face with minimal makeup, and neatly dressed in a plain blouse, skirt, and sensible shoes. She was the kind of doll who made an impression without trying, and who didn't need you to tell her so. She raised her eyebrows at the stark condition of my office.

"Miss Hunbatz? Come in, please. You'll have to excuse the place. As I said on the phone, I'm still working on getting the place back into shape. Won't you sit down?"

I led her to a chair and asked her if she wanted coffee. She accepted a cup—cream, no sugar—and I took a seat on the other side of the desk.

After we'd each taken a sip of the icebreaking brew, I asked her why she'd offered to meet with me.

"I have a twin brother who I haven't seen in many years, Mr. Southerland. I have a feeling he may be the man you met."

I studied the face of the attractive woman sitting across from me, searching for a hint of a resemblance to the burly, hairy man who had helped prepare me to be sacrificed to a bloodthirsty spirit.

"You don't look a bit like him, Miss Hunbatz," I said.

"We aren't identical. He takes after our father, and I'm a dead ringer for my mother. But I was born just three and a half minutes before he was."

I nodded. "Can you describe him?"

"I haven't seen my brother since we were sixteen years old. That was fourteen years ago. I doubt if he looks the same anymore. He was taller than me, and his hair was much darker than mine. His eyes were a little darker, too." She shrugged. "That's about all I can tell you."

"Did he have facial hair?"

She smiled, a small one that hid something sad. "No, but he had to start shaving when he was twelve. By the time he... left, he was shaving twice a day."

"Could be the guy. The man I'm looking for has a mane that would make a lion kick down a brick wall."

Miss Hunbatz eyes widened. "When did you see him?"

"Two nights ago, after midnight. At a meeting of the cult I told you about."

Her hand shook a little as she picked up her coffee cup. She took a sip and didn't say anything.

"Miss Hunbatz, you say your brother 'left.' What did you mean by that?"

Rather than answer my question, Miss Hunbatz reached up, absently twisted strands of light brown hair with her fingers, and asked one of her own. "Was he... okay? When you saw him?"

"He was in better shape than I was," I said.

A haunted look came over her face. "What was he...."

She couldn't seem to finish the sentence, so I did it for her. "What was he doing? He was helping a very nasty and very powerful spirit conduct a sacrifice to an even more powerful spirit. I was the guest of honor. Things didn't go well for them, and he and the spirit vanished, leaving me strapped to an altar. Well, a makeshift altar. Just a tabletop with metal restraints, but it was serving its purpose."

Miss Hunbatz dropped her hand into her lap. "Were you hurt? I mean, did Duffy hurt you?"

"Duffy?"

"That's my brother's name." A smile came and went. "My mother's idea. My father got to name me, and my mother.... But... you got away from him, right? I mean, here you are, and...."

"Like I said, things didn't work out for them. I'd like to find him, though."

Her eyes narrowed. "What are you going to do with him? I mean, if you find him?"

I stared straight into her hazel eyes. They were troubled. Pretty, but troubled. "I don't know yet, Miss Hunbatz. That depends."

"Depends? On what?"

"On a lot of things. You never answered my question. What did you mean when you said your brother left?"

Miss Hunbatz noticed that her hands were sweating, and she wiped them on her skirt. She looked at her cup, but decided to leave it where it was. She looked back at me, her jaw set, her pretty eyes hard. Her words were hard, too, when she spoke. "Duffy disappeared fourteen years ago after our parents were killed. I found their bodies in their bed. They'd been... cut. Slashed by an animal, or by several animals. That's what the cops said. Pieces of them were missing, like they'd been bitten off and eaten. I'd seen Duffy the night before, but he wasn't there when I found the bodies. He'd disappeared sometime during the night. There was no evidence of violence in his room, and they didn't find his blood anywhere in the house. All of his things were still in his bedroom, packed away and undisturbed."

Miss Hunbatz's lips twisted into a scowl. "Duffy was never very bright, but he was very neat, almost compulsively so." She shook her head. "We might have shared the same womb, but we couldn't be more different. I used to think he was a changeling, and that my real twin had been brought up by fairies."

"Uh-huh. You say he disappeared?"

"That's right. The police told me he ran off and hid when he heard whatever it was that killed our parents. He never came back. The police searched for him for a while, but eventually they gave up. I haven't seen him since."

She dropped her eyes and stopped speaking. After a few moments, I asked, "What do you think happened to your brother? Do you think he was carried off by whoever killed your parents?"

She raised her eyes. "No, Mr. Southerland. It was Duffy who killed our mother and father. And then he ran away."

I held her eyes for a few moments before asking. "Why do you think your brother killed your parents?"

Miss Hunbatz reached for her coffee and took a sip. Her hands were steady this time. "When my brother was fourteen, he discovered that he was a shapeshifter. It happened suddenly. One night he had a dream. In the dream, he could see the world around him in every direction from different perspectives, all at the same time. He said that different parts of himself were arguing with each other, screaming at each other, like he'd broken into pieces, and every piece had something to say about it. When he woke up, he found out that the dream had been true. During the night, he'd transformed into seven howler monkeys. Do you know anything about shapeshifters, Mr. Southerland?"

I nodded. "I know a guy who transforms into more than a hundred rats. He says that when a shapeshifter first discovers what he is, it's a very disturbing experience. He told me that a lot of shapeshifters go mad."

Miss Hunbatz nodded. "That's correct, Mr. Southerland." Her voice became clinical, like someone who had done their research. "It happens somewhere near puberty, which is a wild time anyway. And it tears you apart, especially when you transform into multiples, like Duffy did. The animals all share a collective human consciousness, but each one also has its own brain and its own thoughts. To a limited extent, each one has its own identity. If the shapeshifter doesn't successfully coordinate those identities and subsume them into the collective brain, the shapeshifter can lose the human identity altogether, and each of the animals goes feral. They aren't truly separate entities, and they can't fully function on their own. But they try. The effort to keep them all together often drives the shapeshifter crazy."

She pushed a strand of hair out of her face and twisted it around her delicate fingers. "Duffy had a lot of trouble controlling the different animals. He would lose himself for long periods. His mind would break into pieces even when he kept his body whole. It was rough for him, but it was rough for all of us, too. Mom and Daddy had a hard time with it." She turned to me, a pleading expression on her face, the clinical tone gone. "They didn't try to understand him. They thought he was inhuman. Evil. They couldn't stand the idea that he wasn't, you know, like them. Normal." She scorned as she spit out that last word. "They wanted to know who to blame. Each other. His friends. His school. The world. Me. Anyone but themselves."

"There's no one to blame," I said. "It just happens. No one has ever been able to explain how or why."

She threw her hands in the air, exasperated. "I know. Believe me, I know. I wanted to help Duffy, but I also wanted to know why it never happened to me. We're twins! I kept dreading that I would wake up one day and be like him. I still worry about it, even though I know I'm past the age where it typically manifests."

"It's nothing to be ashamed of," I said.

She glared at me. "That's easy for you to say. You've never had to deal with it. Not directly. You say your friend is a shifter. How'd he turn out?"

"Pretty well, all things considered. He says he had some tough times. He doesn't talk about the early days of his transformation much. I gather from hints that he did things he was later ashamed of. Eventually he came to terms with it. He used to own a jewelry store in Placid Point. Beyond coming off as a little eccentric, he seems like anyone else most of the time."

"He's lucky. Most shifters aren't. Duffy wasn't. You can't imagine what it was like for him, growing up with parents who thought he'd been possessed by a demon. They tried to starve the demon out of him. They tried to beat it out. When that didn't work, they brought in doctors. They brought in shrinks. They brought in witches and healers. Most of them were con artists. My parents went broke trying to 'cure' him. It went on for years. And then, Duffy couldn't take it anymore."

"You think he killed your parents?"

"I know he did. As soon as I saw them, I knew. He attacked them and tore them apart. It wasn't a mystery. The police knew it, too, despite what they told me. They just never caught him."

She fixed me with her pleading eyes again. "I want you to find Duffy, Mr. Southerland. I want you to find him and bring him to me."

"I'm already looking for him, Miss Hunbatz. I don't know about bringing him to you, though. I don't know if I can keep him safe even if I wanted to. He has a few things to answer for."

She shook her head. When she looked at me again, her pretty eyes were fierce. "You don't understand, Mr. Southerland. I don't want to help him. That son of a bitch killed my parents. He ruined my life. I want you to bring that monster to me so I can watch him die."

"I'm not an assassin, Miss Hunbatz."

"You don't have to kill him, Mr. Southerland. Just bring him to me, and I'll take care of the rest."

"That still makes me a killer. If I get him, I'll turn him over to the police. If he's guilty of murdering your parents, then he'll get what's coming to him."

Miss Hunbatz leaned toward me over the desk. "What's the difference between turning him over to the police and turning him over to me? It all turns out the same for him either way."

I sat back in my chair to restore the distance between us. "Justice is the government's job, not yours."

"No, Mr. Southerland. Justice is everyone's job."

"You don't want justice, Miss Hunbatz. You want revenge."

Miss Hunbatz bolted to her feet and leaned further over the desk. Her lips curled, exposing the tips of her teeth. "What I want is to look into his eyes when I rip the life out of them!"

I reached for my coffee and took a slow sip. After a few moments of silence, Miss Hunbatz lowered herself back into her chair. She reached into her purse and pulled out a cigarette. "Got a light?" She asked me.

I found an undamaged book of matches in my desk drawer and lit her cigarette for her. "I'm afraid I don't have an ashtray," I told her.

She took a puff and knocked the ash into her coffee cup. "I want to hire you, Mr. Southerland. Find Duffy. If you don't want to bring him to me, at least call me before you call the cops. I want to be there when they pick him up. That okay with you?"

"We'll see how the cards fall," I said. "If they come up right, I'll give you your chance to see him get hauled away. That's the best I can do."

Chapter Sixteen

I'd identified Ixquic's hairy bodyguard, or whatever he was to her, but I was no closer to figuring out how to keep her from killing me, short of giving her Chivo's heart and liver. Thinking of Chivo reminded me that I should check to see how he was doing. The summoning ritual seemed to have exhausted him. It also seemed to have brought some of the human part of him to the surface. He'd tried to speak to me earlier, something he'd never done before. I was anxious to explore the extent of his ability to communicate with me.

When I opened the door to the laundry room, Chivo was still curled up in his bed, sleeping. Siphon was stretched between him and the window, bathing him with a cool breeze.

Chivo's head jerked when I entered the room, and he stared in my direction, his red eyes blazing. When he saw it was me, his eyes dulled, and he sat up. His mouth opened, and he bleated, "Baaalleck."

"Chivo," I answered.

He stepped out of the bed and rose on his hind legs. Siphon moved away from the window and hovered over Chivo's shoulder as he stepped toward me.

I had a hundred questions and didn't know which one to ask first. Chivo beat me to the punch. "Uuunggerrr."

"You're hungry? I'll get you some yonak." I picked up Chivo's bowl, happy to have something to do that didn't involve speaking. After I'd filled it, I turned, uncertain. Somehow, putting the bowl on the floor seemed inappropriate. But Chivo lowered himself to all fours, and, after I placed the bowl in front of him, he lapped at the yonak in his usual manner.

I turned my attention to Siphon, who had followed Chivo and was still whirling above his shoulder. I formed the sigil for its name in my mind and called out to it mentally. Something brushed against me, like a fish nibbling at a baited hook, but it was gone in a flash. I closed my eyes and continued to reach out, but whatever connection I'd almost made vanished. Further straining only threatened to bring on a headache, and I stopped trying.

When I opened my eyes, Siphon was pressed closer to Chivo, as if seeking the creature's protection. That was interesting. When Chivo had licked his bowl clean, I caught his attention.

"Chivo. Can you talk to Siphon?" I indicated the elemental.

Chivo turned toward the whirling funnel of air. He bleated, a normal-sounding goat's call rather than an attempt at a word, and Siphon moved closer to me. Chivo bleated at the elemental again, and Siphon's familiar voice, like an echo rising from the bottom of a well, emerged from the swirling wind. "Siphon will speak my words."

The hairs on the back of my neck rose to attention, and a grin spread across my face. "That's excellent, Chivo. Or should I call you Lord Cadmael?"

Chivo bleated, and Siphon's voice intoned, "You may continue to address me as Chivo. I have grown fond of the name."

***

Using Siphon to pass Chivo's words to me, the two of us had a long conversation. When we were done, and the last rays of the setting sun were casting an orange glow through my laundry room window, Chivo disappeared out the back door and into the alley. There were things I wanted to do—needed to do as quickly as possible—but it had been three days since my last decent sleep, and I didn't think I'd be capable of doing anything at that moment except stumbling upstairs to my bed.

I hoped my sleep would be dreamless. I was desperate for a few uninterrupted hours of blissful repose. I sent messages out into the night: "Do not disturb!" "Nobody home!" "Closed for repairs!" "No solicitors!" "Keep out!" I sent out a mental call to Cougar, pleading with him to wall me off from nocturnal intrusions.

Sometimes you just can't catch a break.

I was back in the Borderland. Why did my dreams keep bringing me there? Hadn't I already served my time? Growls from howler monkeys filled the night. A troop of them, a half dozen or so, leapt through the trees, flying from branch to branch over my head in a blur of motion. A half dozen? Seven of them, more likely, I thought. I ran in a direction I hoped would take me out of the jungle.

The howler monkeys followed me until I emerged into a clearing. A waning moon glowed red over the treetops in front of me. I turned to retrace my steps, but the monkeys dropped to the ground and surrounded me, hemming me in. I tried to push my way past, but the air was so close and so hot, and I was so tired. I fell to my knees, trying to breathe. Ixquic stood in front of me, the light of the moon beaming over her shoulder. Her silver hair spilled over her pointed ears and fell at her shoulders. Her pallid beaklike face seemed to shine with a pale light of its own.

"I hunger, mortal," Ixquic hissed through blood-red lips spread to expose pointed teeth.

I couldn't speak, but I sent thoughts in her direction. "Back off, bitch! You can't kill me."

Her cruel smile didn't leave her face. "That is true, mortal. I am prohibited from killing you until the full moon rises. That will be soon." Her face softened, and the tips of her teeth withdrew behind her dark lips. "I hunger, but it is not your life I prefer. The creature you call Huay Chivo would be a most fitting offering for Itzamna, the father spirit. You have spoken to the Huay Chivo. He trusts you. It would be a simple matter for you to stab the monster in his sleep and take his heart and liver. You will live. And yet, you are reluctant. I do not understand. He is a burden. You never asked to be his guardian. Let him go. He is nothing to you. It is your resistance that prevents you from attaining your much needed rest. Let yourself be free of your burden. Promise to do as I ask and you will sleep again, undisturbed."

A warm breeze blew over me from the direction of the rising moon. The weight of Ixquic's words was overwhelming. My objections to sacrificing Chivo's life in order to preserve my own seemed foolish and petty. Every part of me wanted to comply with the wishes of the Blood Moon and sink into the soothing embrace of a golden slumber. The surrounding jungle faded, replaced by a warm orange glow. All sounds faded as mud flowed gently into my ears. I heard only a whisper in my mind, urging me to comply with Ixquic's reasonable request. Give her your promise. Give her the Huay Chivo. And then I could rest.

I broke into a smile and let out a chuckle. The whispering stopped. I chuckled again. Ixquic's confusion and irritation swept through my mind like gravel spilling on concrete. "You can't touch him," I thought out loud.

"What did you say?" The sound of Ixquic's voice cleared the muck from my ears.

"Chivo. The Huay Chivo. You can't touch him. You need *me* to kill him for you."

I listened to Ixquic's silence for a few moments before continuing. "Why do you need *me* to do it? Are you afraid of confronting Chivo yourself?"

The monkeys roared, low-pitched growls loud enough to drown out thought. I tuned them out as best I could. I stared into Ixquic's eyes and focused on broadcasting my thoughts into her head. "You want Chivo's heart and liver? Go ahead and take them. But you can't, can you. Why not? Is he too strong for you? Would it break some kind of rule you spirits have to follow?" Rage floated up from somewhere deep inside me, and I opened the gates to let it run free. "Yeah, about those rules.... You wouldn't happen to be violating any right now, would you?" I stopped throwing my thoughts and spoke out loud. "I thought you weren't supposed to do me any lasting harm until the rising of the full moon. Well, I gotta tell you, lady, my ticker isn't feeling all that strong right now. You hear how it's pounding? You and your monkeys are scaring the shit outta me!"

Ixquic's eyes darted from one side to the other. She opened her mouth to say something, but I didn't give her the chance.

I raised my voice, sputtering a little. "Is Cizin seeing this, you fuckin' bitch? Is Itzamna?" I poured it on, reaching deep down for the pain and frustration that had been building inside me since I'd found myself strapped to a tabletop, feeling the heat leaving my body. Since I'd seen Badass disappear forever into the maw of a demonic spirit. Since I'd heard about the grisly death of an innocent woman, whose only crime had been to trust me to help her son. Since I'd come home to find my office trashed, with a traumatized Siphon left behind in my laundry room. Since I'd endured a bloody ritual to summon Chivo, only to watch him run away in confusion and fear. Since the Blood Moon had invaded my dream for the second time and given me the choice of sacrificing my friend or dying myself. And now, driven to my knees, my senses overwhelmed by spirit magic, the howls of jungle beasts, and the threatening whispers of a deadly spirit. "I don't know how much more of this I can take!" I shouted, my voice scraped raw. "I haven't slept in days! Keep this up and I'll have a stroke! Or a heart attack! What would happen to you if I kicked off right here and now?" I dialed it up a notch until I was howling at the top of my lungs. "What would be the penalty for you if I up and croaked? What would Cizin do? What would Itzamna think?"

I grabbed at my chest and made choking sounds. I dropped to my hands and knees. My heart was pounding so hard and so fast that I almost convinced myself I'd induced a coronary.

The orange glow around me dissipated, and I saw Cougar standing with his side to Ixquic, his back arched, his ears flat, his tail hanging low and sweeping side to side. He glowered at the Blood Moon spirit through black eyes and bared his teeth. The howler monkeys all fell back at the sight of him. I looked up into the night sky. Stars, like eyes, glared down into the clearing, their light causing the glow of the moon on the treetops to dim. Cougar paced back and forth in front of Ixquic, keeping his head on a swivel and his eyes fixed on hers each time he turned and reversed direction. A low rumble, below the range of human hearing, rolled out of the jungle from every side of the clearing, and the earth trembled. Ixquic watched Cougar, wide-eyed. I could look right through her to the trees at her back. As the monkeys fled into the shelter of the jungle, Ixquic vanished from both my sight and my magical senses.

I sat bolt upright in my bed, gasping for air and knocking aside my sweat-soaked sheets. I was alone in the darkness of my bedroom. Nothing remained of my dream except a vivid memory and the lingering scent of tropical jungle. I reached into the drawer of the end table next to my bed and took out a half-empty pint bottle of rye. After staring at it for a few seconds, I unscrewed the cap and threw back a king-sized swallow. The burn ripped the air out of my lungs, and my heart threatened to jump out of my chest, but I forced myself to stay calm until I could breathe again. I tossed back a more moderate gulp and screwed the cap back on the bottle.

I broke out laughing. I'd been bluffing when I'd told Ixquic I was on the verge of dying, and she'd either believed me or been confused by my resistance. My bluff had been convincing enough to Cougar, as well as other spirits. Or maybe I really had been on the verge of a heart attack. I held up a hand and watched it shake.

A glance at the clock on the end table showed that I'd been 'sleeping,' if that's what you wanted to call it, for less than an hour. How much of my life energy had Ixquic drained from me this time? I sighed, knowing sleep would not be returning that night.

***

Too much had been happening too fast, and I needed to sort it out. I got out of bed, tossed on some clothes, and went outside for a walk in the brisk night air.

The Yerba City sky was clear for a change. Air streams from the southeast had steered the usual blanket of low-lying clouds out into the ocean, and a canopy of stars glittered overhead. The brighter ones anyway. The ones that could compete with the all-night glare of the city lights. I put my hands in my coat pockets and headed in the direction of the Downtown City Center.

I thought back on my conversation with Chivo. He had been surprised to discover that he'd been living in the body of a monster for the past five hundred years. His memories of those years were dim and scattered, mere glimpses of wandering, hunting, and hiding from the sun. His memory of the past year, since I'd found him rustling through the garbage cans in the alley behind my office, were stronger, like a vivid dream. Even his recollection of his life as Lord Cadmael, the last ruler to stand between Lords Ketz-Alkwat and Manqu and mastery of the Western Hemisphere, was faulty and filled with gaps. He knew it had been Lord Ketz who had captured him and transformed him into the Huay Chivo, using Cadmael's own sorcerous shapeshifting enchantments against him. Chivo remembered a long period of captivity, but whether he'd escaped or been released he couldn't say.

Chivo thought he knew why Cizin and Ixquic were fighting over him. Ixquic had summoned Ketz-Alkwat and Manqu from Hell and thought of them as her sons, but the Dragon Lords didn't hold her in the same regard. Ixquic had brought them to our world against their will, according to Chivo, and even though the Dragon Lords were happy enough to carve out their own realms once they got here, they weren't particularly grateful to Ixquic for tearing them away from their old homes. It had been a painful process, and dragons were notorious for holding grudges. Ixquic hoped that by sacrificing their old enemy to the father spirit, the Dragon Lords would elevate her into their good graces. Chivo didn't know why that should matter to her, but, clearly, it did. A maternal thing, he supposed.

Cizin, the ruthless and supremely powerful lord of Xibalba, had chosen the young Cadmael to be one of his own. Later, after the Dragon Lords had humbled Cizin, the diminished spirit had been cut off from all of his chosen ones, including Cadmael, which had led to Cadmael's own defeat at the hands of Ketz and Manqu. When I'd filled Chivo in on Sonoma's quest to find and cure him, Chivo concluded that Cizin was trying to restore their connection so that the old death lord could use him against the Dragon Lords. I agreed it was a reasonable assumption and that he was probably right.

When the Children of Cizin had summoned Chivo and offered him their blood, it had been like waking from a nightmare. A fog had lifted from his brain, leaving him disoriented and confused. When I asked if that's why he had run, however, he'd hesitated to answer. It had been that, but more, he'd finally said. It was as if a cold mist had descended over him, covering him like a wet blanket. I'd asked if it had something to do with Jalen, but Chivo couldn't say for sure. He'd barely noticed the boy, he'd told me. He'd been struck by a wave of fear, and he'd panicked. When I pointed out that Jalen was a chosen of Ixquic, Chivo had shrugged.

When I told Chivo that Sonoma and Jalen were his direct descendants, he'd made a noise that sounded like a cross between a cough and a laugh. He bleated at Siphon, who said, "I was quite active in my day. I'm certain after all this time that I must have many hundreds of descendants. Thousands, perhaps."

Made sense to me. "Sonoma was trying to use her son to help open communications between Ixquic and Cizin," I told him.

A snort escaped through Chivo's snout. "Oood luggg widd daddd," he bleated.

Siphon's translation had come out as, "Best of luck to her, but her success is highly unlikely."

I looked up from my thoughts to find that I was standing outside The Black Minotaur Lounge, my favorite watering hole. I debated going inside but decided to keep walking. Falling into a booze-induced stupor was appealing, but it wasn't going to do much to clear my head and help me put the events of the past few days in order.

I'd told Chivo about Ixquic's desire to offer up his heart and liver to Itzamna as a sacrifice and her threat to substitute my own if I didn't deliver his up by the next rising of the full moon. Chivo told me that Cizin would protect him from Ixquic, and that he was safe as long as Ixquic couldn't convince me to cut him open. He'd looked into my eyes then, and I'd tried to reassure him I'd never do that. I'm not sure he was convinced. I couldn't blame him. I wasn't sure of it myself.

Chivo said he would try to connect with Cizin and see if the ancient spirit could find a solution to our dilemma. I told him I would try to get back in touch with Sonoma and see if she had any suggestions. That's where we'd left things.

I walked some more and found myself in South Market, the bustling home of the City's financial center. The offices were mostly dark now, with only a few lit windows giving evidence of maintenance workers and ambitious middle managers burning the late-night oil. My thoughts drifted toward the air elemental that Walks in Cloud thought might be keeping tabs on me. I stopped in my tracks and put together some sigils in my mind. My vision of the summer night sky changed, and I perceived hosts of air elementals drifting with the wind currents. I tried to focus my perception, to detect something no larger than a teardrop, but it was no use. It was like looking for a drop of rain in the ocean. I abandoned my efforts and instead cast my perception as far as I could, hoping to find Badass hovering somewhere in the distance. Eventually, I gave up and continued walking. I searched inside myself for a hint of sadness and found only a simmering rage wanting to rise to the surface. With an effort, I pushed it into a cage and locked the door. But I kept the key close at hand.

After another half hour of walking, I reached the Downtown District, heart of the city's governing agencies, hotels, shopping, entertainment, and tourism. It was well after midnight, but the air crackled with the living energy of Saturday in the City on a summer night. Taxicabs, buses, and private vehicles of every size, shape, and model jammed the streets. Horns blared at every congested intersection. Brake lights flared red, tires squealed, and drivers shouted death threats and curses out their windows. I watched as a drunk threw a bottle into the street and laughed with his fellow drunks as they staggered along the sidewalk. Near where I was standing, a young woman wearing a faded shawl over a worn sleeveless shirt more suited for the warmer climes of Southern Caychan than the windswept Central Coast ran a bow over the strings of a violin and sang an old folk melody as tourists tossed coins into her instrument case. I thought her song was pretty, and I tossed in a bill of my own. She stopped playing long enough to wink at me, stoop, and weigh the bill down with a few of the coins. I gave her a brief smile and continued walking.

In the distance, I heard a voice rising above the general din of the streets. Frowning, I made my way toward it. After a couple of blocks, I came upon a crowd watching a familiar figure shouting at them from the top of a wooden crate. I stared at him in disbelief. Sure enough, it was the one-armed firebrand I'd seen the night before in the Humback.

"Lord's flaming balls," I thought to myself. The Humback was one thing. People expected a certain amount of rabblerousing there. But downtown? In front of affluent out-of-towners? I shook my head. This was going to go over like a blowtorch in a fireworks factory.

Chapter Seventeen

The onlookers weren't blocking traffic this time; instead, they were gathered in the courtyard of a government office complex. I spotted a polished black sedan double-parked on the street near the crowd and made a beeline for it. I couldn't see through the tinted windows of the car, but with my elf-enhanced awareness I could "see" Stormclaw sitting in the driver's seat. The troll noticed me coming and lowered the driver's side window.

"Good evening, Mr. Southerland. I guess you just can't get enough of our boy."

I leaned against the car. "He sure gets around. What's he doing downtown?"

Stormclaw nodded toward the passenger side of the car. "Why don't you get in and I'll tell you about it."

"You sure? Won't you need to be coming to his rescue in a few minutes?"

"You forget, son. We got the mayor in our pocket. He's arranged to keep the cops off the boy's ass for another fifteen minutes."

"What about the LIA?"

"They're more likely to shoot him from a rooftop than arrest him. And there ain't nothin' I can do about that."

I pushed myself off the car and walked around to the passenger side.

"So what's the story?" I asked, once I was settled inside.

Stormclaw didn't answer right away. He removed his shades and cleaned them with a handkerchief he pulled from his shirt pocket. He took the time to examine the lenses carefully before pushing them back over his face and turning his attention to the gathering crowd. Just when I thought he'd forgotten my question, the old troll began speaking. "The 'story' is that young Mister Colton Randolph over there attracts the marks, and then the Hatfield agents in the crowd start passing around the latest product from their labs. A very pleasant designer narcotic, they tell me. I wouldn't know, myself. I stopped hopping up my head a long time ago, and this junk they put on the streets nowadays, well, it's more than an old troll like me can handle. Not that I ever did myself any favors with the shit I used to take back in the day. But these kids gotta have whatever's new and hip. The first one's free, of course. Can't pass up free, now, can you?"

I stared at the troll. "Are you saying this whole citywide antiwar tour is just a promotional stunt to push drugs?"

Stormclaw shrugged. "A lot of upper-crust children with fat wallets in that Saturday night crowd. Kind of clever, if you ask me. I hear the Hatfields are expecting to rake in some serious dough tonight."

I let out a long breath. "Lord's balls."

Stormclaw shot me a glance. "You okay, son? If I didn't know better, I'd say you were disappointed. Did you really believe the Hatfields were using this boy to inconvenience the powers that be?"

I snorted. "Nah. Where's the profit in that? Using political protest as a front to deal drugs to rich kids is right up their alley."

The troll's laser eyes peered at me through the shades he wore both day and night. "You were a soldier, weren't you?"

"Yep."

"I missed all that. Kept myself one step ahead of the government. Traveled to the other Realms and stayed one step ahead of their governments, too. See action?"

"In the Borderland."

Stormclaw nodded. "Thought so. You know, that conflict goes way back. They were fighting over that land back in my day, a long time before you were born."

I stared in his direction, though his attention was back on the crowd. "So it's true. They've been fighting that war a lot longer than they let on."

"Yep. But I was elsewhere."

"What were you doing?"

"A little of this, a little of that. Seeing the world. Learning about things."

I smiled. "Sounds like you might have been a spy."

Stormclaw turned his head toward me and coughed out a laugh. "A spy? Nah. I've seen them in the movies, shooting up the bad guys and kissing the dames. Nothing so exciting for me, unless you count the time I tossed a regional warlord over a hotel balcony. Made me a local hero for a while, but it also meant a prolonged stay in a Nihhonese prison." He stared over my head at the memory. "Got me a real education in that joint." A shake of his head brought him back to the present. "Anyway, point is, whether you were cutting down enemy soldiers in the jungle or knocking off corrupt officials in foreign realms, I don't know that neither of us was making much of a difference in this world. An even worse warlord took the place of the one I did away with, and the fight for the Borderland is still going on. I'm two hundred years older than you, and year after year the same ol' shit keeps rolling down the mountain and into the village streets. I can't see how it's ever gonna stop."

I nodded toward the agitator haranguing the crowd from his makeshift platform. "Sounds like you sympathize with your firebrand up there."

"Don't you?"

"Me? I don't have any stake in his game."

The troll snorted. "Sure you don't."

Something outside the car window caught my eye. "Uh-oh, buddy. I think you might have to go into action a little sooner than you were thinking."

Stormclaw jerked his head toward the milling crowd, and then beyond it. "Damn! Those motherfuckers are jumping the gun." He opened the door and shot out of the car. I followed suit.

A platoon of hard-faced bulls with "cop" written all over them were advancing toward Randolph from the lobby of the office complex. It appeared they'd been holed up there waiting for the word to move, and now they were coming out in force. I could have walked away, but I didn't. I don't know why. Maybe I was swept up in Stormclaw's wake. At any rate, I found myself chasing after the troll as he pushed his way through the crowd toward Randolph, who, unaware of the impending threat, continued to rant at the growing crowd.

Stormclaw stopped in his tracks and whirled on me. "Get him out of here." He grabbed me by the arm and forced a car key into my hand.

"What? Wait!" I said, but the troll was already shoving people out of his way and making straight for the oncoming cops.

Randolph had stopped his haranguing and was searching the increasingly agitated crowd for the source of the disturbance. When he saw Stormclaw making for the bulls marching through the courtyard, his eyes widened in alarm. He stepped off the crate to run in the opposite direction, but he couldn't fight his way through the onlookers.

"Well, shit," I thought to myself. Raising my voice, I shouted, "Bomb! Watch out! He's got a bomb! Run!"

Screams rang out and bodies scrambled. I made my way through the swarm and grabbed Randolph by his armless sleeve. "Quick! Come with me."

Randolph tried to yank himself away. "Let go of me, you fuck!"

I held up the car key. "Stormclaw's holding off the troops coming this way. I'm gonna get you out of here. Move!" I wrapped my arm around his shoulders and forced him through the panicked mob toward the sedan. Randolph decided to cooperate. Maybe it was because I had an honest mug. More likely it was because I had invoked Stormclaw's name and was steering him toward a familiar vehicle. Either way, we made it without much fuss. As I fired up the car, I glanced out into the courtyard and saw a dozen cops swinging their billy clubs at a surging crowd of narcotics-fueled protesters. Stormclaw was nowhere in sight.

I didn't speed away. I pulled smoothly into the line of passing cars and let the flow take me along at its own pace. When I heard sirens, I pulled over with the rest of the traffic and gave the cop cars a clear path to the altercation. Randolph ducked below the dashboard until they'd gone by.

"You don't have to do that," I said. "The windows are tinted."

He glared at me. "Who are you with—the Hatfields?"

I kept my eyes on the road. "What if I was? What do you think you could do about it?"

His gaze burrowed into the side of my head. "Nah. You're not a Hatfield. You're with the LIA."

"Oh for two," I said. "Nah. I'm just helping out an old pal."

"Stormclaw? He's a friend of yours?"

"I hardly know him. But, yeah, I guess you could say that. We've worked together before, and I kind of like the old geezer."

Randolph relaxed a little. "He's a pain in the ass."

I shot him a quick glance. "He threw himself at a herd of bulls to keep them from putting the arm on you."

Randolph shrugged. "That's what they pay him for."

"Yeah? Well, they aren't paying me. I'll let you out at the corner."

He yanked his head in my direction. "No! Wait. Take me to the Tanielu."

"Fuck you, kid."

"I'll... I'll pay you. How much do you want?"

"I don't want your money. Stormclaw asked me to get you away from the cops, and I did. As a favor to him." I pulled into an alley and stopped the car. "Get out."

Randolph held up his arm. "Hang on a second, man. Those cops are still too close. I need to get away from downtown. Just take me to the Tanielu. You can drop me off anywhere there."

"And what about Stormclaw? All he did was save your sorry ass. I'm going to go back and make sure he's okay."

"He's a troll. He can take care of himself."

"I counted twelve cops, and one of them was a troll."

Randolph shrugged. "If those bulls take him to the pens, the Hatfields will bail him out."

I nodded toward the door. "Beat it."

"All right! All right! Just let me make a call first." He pulled a phone out of his shirt pocket.

"What for?"

"I'm not walking all the way to the Tanielu. I need a ride."

"You calling the Hatfields? Ixnay on that, punk."

Randolph grinned. "You really *aren't* with the Hatfield family, are you."

I didn't say anything.

His grin got wider. "Thing is, you're driving one of their cars. One phone call, and they'll be looking to get it back."

Score one for him: he had a point. "You live in the Tanielu?"

"No, but I've got friends there. Come on. It's not that far. And there's nothing you can do for the old stick-in-the-mud now. He told you to get me out of harm's way, right? Well, I'm not out of the fire yet. Dump me in the Tanielu and we'll call that a good day's job."

To be fair, he was right about Stormclaw, and the Tanielu was only a few blocks from downtown. "Fine," I said. "But I'm driving myself home in this car. The Hatfields can pick it up when they find it. I'm sure they've got a tracker on it."

Randolph settled into his seat. "Thanks, man. I owe you one."

"Forget it," I said. "I'm not doing this for you."

I felt his eyes on me. "Say, what's your beef with me anyway?"

I didn't answer.

"You a vet?" he asked.

I kept my concentration on the traffic.

"Borderland, I'll bet. You've got that look. I lost my arm there."

"Bullshit," I said.

"Three years ago. I was on patrol, searching for insurgents. I found some."

I shot him a quick glance before turning my attention back to the road.

"What's your name, soldier?" he asked.

"Forget it, chump. We're not going to get that close."

157

"Suit yourself. I'm just trying to be polite."

I changed lanes to avoid a double-parked delivery truck.

Randolph continued with his war story. Some people live to talk, and, unfortunately, Randolph was one of them. "Five of my buddies bought it," he said. "We got a few of them, too. Just another day in the jungle." He drew in a long breath. "You know the score. They get some of us, we get some of them, and on and on it goes, year after year after year. And for what?" He turned to me. "What's the fuckin' point? You were there. Did it ever matter to you which Dragon Lord controlled what piece of real estate? If Ketz surrendered the Borderland to Manqu tomorrow, would it matter? Would you care? Would it change your life in any meaningful way?"

The light at the intersection turned red, and I hit the brake a little harder than I needed to. Randolph had to brace himself with his one good arm to keep his head from bouncing off the dash. "Look," I said. "My time in the Borderland was a long time ago, and the last thing I want to do with you or anybody else is stir up old memories."

"Sure, that's fine for you. But what about the young men and women who get sent into that meat grinder day after day? You got kids? Nephews? Nieces? You want them winding up like me? Or worse? For no good reason?"

An image of Antonio in the alley behind my office, cigarette dangling from his lips and a cold bottle of beer in his hand, popped unbidden into my head. If he didn't get selected for jet engine maintenance, he could end up with a rifle in the jungle. I shook the image away. "I don't have any kids," I said.

Randolph studied me with narrowed eyes. "Maybe not. But you know someone who does. And you don't want them to be cannon fodder for the Realm of Tolanica."

I had to hand it to the punk. He was perceptive. "All right," I conceded. "I'm not a fan of a pointless conflict that has been going on for decades—maybe centuries—with no end in sight. But you aren't going to stop it by clowning for the Hatfields so they can deal expensive designer drugs to the tourists. Quit fooling yourself, kid. Your act is nothing but a floor show to hook the right kind of consumers."

Randolph had the decency to blush. "I know what the Hatfields are doing, and what they're getting out of it. But my message is real. Sure, they're using me, but I'm using them, too. Sometimes you gotta dance with the demons in order to do good."

I turned to look at him. "And you think you're doing good?"

"I know I am." He sighed. "Revolutions don't succeed overnight. But someone has to speak out against injustice. And the word is spreading. Tonight was my biggest crowd yet."

"I counted about fifty people, and most of them were there to get high."

"But last night's crowd was only half that. You know that. You were there. Yeah, I remember you." He chuckled. "That was crazy. I called you a gray man and set the crowd on you."

"You thought I was Leea?"

He snorted. "I had no idea. But you were in the right place at the right time, with your suit and tie, and your shiny shoes and hard looks, and I had to take advantage. Someone got the brawl on their cellphone and posted it on social media. It was good publicity. And the best part is they didn't get a good shot of your face. That means no one knows you. Come to my next rally and we'll do it again. I'll finger you for an undercover cop, and maybe we'll get a full-blown riot going. If we can get a local TV crew there, we could even make the evening news! Whaddaya say? Are you game? We might get this revolution going sooner than you think!"

The light changed and I gunned the sedan through the intersection. "No thanks, bud. I'm not interested in your revolution."

Randolph nodded. "I see. So you're jake with Lord Ketz. Everything is copacetic. All hail the mighty benevolent Dragon Lord."

When I didn't respond, he muttered, "Stooge."

I took my eyes off the road long enough to give the punk a good glare. "I'm doing you a favor, kid. Don't bite the hand that's feeding you."

"Sure you are," he drawled. He sat up straight. "I don't get it. You seem like a smart joe to me. How can you not see what's going on right under your nose? You knock me for using my rallies to front for the Hatfield family's drug deals. All right, maybe that's a fair point. But at least I'm getting my message out. But where's your outrage when Lord Ketz sacrifices human lives in a war that has no purpose except lining the pockets of Lord Ketz and his corporate supporters? The war pigs bid for defense contracts, which are funded by the taxpayers. And as long as the government publicists can fan nationalist fervor for the Realm, the government can keep the tax rates for the middle class high. That way his corporate buddies who are getting rich on the war don't have to bear the burden. And where do the soldiers come from? You served. How many of your fellow grunts were from the fat-cat class?"

I crossed into the Tanielu, and the sudden change from the bright lights and vibrant buzz of downtown to the dreariness of the working-class district was jarring. In the Tanielu, pale lamplight glowed through a few dusty windows, but the buildings along the street were otherwise dark. In contrast to the crowded promenades I'd left behind, where sharp-dressed revelers flowed like neon through the radiant streets, only a few furtive individuals, hat brims pulled low and hands stuffed into the pockets of well-worn coats or sweatshirts, shuffled over the dirty cracked sidewalks of the Tanielu, searching for drug connections, hookers, or a quiet doorway where they could cover themselves with tattered blankets and bed down on flattened cardboard boxes for the night.

I pulled up in a space in front of a fire hydrant. "Okay, we're here. Get out."

Randolph let his head plop back against his cushioned headrest. "Come on, man. Two more blocks. My friends have a pad just up the road."

"Look," I said, turning to speak to the oh-so-sincere activist face-to-face. "You give a nice speech. And I don't disagree with you. We all know the system is rife with corruption. And the war in the Borderland is only a part of it. What they are doing to the adaros..., well, I don't want to get into it. Have you been to the settlement? Yeah? Then you know. And it's worse since a bunch of them escaped back to the sea during the big storm." I'd played a role in that, but now wasn't the time to talk about it, so I waved it off. "I don't know anyone outside the government cheerleaders in the media who can drum up a lot of enthusiasm for the war in the Borderland. But Lord Ketz is a fact of life, like the rising of the sun in the morning. Your speeches are more likely to land you in an LIA detention camp than end the war. You think you're going to scare a hundred-foot-long fire-breathing master of magic who conquered the spirits of nature itself?"

Randolph's eyes flared. "If my speeches weren't ruffling the old lizard's scales, then how come his bulls are so keen to stop me? Come on. I'm not safe here. Two more blocks, and I'll never ask you for another favor." He smiled. "Although if you ever want to help me fire up the crowd again...."

I sighed. "All right. Two more blocks. But only if you promise to keep your yap shut until we get there. The second you try to recruit me into your bullshit revolution again, I'll put a bullet in your brain."

Randolph chuckled. "You're not armed."

"How do you know?"

"Who do you think you're talking to? I'm not some dumb rich kid rebelling against his parents. I've lived a life."

"Right. You're the real deal." I pulled the car away from the curb. "Two blocks. That's it."

A block and a half later, Randolph pointed at an apartment building. "That's it up there."

"All right."

A second later, I added, "Uh-oh."

Randolph saw it, too, and I knew I was going to have to stop underestimating the kid. He pointed at a dark green sedan double-parked near the building we were headed for. "Bulls!"

"Yep. And one lounging near the entryway. Looks like they want you pretty bad."

"Lord's balls. How did they get here so fast?"

"They got these things called radios," I explained. "And people called dispatchers. You'd be surprised how organized the YCPD is when it comes to running down fugitives from the law, especially when they try to incite a riot in the heart of downtown on a Saturday night."

Randolph turned to me, his eyes pleading. "You can't drop me off there."

I sighed and made a right turn at the intersection. Randolph smiled. "Thanks, buddy."

"Got any other friends in the area?" I asked.

A look of worry took the smile off Randolph's mug. "They'll be staking them out, too. Can't we just park somewhere for a while? I'll call someone to come and get me."

"Forget it. I'm not going to babysit you until your Hatfield friends come to take you off my hands. I could be here all night."

To be honest, I don't know why I didn't kick the punk's sorry ass out into the street and let him fend for himself. I didn't know him. He wasn't my friend. His "cause" had nothing to do with me, and, even if I halfway sympathized with him, his naïve eagerness was getting on my nerves. Stormclaw had put him in my hands, but what of it? I didn't really know Stormclaw, either. I'd worked with him one time, and it hadn't exactly been a swell experience. For whatever reason, however, I needed to get the punk somewhere halfway safe before I could dump him. It would only be a matter of time before his so-called "rallies" got him dead or thrown in a hole. The simple truth is that I didn't want it to be on my watch.

Besides, I had an idea where I could take him.

Every time the kid started to open his mouth, I stopped him, either with a look or by raising my hand and making a shushing sound. If I was being honest with myself, I think I was enjoying it. His heart was going to explode if I didn't let him yak at me some more.

It took me ten minutes to get to Sonoma's basement hideaway, and the punk never said a word. I parked the sedan as close as I could and turned off the engine. After scanning the neighborhood for cops or other potential trouble, I turned to my passenger. "Get out and follow me."

When we were out of the car, Randolph asked, "Where are we going?"

"There's a basement apartment under that secondhand store up there. It's got a couch you can flop on. Some people I know were hiding there last night, but they were planning on moving on this morning. It should be empty."

Randolph looked at me. "You've got a key?"

"No," I admitted. "We'll have to improvise."

"Terrific."

Chapter Eighteen

I always carried a set of lockpicks in my coat, but it turned out I didn't need them. By the time I reached the basement apartment, I knew it was occupied.

I rapped on the door. "Sonoma? It's Southerland. Can I come in?"

Footsteps approached from inside the apartment. A metal bolt slipped through a sleeve, and the door opened a crack. Sonoma peeked through the opening. "I wasn't expecting company," she said. Looking past me, she asked, "Who's your friend?"

"I'll explain inside. That okay?"

She frowned but pulled the door open. "Come in before anyone sees you."

Jalen was waiting near the doorway, wearing pajamas with no slippers, a white-knuckled grip on a kitchen knife. When we were all inside, Sonoma rolled her eyes at him. "Put that thing down before you hurt yourself."

Jalen scowled and lowered his hand without releasing his grip on the knife.

I turned to Sonoma. "I didn't think you'd still be here."

Sonoma looked as tired as I felt. Her eyes were puffy, and her mouth drooped. "The cops are watching my friends," she said in a flat voice. "We couldn't get away today."

"Yeah? There's a lot of that going around." I indicated Randolph. "They're watching *his* friends, too. I was gonna put him up here until he could phone someone to come and get him, but I guess we'll have to make other plans. Maybe I'll dump him in Bunker Park."

Jalen was staring at Randolph, his eyes wide. "Hey," he said. "You're that crazy antiwar asshole." His eyes glanced off Randolph's empty sleeve.

Randolph noticed and smiled. "I like to think of myself as a revolutionary, rather than a 'crazy antiwar asshole.'"

I turned to him with a straight face. "If the shoe fits."

Sonoma glared at me. "If you've led the cops here...."

"Nah, we're clear," I assured her, hoping I was right.

Sonoma's shoulders slumped. "Fuck me," she muttered, frustrated. "It's been a hell of a day."

Tell me about it, I thought to myself. Out loud, I said, "Why are you still hiding from the police? You didn't kill your wife."

She shook her head. "I told you before. Things I did... things I set in motion.... They might hold me responsible for Clara's death, and they might be right."

"We talked about this, Sonoma. Even if your attempts to bring Cizin and Ixquic together to resolve their issues somehow led to unforeseeable consequences, the law isn't going to charge you with a crime no matter how guilty you feel about it personally."

"You can't be sure of that," Sonoma muttered.

"Have you been here all day?" I asked. "Do you have a plan?"

"I'm hoping to get in touch with Manaia. She has friends who can hide us."

I nodded toward the ceiling. "What about your friends upstairs? Didn't you say they owned the place?"

"They think we left this morning. They didn't come in today, and I don't know the people who work for them."

"You can't hide here forever, and the longer you try the worse it looks for you."

Sonoma continued to shake her head, but I could see that my words were having an effect on her.

"I'll tell you what," I continued. "I'll get my lawyer to help you out. Turn yourself in, and I'll make sure he takes care of you. He's the best mouthpiece I know. Hell, he's managed to keep *my* ass out of the joint. Just do what he tells you and you'll be fine."

Sonoma looked up at me. "I've been foolish, haven't I? I should never have run off with Jalen like that. I panicked. They're not going to like it that I've been hiding, are they."

"Lubank, that's my attorney, he'll take care of that. Do what he tells you to do and say what he wants you to say, if anything."

"Is he expensive?"

"Don't worry about that. If he tries to chisel you, he and I will have words."

Sonoma closed her eyes and let out a long breath. "All right. I'll do it. You'll call him?"

"First thing. You have your phone?"

"Yes, but we've switched them off so the cops can't track us."

"All right. Stay here and I'll send him by in the morning." I glanced over at Randolph, who had watched the exchange in silence. "In the meantime, Joy Boy and I will get out of your hair."

Randolph grimaced. "Terrific. Where do we go now? You can't just leave me by myself in the park."

"Why the hell not? I don't owe you anything."

Sonoma looked Randolph up and down, studying him with a frown. "You're on the run?"

Randolph shrugged. "Just a little misunderstanding."

"He started a riot downtown," I said.

"That's not true," Randolph objected. "I was holding a peaceful rally, and the bulls came out of nowhere and started busting heads."

Jalen pointed his knife at Randolph. "He's that crazy asshole... sorry... *revolutionary* who's been speaking out against the war in the Borderland."

Sonoma's eyes narrowed. "You think it's wrong what the Dragon Lords are doing down there?"

"You bet I do. What right do the Dragon Lords have to send innocent men and women—"

"Don't get him started," I interrupted. "Once you wind him up, he doesn't stop."

Sonoma's lips extended into a slight grin. "I've heard about you. I grew up near the Borderland and saw firsthand what the fighting has been doing to the people there. Did you serve there?"

"Yes, ma'am. I did." He nodded toward his empty sleeve. "I left a piece of me behind."

Sonoma nodded. "It sounds like you've got something to say about that, and I wouldn't mind hearing about it. There's not much room in here, but if you promise to behave, I'll let you curl up in a corner until morning. But you'll have to stay until then. I don't want anyone else coming to our door tonight. And you have to switch off your phone. No one knows we're here, and I want to keep it that way until Jalen and I are ready to leave, and that won't be until morning. Agreed?"

Randolph took out his phone and switched it off. "No problem. There are worse places I could be."

Sonoma nodded. "All right. I've got to warn you, though, we don't have anything to eat. In fact, neither of us has eaten all day. We haven't been able to go out, and we didn't want to risk having anyone come by." She turned to me. "Maybe your lawyer can bring something by when he comes to get us."

"I'll mention it." I gave Sonoma a hard look. "But are you sure about this? All I know about this punk is that he'll talk your ear off, and the cops are looking for him, hard. Harder than they're looking for you."

"All the more reason to keep him off the streets until morning," Sonoma said. "I don't want anyone to catch him leaving this place."

I scratched at my chin. "What about me? I don't plan on staying."

"Then don't get seen leaving."

I wasn't happy about dumping Randolph on Sonoma, but I'd taken care of my obligation to Stormclaw to get his boy out of harm's way, and, as for Sonoma, I'd make good on my promise to call Lubank first thing. All I had to do was to get to my car without a cop seeing me leave the basement studio.

I looked around the room, considering the situation. "All right," I said, finally. "I'll leave you to it. I'll go as soon as I know the coast is clear."

I opened my awareness to whatever lay beyond the door. I sensed no disturbances, nor any signs of magic. The traffic was relatively light in this part of town, a district locals and tourists tended to avoid at night unless they were looking for something illegal. At an opportune time, I cracked the door a notch and peered out, searching for watchful eyes. Finding none, I slipped through the door and made my way to Stormclaw's shiny black sedan without incident. All-in-all, I was feeling good about things. I felt like everything was in hand, at least until morning.

***

Back in my apartment, I climbed out of my clothes and into a robe. I entertained the idea of sleep and dismissed it. I wasn't keen on giving Ixquic another shot at me in my dreams just yet, not until I had a better idea how to protect myself from the bloodthirsty *wayob*.

With nothing better to do until morning, I went into the kitchen and poured myself a drink. Lubank wouldn't be up and around on a Sunday morning until dawn, and that meant I had a few hours to kill. I decided to spend it sitting on my couch with a drink in my hand and empty thoughts running through my head.

Despite my best efforts, I must have nodded off. Later, I would have a vague recollection of wandering through the Tanielu District, ducking away from cop cars cruising up and down the street. I walked past street people lying on the sidewalk or propped up against the walls of stores with barred windows and doors. A whistle pierced the night, rising in pitch and volume, then falling: the call of the lapa, sounding as if it were coming from my own lips.

I woke with a start to utter silence. Had I dreamed the whistle? It seemed so. I rose from my sofa and stretched. I turned on the kitchen faucet and splashed my face with cold water. I dropped to the floor and knocked off fifty push-ups, turned over and followed up with fifty sit-ups. I went into the kitchen and made myself a cup of coffee. I sat back down on the sofa with a deck of cards and dealt out a hand of solitaire. Black jack on the red queen. Red seven on the black eight. No way was I going to sleep again that night. For whatever reason, Ixquic hadn't invaded my dream this time, and I didn't want to risk giving her a second chance.

Two hours later, despite my best efforts, I was drifting off when my phone rang. It was Detective Kalama.

"Are you at home?" she asked, her voice tight.

"Where else would I be at four o'clock in the morning?"

"Don't go anywhere. I'm on my way."

"What? What's going on, detective?"

"We found where Sonoma Deerling and her son were staying. They're in the wind."

Fuck. So much for having everything in hand. "All right, but what does that have to do with me?"

"You were seen driving away from an altercation downtown with a local agitator called Colton Randolph. He was wanted by the police for creating a disturbance."

"Okay.... I'm not saying I was and I'm not saying I wasn't, but—"

"Button it, Southerland. Randolph was found in a basement apartment in the Tanielu. Subsequently, we found out that Deerling and her son had been hiding out there."

"You've got Randolph?"

"Oh, we've got him all right. What's left of him."

"Wait. You mean...."

"He was murdered this morning. And his body was mutilated. The heart and liver are missing."

I groaned. "Lord's balls."

"We'll be there soon. I suggest you call Lubank. You're going to need him."

As soon as Kalama disconnected, I punched in Lubank's number. He was thrilled to hear from me.

"Alkwat's balls!" he screamed. "Th'fuck you want, Southerland?"

"I just got off the phone with Detective Kalama. She says she's stopping by for a visit and suggests I'm going to be needing you."

"Th'fuck you do this time?"

"Nothing. But a nice young punk was murdered this morning, and I was seen driving him to the murder site last night."

"Fuck. I gotta go to the can. Gimme the details while I'm doing my business."

I spent the next ten minutes giving Lubank an abbreviated account of the past two days. "So what do you think happened?" Lubank asked over the sound of a flushing toilet.

"Hard to say. Ixquic has a shapeshifter working for her who transforms into seven howler monkeys. He probably murdered his parents a while back. Maybe he killed Mrs. Novita and Randolph, too. I'm leaning in that direction, but I want to keep an open mind."

"Howler monkeys? Lord's flaming pecker!" Lubank sighed. "All right, I'm on my way. If the cops get there first, don't say nothing. Laurel warned you she was coming, so she's probably not going to arrest you unless you give her a reason to. But she also advised you to have your attorney present, which means if she's forced to arrest you, she wants someone to keep you from disappearing into the system. My guess is she's being pressured by the higher-ups to haul you in, but she talked them into letting her make the call. So sit tight and keep your lip buttoned until I get there."

Lubank disconnected. I dressed, microwaved a frozen roast beef sandwich for breakfast, and carried my coffeepot downstairs to my office. I assumed Detective Blu would be tagging along, and I made sure I had enough chairs to go around. I also peeked into the laundry room, but Chivo was still out. I hoped he'd stay clear until the detectives had come and gone. We needed to establish some sort of signal, I thought. Maybe tack a red ribbon on the back door when the cops were in the building.

Kalama and Blu arrived first, and I was ready for them. "Coffee's on," I told them. "Come on in and take a load off. Lubank's on his way."

After we were all seated, I poured the coffees and made sure Kalama had a bowl of sugar cubes handy. I also set a pitcher of cream next to Blu's cup. I couldn't have been a better host. "I could've come down to the station," I told Kalama.

"The coffee's better here," Kalama said. "Anyway, I just have a few questions. Nothing formal."

I looked back and forth between the two detectives. "Really? For a material witness? With his attorney present?"

Kalama blew over the top of her cup to cool the coffee before taking a tentative sip. "I didn't see the need to interrogate you in front of a camera with a tape machine running. Not yet at least."

For the next fifteen minutes, Kalama and I chatted about the nice weather and how well the city had recovered from the massive flooding three months earlier. Blu slurped from his cup, sniffed a few times, and said nothing. Nobody said anything about a mutilated body in a basement apartment.

I was refilling our cups when Lubank burst through the door without knocking and sized up the situation with a few quick glances. "You tell them anything? Hello, Laurel."

Kalama smiled at Lubank from her seat. "Good morning, Rob. Sorry to get you up so early on a Sunday."

"Always a pleasure to see you." Lubank nodded toward Blu. "And who's this?"

"Detective Blu, my new partner. Detective Blu, meet Rob Lubank, the most corrupt attorney in Yerba City."

Lubank narrowed his eyes at Blu, who remained seated. "Blu? Conner Blu? They took you out of vice?"

Blu slurped some coffee without answering. "You know Detective Blu?" I asked.

"Only by reputation," Lubank said, his eyes darting to the forty-five in the detective's hip holster. The gnome hopped onto a chair I'd prepared for him by padding it with an extra cushion. His feet dangled a foot off the floor, but he could meet everyone's eyes without being forced to look up.

I poured some coffee for Lubank, and he warmed his hands on the cup. "All right," he said. "We're all present and accounted for. Laurel? Shall we get this shindig started?"

Kalama held up a finger while she swallowed some coffee. When she was done, she asked, "What were you doing with Colton Randolph? Was he a friend of yours?"

"I never met him before last night."

"And you just decided to give him a ride?"

"I was doing a favor for a friend."

"A friend who works for the Hatfields?" When I didn't answer right away, the detective added, "One of our cops got the license number of the car you were driving."

I shrugged. "My friend hasn't always worked for the Hatfields."

"Where did you know him from before?"

I caught Kalama's eyes. "I don't remember. What'd he tell you?"

Kalama shot me a taut smile. "Other than giving our boys some advice concerning their private lives, he hasn't been as forthcoming as we'd like. We're still working on him."

I suppressed a grin. Good luck trying to force anything out of the old troll if he didn't feel like sharing.

Lubank had been listening to our exchange, but he'd had enough. "Unless you can put my client at the scene of the murder while the murder was taking place, he's got nothing more to say about it. Th'fuck! Is this what you got me out of bed for, detective?"

Kalama ignored him. "Did Randolph have a cellphone on him when you last saw him?"

I remembered the firebrand switching his phone off. "Yes. Why? Didn't you find one on him?"

"It was conspicuous by its absence."

That seemed interesting, though I didn't quite know why. I turned to Lubank, who shrugged.

Kalama set her coffee cup on the desk and met my eyes. "When's the last time you saw the Huay Chivo? Straight up, Southerland. No cleverness. We've got another mutilated corpse on our hands."

I looked at Lubank, who nodded. "I spoke with him yesterday afternoon."

Kalama's eyes widened. Blu's mouth twitched. Just a slight tic, but for the usually unflappable detective it represented a staggering display of astonishment.

"What do you mean you 'spoke with him'?" Kalama asked.

"The man inside the beast is waking up." I explained how Sonoma and the Children of Cizin had summoned the Huay Chivo, and what they had done to partially reverse the enchantment Lord Ketz had cursed him with.

Kalama took it all in. "And he can talk?"

"In his own way." Without going into the details of our conversation, I described how I'd been able to communicate with Chivo by using Siphon as a go-between.

"And where is he now?" Kalama asked.

"I don't know. He's not here, and I don't keep tabs on him."

Kalama frowned. "He's still a danger."

I shook my head. "Maybe. But he's not the only danger out there." I told her about Ixquic's assistant. "Check your cold-case files for Duffy Hunbatz. That's his name. Fourteen years ago, his parents were murdered in their beds and mutilated. Hunbatz disappeared, and the police never found him. Now he's back in town, if he ever left. And he's acting as a servant to a powerful spirit who's hungry for human lives."

Lubank slapped the top of my desk with the palm of his hand. "There you go, Laurel. I'll lay you five to one this shapeshifter is your man. Or monster."

Kalama pursed her lips and glanced at Blu, who was studying the top of my desk as if it held the secret to life. She turned back to me with a frown. "Why, though? Why would the Blood Moon spirit's assistant attack Clara Novita? And Randolph? What's the connection? Sonoma Deerling?"

I shrugged. "Sonoma Deerling and her son. Here's what I know, or at least what I think I know. Cizin is Sonoma's spirit guide. Relationships among spirits are more complicated than they sound, but in terms that make sense to us earthly folk, Cizin is Ixquic's father. The two spirits have been on the outs, and Sonoma is trying to facilitate some sort of reconciliation between them. To further her efforts, she somehow convinced Ixquic to accept Jalen as one of her chosen. Sonoma communicates with Cizin, Jalen communicates with Ixquic, and Sonoma and Jalen communicate with each other. That's the plan, anyway. As I understand it."

Kalama frowned. "It sounds to me like Deerling has bitten off more than she can chew. First her wife gets brutally murdered, and then Randolph, who can't have been anything except an innocent bystander. Both bodies are missing the heart and liver, which implies a serial killer. Maybe Deerling and her son are dead now, too. We don't know."

"Any evidence that the two of them were attacked?" I asked.

"We're still waiting on lab reports, but nothing obvious. They were either carried off or they escaped. You haven't heard from them?"

"Nope."

"Is Sonoma your client?"

"He doesn't have to answer that," Lubank said.

"This is a murder case, Rob."

I interrupted Lubank before he could argue further. "It's all right. Sonoma isn't my client, detective. I'd arranged for her to turn herself in this morning." I nodded at Lubank. "I was going to ask Lubank to accompany her. She feels guilty about the death of her wife."

Kalama's eyes widened. "Are you saying she did it?"

"No, not directly. She's afraid her wife's death has something to do with all this messing around she's been doing with spirits. But Mrs.

Deerling can't be held responsible for what Ixquic or her howler monkeys might have done. I think she could help you find out what really happened if you can find her."

Kalama's jaw hardened. "It doesn't look good that she snuck her son out of the station and went into hiding."

"She knows that. That's why she was going to turn herself in."

"But now she's running again, if she wasn't killed or carried off."

I shrugged. "She probably saw whoever attacked Randolph. She took her son and lammed out of there as fast as she could. She might be running for her life."

"Any idea where she might have gone?" Kalama studied my face like she was trying to guess whether I'd drawn to an inside straight.

I met her eyes. "Nope. But if I hear from her, I'll let you know."

Her eyes narrowed. "You aren't thinking of looking for her, are you?"

I shrugged. "It's not my case."

Kalama bit at her lower lip and turned to her partner. "What do you think, Blu?"

Blu remained expressionless.

Kalama turned back to me. "Blu's got some concerns, but he appreciates your cooperation."

"How can you tell?"

A half smile appeared on Kalama's lips. "Well, for one thing, he hasn't shot you."

Detective Blu picked up his coffee cup and drained it with three big gulps.

Chapter Nineteen

Lubank stayed behind when the detectives left. "Alkwat's balls, Southerland. You look like you've been raised from the dead. If your eyes were any redder, I'd think you were a troll." He looked me up and down. "A really sick troll."

"I've been having some trouble with my sleep."

"What kind of trouble?"

"I haven't been getting any."

"Good man. Sleep is overrated. Look at me: I only sleep two or three hours a night. I spend the rest of my time working. That's the secret of my success."

"That and your blackmail files."

Lubank shrugged. "What's your point?" He took a pack of cigarettes out of his shirt pocket and tapped one out. "Listen to me. Kalama doesn't believe that bullshit about you not knowing where this Deerling broad is hiding. She's too smart for you. The only reason they aren't dragging you to a downtown sweatbox is she's hoping you'll lead her to the broad and her son."

I shrugged. "I don't know where she is. She might have been carried off by whoever killed Randolph. She might be dead."

"Or she might have killed Randolph and run off."

"What possible reason could she have for killing Randolph? She only just met him when I brought him over."

"Maybe he did something to piss her off. I've heard of that silver-tongued troublemaker. He's got a mouth on him, and he likes to use it. I've got a bad feeling about the broad." Lubank blew smoke out the side of his mouth.

I frowned at him. "You don't even know her."

"She's a chosen of one of the old lords of death. And she pushed her son into the grips of this Blood Moon spirit. I don't trust her. She's got a cause, and she's passionate about it. You can't trust anyone who's so passionate about a cause that they'll put that cause above their own loved ones. And that mouthy antiwar fanatic had a cause that he was passionate about, too. You shouldn't have left those two together in the same room, especially one that's too small to contain all that passion. It's like putting oil and gasoline in an oven. One might burn blue, and one might burn red, but they'll both burn."

Lubank had a point, and it was stabbing me right in the gut. Sonoma had struck me as levelheaded and composed. She didn't have the same fanatical gleam in her eye as Randolph. But under the guidance of a spirit of death she had traveled thousands of miles from the land of her birth to Yerba City in pursuit of the Huay Chivo. She had searched for him for years, and when she'd found him she'd acted immediately to form a blood bond so that she could summon him and free him from the Dragon Lord's enchantment. And all at the request of her spirit guide. What was in it for her beyond the fulfillment of a task that had been imposed upon her? In the meantime, she was acting as an arbiter to reconcile a centuries-old dispute between her spirit guide and another powerful spirit. For what reason beyond duty? Wasn't her devotion to Cizin every bit as fanatical as Randolph's opposition to the war in the Borderland? Maybe more, given how long she'd been at it and how far she'd had to go to do it.

Lubank interrupted my thoughts. "Hey, you make a pretty good case that the howler monkey might've done in the Novita dame, and maybe Randolph, too. I could sell that to a jury, no problem. A monster like that. But what makes you so sure this fuckin' Huay Chivo character of yours isn't the guilty monster here?"

I looked away from Lubank and picked up my coffee cup. The brew was cold, so I set it back down. I took in a breath and let it out. "I'm not as sure about it as I let on to the detectives."

"What do you mean?"

"Chivo has this trick he does where he opens locked doors like the locks don't mean anything to him. He turns the handle and walks in. And when he closes the door behind him, the locks are all locked and the bolts are all in place."

"No shit? That's a neat trick! Could come in real handy. Can he get into locked safes, too?"

I stared at him.

Lubank shrugged. "Just curious."

"Right. Anyway, when Jalen walked in on his mother the night she was killed, the door was locked, just like it always was. I made a point of asking him about it, and he has a clear memory of having to unlock the door. It takes three keys to do it."

"Okay, so what?"

"So whoever killed Mrs. Novita got into the apartment through a locked door and locked it behind him when he left."

Lubank lifted a hand to stop me. "Okay, I get it. But that doesn't mean it was your Huay Chivo. It could have been anyone with the keys. It could have been Deerling. Hell, it could have been the kid."

I shook my head. "And then he calls the police? I don't think so. And Kalama told me he was in shock when she got there. She doesn't think he was acting."

"Okay, but that still leaves Deerling."

"Maybe. But it doesn't leave out Chivo. It would make me feel better if the door was unlocked when Jalen got home. That would have meant that someone without the keys to the place had taken care of Mrs. Novita and run out. And that someone wouldn't have been Chivo, because he would have left the door locked behind him."

"Someone like a howler monkey?"

"Exactly."

"Don't you think the locked door eliminates the howler monkey as the murderer? How likely is it that he would have murdered the broad and then locked the door behind him on his way out?"

"Unless he got out some other way. Jalen was getting in and out of the apartment through the Blood Moon's portal. Maybe Hunbatz did the same thing."

Lubank let out a short laugh. "I'd love to represent the defendant in this one. We've got reasonable doubt up the wazoo! I could represent any of your suspects and get them off in a minute. The fuckin' case would never even get to trial. Any competent judge would laugh it out of their chambers."

Great, I thought. And the elf had told me that finding out who killed Novita was the key to saving my life. I was no closer to solving this murder than I'd been from the beginning. A wave of weariness swept over me, and I stifled a yawn.

Lubank reached up and slapped me in the chest. "You're a mess, Southerland. Get some rest. You need it."

Rest, I thought. Right. Tough to get when every time I close my eyes, a dream-traveling parasite pops in to suck some life out of me.

***

After Lubank had left, Chivo came in through the back door and made his way into the laundry room. I hustled in after him and found him climbing into his bed. Siphon had taken up its old position under the window to keep the air in the room circulating.

I stood in the doorway and crossed my arms. "You know the police are looking for you, don't you?"

Chivo shrugged and settled onto his cushion.

I let out a breath. "You hungry?"

Chivo shook his head.

I scanned the room. I needed to replace my washer and dryer, but what I missed more was the heavy bag. I missed the satisfaction I experienced when the packed sand gave beneath my knuckles as I launched punch after punch.

I let my eyes settle on Chivo. "Look, Chivo. Normally I would say it's none of my business what you do with yourself when you go out at night, but we're both wrapped up together in this thing with the Blood Moon. It's getting serious. She invaded my dreams again during the night and tried to convince me to turn you over to her. She reminded me that it's either you or me. Option one and option two. She got into my mind and fighting her off wasn't easy. I'm not looking forward to a rematch, but I don't know how much longer I can stay awake. I need to find a way to stand up to her. Or, better yet, I need a third option."

Chivo stared back at me, his eyes growing dull.

"And then there's Ixquic's shapeshifter. Hunbatz. He transforms into a pack of howler monkeys. His twin sister says he killed their parents. He might be the one who murdered Mrs. Novita, too. And maybe Randolph."

Chivo lowered his head onto his front legs and stared up at me through half-closed eyes.

"That's it?" I asked. "No advice for me? You're just going to sleep?"

Chivo turned his head toward Siphon, and the elemental's voice emerged from the funnel of wind. "You'll find a way."

Chivo's eyes closed shut. The spikes along his spine flattened, and his sides expanded and contracted, expanded and contracted.... A minute later, I blinked my eyes open, startled to find that I'd nodded off on my feet. I left the room, closing the door softly behind me. For the briefest of moments I thought about going upstairs and taking a nap. I quickly shook off the thought and went out the back door into the alley, locking the door behind me.

***

The washer, dryer, and chairs I'd left in the alley were gone, probably dragged away by neighborhood scavengers. I wasn't that surprised. The easiest way to get rid of unwanted household items in the neighborhoods of the Porter District was to leave them out on the curb, especially during the tough times. And for most of us in the Porter, the times were always tough.

I walked aimlessly down the alley toward the street, wondering where I was going. Not that the morning wasn't pleasant. It was unusually so. Later, the wind blowing off the Nihhonese Ocean would drag along a marine layer to cool the night, but for now the sun shone bright in a sky dotted with a handful of puffy cumulus clouds. I sensed sparkles of magical enchantment in the air, too, and I wondered at that. The flickering sparkles seemed harmless enough: the lingering aftereffect, perhaps, from some larger spell, like mist after a rainstorm. A deep breath cleared the fatigue from my head and brought a smile to my face. I was sharp and crisp, ready to face the world.

When I reached the end of the alley, I made a right turn for no good reason and continued without breaking stride. Traffic on the street was light, and I was the only pedestrian on the block. I walked past hundred-year-old wooden houses that had been subdivided into apartments, each with a barred bay window facing the street. The buildings came right up to the wide sidewalk and were packed side-by-side all the way down the block. I made a few turns at random, and the subdivided houses filled every block I came upon.

Somewhere in the back of my mind, it occurred to me that none of the apartment buildings were familiar.

As I walked, I passed by clusters of apartment residents gathered on the stairways leading to the front entrances to their buildings, lounging and enjoying the open air. I nodded or waved at them as I strolled by, and some of them nodded or waved back. But when I crossed an intersection to a new block with similar housing, the residents clustered on the stairs all turned to stare at me with hooded eyes and stony faces, as if I were an unwelcome intruder into their neighborhood. Their stares caused my skin to prickle, and the smile disappeared from my face. The hostility in those stares cut through the clear enchanted air and fell on me like an icy sludge. What about me was upsetting them, I asked myself. Was it the unsheathed machete I was carrying in my hand?

Wait. A machete? When had I picked up a machete? I hadn't been holding one when I left my apartment. I didn't even own one. I didn't remember finding one during my walk. I stopped in my tracks and squeezed the leather grip, marveling at how supple and natural it felt in my hand. I examined the eighteen-inch naked steel blade reflecting the light of the sun. Where had it come from?

Aware of the eyes on me, I turned and backtracked in the direction of my apartment. As I passed by the tightly packed houses, I saw more and more figures on the stairsteps. They all wore dark cloaks, and many of them peered at me from the depths of hoods. The sun disappeared from the sky, and I found myself stumbling along a dark and unfamiliar street. The alley should have been just ahead, but I must have made a wrong turn on the way back or missed the alley somehow. I stopped to look around me and realized I no longer knew where I was.

I resumed walking, picking up the pace, as if walking faster would bring me to more familiar surroundings. Traffic in the streets whizzed past me at ridiculous speeds. The dark figures on the stairsteps were all watching me with angry glares, and many of them had risen to their feet. I searched for street signs at the corners, but whenever I saw one the letters seemed to jump around or disappear in the darkness, making them impossible to read. I turned corners at random, hoping to stumble onto a street I knew.

I was in the midst of some kind of enchantment, I thought. Someone was imposing their will on me. I could get out of it if I fought back. As I walked, I tried to recall the entrance to the alley behind my building and the familiar structures leading up to it. I envisioned the white two-story subdivided house with the light blue trim at the entrance to the alley, right next to the fire hydrant. Reaching out with my elf-enhanced awareness, I tried to find it. Feeling a tug, I jogged in what I thought must be the right direction and tried to force the house, fire hydrant, and alley entrance to appear ahead of me.

The sharpness I'd felt at the beginning of my walk had long disappeared, and the fatigue had returned. A lethargy had fallen on me, and my jog slowed to a sluggish walk. Wanting nothing more than to curl up on the sidewalk and await whatever was coming, I forced myself to keep moving, to keep dragging myself, one slow step at a time, through the unnatural night.

At long last, I spotted the house next to the alley and made my way toward it. Just past the house, a shadowy figure loomed in the entrance to the alleyway. It grew as I approached it until it filled the alley entrance. Anger boiled inside me, and my hand squeezed the handle of the machete. I didn't know what it was that awaited me, but I was determined to get past it and reach the safety of my home. An oily black liquid poured from the dark shape in front of me, gleaming with malevolence. I stepped into the oozing slime and raised my machete, prepared to slice my way through the obstructing presence.

A gust of wind blew into my face and kept blowing. My eyes watered under the pressure, and I was forced back a step. Determined, I pushed myself forward, and something struck me in the forehead, knocking me to one knee. I smelled something foul, like rotting flesh. I roared at the dark figure in front of me and rose to my feet. A voice filled my head. "Nooooo, Aleksss. Wake up!"

I recognized the voice: Siphon! The wind from the elemental narrowed and focused on a spot between my eyes. "Wake up, Aleksss."

The darkness lifted. I raised a hand to block the wind pounding on my forehead. "Stop, Siphon. It's okay. I'm awake."

The elemental pulled away from me, and I found myself in my laundry room staring through the whirling Siphon at the sleeping figure of Chivo. A chef's knife from my kitchen was in my hand. I let it go, and it fell to the floor with a clatter. Chivo stretched, and his eyes opened into slits. They widened when he saw me. He sniffed the air, and his eyes turned red. Nausea filled my senses. I fell to my hands and knees, my limbs trembling. My stomach clenched, and a black goo poured out of my mouth and nose to the floor.

I turned away from Chivo and raised a hand, palm out. After coughing and retching until my airways were clear, I sputtered, "Stop it, Chivo! Lord's flaming balls! Stop already, you mangy sonuvabitch, or I'll kick your ass!" I retched again and spit more of the black goo to the floor, noting that there was less of it, and it was more gray than black.

"Shi-i-i-it," I rasped, my voice scraping at the gunk in my throat. "I need a drink."

Chapter Twenty

My sleep, if that's what it was, hadn't refreshed me. Weak and exhausted, I trudged upstairs to the kitchen to find a bottle of rye. All I found were some dead soldiers in my wastepaper basket, so I slogged back downstairs to my office to brew a fresh pot of coffee. I made an important decision: finding a new coffeemaker for the office so that I could return my kitchen coffeepot to its rightful place was going to be a top priority, but I had something else I needed to take care of right away.

Ixquic had tried to trick me into killing Chivo. Apparently, playing me for a sucker wasn't against the rules. I wished I had a better idea about the rules of this game we were playing. Who was making these rules, anyway?

Sonoma probably knew. I could ask her if I could find her. Lubank thought Kalama was waiting for me to try so that I could lead the cops to her. He was probably right, but I didn't care. Sonoma wasn't my client, and I didn't owe her anything. That thought reminded me that I *did* have a client. Cozumel Hunbatz wanted me to find her brother. Jalen was still my best lead for finding him, and Jalen was probably with his mother. Of course, Jalen and Sonoma might be dead, killed by whoever had left Randolph's mangled corpse behind in the basement hideaway. Or maybe they were being held captive. But if they had escaped the basement, I had a good idea where they might have gone.

I went upstairs to my bathroom and stared at myself in the mirror over the sink. I looked like shit. More specifically, I looked like a man who hadn't slept in a week. My eyes were bloodshot, my hair was greasy, and I needed a shave. I turned on the faucet and splashed my face with cold water. I splashed some more over the top of my head and ran a comb through my hair. I ignored the stubble on my jaws, chin, and neck. It hadn't started to itch yet, so I figured it could go another day. After drying off, I stepped into my bedroom and let my eyes linger on my unmade bed, my warm, comfortable doorway into slumberland. Having been thwarted, maybe Ixquic was done with me for the day. Maybe I could pick up a safe and dreamless forty winks. Right. And maybe I'd find a pile of shiny gold coins under the sheets. I grabbed my hat and made my way downstairs.

Forty-five minutes later, I pulled the beastmobile into an empty parking space across the street from the meeting hall of the Children of Cizin. The used bookstore on the ground floor was still closed, and I was wondering if it ever opened. I crossed the street and found a sign indicating that the bookstore's business hours were ten to two, Monday through Friday. Nice hours if you can get them. I peered through the window and extended my awareness. The bookstore was empty.

After a good look up and down the street, I climbed the stairs on the side of the building to the second floor. The door was locked, but I'd brought along my lock picks. Two minutes later, I was inside the loft.

The place still reeked of chickens, sweat, and blood, but no one was in the building. I crossed the room to the door on the back wall and tested the handle. It was unlocked, so I opened it and found myself peering into a small office with a desk, a landline phone, and a computer. Turning the computer on brought me to a four-space passcode prompt. I figured that would be the case, but I had to give it a shot. I tried 1111, 9999, 1234, 4321, and 9876 before giving up and turning off the computer. I rifled through the desk drawers and found what I was looking for: a printed directory with names, addresses, and phone numbers.

The name I was looking for wasn't listed. Sonoma had told me that she was hoping to contact Manaia, and I thought that's who'd she go to if she was on the run. The adaro wasn't an official member of the Children of Cizin, but I'd hoped that I could find her contact information in their office. After more futile searching, I knew I'd have to try something else.

I retrieved the membership directory. Looking it over, I settled on a name and used the office phone to make the call.

A familiar female voice answered. "Hello?"

"Is this Tayanna?"

"Who's asking?"

"It's Alex Southerland. Remember me from the ceremony the other night?"

"Mr. Southerland! Of course I remember. What can I do for you?"

"Well, first off, you can call me Alex."

"All right, Alex."

"I don't know if you've heard, but Sonoma and Jalen have gone missing. Any idea where they might be?"

"Missing? Seriously? No, this is the first I've heard about it. I haven't seen either of them since Friday night."

"I see. Would you tell me if you had?"

"Maybe. Maybe not. What happened?"

"I'm not entirely sure, but I'm hoping to find out."

Tayanna was silent for a moment as she processed what I was telling her. "I'm sorry, Alex, but I don't think I can help you. Let me know if you find out anything, though."

"Actually, I was hoping I could see you. I have a few questions I'd like to ask. You might be able to help me more than you think you can."

"You think so? Hmm. Well, I'd like to help if I can. I was just about to eat some lunch. Would you care to come over and join me? It's not much, just some chicken soup, but I've got plenty."

I hesitated. "Chicken soup?"

I heard a chuckle on the other end of the line. "What do you think we do with the chickens we sacrifice, Alex. Let them rot in a dumpster?"

"I... uh..."

"Oh, come now, Alex. It's really very good. I've added some potatoes, mushrooms, paprika, parsley, thyme, coriander, winter savory, and onion powder. Plus a little rue to ward off any lingering effects from the summoning ritual. I also grind my own coffee beans, imported from the central Antis Mountains in Qusco."

My mouth watered at the suggestion of fresh-ground coffee. "Okay, Tayanna. You talked me into it."

After confirming that the address listed in the directory was still current, I left the hall and locked the door behind me.

After I pulled the beastmobile from the curb, I spotted a nondescript sedan a block away do the same and follow me without closing the gap between us. "You coppers aren't even trying to be subtle," I muttered to myself.

Keeping an eye on my tail, I drove until I reached Bunker Park, where I parked in the first spot I found. We citizens of Yerba City are proud of Bunker Park. More than a thousand total acres, the urban park is the largest of its type in the realm of Tolanica. A mixture of grass, concrete, and asphalt, it features museums, restaurants, gardens with exotic flowers imported from all Seven Realms, and a maze of forested areas. It took me no more than twenty minutes to lose the cops on my tail and cut across the corner of the park to the suburban neighborhood in the Yelamu District where Tayanna lived. After another ten minutes of hoofing it, I was on her front porch ringing the doorbell.

A smiling Tayanna, wearing a long floral print dress and sandals, pulled the door open and invited me inside. The scent of soup and coffee spilling through the doorway made the invitation impossible to resist, even if I'd wanted to.

"Lunch is served," Tayanna said. "How do you take your coffee?"

"Black," I said. "I like it to taste like coffee."

Her smile broadened. "Have you had real Quscan coffee before? I'm not talking about the crap they harvest in Azteca and pass off as Quscan. I'm talking about the real deal. It's been boycotted by the Tolanican government, but you can still get it on the black market. They smuggle it past Ketz-Alkwat's trade officials on secret paths through the jungles in the Borderland."

Two bowls of soup were waiting on the kitchen table. Indicating a chair, Tayanna said, "I insist you try the soup." She held up a finger. "No soup, no coffee."

I stood by the chair. "I have to admit, it smells great."

"Sit. I'll be right back with the coffee."

When we were both seated, I wiped my mind free of the memory of headless chickens spilling their blood on the floor of the loft and lifted a spoonful of broth to my mouth. "This is delicious," I said after a swallow. "Thanks. It really hits the spot."

Tayanna's eyes lit up at the compliment. "Try the coffee. You might find it bitter. I can still sweeten it if you'd like. Don't be afraid to ask for cream or sugar."

The coffee was indeed bitter, which was exactly the way I liked it. It had a nuttier taste than the darker Ghanaian brew Walks in Cloud liked, and I found I liked the Quscan every bit as much. Of course, even bad coffee is better than none at all, but I could get used to a life of having to choose between Ghanaian and Quscan every morning.

"This is terrific," I told Tayanna, meaning it. "It must cost an arm and a leg."

"It's not cheap," Tayanna admitted, sipping her own. No cream or sugar for her, I noted.

"But it's worth it?"

She smiled, deepening the creases around her eyes. "You bet it is. It reminds me of home."

I raised my eyebrows at her. "You're from Qusco?"

She nodded. "A little village in the Antis. I haven't been there since I was a young woman."

"What made you leave?"

"I went on a spirit quest. Cizin chose me and instructed me to go north. So, I said goodbye to my family and friends, and here I am."

"Just like that?"

"Just like that. It's how we do things where I'm from." She scooped up a spoonful of soup and blew over it gently to cool it.

"How long have you been living in Yerba City?"

"Twenty? Twenty-five years? Something like that. Long enough to grow accustomed to it." She chuckled. "It took me ten years to get used to the damp air and the fog off the ocean. Not that we didn't have fog in the mountains, but Yerba City fog is its own animal. Dank and salty. But I grew to love it. The sea breezes, too. I'd never willingly go back to Qusco now, although I still think of it as home. And I can still get the coffee. Chocolate, too. If you're Quscan, the chocolate from Qusco never releases you from its grip. I get it from the same people who keep me supplied with coffee. And coca leaves, of course. For my tea. Coffee in the morning and midday, tea in the afternoons and evenings, and chocolate whenever I please. As long as I have coffee, coca leaves, and chocolate, I'll always have Qusco." She smiled and dug into her soup.

When I was halfway through my bowl, I asked, "How long have you known Sonoma?"

"I met her eight years ago. She had just arrived with little Jalen. Cizin brought us together. I'd learned to channel Maurice by then, and Cizin revealed that he had been preparing me to help Sonoma with her search for the Huay Chivo." She took a sip of coffee. "We didn't think it would take this long. But she put together the Children of Cizin, and we held our monthly meetings. Twice a year we'd sacrifice chickens to Cizin, just to remind us all that we were more than a social club. But truthfully most of us had stopped taking our mission seriously until Sonoma rang us all up on Thursday night with the big news."

"That she had found the Huay Chivo?"

"We couldn't believe it. We'd been prepared for the summoning ceremony for years, but I don't think many of us still believed we'd ever actually do it. Friday night was...." Tayanna shook her head, unable to come up with the right word.

"Unexpected?" I offered.

"That, too. But it was like the fulfillment of our entire lives! I guess we're not done yet, though. When the Huay Chivo ran out of our hall, it was a crushing experience for all of us." She met my eyes. "Have you been able to figure out what happened?"

I smiled. "You're asking me if I've seen him, right?"

"And...?"

"I have. The ritual changed him. Brought the human in him out from wherever it had been hiding. Or banished, I guess. But he's still got a lot of the beast in him, too. I can talk to him through an air elemental that he controls. Funny thing. Chivo's been staying at my place for a year, and I didn't know he could command air elementals."

"Air, water, and earth," Tayanna said. "Everything but fire. That's what the stories about Lord Cadmael say, at least."

"Really? I guess I've never gotten to know him all that well."

Tayanna leaned toward me. "What's he like?"

"Chivo? Just your average mangy goat-headed monster with ram's horns, spikes on his back, and a hairless tail. He can make you sick with his eyes, and he's not above ripping out your throat if he thinks you're a threat. I've seen him kill a troll and drag it away to eat it."

If I expected Tayanna to be taken aback by my less than reverent description, I was mistaken. Her eyes beamed. "He sounds like quite the beast. And he's been living with you for a year?"

"He's been staying with me. I've been feeding him in order to keep him from killing off the neighborhood pets. I don't know how effective I've been, but I haven't seen any lost kitten signs posted on my block. I don't know where he goes at night, though, so maybe he ranges into other neighborhoods to hunt." I picked up my coffee cup and took a sip.

Tayanna studied my face. "Do you know what happened the other night? Why he ran?"

"He was spooked by something. He said that he felt threatened, but he didn't know the source. I asked him if it had something to do with Jalen, but he said he'd hardly noticed him."

A frown settled on Tayanna's forehead. "Hmm. I wonder." She resumed eating her soup.

I wiped at my mouth with a napkin. "Can I ask you about something?"

She swallowed. "Sure. Fire away."

"When you were living in Qusco, did you ever hear about someone called the Whistler?"

Tayanna's eyes widened. "El Silbón! The Whistler! Of course! It was a popular story in our village. Our mothers would scare us all to death with that crazy story. I haven't heard it in years." She looked across the table at me. "I'm surprised you have."

"I don't know it in detail. The way I heard it, a young boy from a poor family killed his rotten drunkard of a father and tried to trick his mother into serving up his heart and liver for dinner. The mother was a witch, and when she figured out what the boy had done she cursed him to an eternity of wandering and hunting for food. He whistles when he's up to no good, but if the whistling sounds like it's near, it actually means the Whistler is far away."

Tayanna picked up the story. "And when it sounds like it's far away, El Silbón is upon you! Yes, and then Mama would turn her head and make a faint whistling call. We children would scream and run to our bed." She laughed. Looking at me, she asked, "Where did you hear it?"

I wanted to tell her about the disorienting whistling I'd heard, but, now that it came to it, I was embarrassed. The whole thing sounded like a child's bedtime story. I decided to press on. "Twice in the past few days I've heard a whistle. My senses aren't normal. They've been magically enhanced. When I heard the whistling, it sounded like it was right next to me. But I couldn't sense the source of the whistling anywhere near me. It threw me for a loop. I mean it really made my head spin."

Tayanna's face had turned serious. "What did the whistling sound like?"

I concentrated on my memory of the whistle, the way it rose and faded, and recreated it as best I could.

Tayanna didn't quite gasp, but she looked stricken. "That is the call of the lapa."

"The what?"

"The lapa. That's what we called it in Qusco. Further north it is known as the paca."

I'd seen pacas in the Borderland. "You mean those big spotted rats?"

"Yes. The men of our village hunt them for food. They attract them by imitating their cry." She pursed her lips and whistled, the sound I'd heard when I was shackled to the altar, and later when I was out walking.

"That's it," I said.

Tayanna leaned over the table. "You must tell me of the circumstances in which you heard those cries."

She was taking me seriously. I'd shared her soup and drunk her coffee. I owed her for the meal and her hospitality, and I felt like I could trust her. So I related in detail how Ixquic had attempted to sacrifice me to Itzamna, and how I'd been out for a walk while my office was being ransacked. I told her how Mrs. Novita had hired me to find out where her son was going at night and how he was getting there and back. I told her everything I knew about the murder of Mrs. Novita. I told her about Duffy Hunbatz. I told her how Ixquic had been invading my dreams, and how she'd given me a choice: Chivo's heart and liver or my life. I told her about Randolph and how he'd been murdered in Sonoma's basement hideaway. Finally, I told her that Sonoma and Jalen were missing, that the police were searching for them, and that the cops had followed me to the loft, where I'd found her phone number and address. "They followed me as far as Bunker Park," I said. "I lost them there before I came here, but the detective in charge of the investigation is sharp, and I'm sure you'll be hearing from some coppers soon."

She'd shrugged at that. "I don't know where Sonoma is. I just hope she's okay, and not just because she's our leader. She's a good person, and she's going through a lot right now. I didn't know Clara all that well, and I know that Sonoma kept a lot of our business from her. It hurt Sonoma to be secretive with her, but that's the way Cizin wanted it."

"How did Sonoma and Mrs. Novita—Clara—get along?"

"Sonoma loved Clara very much. It's odd. When you see the two of them together... Clara was such a tiny woman, and Sonoma's a big girl. But don't be fooled. Clara was the dominant partner in that relationship. She was a little general, and Sonoma is surprisingly delicate."

"How did Jalen feel about the two of them?"

Tayanna's face darkened at the question. "I don't know Jalen well. He's rather a brat, in my opinion. Sonoma spoils him, and the two of them are very close. Clara wasn't the type to coddle a child, but I never heard Jalen complain about her."

I decided to bring up something that had been bothering me for a while. "Mrs. Novita told me right out that she was a strong believer in discipline. But she said that neither she nor Sonoma believed in physical punishment. After the summoning ceremony, both you and I saw Sonoma slap Jalen in the mouth."

Tayanna grimaced. "Yes. I'd never seen her do that before. It's out of character. I think Jalen was more shocked by it than anybody." Some strands of gray hair had fallen over her forehead, and she reached to brush them out of her eyes. "Sonoma is going through a lot right now. How much do you know about her?"

I shrugged. "Not much. I know she's from a village in the Cutzyetelkeh Peninsula. She married young and had a son. Her husband ran off on the two of them, and Cizin sent her north to find the Huay Chivo. She met Clara Novita in Yerba City, and the two of them were married." I shrugged again.

Tayanna nodded. "Finding the Huay Chivo has been her life's mission since I've known her, and she's fanatical about it. Suddenly, she finds him in the office of a private detective. It was an overwhelming experience. She immediately calls us together. We haul our ceremonial robes out of the closets where we've been storing them and get ourselves ready for the summoning ceremony we've been rehearsing for years. And then...."

Tayanna shook her head. "And then, Clara is murdered. Her body is mutilated. Word travels fast in our group, and the word is that the police think the Huay Chivo did it."

Tayanna paused, and I asked, "What did Sonoma think?"

"It's hard to say. Sonoma has always been good at keeping her feelings hidden. I know that she loved Clara. She may not have shown it, but she was devastated by what happened to her. But she had a duty to Cizin. You don't know how hard it was for her to soldier through the ritual, knowing that she was summoning the creature who may have done that awful thing to her wife. And she was going to help him. Cure him of his curse. And then to lose the Huay Chivo at the end of it, well.... I don't know how she's managing."

I nodded. "And when Jalen started giving her some lip?"

"Right. I think she just snapped."

I didn't say anything. I reached for my coffee cup and finished off the last cold swallow. After a few moments Tayanna looked across the table at me. "You're a private investigator. What do your instincts tell you? Are Sonoma and Jalen still alive? Are they being held captive? Are they running?"

I held her eyes. "I wish I knew. But, if it helps, my gut tells me that they are on the run. I can't tell you why, except that the police didn't find their bodies at the scene, and I can't think of a good reason why anyone would be holding them."

Tayanna looked down, breaking eye contact. After a moment, she looked back up again and asked, "Do you think the Huay Chivo did it? Do you think he killed Clara and this other fellow?"

I shook my head. "I don't think so, but I wish I had something more to go on than a feeling."

Tayanna's grin was taut, but her eyes twinkled. "But your instincts say he didn't do it?"

I returned her grin. "That's right. My instincts. I've got a lot of instincts, but few facts."

Tayanna's grin broadened. "That's all right. I believe in instincts, and I think you have a lot of faith in yours. If you trust them, then I do, too. You think it was the shapeshifter? The howler monkeys?"

"Maybe. But there's another possibility we have to consider."

"What's that?"

"The Whistler. El Silbón. I need to hear more about him."

Tayanna nodded. "Yes. You're missing some important details of his story. As you said, he was cursed to wander the countryside, always hungry, always hunting, calling out with the cry of the lapa in order to attract his prey. He was cursed not by his mother, but by his mother's father, who was a powerful sorcerer. When the grandfather discovered what the boy had done, he tied the boy to a tree and lashed him, splitting open his back. He then stuffed the father's remains into the boy's wounds and set a pack of dogs on him, forcing him to run. The dogs caught him and tore him to pieces, killing him. But the boy's evil spirit escaped, still bearing the curse. It is said that the evil spirit is drawn to those who are hungry, and when he possesses them they will kill whoever they are with and eat them. But El Silbón is never satisfied. He is doomed to wander for eternity, always hungry, always hunting for hungry boys to possess. Especially boys with abusive fathers...." Her eyes widened. "Wait a minute. Are you suggesting...?"

I'd miscalculated earlier. The stubble on my neck was already starting to itch, and I reached up to scratch at it before answering Tayanna. "My gut tells me Chivo didn't kill Mrs. Novita or Randolph," I said. "I could be wrong, but I'm leaning away from him as the doer. It might have been Hunbatz, the shapeshifter. I've seen those howler monkeys up close, and they're capable. Plus, it's likely that he killed his parents. When they found out their son was a shapeshifter, they weren't happy about it. I'm told they tried to starve and beat the demon out of him."

Tayanna frowned. "Are you saying that you think Hunbatz is possessed by El Silbón?"

I paused, resisting the urge to scratch my neck again. "Maybe. I like the idea. And whether he is or isn't, I think it's more likely that Hunbatz is our killer than Chivo. But we have to consider the possibility that Jalen is the one who's been possessed by the Whistler. He grew up in poverty, and, according to Sonoma, his father was an abusive drunk. It's possible that Jalen killed his mother and Randolph and ripped out their hearts and livers while under the control of the Whistler. He might not even be aware that he did it. And if that's the case, Sonoma may be in great danger right now, if she isn't already dead."

Chapter Twenty-One

When I got back to the beastmobile, the cops were waiting for me. One of them held a cellphone out for me to take. "Detective Kalama wants to talk to you," he informed me.

I took the phone. "Detective?"

"Did you find Mrs. Deerling?" Kalama asked.

"Was I supposed to be looking for her?"

"No. You're a possible material witness, and you're supposed to be keeping your nose out of it. Did you find her or not?"

"No."

"Is she still alive?"

"Far as I know."

"You'd tell me if you knew where she was, right?"

"Of course, detective. No one's paying me to find Sonoma Deerling."

"That's right. What about Hunbatz? Anyone paying you to look for him?"

I hesitated. I was under no obligation to answer Kalama's question, but I didn't have a good reason not to, as long as I didn't reveal the identity of my client without her permission. And maybe the detective could save me some time and effort. "I'm looking for him," I admitted. "You happen to know where he is?"

"Not at the moment. But I can tell you two things. First, we don't have a warrant out for his arrest, but we're extremely interested in bringing him in for questioning in the murder of his parents. The case may be cold, but it's still open."

"All right. What's the second thing?"

"His last known address was the apartment where we found you strapped to the table in your altogether. He flew the coop after our raid, and we don't know where he landed. He may have left the city. The problem is, no one has time for this case at the moment. It's July, and you know what that means."

I did. "Summer heat makes for short tempers."

"Summer is murder season. Last night, some mug bashed his best friend over the head with a five-iron because he ate the last slice of pizza without offering it around first. I've got six fresh cases on my desk and new ones coming in every day. And it's the same for everyone else around here. Fourteen-year-old cases have to fight their way off the back burner. So what I'm saying is, if you happen to run into Hunbatz, I'd appreciate it if you let me know."

"Believe me, detective: if I find him, I'm going to need all the help I can get."

***

As I drove away from Bunker Park, I took some time to assess my priorities. My visit with Tayanna had been illuminating in some ways, but I was no closer to knowing the current whereabouts of Sonoma and her son. It wasn't my job to find them, but Jalen was a potential lead to Hunbatz, whom I'd been hired to find. Unfortunately, it didn't look like the kid was going to be available anytime soon. For the moment, I set Sonoma and Jalen aside.

I had a strong incentive to find Hunbatz, beyond the fact that his sister was paying me to do it. The shapeshifter was close to Ixquic, and he might know a way I could protect myself against her. He might even know her weaknesses, if she had any. Of course, I'd have to find a way to compel him to reveal them to me. According to Kalama, Hunbatz had been residing in the apartment where Ixquic was holding her cult meetings. Kalama's crew had been all through the place, and I knew that the chances of me finding anything useful there at this point were slim, but it was a place to start.

To be honest, I had another reason for wanting to return to that apartment. Badass had vanished there. I had no logical reason for believing the elemental might have left a piece of itself behind for me to find, or that I might be able to discover what had happened to it by going back to the last place I'd seen it, but I wasn't in the mood for logic at the moment.

It was late afternoon by the time I reached the apartment where the Blood Moon had tried to send my life force to the toothless old spirit who brings nothing but good, or so they say. The place was no longer a crime scene, and the front door of the apartment was no match for my lockpicks.

Hunbatz had moved out of the apartment in a hurry, and it wasn't unreasonable to expect he'd left something useful behind. One look at the place dashed those hopes. Either Hunbatz had lived a severely ascetic life, or the cops had picked the place clean. No one had left any convenient clues for me to run across: no scraps of cloth or distinctive buttons ripped from jackets or shirts, no engraved bracelets hidden under the radiator, no matchbox with an address scrawled on the inside of the front cover waiting for me to pry it out of the woodwork in the corner of the closet. No furniture had been left behind. The refrigerator, oven, and kitchen cabinets were not only empty, but scrubbed clean.

The last room I searched was the one in the back where the ceremony had taken place. Not only was the makeshift altar gone, but I was surprised to discover that all the glass from the window Badass had burst through had been swept from the floor. The police weren't that thorough, which meant Hunbatz had taken extra care with Ixquic's meeting room. I remembered Cozumel Hunbatz telling me about her brother's compulsion for cleanliness. Fat chance of me discovering any physical evidence there.

Maybe I could find something of another nature. I stepped to the spot where I'd been laid out to be sacrificed and listened to my surroundings. When I picked up a faint buzz of magic, I wasn't surprised. I wasn't a trained practitioner of magic, but my spiritual connection to Cougar had left me sensitive to the presence of magical energies. Ixquic was a powerful spirit, and she had conducted long and elaborate rituals in that room. She had opened an interspatial portal and walked through it, taking Hunbatz with her. It was inevitable that she would leave traces of herself behind that even a compulsive cleaner like Hunbatz couldn't remove. The question was whether I'd be able to do anything with those traces.

A witch like Madame Cuapa would have been able to read those traces like a book. She could have pulled on the strands and forced them to dance for her. I could only see how they distorted the light in that part of the room and feel the vibrations they produced in my back teeth and inner ear.

I felt for the vibrations and let them lead me to where they were strongest. When my hand passed through a spot about head-high from the floor, I experienced a slight tingling, as if I had passed through a field of static electricity. After some experimentation, I located a disk-shaped distortion, about six inches in diameter, that proved to be the strongest source of the supernatural energy. The disk hovered parallel to the floor, and the visible wave of distortion it produced could only be seen from above or below. Poking my finger through the distortion only produced more tingling, slightly unpleasant, but not painful. Interesting, I thought, but not very helpful.

I gave the room a last once over, but short of noting the window that Badass had broken still needed to be replaced, I found nothing of interest. Disappointed, I turned to go. I thought I would visit the beauty parlor on the ground floor and see if they knew who owned the apartment above them. Maybe the shop and the apartment were owned by the same person, or maybe they paid rent to the same property management company. It didn't seem unlikely.

I was halfway to the door when a burst of energy filled the room. I spun on my heels to see the disk I'd been examining open wide. A dark, hairy creature wearing a baggy pair of high-waisted shorts fell through the disk to the floor and fixed me in his gaze, his jaws open wide. The creature stepped to one side, and an identical creature fell through, minus the shorts. Then another, and another. I soon found myself facing seven howler monkeys, who had maneuvered me away from the door and toward a corner of the room. Individually, they weren't that large—each was only about two feet tall, with another two feet of tail—but I was more than a little impressed by the size of their claws, and even more by the ivory fangs exposed behind their curled lips. With my only escape route cut off, they closed on me slowly and deliberately, taking care to stay out of range of my reach.

I was considering the wisdom of leaping over their heads and racing to the door, when the one wearing the shorts raised a tube he'd been holding to his lips and blew. Something sharp pierced the skin next to my throat, and I had just enough time to pull a thorn from my neck before a freeze descended over the top of my head. The walls and ceiling pulsated and swirled. I sat down hard and watched the lights dim.

I was conscious, but I couldn't move. Brown balls of fur melted together until a single figure stood in front of me, a burly apelike man in a pair of white shorts with a mane of hair surrounding his ugly mug.

The voice that emerged from the mug was surprisingly mild and childlike. "You shouldn't be here. She'll find out."

I tried to talk and found I could squeeze out some words with an effort. "Why... did you... kill... Novita?"

Hunbatz raised a finger to his lips and made a frantic shushing sound. "Shhh! Stop talking! She'll hear you!" He turned his head one way and then the other, as if Ixquic might drop into the room at any moment.

I drew in a noisy breath. "So what?... Let her come."

"Shh! Don't say that! I have to get you out of here."

The shapeshifter rushed forward and scooped me off the floor. I sagged like a sack of potatoes as he slung me over his shoulder and made a dash for the door. After a bumpy ride through doors, down a flight of stairs, and into the open air surrounded by the sounds of traffic, I was dumped unceremoniously to the asphalt against a wall. By then, either the effects of the drug I'd been hit with were beginning to wear off, or my enhanced awareness was working its healing magic on me, relaxing muscles, releasing adrenaline and white blood cells, and pumping blood to the right places. Though still too weak to move my legs, I could turn my head, and my vision was almost clear. I was in the alley behind the beauty parlor near the trash bin where Clearwater had dumped me three nights earlier. Hunbatz was standing above me, a worried look clouding his ugly mug.

"You can't be here," he hissed in a forced whisper, as if he feared being overheard. "You can't let her find you here. You have to leave."

"Why not? And why do you care?"

Hunbatz was frantic. "You can't be here!" His hiss was louder. "She'll find out!"

I lifted my head to meet his eyes. "Hunbatz! Slow down. What will she find out?"

Hunbatz leaned down to speak without being overheard. "She'll find out you were here." He glanced up meaningfully toward the second-floor apartment. "She'll know you came back. She'll be mad. You can't be here."

"Why not? I didn't find anything?"

His eyes widened. "It doesn't matter. She can't find you here! Go away! Don't come back." He picked me up and dragged me to the dumpster I'd fallen into when I'd stepped through the portal in Clearwater's office. He pulled a purple jewel—an amulet of some kind—from his pocket and muttered some words over it in a language I didn't know. When he was finished, the air in front of him began to shimmer and buzz with unnatural energy. Hunbatz pointed toward the distortion. "Go now!"

I tried to stand, but my legs weren't having it, and I collapsed back to the ground. Hunbatz frowned down at me. Grabbing me by the shoulders, he tossed me through the undulating air with more strength than I would have guessed he had in him.

The light dimmed, and the air around me grew closer and warmer, the odors of the alley replaced by the faint smell of cigar smoke and the fainter scent of alcohol. My ears popped, releasing pressure. I dropped in a heap to a carpeted floor.

"What are you doing here?"

I turned to identify the source of the voice and found myself staring at the portly form of Armine Clearwater, his eyes narrowed and his lips pinched in annoyance.

***

"Are you drunk? Get off my floor!"

I groaned. "I'm working on it. I think I was poisoned."

Clearwater snorted. "Why come to me? If you were poisoned, you should have gone to a doctor."

I tried and failed to rise to my knees. "None of this was my idea."

Clearwater sighed. "I can't speak to you while you're sprawled on my carpet. Crawl over to the sofa."

I looked up at him. "I don't suppose you'd like to give me a hand, would you."

"Certainly not." Clearwater shook his head. "Try to show a little dignity, my boy. It's a short crawl. You're practically within reach of the sofa already. Once you're there, I'm sure you'll have no trouble lifting yourself into it." He adjusted his monocle and began reading over some papers on his desk.

It took me the better part of five minutes to push myself across the floor to the sofa and pull myself to an upright sitting position on the cushioned seat. I had questions, but before trying to ask them I took some time to slow my breathing until my heart stopped pounding.

When I was ready, I cleared my throat and asked, "Why did Hunbatz send me here?"

Clearwater looked up from his work. "Hmm? Hunbatz you say?" He frowned. "I suppose he wanted to keep Ixquic from finding you. I'm assuming you went back to the place where she's been meeting with her little cult of school children?" He shook his head. "What is that woman thinking." Looking at me, he added, "You can see why I refuse to help her with her plans. She's quite foolish."

"And Hunbatz?" I prompted.

"Hmm? What about him?"

"Why didn't he want Ixquic to find me?" It was getting easier to speak.

"Because I told him to protect you, of course. Are you entirely ignorant of your situation? You know she wishes to give the Huay Chivo's life energy to Itzamna, don't you? She can't take it from him herself, so she's been trying to manipulate you into doing it for her."

"I'm aware of that," I said.

"Well, then... there it is." Clearwater picked up a pen and went back to studying the papers on his desk.

"Clearwater, you've either overestimated my intelligence, or my brain is clogged from not having a decent night's sleep in... let me think... today is Sunday? So, four days?"

The portly little man let out an irritated breath and set his pen down on his desk. "What are you babbling about, Southerland? And why are you even here? Don't you know I've got a business to run?"

"Hunbatz pushed me through a portal. It wasn't my idea."

"Hunbatz sent you here? Nonsense. Why would he do that?"

"That's what I...." I stopped and shook my head. "Let me get this straight. Ixquic tried to get you to help her with her plans, but you've refused. Okay, I got that. But where does Hunbatz fit in?"

Clearwater regarded me through his monocle with the false patience of a schoolteacher who's heard one stupid question too many. "Hunbatz is with *me*, of course. I should think that would be obvious no matter how much gray matter you've lost because you've decided to forego sleep."

"I thought Hunbatz was Ixquic's assistant, or bodyguard, or something like that."

"Ye-e-s," drawled Clearwater, guiding me along. "And I've convinced him that Ixquic's ambitions are not in his best interests. He serves me now, unbeknownst to Ixquic. Do try to keep up."

"Why does Ixquic want Chivo?"

Ixquic sighed. "We've gone over this, Southerland. She wants to release his energy to Itzamna."

"Yes, I've got that. But... why? What does she expect to get from Itzamna in return?"

Clearwater shrugged. "His blessing, of course. That's worth quite a lot, you know. Lord Ketz-Alkwat and Lord Manqu brought almost all the rulers and spirits of southern Tolanica and northern Qusco under their control, but Itzamna remained out of their reach. He's the most potent spirit in the region, but he's a passive spirit, so the Dragon Lords ceased bothering with him. But, as you know, Ketz-Alkwat is attempting to reproduce himself." His lips stretched into a wry smile. "You very cleverly prevented me from giving him a key alchemical formula that would allow him to do so. Have no fear. I've forgiven you for that. Especially now that he's found a work-around."

I sat up. "What?"

The smile on Clearwater's face broadened. "You didn't know? An engineering firm up north came up with a substitute for the reifying agent that will do the trick just as well, provided Lord Ketz's people can hook their cellular regeneration device to a suitable source of power. If Ixquic's plan is successful, the Blood Moon will be able to channel Itzamna's immense power into the device, allowing it to function and give the Dragon Lord a little baby Ketz. Kind of sweet, when you think about it. Lord Ketz will be the first Dragon Lord on earth to reproduce."

Much of the fog from my head had cleared and my thoughts became more focused. "What will that mean, exactly?"

Clearwater leaned back into his chair and folded his hands over his lap. "Oh, my boy. Have you no understanding of dragons? They are extremely acquisitive and possessive creatures, as I'm sure you know. And they are extremely jealous creatures, too, which is a big reason why they can never form proper alliances with each other. If one of them acquires something unique, something shinier than anything possessed by any of the other Lords, the rest of them become positively enflamed with envy. Ever since it became known that Lord Ketz was attempting to reproduce, the other six Lords have been consumed with the desire to do the same, and to do it first."

I frowned. "Why haven't they?"

Clearwater shrugged. "Dragons aren't the most creative of thinkers. They are more concerned with preserving what they have than trying to dream up new things. I don't know how Ketz got the idea of producing a clone of himself—and, technically, that's what he's trying to do—but he was far along the path toward completion before the other Lords got wind of it. Then the others spent decades convincing each other that Ketz was mad, and that he couldn't possibly succeed."

Clearwater leaned back and gazed at something only he could see. Future possibilities, perhaps. "Now, at long last, Ketz-Alkwat is close to achieving his goal. If he succeeds, it will shake the other Dragon Lords out of centuries of complacency. If he plays it right, Lord Ketz could surpass Ao Qin in the dragon hierarchy. That would be quite a coup for the old boy." He turned back to me. "And all he needs at this point is for Ixquic to receive Itzamna's support, and access to his immense untapped power."

"And for that..." I began.

Clearwater finished my thought. "He needs the life energy of Lord Cadmael, the Huay Chivo."

"Are you telling me that this is all about Lord Ketz-Alkwat creating a shiny object that none of his brother Lords have?"

Clearwater shrugged. "That's the gist of it, yes. Having a clone at his side might also make him a lot more powerful in his own right, but the real point is to possess something in his hoard that the others don't have. And what could be a shinier new possession than a newborn version of yourself?" He leaned forward on his desk. "Trust me, my boy. If Lord Ketz succeeds, he'll drive the other Dragon Lords insane with jealousy. All six of them could even align against him."

A shiver went up my spine and exploded in my head. "Are you saying six Dragon Lords could invade Tolanica?"

Clearwater beamed. "Oh, I'm certain of it."

Chapter Twenty-Two

"You don't seem all that upset by the prospect of an invasion of Tolanica by the Dragon Lords."

Clearwater laughed. "On the contrary, the possibility fills me with terror! But, also, I must admit, a certain amount of excitement. Many opportunities become available during wartime if one is skilled at recognizing them and taking advantage. Still, an invasion of our land by an alliance of Dragon Lords is only one possibility among many."

"But still a possibility."

"Yes. Still a possibility. And not an unlikely one."

"Is that why you turned against Ixquic?"

Clearwater's smile flattened. "That's one reason. But, to put it bluntly, I've never liked the bitch. With her it's always been, 'Boo-hoo, my father doesn't pay any attention to me. Waa-waa, my father doesn't love me enough.' Talk about daddy issues."

"You're referring to Cizin, right?"

"Right. The Lord of Death. You know, it just may be possible that he's got more important responsibilities than pampering his demanding brat of a daughter. But she's miffed at him for ignoring her, so she summons Ketz-Alkwat and Manqu from Hell as an act of revenge. The Dragons emasculate her father and reduce him to a pale shadow of his former greatness. But then the two of them set up their realms, and now she's whining about how her ungrateful children aren't giving her the respect she thinks she's due. This attempt to help Lord Ketz produce his child is nothing but a pathetic attempt to make him love her the way her daddy never did." Clearwater scowled. "It's unseemly."

The effects of the poisoned thorn were wearing off quickly, and tiny jolts of electric current ran through my legs as the numbness receded. I stretched them to pump more blood down their length. Looking back at Clearwater, I said, "It wasn't that long ago that you were hell bent on securing Lord Ketz's favor."

Clearwater shrugged. "My attempt to get back into Ketz-Alkwat's good graces failed. I no longer see any benefit to be gained by aiding him."

I thought about the elf's schemes to overthrow the Dragon Lords. "Does that mean you would support opposition to his rule?"

Clearwater snorted. "Opposition? By whom? Yes, I know that certain forces are scheming against the Dragon Lords. I can read the currents in the winds as well as anyone." He shook his head before meeting my eyes. "Let me give you some valuable advice, my boy. Any attempt to move against a Dragon Lord by anyone other than another Dragon Lord—or, better yet, an alliance of Dragon Lords—is doomed to fail."

"I see," I said, considering the underlying meaning of Clearwater's assessment of events. "Let me see if I've got this straight. If Ixquic is successful in gathering the power she's looking for from Itzamna, she'll use it to help Lord Ketz clone himself. This is likely to drive the other Dragon Lords crazy with envy. So much so, that some or all of them might team up and invade Tolanica. If this invasion succeeds, it would get rid of Lord Ketz and create new opportunities for yourself."

Clearwater nodded. "Correct."

I rubbed at my neck, which was still swollen and inflamed where the thorn had pierced it. "I'm a little confused."

"Oh? How so?"

"You started out helping Ixquic, but you turned against her, because you were tired of her daddy issues, or something like that. But it doesn't make sense. I mean, I get that you don't like her, but why aren't you continuing to help her anyway? If she gets what she wants, don't you get what you want, too? It seems to me that you would welcome an invasion of Tolanica by the other Dragon Lords."

"Does it?" Clearwater removed his monocle, breathed on it, and then wiped it with the end of his tie before replacing it over his eye. Turning back to me, he said, "There would be, as I said before, a certain excitement inherent in that prospect. But, in the end, it would be too much. Too much damage to the land. Too much devastation. And, if Ixquic is the one to give Lord Ketz what he wants, too little reward for me. If I had succeeded in giving Ketz the reifying agent he needed to ensure his reproduction, that would have been one thing. But to be nothing more than a minor player in his power game while Ixquic gets all the credit?" He shook his head. "No, my boy. I don't see the profit in it. I will not oppose the Dragon Lord directly, but I will oppose any efforts by the Bitch Moon to grab the glory."

A broad smile spread across Clearwater's face, reaching all the way from his pudgy cheeks to his eyes. He leaped from his seat and stepped toward the bar across the room. "We have been far too long without a drink, my boy. I will remedy that situation immediately. I believe avalonian is your preferred spirit?" He winked at me to acknowledge his not-so-subtle pun.

He brought me a drink and extended his own glass. "A toast," he proclaimed. "To obstructed schemes and broken dreams, and a century of peace and prosperity."

I drank to that. I would have drunk to anything. The avalonian chased the last of the thorn's poison from my system and replaced its lingering queasiness with a warm, pleasant glow.

I drained my glass in three swallows, and Clearwater refilled it before I could stop him. I gazed at the amber-colored elixir with something akin to lust but hesitated before taking another drink. The danger now was that I wouldn't be able to stay awake. Sleeping meant dreaming, and dreaming opened me up to the Blood Moon.

I said as much to Clearwater, and he scoffed. "I have given you some fortification, and you are a more formidable character than you give yourself credit for. You've succeeded in avoiding her snares so far. Sleep without fear. You'll be fine."

That was easy for him to say. "All the same," I said aloud, "I think I'll keep my wits about me." With great reluctance and a last lingering look, I set my glass down on his desk.

I looked across the desk at Clearwater, spirit of the Night Owl, who had recently intended to kill me, and who had come close to succeeding. "Clearwater, I'm having a hard time with the idea that we might be on the same side in this thing. Are we?"

Clearwater sipped at his whiskey, an amused gleam in his eyes. "Side? My boy, you talk as if there were only two sides in the game. That's so human of you."

"So as long as our interests are aligned..."

Clearwater set his glass down. "Let me put it this way. As long as you are useful to me, I will use you to my advantage. If you oppose me, I will crush you. And if you are neither useful to me nor trying to interfere with my plans, I will pay you no mind at all. Does that clarify the matter for you?"

I nodded. "It does. Most satisfactorily."

Clearwater beamed up at me. "Excellent. You learn fast. And your next question is...?"

I didn't have to think about it twice. "How can I be useful to you at the moment?"

The portly spirit surprised me by leaping nimbly to the top of his desk. "That is the correct question, Mr. Southerland." He removed his monocle and peered at me beneath his bushy brows. "And here is your answer. Find out who killed Clara Novita. Do it before the rising of the full moon."

Before I could stop them, words slipped past the defenses of my sleep-deprived and alcohol-soaked brain. "The elf told me the same thing," I said.

I caught my breath and whipped my head around to catch Clearwater's eyes. "Did I just say that out loud?" I asked.

Clearwater's face lit up. "You did indeed, my boy. An elf, is it? Well, well, well. I suspected as much. I sense an elf's influence over you, and the gifts he has given you. I knew you had help taking Thunderbird from me. No mere human could have done that on his own, not even one chosen by Cougar, who is no match for me. The Dragon Lords insist that the elves were all destroyed, but I never took their claims seriously. Elves have never held as much influence in this part of the world as they have on the other side of the seas, but I've sensed more activity and involvement from them around here recently."

As I watched, openmouthed, Clearwater's head began to glow and shimmer. It melted and reshaped itself into the face of an owl. The owls' beak opened, and Clearwater's voice emerged. "Tell me what the elf has been planning."

I shook my head, but I felt myself falling into a dark hole. From a distance, it seemed, my mouth opened, and I could no longer prevent words from pouring forth. It was as if someone else were doing the speaking. I listened, horrified, as I told Night Owl everything I knew about the elf's plot to seize control of the earth they'd once ruled from the Dragon Lords who had taken that control from them six thousand years before.

When I was done speaking, Night Owl continued to stare into my eyes. After the silence had stretched for what felt like an eternity, Clearwater's frowning face replaced the bird's. "That's it?" he asked. "An elf has aligned himself with the Hatfield Syndicate to use their labs and personnel to alter stem cells from elf/human hybrids in some manner unknown to you as part of a long-range plan to topple the Dragon Lords from their perch? He's raising the newly born Thunderbird as part of this scheme? The nirumbee warrior chosen by that little shit Badger and an adaro prince are also serving him? He's gone to extraordinary lengths to keep *you* alive and out of serious trouble? And now he wants you to find out who killed Clara Novita, a woman who was married to one of the chosen of Cizin?" Clearwater removed his monocle and raised his eyebrows. "That's it? That's all you know?"

I was in control of my voice again. "I guess so."

Clearwater's face fell, and he reattached the monocle. "Hmmph! You've certainly been useful to him, but he's clearly kept you in the dark. He must not think that highly of you beyond your ability to perform small routine tasks here and there. It's a wonder you've committed yourself to his ridiculous cause. I should think you'd have more self-respect."

Clearwater snapped his fingers, and his face brightened. "I've got an idea. Why don't you betray the elf and serve me instead? It will certainly be a lot more fun, and maybe we can succeed where he's doomed to fail."

"Can't do that," I said.

Clearwater frowned. "Why not?"

"I owe him. He gave me some very useful magic, and he's saved my life a few times."

Clearwater's lips pursed. "I gave you protection against the Blood Moon. I saved your life."

"Maybe. But the elf has never tried to kill me. You have."

"And you're holding that against me?" He shook his head. "I thought you'd be a big enough man to let bygones be bygones."

I suppressed a chuckle. "Here's the bottom line. You're too flighty, Night Owl."

Clearwater scowled. "Is that supposed to be funny?"

"What? Oh, I see. Excuse the pun. It was inadvertent."

"Hmmm."

"What I mean is, you change sides too easily. First you're helping Lord Ketz, then you're not. Then you're serving the Blood Moon. Then, on a whim, you decide not to. At least I know where the elf stands."

Clearwater shook his head. "Don't you see? Your elf can't win! He's opposed to all seven of the Dragon Lords, and the only way to defeat one is to enlist the aid of the others. That's how I'd do it. And you could help me. We'll walk right up to Lord Ketz-Alkwat and spit in his eye. It will be fun!"

"And if it ceases to be fun, what then? You'd betray anyone following you to save your own ass."

Clearwater's glare was murderous, and I cursed myself for failing to govern my big mouth. I wasn't usually so reckless. Lack of sleep and too much booze, I reminded myself.

I took a deep breath and let it out. "Look, Clearwater. I'm just a private investigator working out of his home in a working-class neighborhood in the Porter. There's not much I can do about rivalries and conflicts between elves and Dragon Lords. I'm not walking into a Dragon Lord's lair, and if I ever get near Lord Ketz I'm certainly not going to spit in his eye. And I can't do much about family squabbles between big nature spirits, either. These things are above my pay grade. The most I can ever expect to do is keep my own house clean and tend to my own neighborhood. But I owe the elf a debt, and I pay my debts. If the elf thinks he can take down the Dragon Lords, that's jake with me. I had my doubts at first. You've seen one boss, you've seen them all. But once I witnessed firsthand what the Dragon Lords have been doing to the adaros, well, that's an injustice I can't ignore. If the elf has a plan that will eliminate the Dragon Lords someday, no matter when that day might come, then I'm happy to help in whatever way I'm able, no matter how small the task."

Clearwater lowered his eyes and shook his head. "You disappoint me, Southerland. You're capable of so much more than you give yourself credit for. You should aim higher. You should follow me. Grab hold of my coat tails and I'll take you to great heights."

A bitter laugh escaped through my lips. "Great heights? No thanks. My feet belong on the ground. You told me yourself that your biggest goal is your own pleasure. No one's going to take you seriously as the leader of a movement for the common good. You'd take me to great heights all right, but I wouldn't survive the fall when you send me crashing back down to earth. I'm grateful that you stepped in when the Blood Moon was feeding on me the first time she came to me in a dream, and I admit your enchantment kept her from finishing me off when she had me on the sacrificial altar. But in my book you were paying off the debt you owed for the times you tried to kill me."

Clearwater arched an eyebrow. "What about the dinner I bought for you and your date at The Gold Coast Club? That was not inexpensive."

I stared at him without saying anything.

He threw up his arms in surrender, "All right. I see your point. You don't feel I've done enough to balance the ledger."

I shrugged. "Fine. Tell you what. Let me keep the protective enchantment you gave me against Ixquic, and we'll call it even. As of now, we're square. But I won't serve you. I'm not going to abandon the elf."

Clearwater rubbed his chin, pondering my offer. "Okay, done. And if this elf severs his relationship with you for betraying him tonight, I will take you under my wing. But only if you come crawling and pleading. Deal?"

I felt myself relax. "Sure, why not? Especially since that will never happen."

Clearwater's smile didn't reach his eyes. "Never say never, my boy. Won't you finish your drink?"

"Maybe," I said. "But I have a question I'd like you to answer first."

Clearwater sighed. "This has been fun, Southerland, but I've got things to do before the club opens. Make it quick."

"Hunbatz. What exactly is he doing for you?"

"Hmm? Oh, him. He's keeping an eye on Ixquic for me. I've told him to do everything she asks of him without hesitation or questions, and then to report everything she's doing to me. He sent you away to keep Ixquic from finding you, but make no mistake, my boy: if Ixquic commands him to murder you in one of your dreams, he'll do it."

"And then he'll tell you about it later?"

Clearwater's eyebrow arched. "Precisely."

After that, Clearwater didn't have a lot to say to me.

I wound up finishing my drink. Clearwater was done trying to recruit me, and I'm not one to let a good avalonian go to waste. He called me a cab and had one of his men make sure I got in it.

Before I left his office, he gave me a parting word of advice.

"Remember, Mr. Southerland," he said without looking up from the document he was signing. "In the end, it's your dream. It belongs to you. You don't have to let anyone wrest it away from you."

Chapter Twenty-Three

That night I dragged a razor over my neck and cheeks, pleased that the inflammation in my neck had cleared, and took a long, hot shower. After drying off, I splashed aftershave on my face even though I wasn't going anywhere that evening, because the sting chases the itch away. It had been a long, long day, and I was desperate for sleep.

I told myself not to worry about dreams. The talon Clearwater had shoved in my forehead would protect me from the worst Ixquic could dish out at me, and the elf and Cougar were in my corner. I hoped. Besides, the Blood Moon was restrained by rules, although she'd proved she was willing to bend them or work around them at every opportunity.

As I fluffed my pillow and pulled the covers over my shoulders, I'd almost convinced myself I'd be fine. In any case, I had no choice. Sleep had a grip on me that wasn't going to let go, and I was either going to fall asleep in bed or on my feet. I pushed my head into my pillow and closed my eyes.

Howler monkeys screeched at me from the shadows of the trees. Above me, the scarlet moon lowered itself from the night sky. As it drew near, its red glow surrounded me until red was all I could see. The light faded, and Ixquic stood before me, clothed in a hooded white robe. She pushed the hood off her head, revealing her ivory beaklike face, pointed ears, and the tips of her pointed teeth.

Ixquic regarded me with eyes pale as ice, her crimson lips pursed. The lips parted, and the voice that emerged was soft as rose petals. "Why do you choose death over dreams?"

I didn't know what to say to that, so I kept my trap shut.

She listened to my silence for a few heartbeats before continuing. "My father, Cizin, is weak. That's how it should be. At the peak of his strength, he was sadistic and harsh. Not content to collect the dead and preside over them in Xibalba, he delighted in meting out cruel punishments. He tortured not only the dead, but the living, dispensing terror and dread. My sons, the Lords Ketz-Alkwat and Manqu, brought him to his knees and tamed him. They transformed him into a caring spirit who guides and tends the dead, rather than torturing them. Yet, in his heart, he has not changed. He has ever sought to regain his old strength, the strength that was torn from him."

She paused, and I took advantage of the opportunity to slip a word in. "Is this your new strategy? Instead of sucking up my life energy you're going to bore me to death with a sales pitch?"

Ixquic's eyes narrowed for a moment, but she continued as if I hadn't spoken. "Cizin gave much of his essence to his servant, Cadmael, so that he could become a great ruler. Cadmael launched vicious wars, which sent great numbers of dead to Cizin for his pleasure. The two found much strength in each other. But Lords Ketz-Alkwat and Manqu succeeded in severing the ties between Cadmael and Cizin, weakening and transforming both the bringer of death and the ruler of the dead. Cadmael was torn from Cizin's sight, but he chose servants from the children of Cadmael to seek him and reunite them. Now, a descendant of Cadmael, whom you call the Huay Chivo, has formed a bond of blood with the weakened bringer of death. She has summoned him and removed many of the protective enchantments laid upon him by my sons. Even now Cadmael and Cizin are drawn to each other, and they seek each other out."

Ixquic glared at me, and her voice hardened. "They must not reunite. If they do, Cizin will regain his old strength. The Lord of Death will once again become a lord of terror. Only by sacrificing the Huay Chivo to Itzamna can Cizin's mad scheme to regain his former strength be stopped."

Ixquic seemed to expand, to grow. She placed her hands on her hips and stared down at me with cold eyes. Her shout pounded on my temples like hammers. "So I ask you again: Why have you chosen death over dreams?"

I endured the shock of her voice and her icy glare. I looked up and spoke. "Chivo seems like an all right gee to me. I don't give a shit about Cizin, and I don't give a shit about you. You spirits got your own games going on, and all the best to you. As for Chivo, well, you say he's Cadmael and a 'bringer of death'—very dramatic, by the way—and I don't know about any of that. But the Chivo I know? He's okay."

Ixquic's jaw dropped, exposing more sharp teeth. She raised a staff I didn't realize she'd been holding and pointed it into the air. Seven howler monkeys, one clothed in baggy white shorts, leaped from the trees and ran at me from all sides. I had nowhere to run, and they fell upon me all at once, bearing me to the jungle floor with their combined weight. I rolled into a ball as teeth and claws slashed at my back, arms, and legs. I've heard it said that you don't feel pain in a dream, but this was more than a dream. I screamed as I felt my skin rip in a dozen places.

The weight lifted from my body. Through a bloody haze, I saw seven furry shapes melt into each other until Hunbatz stood over me staring down with something that looked like sorrow in his eyes. He reached inside his coat and brought out a blowgun. With a sigh, he reached into the pocket of his baggy shorts and pulled out a thorn.

Ixquic's voice cut through the night. "Not that one! The other one."

Hunbatz grimaced as he put the thorn back into his pocket and brought out a second, darker one. From the grim expression on Hunbatz's face, I knew this thorn would do more than leave me temporarily paralyzed. Working deliberately, Hunbatz placed the thorn into the blowgun and brought it slowly to his lips.

Clearwater's voice sounded in my head: "In the end, it's your dream."

The blood haze lifted from my eyes. "It's your dream," I thought to myself.

I covered my mouth with my hand and pursed my lips. I whistled, softly, a low tone that rose in pitch and volume before falling and fading. The call of the lapa. And because it was my dream, both Hunbatz and Ixquic heard it as a sound in the distance.

Hunbatz lurched just as he blew, and I felt the thorn whiz past my ear to the jungle floor. Ixquic shot a glance to one side, and then to the other. She spun to see if anyone was behind her.

My wounds were gone, and my head was clear. I took control of my dream and caused the grass to extend over me, hiding me from view. I let myself sink into the earth, and I fell into blackness.

I awoke in the safety of my bed with sunlight spilling on me through the open blinds on my window. I picked up my phone from the end table where I'd left it and checked the time. Hours had passed. If any dreams had descended on me during those hours, they'd said their goodbyes and departed without leaving any memories of their visit behind. I drew in a slow breath, feeling better than I had in days.

***

I took my time with my breakfast, and Chivo was already curled up in his bed when I made my way downstairs to check on him. I decided not to wake him. It would have been rude, and, anyway, I didn't have any pressing questions for him at the moment.

My plans for the morning included shopping for a new coffeemaker. Shopping for anything wasn't my idea of a good time, which is why I'd put it off as long as I had, but coffee was one of life's vital necessities, and I didn't want to keep running my portable kitchen coffeepot up and down the stairs. I grabbed my hat and was heading out the door when my phone buzzed. It was Cozumel Hunbatz, and she wanted to know if I'd made any progress finding her brother.

"I've got some strong leads," I told her. "I'm going to follow them up later today."

"Is he still in the city?" she asked.

"I believe so."

"Is he still involved with that... cult or whatever?"

"Miss Hunbatz, you need to give me a chance to work my investigation. These things take time. I don't work well on a short leash, but when I know anything important, you'll be the first person I'll call."

Miss Hunbatz fumed on the other end of the line. "Fine," she said at last, and disconnected the call without another word.

I looked at my phone and sighed. I could have told Miss Hunbatz that her brother had laid me out with a blowgun and thrown me through an interspatial portal, or that he had attacked me during a dream that was more than a dream, but not without spending the better part of the day filling her in on a lot of context I didn't feel like going over with her. Still, I thought, maybe it would be a good idea to uncover some information that might keep her satisfied with my progress before she canceled our contract. The coffeemaker, I decided, could wait.

I needed to find out for sure if Duffy Hunbatz was residing somewhere in the city. It wasn't a lock that he was. For all I knew, Ixquic was hauling the shifter in from the jungles of the Borderland. I didn't think so, though. Hunbatz hadn't smelled of the jungle when he'd attacked me in the Tanielu apartment, and the jungle in my dreams wasn't a place on this earth. Maybe Hunbatz wasn't living anywhere on this earth, either, but my gut instincts told me he was near at hand, probably with Ixquic. I didn't fully understand the powers that spirits like the Blood Moon and Night Owl possessed, but it seemed to me when they traveled through portals, they didn't travel very far. When Night Owl had kidnapped Thunderbird and brought him to Yerba City, he hadn't simply created a portal and carried him through. Instead, he had transported him by car. The Blood Moon might be a more powerful spirit than Night Owl, but probably not by much. I had a strong feeling that both Ixquic and Hunbatz could be found somewhere in Yerba City.

I decided to finish what I'd set out to do the day before: find out who owned the Tanielu apartment where Ixquic's cult had been meeting. Walks in Cloud hadn't called me about my computer, and I knew better than to press her. She'd let me know when she'd finished putting it back in working order. I had my phone, but I didn't like using it for extensive work on the internet. The screen was too small to read, and operating the electronic keyboard with my fat fingers for any length of time was about as appealing to me as sewing a button on my shirt. I mean, I've done it, but only when I had no other alternatives, and it cost me hours I could have spent doing something more exciting, like watching paint dry.

Which is why I picked up the beastmobile from Gio's lot and drove to the Tanielu District.

I found an available parking spot no more than a block and a half from the beauty parlor on the ground floor beneath the meeting place for Ixquic's cult. A dozen sets of curious eyes belonging to hostesses, beauticians, assistant beauticians, and women of various ages and species with heads of hair getting curled, combed, cut, dyed, and dried by blasts of hot wind followed me as I walked into the shop, hat in hand. A human woman who appeared to be half my age smiled at me from behind a counter.

"Are you here for someone?" she asked, an amused expression on her face.

"What makes you think I don't need my hair curled?"

Her smile broadened, deepening the dimples in her cheeks. "Do you have an appointment?"

"You don't do walk-ins?"

She gestured toward the business end of the room. "We're a little busy at the moment. On the other hand," she pretended to study my short-cropped hair, "you don't look like you'd need more than a minute or two. Are you thinking of a new style? Or maybe a dye? Dark orange tiger stripes would go good with your eyes."

"Actually, I was hoping for a word with your manager."

Mischievous crinkles formed on either side of her nose. "How about the owner?"

"That'll work."

"Speaking. How can I help you?"

I paused, studying her. "You own this place? I had you figured for the owner's daughter."

She pointed at a middle-aged woman holding a blow dryer at the back of another woman's head. "That's my mother. I bought the shop from her after I graduated from business school."

"I might have underestimated your age," I said.

Her face, already bright, practically glowed. "Many people do. I'm Mrs. Hirano. And you are...?"

"Alexander Southerland. I'm a..., wait. You're married?"

She extended a left hand to show me a gold wedding band. "Happily."

I took her hand and made a show of studying the ring. I let my face fall to show mock disappointment. Maybe not entirely mock.

She pulled her hand away and let out a laugh that sounded like little bells. "And so, Mr. Southerland, why do you wish to speak to the owner of this establishment?"

I focused my mind on the reason I'd come there. "Mrs. Hirano, I noticed that the apartment above you is vacant. Would you happen to know who owns it?"

She made a show of looking me up and down. "Hmm.... You don't have a wedding ring, or an impression from one, either, so you're probably not recently divorced.... You're too young to be looking for a place for a son or daughter.... Are you moving into the city?"

"I've lived here for about ten years."

Her face brightened. "Aha! Then you're looking for a secret hideaway to stash a young woman. You can't bring her to your place because the neighbors will gossip."

"Nothing as exciting as that, I'm afraid. I'm on the lam and need a place to hole up until the heat dies down."

She gave me a knowing look. "Oh, I see. Well, you've come to the right place. All of the spaces in this building are leased by the Peninsula Property Management Company, which is owned lock, stock, and barrel by—"

"The Hatfield Syndicate," I finished for her.

She pointed a finger at me as if it were a gun, and pulled the trigger. "Give that man a cigar. And since you're on the lam, they'll be the perfect landlords for you. Of course, they're likely to want a piece of your action. Did you rob a bank?"

"A bank? No. I'm a cat burglar. I steal jewels from rich old widows who live in oceanfront penthouses."

She narrowed her eyes. "Even better! It's going to be fun getting to know you. You sure you don't want me to dye your hair? By the time I'm done, no one will recognize you."

"Tiger stripes?"

"No, silly! A cat burglar can't stand out. Tiger stripes would be too obvious." She placed a firm hand on my chin and turned my head one way, and then the other, scrutinizing my face and hair. "We'll go with a nice gray to make you look like an old dockworker. Hang out in the Marina and no one will look at you twice."

"I'll think about it," I said. "Say, you don't happen to know who lived in that apartment before it became vacant, do you?"

Mrs. Hirano's open face turned guarded. She studied me for a few moments before giving her head a slight shake. "You're not a cat burglar at all, are you Mr. Southerland. I'm beginning to think you might be a policeman."

"Not quite," I said. Playtime was over, and it was time to be direct with the deceptively perceptive young shop owner. "I'm a private investigator. I'm looking into certain activities that have been taking place in that apartment."

This got me a new kind of stare as Mrs. Hirano re-evaluated my appearance. "Do you have a business card, Mr. Southerland?"

I handed her one, and she gave each side a quick scan. "Not much information here."

"Just the essentials. I've got a license, too, if you want to take a look at it."

She put the card under the counter. "That's okay, I believe you. I can't tell you much about what's been going on in that apartment. I know someone's been living there, but I've never seen him. It's empty most of the time, at least during the day when the shop is open. But I worked late one night a couple of weeks ago on the end-of-the-month books, and I heard noises from upstairs. Footsteps and scraping furniture. Some kind of gathering. Not a party, though. More like, I don't know, a meeting of some kind, but why they were holding it after midnight, I couldn't tell you. Anyway, it got quiet, and then this chanting broke out. I couldn't make out the words, but it was all kind of weird."

Mrs. Hirano turned to look me square in the face. "You're going to think it sounds stupid, but I could feel the air down here get all tense, like just before a storm." She leaned toward me and lowered her voice a notch. "I think they were witches. It's the only thing that makes sense." Leaning away from me again, she went on in a normal voice. "And the police were all over the place the other morning. You wouldn't happen to know what that was all about, would you? Mr. Private Investigator?"

I shook my head. "Afraid not. Your witches are probably gone now, though."

She pushed a strand of hair off her cheek. "I hope you're right. Having cops around tends to upset our customers."

I nodded toward the buzz of activity in the shop. "It doesn't seem to be keeping anyone away."

"True," she agreed. "One incident arouses curiosity. Too much of it would be bad for business."

"Uh-huh. Well, I think the worst is over. Thank you for the information." I started to put my hat on my head.

Mrs. Hirano put a hand on my wrist to stop me. "Not a problem. But if you ever do find yourself on the run, don't forget about me. I'll give you a new look that would get you past every police roadblock in the city!" The smile she gave me lit up the room.

Chapter Twenty-Four

When I was outside, I used my phone to find the number of the Peninsula Property Management Company. As I debated the wisdom of contacting the company directly, I decided, since I was in the neighborhood, that I would first swing past the basement apartment where I'd last seen Sonoma. It was only a handful of blocks away, so I took advantage of the sunlit summer day and hoofed it down the sidewalk.

The ragged figures camped alongside the crumbling structures of the Tanielu, humans mostly, but a few dwarfs and even a down-and-out gnome, watched me with vacant eyes, or ignored me entirely. Some had worn cardboard signs suggesting they'd accept any spare change I might have on me. One sign read, "I'm not going to lie, I need a fix." I appreciated his honesty but kept my dough in my pocket. You give to one, you've got to give to them all. The massive amount of people living on the street in the Tanielu was not a problem I could solve.

Eventually I reached Mandy's Closet and took the stairs down to the basement apartment. I picked the lock and pulled the door closed behind me after stepping under the crime tape crisscrossing the doorway. The apartment was dark, but with my magically enhanced senses on full alert I didn't need light to "see" the smeared blood drying over most of the cement floor. When I alerted myself to the presence of magic, a faint buzz tingled my back teeth and inner ear, the lingering trace, perhaps, of something unnatural. Or maybe just a strand of stray magic floating in from the street, or down from the used clothing store.

I looked toward the ceiling and noted the trapdoor I'd seen the first time I'd been there. The ceiling was low enough for me to just reach the clasp. It wasn't locked, and when I swung the door open a set of wooden stairs unfolded until it reached the floor.

I faced the stairs and studied the steps carefully. I even used the flashlight on my phone to light up the steps so that I could see them in the normal way. Dried blood from the soles of a single pair of bare feet trailed up the steps to the room above. I pocketed my phone and followed the bloody footprints up the stairs.

I emerged inside a small office. Used clothes were piled up in a corner, and papers were strewn across a desk. No one was present. The office door was closed, but the walls were thin enough for me to hear customers shuffling through the aisles. I examined the hardwood floor of the office. Someone had made a halfhearted attempt to clean up, but I could detect enough traces of blood to conclude that whoever had climbed through the trapdoor had crossed the office and walked into the store.

When I'd last seen Jalen, he'd been barefoot and wearing pajamas. After walking into a store filled with used clothing, he'd be fully clothed now. What bothered me was that only one set of footprints led out of the basement and into the office. What had happened to Sonoma, and where had she gone? And more to the point, why hadn't she left the basement apartment with her son?

Kalama wouldn't have missed the bloody footprints on the stairs, nor what the single set of prints implied. She hadn't shared that knowledge with me in my office, though. I had to tip my cap to her. She'd only told me enough about her investigation to get me to reveal what I knew. Hell, she was probably hoping she'd aroused my curiosity to the point where I'd come back to the scene of the crime to give it the once over. For all I knew, she had people watching the place to see if I'd show up.

I climbed back down to the basement and closed the trapdoor. Turning the flashlight on my phone to the basement floor, I quickly realized the futility of trying to find footprints in the dried blood. Not after the cops had come and gone. Maybe Kalama's forensics team had found something useful when they'd first arrived, but after taking their pictures and gathering their evidence they'd walked in and out of the doorway and left their own prints throughout the room.

I made one last sweep of the place and stepped outside. I found no blood on the steps leading out of the basement apartment or on the sidewalk. Someone, presumably the owner of Mandy's Closet, had done a thorough job of cleaning. That made sense. Even in the Tanielu, visible blood was bad for business.

I scanned the street before leaving but saw nothing of interest. If any cops were looking for me, none of them stopped me as I started back toward the beastmobile.

I'd walked three blocks and ceased to notice the street people sitting against the buildings and staring at the ground with dull eyes, or curled up on flattened cardboard boxes and covered by thin blankets. I was mulling over scenarios in which a barefoot Jalen climbed through a trapdoor into Mandy's Closet while Sonoma walked—or was carried—through the front door, when a familiar voice disturbed my speculations.

"You just going to walk on by, champ?"

I stopped and turned. "If you're going to pass for destitute, you need to lose those expensive shades."

Stormclaw climbed to his feet. "I ain't passing for nothin'. I'm just resting my weary bones for a spell. I'm not as young as I used to be, you know."

"Let me guess," I said. "The Hatfields sprung you?"

"Those Hatfields has got some good lawyers on the payroll."

I grunted. "I don't doubt it. I'm assuming they retrieved the car?"

Stormclaw pointed down the street with his chin. "Got it parked around the corner. I was just waiting for you to finish looking that apartment over. Find anything interesting?"

"Nothing the cops don't already know."

"Too bad. They don't know much." He dusted off his pants and turned. "Let's go."

I didn't move. "Go where?"

"Benning is waiting for you. I'll drive."

I still didn't move. "Why would I want to talk to Benning?"

"He wants to talk to you, son. He told me to carry you in if I had to. But I'm not going to have to, am I?" He stared down at me from a step away, and I had to tilt my head back to look him in the face.

I sighed. "No, that won't be necessary. Where did you say you were parked?"

***

Inside the Hatfields's black sedan, I turned to the motorman. "The last time I saw you, you were charging into a squad of our city's finest."

Stormclaw kept his eyes on the traffic ahead of him. "Did a little damage to them, too, while you were getting our boy away."

"You owe me for that."

Stormclaw didn't blink. "Do I? He didn't stay alive for too long after."

"I did what you wanted. I got him away from the cops."

"Would have been nice if you'd'a stayed with the boy until someone came to retrieve him."

"Is that what Benning wants to talk to me about? Well, screw him. I'm not on his payroll."

Stormclaw smiled. "Nah. He's got no beef with you. He just wants to know some things."

"Like what?"

"That's his business. I just drive the car."

"And pick up his packages," I said.

Stormclaw gave me the briefest of sidelong glances. "That's right, Mr. Package."

Anton Benning, attorney for the Hatfield family and the mayor's fixer, worked out of his disarmingly modest one-story stucco house in a nearly hidden cul-de-sac near Midtown. In every way that was important, the Benning home was located in a different universe than the one occupied by the bloodstained hideaway beneath the secondhand clothing store. Geographically, however, it was less than a mile from the heart of the Tanielu District, and even on a busy weekday we'd reach it in less than fifteen minutes, especially with Stormclaw behind the wheel. The old motorman maneuvered through the thick traffic as if he were using sorcery to create openings. I knew that Stormclaw was no wizard, but more than a hundred years of driving experience provided him with all the magic he needed.

I didn't figure he'd be distracted by questions, so I decided to ask a few. "How long did you have to wait for me?"

Stormclaw switched lanes with a flick of his wrist. "Not long."

"How did you know where I was?"

"Got a call from Benning."

"He told you I was at the apartment?"

"He said you were headed there."

"How did *he* know?"

Stormclaw shrugged. "I didn't ask."

I mulled that over. Had Mrs. Hirano called Peninsula Property Management and told them I'd been nosing around? Maybe she'd watched me walk in the direction of the basement apartment and passed that information along. But wouldn't they assume I was simply heading for my car?

My questioning didn't seem to be bothering Stormclaw any, but I waited for him to breeze through the front end of a red light before resuming. "Randolph's phone was missing when the cops found him. Any idea who might have taken it?"

Stormclaw shot me a sidelong glance. "How would I know something like that?"

"Benning didn't mention it?"

"We ain't pals. He gives me my instructions, and I follow them."

"Last time I saw Benning, he had another troll driving for him."

The hint of a smile appeared on Stormclaw's face. "Bronzetooth."

"What happened to him?"

"He got promoted. He's Benning's personal bodyguard now."

"Are the two of you pals?"

"Nope."

Stormclaw turned off the main road we'd been on for the past ten minutes and pulled into a wide alleyway. I looked at him with a question in my eyes.

"Shortcut," he explained.

I nodded. "How long did the cops question you?"

"A few hours."

"They get tough?"

He grinned. "They tried."

"Did you tell them who killed Randolph?"

Stormclaw grunted. "Wouldn't have even if I knew. Which I don't."

"No ideas at all? You've been with him at his performances."

"Might have been someone who didn't like what he was saying."

"Like the LIA?" I suggested.

Stormclaw steered the car through a drugstore parking lot that was only half filled and turned onto a quiet two-lane street. "Or a war veteran who felt like he was being dishonored. Or maybe the husband of some broad he'd been screwing."

"Are there many of those around?"

"A few. Our boy could attract the ladies."

I wondered how many cuckolded husbands would take the time to claw the heart and liver out of their victims. A few, perhaps, but not many.

Stormclaw pulled up to a gated driveway. "We're here," he announced. He punched some buttons on a security call box and, when the gate opened, eased the car along a brick driveway to the home of Anton Benning.

I turned to Stormclaw. "You don't suppose Benning will be serving lunch, do you? I haven't eaten since breakfast, and that was too many hours ago."

Stormclaw didn't bother to answer. After stopping the car near the house, he walked me to the front door, which opened before we got there. A troll in an elegant three-piece gray suit and stocking feet stood in the entryway.

I put on my most neighborly smile. "Hello, Bronzetooth. Long time no see." I raised my arms to my side.

The troll did not smile. Instead, he patted me down without a word and took my cell phone. "You'll get this back when you leave. Please remove your shoes and wait here until I come back for you." He turned to Stormclaw. "He wants to see you first."

I didn't have to wait long. Five minutes after I'd added my shoes to the collection near the front door, Bronzetooth returned and led me down a carpeted hallway to Benning's office and followed me inside.

Anton Benning, wearing a dark suit with a diamond stickpin in his tie and a white carnation in his lapel, was seated behind a polished mahogany desk that could have consumed the desk in my own office as an appetizer. Stormclaw, still wearing his shades, sat comfortably in an easy chair on one side of the desk, his shoeless feet crossed. Both men had half-empty whiskey glasses in hand. Benning set his down and stood as I entered, a thin smile beneath his bushy salt-and-pepper mustache.

"Mr. Southerland. How nice to see you again." He gestured toward a padded chair in front of the desk. "Please. Can I get you a drink?"

"Depends," I said, easing myself into the chair. "How long am I staying?"

"Long enough for a glass of shawnee. Bronzetooth?"

The troll poured me a glass at the portable bar and set it on a coaster within my reach on the corner of the desk. Having done his duty, he took up a position standing at his boss's side. I picked up the glass and took a taste, letting the cool liquid soak into my tongue before sending it pouring down the back of my throat to my empty stomach. I closed my eyes and grimaced as the air left my lungs and a flame shot from my midsection to the back of my neck, detonating a keg of gunpowder inside my skull.

When my breath returned, I took another drink to put out the inferno, but, of course, it just lit another fuse. Oh, that's right, I remembered. You can't put out a fire by dousing it with gasoline. Silly me. I took a third sip to confirm the truth of that maxim, and it held up.

Benning nodded at me, pleased to see his guest enjoying his hospitality. "Let me explain why I sent for you, Mr. Southerland." He sat up straight in his chair and rested his folded hands on his desktop. "First, I want to thank you for extricating Mr. Randolph from the hands of the police. They were a bit overzealous and exceeded their instructions. I believe the leader of the police patrol may have been drunk. Rest assured, there will be repercussions."

Benning paused to catch my eyes. "Second, I'd like for you to explain to me what went wrong once you reached the Tanielu District. I'd hate to think that, for obscure reasons of your own, you deliberately acted to bring about Randolph's untimely, and, apparently, brutal demise."

I met the fixer's stare. "Of course not. I had no reason to want Randolph dead. I didn't even know him. I only drove him out of there as a favor to Stormclaw. When his own havens proved to be compromised, I improvised and took him to a location where I believed he would be safe. I'm as mystified by his death as you are."

Benning studied me closely for a few moments before speaking. "Tell me what happened. In detail."

Aware that I was in the stronghold of a high-ranking member of the Hatfield Syndicate with two trolls ready to respond to his orders, I allowed myself to be thoroughly debriefed. I explained all my movements from the time I escorted Randolph to Stormclaw's car until I returned to my apartment. Except for asking me to clarify a few points, Benning allowed me to explain the events in my own way.

"And that's it," I concluded. "When I left Randolph with Mrs. Deerling, I thought everything would be jake until morning."

Benning unfolded his hands and rubbed his chin, considering my story. "I see...."

I leaned forward in my seat. "If you don't mind, I have a couple of questions of my own. Did Randolph call you or any of your people after I left him?"

Benning refolded his hands. "Not as far as I know." He turned toward Stormclaw, who shook his head.

"The police didn't find his phone on his body," I said.

Benning didn't say anything to that, so I continued. "I can think of two explanations. First, whoever killed Randolph ran off with his phone. I can't think of any reason why he would have, but it's still a possibility. Second, one of your people came to the apartment after Randolph was dead and took his phone. I like this explanation. But you say he didn't call any of your people."

Benning lowered his eyes and let out a breath. "He didn't have to. Stormclaw wasn't the only person we had at the rally. When I heard what had happened, I passed down instructions for him to trace Randolph's phone and find out where he'd gone."

"I watched Randolph turn his phone off."

Benning's lips pressed into a flat smile. "It didn't matter. He had a tracer in his phone. It ran off its own battery."

I nodded. "I see."

Benning continued. "Our man found the apartment not long after you left, empty except for Randolph's body. Randolph had information on his phone we didn't want landing in the hands of the police, so our man took the phone with him when he left. He called his handler and explained the situation. His handler called me, and I instructed him to leave an anonymous tip with the police."

"You called the police?"

"Not me personally, but yes. Believe me, I'm as anxious to find out who killed Randolph as anyone. He was the front man for a potentially lucrative operation. An operation I designed myself." His thin face hardened. "I'm not pleased with the way it's turned out."

I reached for my glass but didn't lift it. "And there's no chance your own man killed Randolph?"

Benning's eyes met mine. "None. Bronzetooth questioned the man himself. We're convinced he reported the situation accurately."

"Was the door locked when your man got there?"

Benning turned to Bronzetooth, who shrugged and said, "Our man says it was, but it didn't give him any trouble. He has a talent for that sort of thing, but he says any amateur could have got past it with a nail file."

I nodded at Benning. "Any chance I can talk to your man?"

"I'm afraid he's unavailable." The fixer took a delicate sip from his glass.

"Right." I leaned back into my seat. "Do you have any further questions for me?"

Benning's lips stretched into a smile. "No. I believe I've learned everything from you that I need to." He picked up his own glass and held it in front of him. "Mr. Southerland, I once offered you a position with the family business, and you turned it down. I appreciate that you enjoy operating as an independent. But allow me to extend you this invitation. I have people looking into Randolph's unfortunate murder, but outside help is always welcome. If you happen upon pertinent information that could lead to the apprehension of the guilty party, I'm willing to write you a check for your services, no strings attached. You would be acting strictly as a freelance contractor. You will receive an additional bonus if you call us with this information before you give it to the police, but I'll leave that to your discretion." He extended the glass. "Do we have a deal?"

I lifted my glass but didn't extend it. "Can I ask you another question first?"

Benning pulled his glass back. "By all means."

"Have you been tailing me with an air elemental?"

Benning's eyebrows raised. "What? Of course not. Why would you ask such a question?"

"How did you know where I was this morning? I've fixed my phone so that it's practically untraceable, and I know you don't have a tracer in it. How did you know to send Stormclaw to that apartment?"

Benning put his glass down on his desk. "I have sources of information I can't share with you."

"Someone told you where I was?"

Benning's words were clipped. "I was informed."

"But you aren't going to tell me who informed you."

Benning's head tilted a degree or two to one side. "Why would I do that?"

"Of course. I was just wondering." I rose from my chair. "I think we're done here, Mr. Benning."

Benning also rose. "I believe we are. Stormclaw will take you to your car. But before you leave, Mr. Southerland...." Benning picked up his glass. "My offer to you still stands."

"I'll think about it," I said.

"Do that. Oh, one more thing. You made some inquiries this morning regarding a tenant in a unit managed by Peninsula Property Management. I have that information for you."

I stopped in my tracks. "Is that so?"

"Indeed. The apartment you were asking about was occupied by a Mr. Duffy Hunbatz. Unfortunately, the managers were compelled to evict him. Quite recently, in fact."

"I knew that Hunbatz lived in the apartment, but I didn't know he'd been kicked out. What I'd like to know is where he is now. Any idea?"

"In fact, the company required a forwarding address from him, as he still owes for damages inflicted upon the property." Benning reached into his desk drawer and pulled out a sheet of paper. "I've been instructed to give this to you."

"Instructed? By who?"

Benning pursed his lips. "That's 'by whom.' And it's information you don't need to know."

Chapter Twenty-Five

Stormclaw was quiet as he drove me back to the Tanielu, and I was wrapped up in my own thoughts. When he pulled up next to the beastmobile, I didn't climb out right away.

"Now that Randolph's out of the picture, what does Benning have you doing?" I asked.

I wasn't sure that the old troll would answer my question, but he shrugged and said, "I've got the rest of the day off. After that, we'll see."

"I've got something I need to do, and I could use a hand," I said.

Stormclaw's eyes narrowed behind his shades. "What do you have in mind?"

"I need to see a guy. He might be reluctant to answer the questions I want to ask him. He might be more willing if I've got some backup with me."

Stormclaw snorted. "You're going to see this Hunbatz fellow?"

"That's right."

"And you need some muscle? I'm a little old for that kind of work."

"You probably won't need to do anything more than fill space and look tough."

"Hmm.... Would it help if I was packing some heat, seeing's how you're not?"

"It might."

He rubbed his chin with a four-fingered hand. "How much you offering?"

"How 'bout I buy you lunch?"

A wide smile split the troll's wrinkled clay-like face. "I know a place. But there's a catch."

I frowned. "A catch?"

Stormclaw nodded. "Yeah. I want to drive that tank of yours. You can follow me in this baby."

Forty-five minutes later, the two of us were sitting at a table in a sandwich joint near Bunker Park called The Ripe Tomato, a place we could have reached in half that time if Stormclaw hadn't led me on a meandering route through the city so he could put the beastmobile through its paces. He'd been reluctant to return my keys.

"Someone's been tricking up that engine," he told me, his glowing eyes gleaming even more than usual. "Maybe you'll let me drive it down the coast sometime?"

The Ripe Tomato had a roast beef sandwich that was more than passable, and Stormclaw's eyes closed in ecstasy as he slurped up some yonak that smelled like a stockyard. I picked up the tab and let the old troll drive me to Hunbatz's new place in my car while I stretched out in the passenger seat. He maneuvered the beastmobile through traffic as if he were driving an economy car.

"I could get used to this," he told me.

"My mechanic's son has dibs on it," I said.

"Hmm. Shame to waste this beast on a human."

We didn't waste any time getting to the address Benning had given me. Hunbatz was now living in a westside apartment in a three-story complex called Redwood Towers, which was located a good hundred miles from the nearest Redwood Tree, and which looked more like a barn than a tower. Hunbatz had moved into Apartment Three Fifteen, a unit on the top floor. The elevator was out of order, leaving me to wonder what the deal was with elevators in this city. The stairs were intact, and Stormclaw took them three at a time while I hustled up behind him, thinking he was awfully spry for such an old man.

No one answered when I knocked on the door, and I confirmed that both visible locks were engaged. No one was stirring inside the apartment, but I called out Hunbatz's name anyway, just to be certain. A door opened across the hall, and a lady who appeared to be at least ninety slid halfway out.

"Are you looking for the young man who just moved in?" she asked.

I put on my most disarming smile. "Yes, we are. We were supposed to help him move some furniture."

She frowned. "Oh, my. He left not more than half an hour ago. He doesn't have any furniture that I know of."

"He's bringing it in. That's why we're here."

The frown didn't leave her face. "Are you friends of his?"

"That's right. Me and Duffy go way back."

Her face softened a bit. "Duffy moved in last night. He introduced himself to me this morning. He seems like such a nice young man."

"Yes, ma'am. Duffy's a right gee."

"And you're here to help him with his furniture?"

"Yes, ma'am. That's why we're here."

The woman leaned a little farther into the hallway. "I hope he doesn't throw parties. The last man who lived there threw the wildest parties. Land's sakes, those kids carried on all through the night! I told him to keep the noise down, and he promised he would, but he never did. Such carrying on!"

I kept the smile on my face. "Don't you worry about Duffy, ma'am. He's as quiet as a mouse."

Relief crept onto the old woman's face. "Well, that's good to hear, and I hope it's true." She pulled herself the rest of the way into the hall, revealing the sawed-off shotgun she'd been concealing behind the door. "I'd hate to have to chase him off the way I did the last guy. Land's sakes, such squealing. You'd think he'd never had a popgun shoved up his ass before."

"No, ma'am. You won't have any problems with Duffy. He's a real homebody."

"Well, that's good to know. I don't know when he'll be back. You'd best wait for him in the lobby." She let the business end of the shotgun drift our way a bit.

"Yes, ma'am. That sounds like a real good idea," I told her.

***

Back in the lobby, Stormclaw let out a cackling laugh. "I may have to go back up there and ask her to marry me," he said. "I think I'm in love."

I looked him up and down. "The two of you would make a cute couple."

His grin caused his pointed ears to rise on the sides of his hairless head. "I wouldn't cheat on her, that's for sure."

"I think you'd have to do all the cooking and cleaning, too."

"I wouldn't mind. Long as she let me do all the driving."

I took a deep breath and let it out slowly, composing myself. "That lady doesn't know what she's in for. Hunbatz is... different."

Stormclaw stopped smiling. "How you mean?"

"He's a shifter."

The troll adjusted his shades. "Mmm.... What sort?"

"He transforms into a troop of howler monkeys."

Stormclaw's eyes widened. "You don't say. I've known a few were-folk in my days, but never any monkeys."

"He's a little nuts, too."

That got me a nod. "Most of them are."

I looked up at the troll. "But the worst part is he serves a real mean spirit. You ever hear of Ixquic?"

"The Blood Moon?"

"Yep."

Stormclaw scratched the side of his nose. "She's a little nuts, too."

"She's got a cult full of high school kids. She tried to sacrifice me to a spirit called Itzamna during one of their meetings."

Stormclaw turned his head and stared at me. "Itzamna, you say?"

"An ancient sky spirit."

The troll nodded. "I'm familiar with him. That's who the Blood Moon was sacrificing you to?"

"Yep. It didn't go that well for her, and she disappeared through a portal with this Hunbatz fellow we're looking for. He's some kind of assistant to her."

Stormclaw frowned down on me. "What are you going to do when you find him?"

"She's still threatening me. I'm hoping Hunbatz will tell me how I can get her to go away."

"Why would he do that if he works for her?"

"His loyalties might actually be a little divided."

A middle-aged man wearing a homburg and carrying a briefcase came through the front door and headed for the stairs without giving the two of us more than a casual glance. Stormclaw watched him until he was out of view, then turned to me. "You planning to get tough with this guy?"

"I hope I won't have to. I just need to talk to him, and I'm hoping he'll be willing."

"And if talking don't cut the mustard?"

I glanced up at him. "We'll improvise."

Stormclaw shrugged. "Okay."

"You're cool with this?"

A smile crossed the troll's face and left just as quickly. "As plans go, it's a little light on contingencies."

I grunted. "I'm not big on overthinking things. Too restrictive. I like to maintain my flexibility."

Stormclaw nodded. "Works for me. I'll just follow your lead." He glanced at the door. "Provided your boy shows up. How long you planning on waiting around for him?"

"I don't know. Not too long."

The door opened, and two trolls in pinstripe suits and unsmiling faces stepped through. They gave us the once over before disappearing down the hall.

"This place is busy," I told Stormclaw. "Too busy for my comfort. Let's wait in the car."

As we started for the door, it opened, and Duffy Hunbatz crossed into the lobby holding a paper grocery sack in each arm.

He didn't see us right away, which gave me the chance to cut off his path back to the door. Stormclaw saw what I was doing and moved to stand between Hunbatz and the stairs. At the sight of the troll, Hunbatz stopped in his tracks. His jaw, nearly buried beneath a mane of thick red-brown hair, dropped.

"Hello, Duffy," I said.

Hunbatz turned away from the troll to me, his face twisted with panic.

I raised a hand, palm out. "Easy there, pal. I just want to have a little chat."

Hunbatz whirled to face Stormclaw, turned back to me, and slumped.

"That-a-boy, Duffy," I said, keeping things friendly. "Shall the three of us go up to your new digs? I hope you have some beer in one of those sacks."

Hunbatz peered at me over the grocery sacks with sullen eyes. "I'd rather talk with you outside. I'll leave these bags here."

"That's fine with us. But don't even think about transforming. Stormclaw's got this thing about monkeys. He's likely to yank the heads off three of yours before he can stop himself."

Hunbatz let out a resigned sigh and lowered his groceries against the nearest wall. Stormclaw placed a taloned hand on Hunbatz's shoulder, and I guided us out of the lobby.

When we were outside, I turned to Hunbatz. "Your sister hired me to find you."

Hunbatz stiffened. "Mel?" His eyes darted one way and then the other. "Is she here? She can't know I'm here."

"Why is that, Duffy?" I asked.

"She... she'll be mad."

"Is that because you killed your parents?"

In a flash, Hunbatz's expression turned from panic to anger. "I didn't kill my parents! I mean... they weren't my parents. Not my real ones."

I stared at him. "What do you mean? Are you saying the people you killed were your stepparents?"

"Yes! I mean… No! I don't know who they were." Hunbatz raised a hand and scratched so vigorously at the bush on the side of his face that I thought he would wear a hole in it.

"Easy now, Duffy. You're not making sense. You killed somebody, right? A man and a woman?"

"They weren't my parents!" Hunbatz insisted.

"But you killed them, right?" The shifter's eyes began darting again, but he didn't respond.

I tried again. "If they weren't your parents, who were they?"

Hunbatz jerked his head to face me. "I don't know. They were bad. They hurt me. They hurt Mel."

"Your sister told me they were your mom and dad."

Hunbatz's hand shot out like a striking snake, and he grabbed me by the collar. "She lied!"

Stormclaw moved in on Hunbatz, but I backed him off with a short shake of the head. Turning back to Hunbatz, I said. "It's all right, Duffy. I believe you. Does your sister lie a lot?"

Hunbatz nodded vigorously. "Yes! She's a big liar!"

"Did she hurt you, too? Like your parents did?"

"Yes! I mean…." Confusion cast a shadow on the shifter's anger, and he released his grip on my collar. His voice fell. "I mean… no. No, Mel is good. She tried to keep them from hurting me. They hurt her. Daddy hurt her. He was going to hurt her some more. That's why I killed them. To protect her." He lifted his eyes to meet mine. "I had to protect her."

I smiled at him. "Then you did a good thing, Duffy. Do you want to see your sister so you can tell her how you protected her?"

Hunbatz backed away from me until he bumped into Stormclaw. "No! No! She can't find me! She'll be mad!"

"What's going on out here, Duffy? Are these men bothering you?"

I turned to see the old woman who lived across the hall from Duffy standing in the doorway and pointing a full-sized slide-action shotgun squarely at my chest.

I raised both arms slowly. "Oh, hello. The three of us are just having a little talk. About his furniture. You see, we were under the impression that he was going to be bringing some over for us to carry inside, but he didn't bring it. I guess we got our wires crossed. Anyway, we were just adjusting our plans." I turned my head to look at Hunbatz. "Isn't that right, Duffy?"

Duffy nodded. "That's right, Mrs. Garza." He indicated Stormclaw and me with his hands. "These are my friends."

Mrs. Garza kept the shotgun pointed at me. "They don't look all that friendly to me. And that one's lying." She indicated me with a jerk of the shotgun. Switching her aim to Stormclaw, she said, "And you keep your paws off Duffy, mister. You wouldn't be the first troll I've put down."

Stormclaw smiled. "*Mrs.* Garza?" He asked. "I was hoping you were single."

"I buried my Thairo nine years ago, not that that's any of your beeswax."

Stormclaw's smile never left his face. "You didn't shoot him, did you?"

"Course not, you big ape. The cancer got him. But that won't mean I won't pump you full of lead if you don't step away from Duffy. He may be new here, but he's one of us now, and the folk here at Redwood Towers stick together."

Stormclaw, still smiling, took two troll-sized steps back, and Mrs. Garza turned her attention, along with her aim, toward me.

"Come inside, Duffy," she commanded. "I believe your friends were just leaving."

Hunbatz turned a panicked look in my direction, and I nodded. "Go ahead, Duffy. Wait." I reached carefully into my shirt pocket and withdrew one of my cards. "Call me later, okay? We still have some things to talk about." I lowered my voice. "Night Owl says hello." When he took the card, I pointed my chin at Mrs. Garza. "Good luck with her. And just so you know, she doesn't like noisy neighbors."

***

Stormclaw was still smiling as he drove me back to The Ripe Tomato. "I bet that woman's got some stories to tell."

"You think she's really put down trolls?" I asked.

"I don't doubt it for a second. That's a tough old broad. I wonder if she can make yonak."

I let out a chuckle. "How tough could that be? You just leave some raw blood-soaked meat in the sun for a few days until it's good and fermented."

Stormclaw cast me a sidelong glance. "It's all in the spices, my man. You humans have no taste."

"I don't want to burst your bubble, but that old broad is human."

"Sure she is. But she's a pistol and a half, ain't she? I have a feeling she could keep an old troll happy if she'd a mind to."

"If she didn't pump him full of lead first."

Stormclaw cackled. Shooting me a glance, he asked, "So what about that shifter fellow? What are you planning to do about him?"

"First thing I'm going to do is let his sister know I found him. That's what she hired me to do. Well, that's one of the things she hired me to do."

"What else does she want?"

"She wants me to hold him for her so she can kill him."

Stormclaw looked at me. "Sweet girl."

"At the very least she wants to be there when the police haul him away."

"You gonna let her kill him?"

"Hmph. I doubt it. Like I told her, I'm no assassin."

"You gonna call the cops?"

I thought about that for a few moments. "I should," I said, finally. "But I want to talk to my client first. I've got a few questions for her."

Stormclaw didn't say anything. After half a minute of silence, I turned to him. "What."

"Nothing."

I stared at him until he spoke.

"It's just that a professional does what his boss tells him to do."

"She's not my boss. She's a client."

"Same difference."

"Do you always do what your boss tells you to?"

Stormclaw started to speak, closed his mouth, and waited until he'd pulled the car to a stop near The Ripe Tomato. He switched off the engine and turned to face me. "Most of the time, I do. Like I told you before, I'm not one for asking questions of the people who pay me. But maybe I might want to know more about why a girl would want to kill her own brother, or to send him off with the cops. Now, that boy back there, he seemed a little simple, and I'm a little confused. Did he kill his mama and daddy or not?"

"That's one of the things I want to talk to his sister about. He killed somebody, and maybe it was his parents or his stepparents, or maybe it wasn't either of those. Whoever it was, he says they were hurting both him and his sister. Maybe I've got a bit of a soft spot for shifters because of a friend of mine who I haven't seen in a while. He told me a few things about what shifters have to go through with their families a lot of the time. Maybe that makes me want to lean a little in a shifter's favor, give them the benefit of the doubt, even if that shifter might happen to have attacked me a couple of times. Maybe that means I'm soft. But he says the people he killed were bad people. Maybe they were abusive, I don't know. He says he was protecting his sister. Before I go blindly following her orders, I want to know more about all that. I guess what I want to know is if the sister is playing me for a sucker. Once I know that for sure, that's when I'll decide whether or not to take her brother out of her life."

Stormclaw nodded. "Sounds fair to me. Thanks for the lunch and letting me drive your automobile. I think I got the better end of our deal. Maybe I can even the scales a little." He reached inside his coat and pulled out a flask. "Let me buy you a drink."

I raised my arms as if defending myself from a punch. "Trollshine? Nix to that, pal. I'd rather drink paint thinner."

He unscrewed the cap and filled the beastmobile with fumes. "C'mon, champ. Just a sip. You look tired. This'll make your mind right."

"It'll turn my mind to mush!" I protested.

He raised the flask to his lips and tossed back a healthy slug, swallowing it with a grimace. "Mmmph! I'm telling you, son, trollshine will put hair on your head."

"Trolls are bald," I pointed out.

"Only on the surface." He held the flask out for me to take.

I eyed the flask as if it were a black widow spider. Stormclaw left it out there, and I felt like it would be rude not to take it. "Maybe a sip," I muttered. "But you'll revive me if my heart stops, won't you?"

"I'll give it some thought," Stormclaw deadpanned.

My only experience with trollshine had come at the hands of a sadistic troll cop who had nearly killed me by forcing it down my throat. Maybe it wouldn't be so bad under more amenable circumstances. I raised the flask and let a drop wet my lips.

It wasn't so bad, at least not at first. Not until my lips went numb and a napalm bomb went off in my sinus cavities. I spent the next several seconds trying to breathe, and the next minute after that trying to speak without squeaking.

"Give some to Mrs. Garza," I said at last, handing the flask back to Stormclaw. "She'll probably drink you under the table."

"Wouldn't surprise me." Stormclaw took another snort of the 'shine and returned the flask to the inside of his coat. "All right, champ. You take good care of this car of yours. Maybe I'll run into you again sometime."

"Thanks for your help with Hunbatz. Take care of yourself. And, hey—watch out for Benning. He's a snake."

"They're all snakes, son. The whole world's a snake pit. The trick is to find the one who pays you what he owes you and who does it on time. See you on the flipside, champ."

Chapter Twenty-Six

Stormclaw had told me his trollshine would make my mind right, and I was amazed to discover he hadn't been bullshitting me. I didn't know what was in that juice, but I'd achieved more clarity of mind from a single drop of the stuff than I'd attained with the previous night's deep sleep. It was more than the alcohol: Stormclaw's 'shine contained some different kind of potency. I wondered if the drink had been enchanted. I hadn't sensed anything, but the telltale vibrations of magical energy could easily have been drowned under the liquor's powerful fumes.

In any event, as I watched Stormclaw drive away in his Hatfield company sedan, I knew what I needed to do next. I'd found Hunbatz, the job I'd been hired to do, but I still hadn't discovered who'd murdered and mutilated Mrs. Novita. No one had hired me to do it, but both the elf and Clearwater had indicated that solving that case would be the key to stopping the Blood Moon from making her sacrifice to Itzamna. And since the intended sacrificial victim was going to be either Chivo or me, I couldn't let it happen. It was already Monday afternoon, and the next full moon would rise on Wednesday evening. My time was running short.

Stimulated by the trollshine, I began organizing my thoughts. I was certain that Mrs. Novita and Colton Randolph had been done in by the same killer, so that solving one of the murders would mean solving them both. My obvious suspects, based on the ravaged condition of the bodies, were Chivo, Hunbatz, and the Whistler.

Both victims had been found behind locked doors. Chivo could walk through locked doors and leave them locked when he left. Despite that, I didn't like Chivo as the murderer. Maybe it was simply because I didn't want him to be, but my gut told me no, and, for better or worse, I trusted my gut.

Hunbatz was secretly working for Night Owl, but he would have killed Mrs. Novita if Ixquic had directed him to do it. This was the idea I'd been leaning toward from the moment I'd discovered Hunbatz was a shapeshifting barrel of monkeys. After the aborted sacrificial ceremony in which I had been the surprise star attraction, Ixquic had taken Hunbatz with her through an interspatial portal. According to Jalen, he was supposed to have been the one on that altar, and a portal had been set up to take him safely back to his bedroom after Ixquic snacked on a bit of his energy. Hungry for another victim after her botched attempt to skim some of the life from *my* body, had Ixquic taken that portal to her chosen's apartment for a quick and messy alternative meal? Jalen hadn't made it back home yet, and Sonoma was off gathering up the Children of Cizin, but Mrs. Novita would have been handy. Had she heard Ixquic and Hunbatz pop into her son's bedroom, or heard them open the bedroom door and shuffle their way into the living room? Had she stumbled out of her room, still groggy from the sedative Sonoma had slipped her earlier, and walked right into Hunbatz's arms? She wouldn't have had a chance.

It all made sense for Mrs. Novita's murder, but I couldn't make it work for Randolph's. Why would Ixquic want Randolph dead? Why would Hunbatz have killed him? If Mrs. Novita and Randolph had been the victims of the same killer—and I was convinced that they were—then Hunbatz wasn't an easy fit, at least not with the facts I had so far.

It was possible that Hunbatz had committed the murders under the influence of El Silbón, the mysterious Whistler, a demon who possessed scarred and hungry boys and forced them to stalk human prey. Boys like Duffy Hunbatz, starved and beaten by his parents after they discovered he was a shapeshifter. Had the Whistler driven young Duffy to murder his parents? Was the Whistler still driving the older Hunbatz to kill?

Or had the Whistler possessed Sonoma's son, Jalen, when he was a ragged child, living in squalor with his mother and a drunken father who brought home rats to feed his family? Was the demon lurking in the boy, taking control of him when the occasion was right? And, if so, would Jalen be aware of it? Jalen had been with Randolph when the agitator was murdered. According to Sonoma, neither of them had eaten that day. Had the boy simply been hungry? Had the Whistler compelled the boy to make a meal of the most convenient victim?

I wanted to get in touch with Cozumel to clarify some points in her story before deciding whether to tell her I'd found her brother. But that could wait. I knew where Hunbatz was, and I didn't think he was going anywhere in the near future. At the moment, I needed to find out what had happened in the basement apartment where I'd left Randolph with Sonoma and Jalen. Randolph had been in my care, and I couldn't shake the feeling that I'd delivered him to his death. Whether or not a possessed Jalen had killed Randolph, the kid had witnessed the murder, and that meant I needed to find him. Stormclaw had left my key in the ignition. I slid behind the wheel of the beastmobile and fired it up. My tires squealed as I punched the accelerator and cut off a luxury SUV on my way into the afternoon traffic.

I drove back to Mandy's Closet. Sonoma had told me that the used clothing store was owned by friends of hers, and I was hoping they'd have an idea where I might find Jalen or Sonoma. I entered the store and walked up to the front counter, where an older woman with dyed red hair was tapping at the screen of her cellphone. I asked her if the owner was in, and she pointed toward the office in the back of the store without looking up from the phone.

The door to the office was open partway. I pushed it open the rest of the way and turned to a familiar figure sorting through the pile of clothing I'd seen earlier that day when I'd entered the office from below through the trapdoor.

"Tlalli? You own this place?"

The short, stocky earth elementalist looked up at me from where he was squatting. "Southerland, right? My wife and I own it. She runs it, but I help out a little. What brings you here?"

I took his proffered hand and braced myself for his grip. "Call me Alex, please. I'm looking for Sonoma and Jalen. I know they were staying in your basement. I visited them a couple of times there."

Tlalli nodded. "Then you know what happened?"

"Not as much as I'd like to. I'm afraid that I'm the one who brought Randolph there Saturday night. He needed a temporary place to hole up, and Sonoma said it would be all right if he stayed till morning. That didn't turn out so well."

Tlalli grimaced. "The police were all over this place yesterday. Mandy—that's my wife—had to close the store for the day."

"I'm sorry about that."

"That's okay. It's not like this place brings in a shitload of dough anyway. Mandy runs it more like a charity than a business. She enjoys it, and my construction company is doing well enough to keep us afloat." He indicated a wooden chair next to his desk. "Would you like a seat?"

I took him up on his offer, and Tlalli sat down on a chair behind the desk.

"That was a bad business with that Randolph fellow. The police say he was some kind of shit-stirrer. Was he a friend of yours?"

"I hardly knew him. He was an antiwar activist. He told me he lost an arm in the Borderland. I don't know if that was true or if it was just what he wanted people to believe. A friend of mine had been hired to drive him around and keep him out of the hands of the police. I was with my friend when Randolph was attracting a crowd downtown. The cops swooped in and I drove Randolph away as a favor to my friend. Randolph said he had people in the Tanielu who would help him, but the cops beat us to them. I thought I could stash Randolph in your basement until the coast was clear. I should have dumped him in the street and called it a night."

Tlalli stared at me, sizing me up and considering my story. "And now you're looking for Sonoma?"

"And Jalen. I think they left your basement separately. I know Jalen came up through your trapdoor and into your store, where he probably got himself some clothes. I think Sonoma left through the front door of the basement. Beyond that, I'm not sure."

Tlalli nodded. "I think the cops came to the same conclusion. They have Jalen's bloody pajamas."

"You talked to them?"

Tlalli snorted. "At length. I'll tell you what I told them. Jalen tracked blood all over the floor in here. I cleaned it up yesterday. His were the only tracks I saw. He let himself out our front door. Left the door open, too. You can't do that in this neighborhood." He shrugged. "We lost a lot of inventory. A lot of the bums out there are a little warmer and better dressed now. No big deal, I guess. We give a lot of our stuff away to them anyway. And they didn't do any damage to the shop. Still, though." He shrugged again. "I'm not real happy with that kid right now. He could have stayed here in the office till morning. Mandy would have helped him out."

"You don't know where he might have gone?" I asked.

"Who knows? I'm more concerned about Sonoma. Why wasn't she with him? I think whoever killed that shit-stirrer might have done something to her. Maybe took her. Maybe worse." Tlalli's jaws set, and his nostrils flared.

"I take it you haven't heard from her. You've talked with the other Children of Cizin?"

"With a lot of them, yeah. I hear you've seen Tayanna?"

"I was with her yesterday afternoon. She made me some chicken soup."

A grin pierced the anger in Tlalli's face. "Of course she did. She's quite the cook. She knows Sonoma as well as any of the rest of us, except maybe Manaia. Have you talked to her?"

"No."

Tlalli frowned. "Me neither. She's a strange one. Doesn't talk much. But if Sonoma is hiding out there somewhere, Manaia might know where. She has connections with some shady types, and Sonoma and her are pretty tight. I can give you her number, but I haven't been able to get anything except her voicemail, and she hasn't responded."

"Do you know where she lives?"

One corner of Tlalli's lips lifted into a half-smile. "I know where she works." He held up a hand. "Not that I've ever... well, you know. Anyway, when she's working you can find her out near the bars on Post Street. On the other end of the Tanielu."

"Out near the Garland Hotel?"

"Right. She might even live in the Garland."

"Thanks," I said. "It sounds like she's someone I need to talk to."

"Right, right." A distant look came over Tlalli's eyes. He refocused and turned to me. "Be careful, though. Like I said, Manaia is a strange one, and not just because she's an adaro. There's something about her."

"What do you mean?"

Tlalli drummed his fingers on his desk. "I don't know what happened the other night. And I don't know if Manaia was anywhere near the place. But if she was, for some reason.... If, let's say, Sonoma called her and asked her to come over because maybe she didn't feel entirely safe with that shit-stirrer in the apartment.... Well, Manaia is fully capable of doing some violence if she thought it was necessary. Fully capable. And it wouldn't be the first time."

My eyes narrowed. "Are you saying Manaia might have killed Randolph?"

"I don't know. All I'm saying is that broad is a lot tougher—and a lot meaner—than she looks. And I get the impression she's quite attached to Sonoma. *Very* attached, if you get my drift."

"Did you tell any of this to the police?"

Tlalli let out a breath. "No. Maybe I should have. But I don't actually know anything, and I didn't want to get her into any trouble if she shouldn't have any coming to her." He grinned at me. "Besides, I'm a little scared of her. If I sicced the cops on her...." He shook his head. "Uh..., speaking of which...."

I smiled back at him. "Don't worry. I won't tell her you mentioned her."

Tlalli breathed a sigh of relief. "Thanks. I appreciate that."

***

It was well into the afternoon when I left Tlalli's, but too early to try to find Manaia, so I took the time to shop for a new coffeemaker. I tried a department store, but one look at the expensive plastic devices with their useless digital displays and settings for exotic brews of coffee I had no interest in told me I was in the wrong place. The only things I wanted from a coffeemaker were durability and a dozen cups of steaming hot joe at a pop without having to read a sixty-page instruction manual to make it work.

I'd just left the store empty-handed when Walks in Cloud called to tell me that my computer was ready.

"I cleared up some space in your memory, so it will run more efficiently," she told me. "You probably won't notice it, though. Also, I installed some enchanted security software that will make it a lot harder for anyone to hack your data or listen in on you in any way, either digitally or with a planted physical device. You can pick it up whenever you're ready."

"I'm on my way. Say, you don't know where I can find a good coffeemaker, do you? Something that might survive the next time my office is ransacked?"

"Your office is a battleground. How many times has it been wrecked?"

"You mean this year?"

"There's an army surplus outlet near here. They might have what you want."

"Hmm. That might just be the ticket."

"I'll tell you where it is when you get here. We'll also discuss payment for my time."

"Sure," I said. "What did you have in mind?"

"Dinner, for starters," she said. "I want salmon steak. Call Skipper's and reserve us a table. I'll be ready by the time you get here."

Two hours later, my repaired computer and a coffeemaker intended for use at a basecamp mess hall were loaded in the trunk of the beastmobile, and I was cutting off a tender slice of bluefin tuna with Walks in Cloud at Skipper's Grotto, an unpretentious seafood restaurant in Nihhonese Heights.

Walks washed down a potato wedge with a sip of coffee. "What I don't get," she said, having spent the better part of the late afternoon and early evening listening to me update her about my recent activities, "is why your detective friend is so convinced that Chivo killed Mrs. Novita. Why would he? What was she to him?"

I swallowed my bite of tuna before answering. "I don't think she's really all that convinced. But she's seen Chivo's work firsthand, and that was the first thing she thought of when she saw the condition of Mrs. Novita's body. Plus, she's never been comfortable with the idea that a monster sleeps in my laundry room. She's never reported it to her superiors, and she feels guilty about it. If Chivo ever causes any harm, she'll feel responsible."

Walks narrowed her eyes and shook her head. "I don't see it. He's not the only monster walking the streets of this city."

"That's what I told her. We can't rule him out, though. It bothers me that both Mrs. Novita and Colton Randolph were found inside locked rooms."

"And locks don't stop Chivo. I get it. But I'm sure there are other explanations." Walks speared another potato wedge with her fork. "What about that kid? He was with his mother and that other joe when they were killed."

"He wasn't with his mother. She was dead when he found her."

"So he says. But he was covered with her blood when the cops found him, right?" She dug into her grilled salmon.

"He tried to revive her. He even tried mouth-to-mouth." I cut off another slice of tuna.

"Mmph," she said around a mouthful of salmon. She swallowed and added, "And both stiffs were missing their heart and liver? That can't be a coincidence. Hearts and livers are centers of energy. That's why they're used so often in sacrifices to the spirits. The fresher and bloodier, the better." She lifted another bite of salmon to her mouth. "Mmm! This is delicious. You want to try it?"

"Sure," I said. "I'll trade you a bite of tuna."

We each cut off a chunk of fish and made the exchange. The salmon was flakier, but I thought the tuna was meatier.

As I chewed, I considered what Walks had just told me. "I've been wondering about that. It's possible that both murders had a ritual purpose. That they were sacrifices. Everyone describes Ixquic as hungry, and Jalen is one of her chosen. Maybe he's feeding her. Or if he's possessed by the Whistler, maybe he's feeding himself. Stories about the Whistler say that he brought his father's heart and liver home to his mother for dinner."

Walks swallowed and reached for her coffee cup. "Your tuna is good. I think I prefer the salmon, though. I was in the mood for it." She sipped some coffee. "My money's on the kid. I think he did them both."

"That's it, then. I'll let the cops know you've solved the case."

Walks wrinkled her nose at me. "Smartass. You'll see. If I'm right, you owe me another dinner."

"I have to find him first. Speaking of which, I'm going to try to talk to someone later tonight who might be able to help me with that. Someone who might know where he's hiding. She might even be hiding him herself."

A sly smile landed on Walks's lips. "A woman you have to meet at night? Sounds intriguing!"

I felt a slight burn in my cheeks as I said, "She's a working girl. An adaro."

Walks's smile broadened. "A prostitute? Oh, you *have* to tell me about *this*!"

"She's a friend of Sonoma's, Jalen's mother. Other mother. Well, his biological mother.... Never mind. Anyway, I met her at that ritual I talked about."

"The one where you were going to get sacrificed?"

"No, not that one. The other one. The one where Sonoma summoned Chivo."

"Ah, right." Walks cut off a bite from a potato wedge.

"So I'm told she works near the Garland Hotel. That seems like a good place to hide out for a while until the heat dies down."

"Your job takes you to such nice places."

"The glamorous life of a private investigator."

She smiled at me across the table. "In the movies, the prostitute would be a knockout, and she and the P.I. would have a torrid love affair. She'd be a good person inside, driven to her sordid life by childhood traumas and poverty. He would rescue her, and they would live happily ever after."

"Right. Well, she's an adaro, so she's attractive enough. And I don't doubt she's had a tough life. I wouldn't count on that heart of gold nonsense, though. As for the rest of it, that crap only happens in the movies."

"So you're not going to rescue her? Like you rescued those other adaros?" Her smile had disappeared at some point.

"I've only met her once, but she didn't strike me as someone who needed to be rescued. Besides, she might even be a suspect."

Walks's eyes widened. "No shit?"

"It's been suggested to me that she and Sonoma may be more than just friends."

"No way." Walks chuckled. "You mean when you get past the cults, ritual sacrifices, dream-hopping spirits, crazy howler monkeys, and legendary cannibalistic demons, this whole thing could come down to a simple love triangle?"

"Let's hope so," I said, finishing off my coffee. "That's something I think I might be able to handle."

Chapter Twenty-Seven

After driving Walks home, I went back to my place long enough to carry my computer and new coffeemaker into my office and scoop some fresh yonak into Chivo's empty food bowl. Chivo was still curled in his bed and woke up only long enough to shoot me a quick glance through one barely opened eyelid. I watched his thin body swell and collapse a few times and listened to his gentle snores before shaking my head and quietly closing the laundry room door as I left. I couldn't reconcile the possibility that the peacefully slumbering critter could have slaughtered and partially consumed two people over the past weekend, and then come home to polish off a couple of bowls of yonak.

I drove back to the Tanielu and found a parking spot three blocks from the Garland Hotel. The Post Street neighborhood was the most notorious part of the Tanielu, known to the rest of the city as a center of cheap illegal drugs and not-so-cheap unlicensed prostitution. On the way to the Garland, I passed at least a dozen hookers in short shorts and tight blouses with half the buttons unfastened, all looking much older up close than they did from a distance. About half of them were adaro nymphs, their feathered gills coated with fluorescent makeup that reflected the garish light from the neon signs over the doors of the bars. A couple of the joy girls had artificial gills: humans trying to pass themselves off as adaros. You'd have to be pretty drunk to fall for that gag, but I supposed it worked often enough. None of them were Manaia, and I politely turned down their kind offers for "dates" and "good times." Whenever I asked if Manaia was around, they frowned, pursed their lips, and told me they were unfamiliar with anyone going by that name before assuring me that anything she could do, they could do better and more willingly.

I decided I needed a drink and walked into the largest of the Post Street bars. The joint was darker than the night and mostly empty. The barflies on the stools sat huddled over their whiskeys as if they were afraid the drinks were planning to make a run for it. They melted into the darkness of the bar, safe from predatory eyes. I spotted a couple of goodtime girls at a table—probably on a break after some early action—but no Manaia.

The bartender was bald as a cue ball with gray eyes and an even grayer mustache. I ordered a shot and put an extra couple of bills on the counter.

"Have you seen Manaia tonight?" I asked

The bartender put one of the bills in the register and pocketed the extra. "Manaia? You mean Maya?"

"Genuine adaro? A little classier than most of the others?"

"Maya's her working name. You a friend of hers?"

"We have a mutual friend. In a non-professional capacity."

The bartender squinted at me. "You a cop?"

"Private," I clarified. "Our mutual friend wanted me to deliver a message to her."

"He couldn't come himself?"

"She. And no."

The bartender turned it over in his mind. "Maya doesn't walk the street, but she cruises most of the bars on the block. If you can't find her in one of the bars, you could try the Garland. In fact, that might be your best bet this time of the night. The bars don't start getting busy till later." He stepped away then, letting me know I'd received all that I'd paid for.

I knocked back the watered-down shot without tasting it and walked out of the protective dark of the bar into a night lit by the perilous beam of a moon just short of being full.

The lobby of the Garland reminded me of a forgotten actress: quite the doll in those old classics, but cast adrift once the pancake makeup could no longer fill in her deepening wrinkles and firm up her sagging jowls. The geezer reading a newspaper behind the check-in counter looked like he could have been an usher when those cinema classics were the talk of the town.

I stepped up to the counter and said, "I'm looking for Maya."

"Got an appointment?" the geezer asked. He looked bored, and his eyes didn't meet mine.

"No, but she won't mind."

The geezer glanced across the counter at me. "Gotta name?"

"Tell her Alex Southerland wants to talk to her."

The geezer gave me a quick once over and plucked the receiver off a telephone that might have been installed the day after phones were invented. After two rings, I heard a female voice through the receiver say, "Yeah?"

"Got an Alex Sonderling down here. Says he wants to talk to you."

"I don't know anyone by that name. Tell him to scram."

"*Southerland*," I said.

"Make that an Alex *Southerland*," said the geezer.

"Southerland, you say? That's different. Him you can send up."

The geezer hung up the phone. "Four oh five. Elevator's around the corner." He went back to his newspaper.

The working elevator elevated my opinion of the Garland a notch, so that by the time I made it safely to the fourth floor, I'd decided the place was a swell old joint. Manaia, wearing a halter top and a red skirt cut from less material than my hat, answered my knock and held the door open for me to enter. I took in the room at a glance: a small, modestly furnished suite with enough clutter to make it look homey. Manaia directed me to a cushioned chair and sat across from me on the edge of a double bed. "Can't say I was expecting you," she told me.

"I'm just here to talk," I said. "I don't know if you've heard, but Sonoma and Jalen are missing."

Manaia crossed her legs at the thighs and leaned back on the palms of her hands. "Usual rates apply."

"Say again?"

"Talk or play, I'm on the clock." With a deft dip of her head, she flipped her hair off one bare shoulder, exposing the gills on that side of her neck.

My nose tickled, and I took a few moments to control my thoughts. Adaros were not human. Adaro women were ocean nymphs, and in their natural habitats they outnumbered the fierce adaro men ten to one. Over the ages, natural selection had favored certain survival traits in the women of the species, including the powerful pheromones emanating from Manaia that were stimulating an uncomfortable sexual desire in me as I breathed in her scent.

I focused on why I was there before speaking. "How 'bout I ask my questions and I decide whether your answers are worth paying for?"

She shook her hair off her other shoulder. "That won't do. Give me a hundred up front as a deposit, and I'll decide whether your questions are worth answering."

"That's a lot of dough for a few questions from a guy who's trying to help your friend."

She raised a knee about an inch, and I gripped the arms of my chair. "It's a third of what I'm worth," she said, purring like a jungle beast, "and it only buys you a few minutes of my time. Which, by the way, you're using up fast."

I shook my head and took out my wallet, consciously relaxing to keep my hands from shaking. "I've only got sixty," I said.

Manaia sat up on the bed. "Seriously?" She huffed out a breath.

"Look, Manaia…" I began.

"Sh! I'm thinking." After a few moments, she looked up at me. "I know who you are. You're the human who smuggled a busload of adaro women out of the settlement and helped them return to the sea."

"I might have had something to do with that."

Her lips curled into a half smile. "You know you really fucked up the settlement. The place is more like a prison than ever now. The settlement is the only place where people like me can access the water without getting tracked and shot on sight. And we've all gotta return to the water at least three or four times a week. Getting in and out of the settlement is a real bitch now, what with all the new checkpoints and procedures."

I shrugged and said nothing.

She looked me up and down. "You know, you've got quite a reputation with us now. A lot of us think you're some kind of hero. They're hoping you'll rescue them and send them home the way you did those others. But others of us think you should be strung up by your balls for stirring things up the way you did."

"What do *you* think?" I asked.

"Hmph," she snorted. "I don't give a shit. I sure don't need rescuing. I'm doing fine."

"You don't want to go back home?"

Manaia glared at me with narrowed eyes. She rolled down the sleeve of the glove she was wearing on her left hand to expose the serial number tattooed across her wrist. "I'm a registered displaced person, and I've got a tracking device under my skin. I'm a member of a conquered species, and we're separated from our men. I'm an unlicensed sex worker living in a cheap hotel and making her money on her back. I guess you think I must hate my life." She pulled her glove back over the registration number once again. "Let me tell you something, buster. Before the Tolanican Navy fished me out of the water and tossed me into the settlement, I was a nobody. My mother scraped barnacles off of rocks for a living. She was raped, and I don't know who my father is, or if he's still alive. I had no prospects with my people beyond working in menial labor. I had no chance to be married, even if I wanted to, which I never did. Adaro men are animals. Fuck them all, and I don't mean literally. Even with all the restrictions placed on me and my kind by your government and military, I have more control over my life here on the land than I ever would've in the sea. So... no. I don't want to go back there. Ever."

I found I had no response to that, so I kept my mouth in check.

She smiled and leaned forward on the bed. "I have to admit, though, that the way you snuck those bitches out from under the noses of the settlement officials was very cool."

I smiled back. "So I'm a hero?"

She snorted. "Fuck no. You're a sucker for adaro pheromones, just like every other human male. The way I figure it, those nymphs had you sitting up and begging them to let you risk your life to set them free."

I chuckled. "No comment."

She sighed. "All right. Tell you what. Give me whatever chump change you've got in your wallet, and I'll answer a question or two about Sonoma. But make it quick, will you? This girl's gotta make a living."

I handed her my three twenties and asked, "Do you know where Sonoma is right now?"

She took the time to put the money into a dresser drawer before turning back to me. "She's safe."

"What about Jalen?"

Her features darkened. "We don't know. She's worried about the little shit."

"Did she tell you what happened to the man that was with them?"

Manaia shook her head. "She doesn't know. That's what she tells me, at least, and I believe her. When I picked her up, she was covered in blood and vomit, but she has no idea how it all got there. I heard about the dead guy later, but she doesn't know what happened. She says she was in the basement under Mandy's store one moment, and the next she was wandering the streets by herself. She called me, and I came and got her."

"Is she here in the hotel? Can I talk to her?"

She leaned against the dresser and folded her arms over her chest. "No and no."

"Can you get a message to her?"

"You'll owe me."

"The sixty doesn't cover it?"

"Not even close."

"Even though I'm a hero?"

She made a noise that might have been a scoffing sound or a sharp laugh. Maybe both at once.

"Just tell her I want to talk to her," I said. "As soon as possible. And that I'm looking for Jalen."

She sighed. "Give me your number."

I fished for one of my business cards, but she ignored it and picked her cellphone off the top of her dresser. "Shoot," she said, and she tapped in my number as I read it off to her.

When she was done, she put the phone back on her dresser and turned to me. "Time's up. Scoot!"

I thanked her for her time and left. On the way back to the beastmobile, I was hit on by four sweet-talking streetwalkers, a baby-faced joy boy, and a dwarf in a bowler hat with a bag of rock cocaine. I tipped my fedora to all of them on my way by, wanting nothing more that evening than a quick route out of the Tanielu.

***

It was with more than a little trepidation and after a pep talk in which I reminded myself that I owned my own dreams, that I climbed into my bed that night and shut my eyes.

The dream must have been lying in wait for me, because it came immediately.

I was back in the restaurant with Walks, watching her cut into her salmon steak. My bluefin tuna lay on my plate in front of me, waiting for me to dig in. And I was hungry. Powerfully hungry. Hunger pressed down on me like a weight, as if I hadn't eaten in a month. It twisted my stomach and caused my hands to shake. My heart was pounding in anticipation and my breath was caught in my throat. I had a fork in one hand and a knife in the other. All I had to do was cut off a succulent slice of the meat and scoop it into my waiting mouth.

I wanted to. The universe was speaking to me, telling me to stab, cut, and eat. Across from me, Walks was ripping huge chunks from the salmon and stuffing them into her mouth with gusto. Scarlet blood poured from her salmon steak, flooding her plate and staining her mouth. Except Walks no longer had a slab of baked meat in her plate, but a whole living fish, which she was slicing with a knife the size of a machete. The tuna in my plate was whole and alive, too, flopping weakly and staring up at me with pleading eyes.

"The liver," whispered a voice that came from everywhere. "Cut out the liver."

The hunger intensified, causing my whole midsection to cramp, and I knew this hunger wasn't natural. It wasn't that I was hungry; the hunger was invading me from outside, penetrating me, taking control. I didn't know if it was a spell or possession. Either way, I was determined to resist it.

Despite my best intentions, I felt myself preparing to stab the belly of the fish with my fork and slice it with my knife. Again, I heard the whisper: "The heart. Cut out the heart." A wave of hunger, stronger than before, swept over me, and I lowered my fork until the tines were pressing on the scales of the fish.

"It's a trick!" I shouted. "Let go of me!"

"You hunger," came the whisper, and my stomach collapsed in on itself. "The liver is life. It is satisfaction."

"Ixquic! I won't be your sap! I'm in control of this dream."

"I am not the Waning Blood Moon. I am your hunger. And I am in control."

I recognized the voice then. It was the voice of my father. I hadn't recognized it before because he was whispering and saying things in a way I'd never heard him speak, but I knew him now. He appeared then, standing next to the table, his breath reeking of alcohol.

"Eat, boy," he said, no longer whispering. "Eat, if you know what's good for you."

"Fuck you!" I shouted, and he nailed me with a lightning backhand slap across the mouth.

"You'll do what I tell you to, you little fuck. Who the hell do you think you are!" He swung at me again, and I ducked my head to absorb the blow with my shoulder.

I'm not a kid, I told myself, wiping the blood off my lip. I'd kicked the stuffings out of the bitter old man the last time I'd seen him before departing for military service, and I was ready to do it again. But before I could rise from my chair, my father was gone.

Walks no longer sat across from me. In her place a silver wolf sat on its haunches and gazed at me with watery orange eyes. A full moon stared down at me from the night sky. Stalks of thick grass rose on either side of the table, and I noticed I was now sitting in a verdant field, a gentle night breeze causing the shadowy blades of grass to roll like waves in the ocean. A faint scent of putrefaction rose from the tuna on my plate. The eyes above the partially open mouth of the motionless fish were no longer pleading, but dull and lifeless. The overpowering sensation of hunger vanished, and I let the fork and knife slip from my hands and clatter to the table.

I wanted to stand and step away from the wolf, but my legs wouldn't cooperate. I was frozen in my seat. The putrid smell of dead fish grew stronger. Nausea crept into my stomach and rose to my throat. A waiter came to my table from out of nowhere. I looked up and saw Stormclaw dressed in a white shirt, black slacks, and a black bow tie. He was sporting his trademark shades, and a lit cigar dangled from the corner of his mouth. "I can't take that," Stormclaw told me, indicating the dead fish. "It's unacceptable."

With the suddenness of a striking snake, the wolf buried his snout into the grass. When he came up again, a blood-soaked rabbit was clenched in his teeth, and he let it fall onto the table. The wolf stood on his hind legs, and his face transformed into a human skull, a cigarette clenched between his teeth. The fur fell off the wolf's body, revealing rotting flesh peeling away from pale brown bones tinged with gray. My eyes began to water, and I was nearly overcome by the fetid corpselike stench wafting through the air.

Stormclaw turned to stare at the figure in front of me. Smoke drifted from the skull's nasal cavities and eye sockets. After a moment, the monstrous figure turned and walked away from me toward the setting moon. As he pushed his way through the grass, the skull-headed figure slowly transformed into a wolf and melted into the darkness.

I turned to find Stormclaw grinning at me, the last light of the setting moon reflecting off his shades. "How 'bout some trollshine, son," he said, extending his flask to me. "It'll put hair on your head."

I ran my fingers over my scalp. I looked at my hand and saw that it held a clump of my hair, which I shook off into the grass. I took the flask from Stormclaw and sipped.

I sat up, gasping. My heart was pounding, and my lungs were on fire. When my head cleared, I saw that I was in my room, sitting up in my bed, surrounded by darkness. I took a deep breath, held it for a second, and breathed it out slowly, letting it carry the vestiges of my dream with it into the night. Bracing myself to climb out of bed, I pushed my hand down into something soft and wet. I jerked my hand away and found myself gaping wide-eyed and openmouthed at the mutilated body of a dead rabbit.

My body clenched, and I was only halfway to the bathroom when I fell to my knees and heaved, spilling the remains of bluefin tuna and coffee over my bedroom floor.

Chapter Twenty-Eight

It was still dark when I pitched the dead rabbit into the alley outside my back door. If the raccoons or stray dogs didn't get it first, I figured Chivo would finish it off when he returned from his nightly prowl.

I didn't feel like eating, but I was dying for coffee, so I set up the new coffeemaker in my office and tried it out. Three cups later, I proclaimed it to be the best purchase I'd ever made.

I also got my computer up and running. Walks was right: I didn't notice any of the improvements she'd made. But it worked fine, and I was satisfied. After losing a couple of games of computer solitaire, I checked my website but found no contacts from potential clients. I wondered about the site. Granted, it had only been up for a few days, but, so far, the new site had brought in one client, and she was dead. Not exactly what I'd been hoping for.

With sleep out of the question and nothing productive to do until after sunrise, I changed into a sweatshirt, shorts, and sneakers and went out for a run. Twenty minutes later, with a stitch in my side and coffee sloshing about in my otherwise empty stomach, I aborted the run and walked back to my apartment. A shave and a shower later, with the morning sun casting shadows through my window blinds, I sat down to a belated breakfast of toasted frozen waffles, banana chips, maple syrup, and more coffee. Despite another restless night, I was awake and ready to tackle whatever the day threw my way.

Duffy Hunbatz called me while I was in the middle of what I swore was going to be my last coffee until at least lunchtime.

"Did my sister really hire you to find me?" he asked.

"She did."

"Have you told her where I am?"

"Not yet. I wanted to talk to you first. We didn't get much of a chance yesterday."

"I'm sorry for that. Mrs. Garza shouldn't have done that."

"That's okay. She was just looking out for you."

"She's a good neighbor. I like her."

"That's nice. What's on your mind?"

"I want to see Mel. I want you to bring her here to see me. Will you do that?"

"Cozumel? Sure," I said. "When?"

"Today. Bring her today."

"I'll call her. But I have to ask, Duffy. Why do you want to see her? I'd hate to think you're up to something."

"No! I'm not up to something. I want to talk to her. She was nice to me. You know, back then. I haven't seen her in a long time. I want to talk to her. I want to tell her things."

"Oh? Like what?"

"Just... things. Bring her to see me today. Please?"

It must have been the 'please' that did it. "All right, Duffy. I'll give her a call and let you know when we're coming. No funny business, right?"

"No funny business."

"And Ixquic? Does she know about this?"

"No! She can't know! I don't want her to know!"

"That's good, Duffy. You won't tell Ixquic, will you?"

"No! I won't tell. I promise."

"That's fine, then." I said. "I'll call you later.

Interesting, I thought. Hunbatz might be planning to ambush his sister, but I didn't get that impression. I knew of some professional shrinks who would give their eye teeth to have a gander at the tangle of worms crawling around in the shapeshifter's brain, but I had a hunch his desire to reconnect with his sister, a warm memory from his traumatic past, was genuine.

I also remembered why Cozumel had wanted me to find her brother, and what she wanted out of their meeting. This reunion was going to be a tricky business. I wondered if I should get the cops involved.

As I was considering my options, my phone rang again. I thought it might be Hunbatz calling me back, but the number was unfamiliar. When I connected, it was Manaia's voice that greeted me.

"I'm surprised to hear from you at this time of the morning," I said. "Long night?"

"As it turned out, I didn't work at all," she explained. "I talked to Sonoma and took the night off."

"How is she?"

"Fine. Tired. Pissed off. She wants to see you tomorrow night." Manaia sounded bitter about it. "The Children of Cizin are going to be holding a candlelight memorial for Clara in Bunker Park. She wants you to come."

"She'll be there?"

"Yes. It's a stupid idea, but she's determined."

"Isn't she afraid the police will pick her up?"

I heard Manaia breathe into the phone. "It's a risk. I don't like it, and I told her so. But the moon will be full tomorrow night. Have you ever been to Bunker Park during a full moon in the spring? It'll be filled with all kinds of groups conducting ceremonies and rituals, dancing in the moonlight, or just cruising through to catch a glimpse of the shows. And other than making sure all the weirdness is contained in the park and doesn't spread into the neighboring communities, the cops usually leave well enough alone. Our group will blend right in. The Children have reserved a spot in what we hope will be one of the quieter sections of the park. We'll let a few wolves roam around nearby to scare the spectators away."

"Did you say 'wolves'?"

"Don't worry about them. They look mean, but they're as gentle as lambs."

Great, I thought. I should have saved the rabbit for them as a diversion. "What time should I be there?"

"No later than eleven forty-five. The Children will begin a funeral ritual at midnight, even though we don't have a body."

"You won't be killing any chickens, will you?"

Manaia let out a brief chuckle. "Nothing like that. I'm told it will be a tame affair. Candles and incense, a little chanting. No bloodletting. Clara wasn't one of Cizin's chosen, and she didn't have much to do with the group. So the whole thing is really for Sonoma's benefit."

"And Jalen's?"

Manaia made a scoffing sound. "Sure. If the little creep decides to show up. He's still missing."

"You don't like him much, do you," I said.

"Jalen? He's a brat. But Sonoma loves the little pecker, so, well, whatever."

"Does he get in your way?"

"What the fuck is that supposed to mean!"

"I've heard that you and Sonoma were, uh, close. I can see where a wife and a teenaged kid could be an inconvenience for you."

Silence shouted at me over the phone. When Manaia broke it, her voice was soft and filled with menace. "Now you listen to me, pigfucker.

Sonoma and I are friends. Good friends. The kind of friends who can talk to each other about anything without a lot of judgment going on."

I interrupted her speech. "Did it ever get physical?"

I was expecting her to shout. Truth be told, I was goading her into losing her cool. If Manaia had murdered Mrs. Novita in a jealous rage, I wanted to see what would happen if I jabbed her a little. Maybe she'd tell me something useful. I was surprised, then, when she laughed, and the menace disappeared from her voice. "You'd like that, wouldn't you? I've heard about you private dicks. You get your kicks peeping through motel windows. Well, buster, if you're looking for some kink from me you'll have to pay for it like all the other johns."

"It didn't bother you that Sonoma had a wife?"

"Sure it did. I didn't like Clara. I didn't like the way she treated Sonoma. Yeah, Sonoma's a big woman, and Clara was a dainty thing. But don't let that fool you: that evil little rodent was a bully. She walked all over Sonoma. There was never any physical violence involved. Clara wasn't like that. She was subtle. Passive aggressive. Sonoma is the gentlest, most vulnerable person I know, and Clara knew all of her buttons and how to push them. But...." Manaia sighed. "Sonoma loved her. Or maybe she fooled herself into thinking she did. Maybe it was just an emotional dependence." She paused for a bit before chuckling. "Listen to me, talking like a shrink. Anyway, it doesn't matter. She's devastated now that Clara is gone. She doesn't show it, not to the likes of you, anyway. But it's there, believe me."

"And you're helping her get over it?"

Manaia responded with a single sharp barking laugh. "I know what you're trying to do, you know. I'm not stupid. You think I killed Clara in order to have Sonoma all to myself. You're not the only one who thinks so, by the way. Half of Cizin's Children are convinced I had something to do with it. You should see the way they all look at me."

"Did you?"

"Would you believe me if I said no? It doesn't matter. Sonoma needs my help, and I'm doing what I can for her. And that includes passing her invitation to you. Whether you come tomorrow night is up to you. I don't give a fuck one way or the other. But I'll tell you this, you son of a bitch: if you bring the police, I'll find you, and I'll kill you. That's a promise!"

"Tell me again when she wants me to be there."

Manaia paused to catch a breath, or maybe swallow a retort, before answering me. "Sonoma won't show herself until just before the midnight ritual, but if you're there at a quarter till, I'll take you to her for a brief talk. That's the best we can do, so take it or leave it."

"I'll be there," I said, but Manaia had already disconnected the call.

***

I'd promised Cozumel Hunbatz that when I found her brother I'd call her before I called the police. As I tapped her number into my phone, I wondered whether I'd regret that promise.

My call went to voicemail, and I left a message saying I'd found Duffy and he wanted to meet with her. She called me back at noon as I was making myself an open-faced peanut butter and banana-chip sandwich covered in honey.

"Where is he?" Miss Hunbatz asked in the breathless voice of someone who was just getting off a busy shift.

"In a safe place," I said. "He wants me to bring you to him."

"I just started my lunch break," she said. "I only get a half hour, so I'll have to see him when I get off work."

"When's that?"

"Five o'clock. I'm a cashier at the Central Coast Drug Store in the Marina. Can you pick me up from there?"

"That should work. Do you want me to pick something up for you to eat on the way over?"

"Don't bother, I'll grab something from the diner. Just get me there and let's get it over with."

She disconnected before I could get another word in. Two in a row. It was my morning to be dismissed out of hand.

I stared at my phone. If Miss Hunbatz thought I was going to bring her to her brother's apartment so she could watch me assassinate him in cold blood, she was going to be disappointed. I thought again about getting the police involved. According to Kalama, no one was actively looking for Hunbatz, but he was still wanted for questioning. I'd told her I would let her know when I found him. But Hunbatz had called me in good faith. It would be a breach of trust to show up at the head of a squad of trigger-happy goons. I decided there would be time to call in the cops after the Hunbatz twins had their long-awaited reunion.

After polishing off my lunch, I went downstairs to check on Chivo, and found him sitting up in bed, awake, but groggy. When he saw me, he turned his head toward Siphon hovering near the window. After a moment, a voice spoke from the midst of the spinning whirlwind: "Where did you get the rabbit?"

He pointed to his food dish, which was now buried under bloody white fur and a pile of bones that had been picked clean. "It was given to me in a dream by a wolf," I said. "And the least you could have done was throw what you didn't eat into the garbage can."

Chivo stared at me with his glowing red eyes, and I readied myself to fight off a bout of nausea. None was forthcoming, however. Instead, Chivo's lips twisted, and, with an effort, he managed to sound out a word: "Rrrooollf?"

"A wolf, right. Except that sometimes he looked like a corpse with a human skull for a head. Smoking a cigarette."

Chivo's lips twisted again. "Kiiis-ziiin."

The creature stepped out of his bed and stood on his hind legs, his posture straighter and more humanlike than I'd ever seen it. He turned toward Siphon, and the elemental's voice sounded: "Cizin has found me again. For the part you have played in bringing us together, I thank you."

I kept my eyes on Chivo. "How are you... feeling?"

Chivo's eyes widened, and the voice emerging from Siphon said, "Feeling? What do you mean?"

"Are you... I don't know... yourself? Are you Lord Cadmael?"

Chivo made hissing sounds that sounded like laughter. He pointed at himself, twisted his lips, and said, "Shheee-boh."

I snorted. "What will you do now?"

The goat creature's lips curled over his stringy beard in what might have been a smile. Siphon's voice said, "You are acceptable company, Alex. For now, I will continue to sleep in this place you have provided for me and dine on your yonak. In return, I will advise you and protect your property as I am able. Is this arrangement acceptable to you?"

I can't say my throat didn't tighten, or that my eyes didn't water a little. It might have been the lingering odor from the remains of the rabbit. "Sure," I choked. I cleared my throat and added, "As long as you like."

He made a slight bow with his head and started back to his bed. Siphon resumed its place below the window, circulating fresh air into the room. When Chivo was settled on his cushion, eyes shut and long rat's tail curled around his goat-like back legs, I carried the remains of the rabbit to the alley and dumped them into the garbage can.

Chapter Twenty-Nine

At five o'clock I walked into the Central Coast Drug Store and lingered near the front entrance. Cozumel emerged from a door behind the soda fountain a few minutes later and acknowledged me with a nod. She stopped to pour coffee into a thermos before walking with me to the parking lot. Her face seemed taut, and her eyes hard.

"Is it far?" she asked.

"It's across town," I said. "Maybe a half hour if the traffic cooperates."

She groaned. "Figures."

"Have you eaten?" I asked.

"I'm not hungry. I want to get this over with as soon as possible."

When we got to the beastmobile, her eyes widened. "This is your car?"

"Yep."

She stared at me, disapproval written all over her face. "I thought you were a private detective. You didn't tell me you were a pimp."

"You want me to call you a cab?"

She huffed out a breath. "Don't be silly." She gave the beastmobile a once over, shrugged, and climbed inside.

"Roomy, right?" I said once I was behind the wheel.

Cozumel looked over her shoulder into the back seat, which was large enough to seat four trolls comfortably. "I thought you private eyes were supposed to be inconspicuous?"

"I am," I said. "Nobody ever looks at me twice."

She stared at me. "They're afraid you've got an army in here."

I fired up the engine and pulled into the street. "It's good in traffic. The other drivers give me plenty of space."

"They have to. Otherwise you'll roll right over them." She reached for my glove box. "What do you have in here? A machine gun?"

"Just license and registration, ma'am. I'm not carrying any weapons."

She jerked her head around to glare at me. "You're unarmed? Then how...."

I turned to meet her glare. "I told you, Miss Hunbatz. I'm not an assassin."

"Then what are we going to do?"

"Your brother wants to talk to you. I'm going to give him his chance."

Cozumel opened her purse and pulled out a twenty-two pistol. "Well, *I'm* not unarmed."

"You will be when I take you to see your brother. Now put that thing away before you get hurt."

"Don't tell me what to do. I hired you. That means you do what I tell *you* to do. Hey! What are you doing!"

I slowed the beastmobile to a stop next to a fire hydrant. "It doesn't work that way, Miss Hunbatz. When you hire me, I make the rules. If you don't like the way I'm doing my job, we can forget the whole thing. I'll return your retainer and drive you back to your car."

Cozumel's face reddened. "You bastard! My brother killed my parents, and he's going to pay."

I didn't like the way she was waving her gat around, so I took it away from her. She didn't like that much.

"Hey, asshole! Give that back!" She reached for the gat, and I used my forearm to force her back into her seat.

"Behave," I told her. "Or I'll put you out on the sidewalk."

When I felt her relax, I released her and dropped the magazine from her piece. After making sure the chamber was clear, I handed the gun back to her. "Put this back in your purse. I don't want to see you pull it out again. Got it?"

Cozumel's lips curled into a pout. "What about my bullets?"

I opened my glove box and put the magazine inside. "You'll get it back when we're done."

Cozumel looked at the glove box. She turned to glare at me. She looked back at the glove box and sighed. She opened her purse and dropped the handgun inside.

"Good," I said. "Now here's what's going to happen. We're going to see your brother. The two of you will talk. What we do after that depends on how things go. All right?"

She stared daggers at me for another moment before settling into her seat. "Fine! Let's just go."

Back in the flow of the traffic, I turned to catch a glance at my passenger, who was staring straight ahead, her eyes hard and her jaw set.

"Tell me about your parents," I said.

She blinked and turned to look at me. "What?"

"Your parents. What kind of people were they?"

"Is this part of your rules? I have to talk to you?"

"Yes."

After a moment, she let out her breath and turned to stare through the window at the traffic. Finally, she began speaking. "There's nothing to tell. I mean, they were like most parents, I guess. They taught us what was right and what was wrong, and we were expected to do right and not do wrong. When we did wrong, they punished us."

"How'd you do? Did you stay out of trouble?"

"Me?" She made a scoffing sound. "Mom and I fought like cats and dogs, but I was Daddy's little angel. At least up until the time Duffy went through his change."

"Did you have other brothers or sisters?" I asked.

Cozumel shook her head. "We were a difficult birth. After Mom had us, she couldn't have any more. She blamed us for that. She never said so out loud, at least not to Duffy or me, but I could tell. That was a big part of the reason why we didn't get on so well. She resented me. Both of us, I mean. When I was six years old, she told me she was going to send us back to the hospital and get some new children. I never forgot that. Later she told me that she hadn't meant it, but you don't say something like that to a six-year-old unless deep down inside that's how you really feel."

"That's a rough thing for a child to hear. I can see how it would be hard to get over it."

She glanced at me. "Do you have kids?"

"Nope."

"Me neither. It must be hard to be a parent. You get angry, you let something slip.... Even if you mean it, you know you shouldn't say it out loud. But you do, and then it's out there forever. A child hears it, and they can't unhear it. For a long time, I believed that I had done something to hurt my mother, to make it so she couldn't have kids anymore. I thought I was a bad person because of that." She turned to look at me. "I know it's all bullshit. I know I didn't do anything wrong. But it doesn't make it hurt any less. And all the *I'm sorrys* and *I didn't mean its* in the world can't make it go away. I spent a lot of time trying to make my mother want me." Her hands curled into fists. "It was all so stupid."

"How did Duffy get along with your parents?"

"Hungh! You mean before he murdered them in their beds and ran away?"

"Right. Before that."

She shook her head. "He was a little... slow. Maybe it had something to do with those complications when we were born. He had a hard time learning things. Not just in school, but everything. I was always the bright one. My parents used to get so frustrated with him. Both of them. And it was weird, because we were twins. But we couldn't have been more different." Her lips stretched into a thin smile. "The funny thing was that he was such a happy little boy. I would sass and brood and scream because I couldn't get my way, and because nothing I did was ever good enough, and because nothing ever went right, and for a million other reasons. But Duffy...." She shrugged. "He just floated along, not knowing any better. He practically worshiped our parents, and he never knew how frustrated they were with him."

"Did you and Duffy get along? When you were kids?"

Cozumel's eyes narrowed. "Where are you going with all this? Yes, when we were children, Duffy and I were best friends. You know how it is with twins. Even though we were different, we were close. Right up until...."

"Right up until he discovered he was a shapeshifter," I finished.

"Don't you try to judge me," Cozumel hissed. "You have no idea what it was like. The Duffy I knew died. He was replaced by those filthy fuckin' monkeys. And those monkeys killed my parents."

Cozumel turned away from me then and shut down. She didn't speak another word until we arrived at the Redwood Towers.

***

After I parked the Beastmobile, I made Cozumel empty her purse on my car seat to make sure she wasn't carrying any other weapons.

"Are you going to frisk me?" she asked.

"Do I need to?"

Her only response was to return the spilled items to her purse.

The front door of the apartment complex was unlocked, and we climbed the stairs to Duffy's apartment. My senses told me that Duffy was inside, and that he was alone. Cozumel's face was grim as I knocked on the door.

Duffy opened the door and stared at his sister, who stared back. I couldn't tell what was going through their minds, but the intensity in the air was like a million screams just out of the range of human hearing. Dogs would have cowered in fear, their paws over their ears. Hell, it seemed like a good idea to me, too.

I gestured past the doorway. "Shall we go inside?"

Without a word, Duffy moved aside to let us enter. The apartment was furnished only with a bare mattress on the hardwood floor in the center of the living room. The shapeshifter had used his coat as a pillow, and his other clothes were in a cardboard box on one side of the room.

He continued to stare at his sister. "You came," he said, finally, his voice echoing in the empty room.

That's all it took to light Cozumel's fuse. "You son of a bitch!" She screamed.

I closed the door behind us.

"Why did you do it? Why did you kill Mom and Daddy? Why did you run away, you sick motherfucking coward!"

"I didn't!" Duffy whined.

"You killed them! You murdered them and cut up their bodies. And then you ran away! You left me!"

"I... No! It wasn't Mommy and Daddy! It was bad people. They hurt me. They hurt me bad!"

"You killed your own parents! Why did you do it? Why did you take them away from me?"

"I didn't!" Tears poured from Duffy's eyes.

"Yes you did, you sick fuck! And you ran! Why? Why did you leave me?"

"It wasn't Mommy and Daddy. They were bad people. I had to protect you from them. They hurt you. They would have hurt you more."

Cozumel shook her head. "What are you talking about? Mom and Daddy never hurt me."

"Daddy did bad things to you. I saw him. But it wasn't really him. It was someone pretending to be Daddy."

"That's not true! No one was pretending to be Daddy. And Daddy never abused me. It only happened in your fucked-up mind. Daddy was always good to me. And you killed him! You killed both of them!"

Duffy reached for his sister, trying to pull her in for an embrace. "I was protecting you, Mel."

Cozumel took a step toward her brother and nailed him in the side of the face with a looping right hook that carried fourteen years of stifled fury.

Duffy barely moved as he took the full weight of the punch, but Cozumel whirled away from him, doubling over and grabbing her own wrist. "Ow! Shit!" she screamed. "Lord's balls—I think I broke my fucking hand!"

Duffy looked stricken. "I'm sorry, Mel."

"Son of a bitch!" she screeched.

"I didn't mean it."

I stepped between the two of them. "If we could just…."

The door flew open, and we all turned to see Mrs. Garza in the entryway, her sawed-off pointing straight at my chest. "What's going on in here?" she shouted. Her eyes shot toward Cozumel, still doubled over and grabbing at her hand. "What did you do to her?"

I held up my hands, palms out. "Take it easy, Mrs. Garza. I didn't hurt her. She—"

The elderly lady jerked her gaze back at me. "Shut your pie hole and step back. Do it, or I'll plug you."

I shot a glance at Duffy. "Uh, Duffy? You want to clear this up?"

A trickle of blood dripped slowly from the corner of Duffy's mouth, and Mrs. Garza's eyes fixed on it. "What did this man do to you, Duffy?" she said, her voice hard as stone.

Duffy's mouth moved, but no words emerged.

Mrs. Garza's hands tensed on her weapon. "I'll cover him," she said. "Go get something to tie him up with."

Cozumel's head turned from Mrs. Garza to Duffy, and I saw her eyes narrow. She straightened and pointed at her brother with a crooked finger. "He fuckin' broke my hand! He murdered my parents!" She turned to Mrs. Garza. "He's crazy! Shoot him! Shoot him!"

Mrs. Garza turned to stare at her. "What? What did you say?"

"Shoot him! He's trying to fuckin' kill me. Shoot him!"

Duffy's eyes widened. "Don't say that, Mel. That's not nice."

Cozumel's mouth was twisted with fury, her eyes feral. "Shoot him!" she demanded.

When Mrs. Garza dipped the barrel of her shotgun toward the floor, Cozumel leaped for it. The older lady tried to pull the weapon away from her, but she was too slow. I rushed them both, and all three of us had our hands on the gun when it went off.

Chapter Thirty

An officer who introduced himself as "Buck" Turlison took my statement in the lobby of the Redwood Towers. I told him I was a private detective hired by Cozumel Hunbatz to find her twin brother, Duffy Hunbatz, and that the sister had started yelling at the brother as soon as I'd brought the two of them together.

"The brother is the shapeshifter?"

"That's right."

Officer Buck scribbled something on his notepad. "What was she yelling at him about?"

"She accused him of murdering their parents. He denied it. Well, he denied that the people he had killed were their parents."

"But he killed somebody?"

"It's complicated."

I explained how Mrs. Garza had burst into the room brandishing a sawed-off shotgun.

"The little old lady had the gun?"

"That's right. Don't underestimate that 'little old lady.' She's a tough broad."

"And she shot the shapeshifter?"

"Miss Hunbatz, Mrs. Garza, and I were all fighting for the gun. It went off."

"And hit the monkey."

"Right. Hunbatz shifted into seven howler monkeys. He was shifting when he was hit, and one of the monkeys took the brunt of it. I'm guessing he was killed instantly. The other six monkeys fled through the door. They were moving fast, and I have no idea where they are now."

"What happened after that?"

"I took control of the sawed-off. Then I checked on the monkey that was left behind and confirmed he was dead. I told Miss Hunbatz and Mrs. Garza to stay where they were and called the cops." In fact, Mrs. Garza had held her shotgun on the two of us until the police arrived. We'd all waited in silence, one of the most uncomfortable half hours of my life.

Officer Buck had me clarify some minor details and asked me to wait in the lobby while they verified my story with Miss Hunbatz and

Mrs. Garza. When he went upstairs, I gazed around the lobby, checking the place out. Who was I to say I'd never need to rent a new place some day? While I was strolling through the place, a snappily dressed young jasper stepped in from outside and, after checking his mailbox, headed for the stairs, taking them two at a time. Oh to be twenty-three again, I thought to myself. I glanced at the elevator, which was still out of order. A definite strike against the place, although non-working elevators seemed to be the norm these days. Next time I saw Benning, I was going to tell him to mention it to the mayor.

Something above the mailboxes caught my eye, and I walked over to check it out. Inside a glass window display, a poster warned occupants that, starting immediately, a fee would be charged to anyone needing to replace a lost mail key. Apparently, this had become a problem. A phone number was posted for occupants who had any questions about the new policy. I thought I recognized the number, and I checked my phone to be sure. I confirmed that the phone number was for the Peninsula Property Management Company. It figured, I thought to myself. The Hatfields owned half the city.

While I was waiting for Officer Buck to return, I called Kalama to let her know I'd located Hunbatz, but his current whereabouts were unknown. She wasn't thrilled with my story.

"You knew where he was when you called me earlier," she said.

"I knew where he wanted me to bring his sister. She'd hired me to find him. I wanted to bring them together before I called in the cops."

"You knew where he was, and you didn't tell me. You knew he was wanted for questioning, and that he was our primary suspect in a double homicide."

I couldn't deny it.

"We're both in the soup now, gumshoe," she said. "You knowingly withheld evidence in a murder case. I knew you were going to meet with the suspect, and I let it happen."

"It wasn't an active case," I pointed out. "No one was working it."

"That's technically true. I hope Lieutenant Sanjaya sees it that way."

"Does he know you talked to me earlier?"

"Probably not. I didn't mention it."

I took a look around the deserted lobby. "Well, if you don't tell him, I won't."

Kalama let out a breath. "Let's leave it there for now. So.... Hunbatz is alive?"

"He's down a monkey, but, yes, he's alive. I figure he can lose two more and still be Hunbatz. After that, he's just a bunch of isolated monkeys running around the city."

"Do you still think he killed Clara Novita?"

"Detective, to be honest, I have no idea."

"Mmm.... What's your take on him? Is he dangerous?"

I thought about Hunbatz trying to comfort his sister before she popped him one. "As far as I can tell, he means well, but he's not playing with a full deck. I don't think he's a bad guy at heart, but he's had a rough life, and he's the kind of mug who gets used. Ixquic—Blood Moon—was using him to keep the kids in her cult in line. Night Owl is using him to spy on Blood Moon. Blood Moon is also using him to threaten me into giving her Chivo. If he killed Mrs. Novita or Randolph, it's a near certainty that he did it because Ixquic told him to. I'm sure he killed his parents, but he says he was protecting his sister."

"What do you mean?"

"From what I picked up, his parents didn't take it well when their son came out as a shapeshifter. Cozumel—the daughter—said something about them bringing in quack doctors and folk healers to try to cure him. Some of the cures might have been extreme. Hunbatz says his father hurt him. It's possible he was abused."

"You mean sexually?"

"Maybe. I don't know for certain. I've only got throwaway comments and vague hints to go on. Hunbatz claims he saw his father doing something to Cozumel, but Cozumel says it was all in his head, and that her father never hurt her. Who knows what was really going on in that family. It's clear that Hunbatz is confused. Maybe delusional. I think he believes his parents changed in some way after they found out he was a shifter. Became different people. And that these 'bad people' who had replaced his parents were a danger to both him and his sister."

"And so he killed them."

"That's what it looks like. But, like I said, I don't have a whole lot to go on."

"Mmm...."

"I think Officer Buck is coming down the stairs to talk to me. My guess is I'll have to go to the local precinct and make a formal statement."

"One thing before you go. Are you going to see Hunbatz again?"

"No idea. He's in the wind. I'm sorry for that. My plan was to get what I could from Hunbatz to satisfy my client and then bring him downtown for a visit if that's what I thought the situation called for. Looks like I fumbled the ball."

"Yeah, you did. But I'm in no position to judge. Here's the thing, though. You probably know this already, but when shapeshifters lose an animal, they literally lose a piece of themselves. It can affect their whole personality. Imagine losing the part of yourself that puts a check on your antisocial impulses and makes you less of an asshole. I'm not saying that's what's happened in this case, but if you see him again, he might not be quite the same person."

She was right: I did know all that. But I appreciated the reminder. "Thanks, Laurel. Tell your lieutenant I said hi."

"You can tell him yourself if I decide to haul you in for obstruction of justice. Keep in touch, gumshoe. And don't leave town."

Officer Buck told me that he was satisfied with my version of events. "The little doll is a fruitcake. She couldn't tell a straight story if we laid down tracks. And you were right about the old lady. That dame is a handful and a half. But between them I think we got the gist of it. We're gonna need you to come down to the station for a formal statement. I'm assuming you've got a car? You can follow us if you want. You've got a P.I. license, so you know better than to try anything funny."

I assured him I wasn't in the mood for comedy and drove myself to the neighborhood cop house. I spent the next hour in a sweatbox, where a couple of detectives threatened me with everything from misdemeanor disturbing the peace to conspiracy to murder. In the end, they wrote the whole incident off as an accident and let me go with a pat on the back and a number to call if I ran into Hunbatz again. The coffee and rolls weren't half bad, and things never got to the point where I needed to call Lubank.

I didn't see Miss Hunbatz at the station, and my call to her went to voicemail.

***

On the way home, I swung by Peninsula Property Management. I figured they'd be closed for the evening, but I decided to check for myself.

One of the things that had been bothering me was how Hunbatz was providing for himself. As far as I knew he didn't have a job, except assisting the spirit of the Blood Moon, and I didn't think she paid him a salary. Yet he'd found another place to live within a couple of days of being evicted from his previous residence. And both his old apartment and his new one were managed by the same property management firm, a company owned by the Hatfield Syndicate. Why had Peninsula Property Management booted him out of one place only to put him in another? And how was he paying his rent?

The offices of Peninsula Property Management were decidedly unassuming. Located on the fringes of downtown, not more than two blocks from the Tanielu, the company was housed inside a rundown two-story complex that also included a title company and a handful of small law firms, one of which advertised on daytime television and offered low rates for victims of accidents, internet scams, and curses. I parked in the building's small, deserted lot and walked up to Peninsula Property Management's front door. When I tried the handle, I wasn't surprised to find that it was locked. I leaned against the door and contemplated the nearly full moon rising in the southeastern sky.

On the next night, the blood moon would rise, and by midnight it would be waning. The spirit of the Waning Blood Moon would demand her sacrifice: the heart and liver of the Huay Chivo. Failing to receive it, she would seek an alternative: the heart and liver of Alexander Southerland, private investigator and working-class joe. I spent a moment wondering how I got myself into these messes, but only a moment. I didn't have time to brood about "fate" or complain about the unfairness of it all. Fairness had no place in my world, and fate was just another word for giving in. I reached inside my coat pocket for my whiskey flask, and then cursed myself for forgetting to bring it along when I'd driven out to pick up Miss Hunbatz. I took in a breath and let it out slowly, knowing that if I was going to figure out a way to ward off the Blood Moon, I was going to have to do it with a clear head and sound, logical reasoning.

Fuck that, I thought to myself. Time was in short supply. I decided to break into the property management office.

If I were Walks in Cloud, I would find a way to hack into the company's computer files and find a rental agreement for Duffy Hunbatz's apartment. I could call the computer wizard, I thought, but decided against it. According to the law, a third party could only obtain tenant information with the consent of the tenant, and I didn't have it. Asking Walks to engage in illegal activity seemed like a callous way to use a friend. Granted, if my buddy Crawford were around, I'd have no qualms about asking him to assist me with a little breaking and entering. The shapeshifting were-rat needed the occasional break from the otherwise tightly controlled and mundane life he'd built for himself as a way of containing his wilder impulses. As he'd explained it to me, he needed to placate the rats inside him by giving them a chance to go wild from time to time, or else they'd gnaw at his collective consciousness until it fell apart under the pressure. But that was before the LIA had forced him to leave the city.

Keeping the brim of my hat low over my brow, I checked for security cameras and found one above the office door. I doubted anyone was actively monitoring the site, but somewhere a computer was receiving a video feed of me standing in the dark outside the office. I'd worry about that later. My more immediate worry was the door security. If I picked the lock and opened the door, an alarm would sound, and a signal would be sent somewhere, either to a security company, the cops, or both. Someone with a flashlight and a gun would be dispatched to check the place out, and it wouldn't take them long to show up. Whatever I was going to do, I'd have to be quick.

I knew that property management companies kept paper copies of all their rental records locked in file cabinets. I also knew that locks on file cabinets tended to be jokes, even in professional offices. I had a set of jiggler keys in the glove box of the beastmobile that would unlock most cabinets in less than a minute. What I didn't want to have to do was spend precious time searching for the file cabinets. I needed to know where they were before I entered the office.

I extended my senses through the door and became aware of the shapes inside. As I expected, I detected no signs of people: no housekeepers, night watchmen, or late-working eager beavers. My enhanced awareness indicated a space beyond the door that felt like a reception area, but I couldn't get a precise read on what lay behind the front desk. Even magically enhanced senses have limits. To find out more, I needed to bring in my most valuable surveillance assistant.

I sent out the call for Smokey and felt the connection lock into place. Figuring the elemental would arrive in about ten minutes, I spent the time moving the Beastmobile to a parking spot a block away from the building. By the time I retrieved my jiggler keys from the beastmobile and walked back to the office of Peninsula Property Management, Smokey had zoomed in from the night to hover over my shoulder.

The elemental's voice hissed in my ear. "Hello, Aleksss. Howsss tricksss?"

"Hello, Smokey. Ready to go to work?"

"Smokey is happy to ssserve."

***

Through its experience with me in other cases, Smokey knew how to identify a file cabinet. What the elemental couldn't do was read. After picking the lock on the front door and entering the office with a pen flashlight, I moved as quickly as I could to the back office, where I found Smokey hovering near a bank of metal cabinets. I'd have to identify the right cabinet and find the file I was looking for on my own. And I'd have to do it fast. Shrill, intermittent beeps rang into the night, and I had no doubt that unwelcome company was on its way.

After sending Smokey out of the building with instructions to let me know immediately if anyone or anything entered the parking lot, it took me almost no time at all to find the file drawers for, "Rental Properties, Apartments." It took me another half minute to find the drawer containing files for Redwood Towers. I inserted a jiggler key into the cabinet lock and jiggled. And jiggled. And jiggled some more.

Lord's flaming balls! Leave it to a Hatfield-owned company to invest in some premium locks.

Who had the key to the files? A file clerk, of course. I looked around the office, searching for a likely workspace for someone whose job consisted primarily of circulating and refiling documents. With the alarm blasts piercing my ears, I spotted a small, simple wooden desk near the bank of file cabinets and next to a copy machine. Moving quickly, I tried the desk's only drawer. It was locked. The clock was ticking, the alarm was driving me nuts, and I was out of patience. I kicked the underside of the drawer in, and the contents spilled to the floor. Among the scattered paraphernalia was a set of keys. I snatched them up and hurried to the file cabinet.

The third key I tried opened the lock for the drawers I needed, and it took me a few more frustrating moments to find the file folder for Apartment Three Fifteen, which, naturally, had been filed out of chronological order. Before I could open the folder, a miniature whirlwind darted through the room to my ear. "Car comesss!" Smokey called, a shrill urgency in the elemental's hiss. I ran from the room, tossing the set of keys over my shoulder on my way out the front door.

Two uniformed officers were emerging from the cop car in the parking lot. Extending my awareness, I tore past the cops into the street as fast as I could run. Horns blared and brakes screeched as I shot in front of a two-door sedan, my enhanced awareness telling me I had inches to spare if I didn't slip or fall and the car didn't deliberately speed up. I pulled up short to let a speeding SUV pass by and hustled across the street with a few yards to spare before a family cruiser could flatten me to the pavement.

    The cops never had a chance. I was out of their sight before they could leave the parking lot.

Chapter Thirty-One

I opened the folder I'd stolen as soon as I was back at my desk. Breaking into Peninsula Property Management had been a desperate and stupid move, not to mention sloppy, and I had no doubt the cops would eventually come around to tell me so. I hoped I would at least have until morning.

I leafed through the paperwork in the folder and found a stack of canceled checks for the monthly rent, along with copies of receipts, all bound together with a paperclip. I looked at the most recent check, and set it aside, confused. The check had been signed on the first day of June by Margarita Garza. I'd taken the wrong folder.

Or had I? I rechecked the apartment number on the folder: Three Fifteen. That was Hunbatz's apartment. I'd seen Mrs. Garza come out of Three Sixteen, the apartment across the hall from Hunbatz. The check I was looking at must have been filed in the wrong folder. I looked at the receipt. It was for Apartment Three Fifteen.

I looked at the next check in the stack. Mrs. Garza had signed it at the beginning of May. I sorted through all of the checks. They had all been signed by Mrs. Garza on the first day of every month without a break for the past eighteen years. Each check was attached to a receipt listing the apartment as Three Fifteen.

Mrs. Garza may have been residing in Apartment Three Sixteen, but, according to the records, she was paying the rent for Apartment Three Fifteen. That feisty little old lady was becoming more interesting to me by the minute. I needed to have a talk with her, preferably while she was unarmed.

The folder also included a rental agreement for Apartment Three-Fifteen, signed by Mrs. Garza eighteen years earlier. As I scanned the agreement, an item caught my attention. While the Redwood Towers was managed by Peninsula, the owner of the apartment complex was identified as a firm called Multispec Holdings. The name screamed "shell company."

The addresses, phone numbers, and operating officers of shell companies are difficult to trace, but not impossible if you know where to search. You can find a lot of information about companies on the internet, but it can be a clumsy process if you don't know how to filter your search results. This was my profession, though, and I'd learned a few things over the years. All legally operating businesses were required to register with the government, and they are listed in public registries. The problem is that companies are not required to provide much information in these registries, and my initial attempts to find out anything about Multispec Holdings turned up nothing more than the company name and a useless identification number.

Reasoning that Multispec might be directly involved with other businesses in the area, I searched the records of other locally based corporations to find entities for which Multispec might be a manager or a member. This was a painstaking process, and after hours of futile searching, I decided to try another approach.

After breaking long enough to savor a steaming cup of coffee from my new coffeemaker, I conducted a deep search in the corporate records of local companies involved in real estate, commercial banking, business insurance, commercial construction, public utilities, and other concerns related to property ownership. To keep myself from being inundated with thousands of photographed documents with tiny print and smudged signatures, I filtered my search inquiry to limit my responses to corporate filings and certain types of regulatory documents issued in the most popular document file type.

At four thirty-seven in the morning, I hit paydirt. An insurance company had filed an electronic record of a claim paid out to Multispec, and the record indicated the name of the company's beneficial owner: Tauri Garza.

I nearly blew a mouthful of coffee out my nose when I saw the name.

A simple internet search revealed that Tauri Garza was the CEO of Tourmaline, Inc., a commercial finance company based in Yerba City with branches throughout western Tolanica. I found a biography of Mr. Garza indicating that he was the son of Tomas and Topaz Garza. No mention of a Margarita, but the last name couldn't be a coincidence. Still, if the gun-toting old dame in Three Sixteen was related to the CEO of a prosperous commercial finance corporation, why was she living in a shabby apartment complex with an out-of-service elevator in a non-fashionable part of town?

I needed to find out. It wasn't just that feeling I get in the back of my neck when my curiosity grabs me and won't let go, it was the way she had taken on the role of protecting the servant of a powerful spirit who was threatening to drain the life out of me in less than twenty-four hours.

I'd wanted to question Hunbatz. The elf had told me that finding out who had killed Mrs. Novita would save my life. Night Owl wanted me to solve the murder, too, for reasons of his own, and it wouldn't hurt to have the enigmatic spirit in my debt. Even though I hadn't made much headway in my investigation, my money was still on the shapeshifting troop of howler monkeys as the killer. But every time I'd been close enough to Hunbatz to ask him about Mrs. Novita, Mrs. Garza had shown up out of nowhere waving a loaded weapon at me. And now it appeared she was footing the bill for Hunbatz's apartment.

I wondered. Who had paid the rent on Hunbatz's previous apartment? The apartment used for Ixquic's cult meetings? Though I found no record of it, I had no doubt that Multispec was owned outright by Tourmaline. The fact that Tourmaline's CEO was the beneficial owner of Multispec all but confirmed it. Apparently, Tauri Garza's company was providing an apartment for Hunbatz rent-free. What was the connection? How far did it extend? It wouldn't have surprised me a bit to find that Multispec also owned the apartment over the beauty salon where I'd almost been sacrificed by the spirit of the Waning Blood Moon to an even more powerful and mysterious spirit called Itzamna, "the toothless one who brings nothing but good." If true, where did Mrs. Garza fit into it all? Was Ixquic directly involved?

Sleep was out of the question. I savored another mug of caffeinated brew and resisted the urge to spice it up with some rye, fearing the alcohol would make me drowsy. The sun would be rising in another hour, and it occurred to me that this might be my last chance to see a sunrise. If that was going to be the case, I wanted to watch it rise over the Nihhonese Ocean from the western side of the city. It occurred to me that the Redwood Towers was located on the western side of the city. I grabbed my coat and hat and prepared to greet the coming day.

***

At eight o'clock sharp, I entered the lobby of the Redwood Towers and walked up the three flights of stairs to the top floor. I paused outside Three Fifteen to listen, breathe the air, and feel for heat and vibrations. I detected nothing to indicate that anyone might be inside.

I turned and knocked on the door to Three Sixteen, hoping I hadn't caught Mrs. Garza in her nightclothes. My experience with older people told me they tended to rise with the sun, but there were always exceptions. It didn't seem likely to me that the hypervigilant Mrs. Garza would be one of them. In any case, I sensed her approaching as soon as I'd finished knocking.

The door opened a crack, and the weatherworn face of Mrs. Garza glared through it. When she saw who it was, her expression hardened.

"Oh," she said. "It's you. What do you want?"

"I'd like to ask you a few questions about Duffy Hunbatz."

"He's not there. He never came back after last night."

"Do you know where he is?"

She pressed her lips together. "Of course not. Why would I?"

"Are you paying his rent?"

"Am I what now?"

"Mrs. Garza, you're listed as the tenant in Apartment Three Fifteen."

Her eyes narrowed. "Who are you? And don't give me that bullshit about being Duffy's friend."

"My name is Alexander Southerland. I'm a private investigator. Duffy's sister hired me to find him."

"So that crazy bitch was his sister? The coppers wouldn't tell me nothing."

"Yes. They hadn't seen each other in several years. The reunion didn't go so well."

She sighed. "No, it didn't." The door swung open. "I guess you better come in."

Thankfully, Mrs. Garza was fully dressed, and she placed the shotgun she'd been holding—the one she'd brandished at Stormclaw and me when we'd first met—in a rack on her wall. An empty space in the rack would have held the sawed-off shotgun she'd had the previous night, but it was undoubtedly in police custody. Two other weapons were in the rack: a twenty-four-gauge hunting rifle and an old-model military-issue automatic rifle similar to the one I'd used during my tour in the Borderland. I walked into a tidy living room where an overstuffed sofa and an old leather easy chair were arranged around an antique coffee table beneath a slowly revolving overhead fan. Against the wall, a vintage radio console played a southern Tolanican ballad at a volume that was barely audible. Mrs. Garza indicated the easy chair with a wave of her arm and told me I could sit in it.

"It was my late husband's, but he don't have no use for it now, so go ahead and take a load off."

When I was seated, she said, "How do you like your coffee?"

"Black."

She grunted and stepped into the kitchen, shuffling a bit. I hoped she wasn't going to reemerge with a combat knife. The old dame might be a little past her prime, but that didn't keep me from feeling a bit uneasy on her home turf.

She returned with cups and saucers for each of us and lowered herself carefully onto the sofa. "Pardon the creaking," she said, a sly grin on her face. "These old bones ain't what they used to be."

Like I was going to fall for a line like that. I eyed my coffee, wondering if it had been poisoned.

Mrs. Garza saw me staring at my cup and let out a cackling laugh. "Don't worry, young man. If I was gonna kill you, I'd'a shot you when you walked in." She picked up her cup and slurped. I took a sip of my own.

Mrs. Garza returned her cup to her saucer and leaned back into the couch. "All right, Mister Alexander Southerland. We've got the opening niceties out of the way. Why don't you tell me why you're here."

I took another sip of coffee and leaned forward. "Are you paying the rent on Duffy's apartment?"

"My nephew's company is. He owns the building. I'm just signing the checks. I'm listed on the company payroll as the vice president of something or another."

"Tauri Garza is your nephew?"

"Yep. Son of Thairo's brother, Taavi. The cancer got him, too. Taavi, I mean. Seems to run in the Garza family. Tauri's still kicking, though. For now."

"He must be pretty well off."

Mrs. Garza's lip lifted in a half smile. "He's stinkin' rich, is what he is. Nice kid, for all that. Nice enough to put Thairo and me up in this cozy little apartment after Thairo retired. Course, he's never actually visited me here, but that's jake with me. He's a busy man, and I don't got that much to say to him."

"Is Tauri responsible for putting Duffy up in the apartment across the hall?"

Mrs. Garza's head shook. "Nope. That's all me."

That surprised me. "You brought him here?"

"That's what I just told you, isn't it?"

My brain scrambled to process the information. "What's your connection to Duffy?"

In response, Mrs. Garza reached for her coffee. After a sip, she shrugged. "The kid's had it rough. He needed help, and I decided to give him some."

"When did you meet him?"

Mrs. Garza put her cup down and frowned at me. "Why do you want to know? You say you're one of those private dicks, but you ain't a real copper, and that means I don't have to answer your questions. So why don't you answer one of mine? Why are you interested in that nice young man that you made me shoot last night?"

I sat back in my chair. "Mrs. Garza, I'm sorry about what happened to Mr. Hunbatz. You're right, he's had a rough go of it. And I'm not going to wave any blame around, even though he was shot by your weapon. What happened was unfortunate. But Duffy Hunbatz very likely murdered his parents, and he might have killed one or two other people within the past couple of days. He tried to have *me* killed a few nights ago. He got the drop on me and tied me to an altar, and then stood by while the woman he was serving tried to sacrifice me to a nature spirit called Itzamna. So, yes, I've got a reason for asking about him. And if you know where he is, I'd like to know about it."

Mrs. Garza's eyes widened. "Did you say Itzamna? You were going to be sacrificed to Itzamna?"

"Yes. By another spirit called Ixquic. She's the spirit of—"

"I know who she is." Mrs. Garza leaned toward me and folded her hands on her lap. Her attention fell on me like a weighted net, and I twitched in my chair. "When did this happen?"

"Thursday night. A couple of hours after midnight, so early Friday morning."

"I see. And what brought you there?"

I'd come to the apartment to question Mrs. Garza, and I felt control of the situation slipping through my fingers. "It happened in an apartment in the Tanielu. A place located above a beauty parlor. Does your nephew own that building? That's where Duffy was living before you brought him here. Was he living rent-free there, too?"

The weight of Mrs. Garza's attention increased. "Answer my question, Mister Alexander Southerland. What were the circumstances that put you in a position to be sacrificed to the spirit Itzamna by the Waning Blood Moon?"

I thought if I gave something to the old dame, I'd be able to regain control of the situation. "I was hired by a Mrs. Clara Novita to find out where her son was disappearing to late at night. Turns out he was recruiting his classmates to a cult dedicated to the Waning Blood Moon."

I wound up telling Mrs. Garza how I'd launched my investigation, beginning with my initial meeting with Mrs. Novita, my first dream that wasn't a dream, my meeting with Night Owl, and my near-death experience on the sacrificial altar.

Mrs. Garza was fully aware that Armine Clearwater, the owner of the newest and hottest nightclub in town, was Night Owl. She'd made a dismissive scoff when I'd told her. "Of course he's Night Owl! The self-loving asshole named the place after himself, didn't he? Does he think he's being clever? Hmph!"

She'd asked me to describe the sacrificial ceremony in detail, and I did. I'm not sure why. It felt right to tell her everything, and I felt better when I did.

"You were attached to your elemental?" she asked.

I nodded. "I was. We'd been through a lot together."

"Interesting. Go on."

I told her about the death of Mrs. Novita and my suspicions. When I started to tell her the story of the Whistler, she grimaced.

"I know the story. Fucking demon!" She frowned. "You heard the whistle? How much time have you spent in Azteca?"

"I did a two-year tour in the Borderland. I lived in Aztlan for a few months. That's about it."

"You heard him when the woman was killed? You're sure?"

"And one other time. Maybe two." I told her about the break-in at my office and the whistle I might have heard when Randolph was being slaughtered. "That one might have been a dream, though," I said.

"You only hear the Whistler when he wants you to. He's chosen you for some reason, and he usually chooses people who are about to die."

"Is he ever wrong?"

"Sometimes."

"Good to know."

She shook her head, and I had to tell her about my other dreams, Chivo, Sonoma, Jalen, and Randolph. By the time I realized I'd given Mrs. Garza a detailed description of nearly everything that had happened to me over the past five days, several hours had passed. My eyes felt as if they were being propped open with toothpicks, and my stomach was as empty as a hooker's smile.

Mrs. Garza took it all in. "And so tonight, you either have to give the Huay Chivo's heart and liver to Ixquic, or she will sacrifice you to Itzamna? And in return she will receive enough raw power to enable Lord Ketz to become a father?"

I let out an exhausted breath. "That's about the size of it."

Mrs. Garza sat back in her seat and adjusted her dress. "Well, Mister Alexander Southerland. It sounds to me like you're screwed."

"Gee, thanks." I leaned back into the easy chair and listened to the soft music coming from Mrs. Garza's radio. It had been playing all morning, but I'd screened it out as I'd told my story. Now that I was done, I was aware of how soothing the tunes were, how gentle and calming. Mrs. Garza had struck me as a crusty, disagreeable old crone, but I'd been amazed at how easy it had been to unburden myself to her. I'd told her much more than I'd intended, freely expressing the concerns, suspicions, and fears that had been building in me since I'd found the incantation to Ixquic in Jalen's algebra textbook. The only part of the story I'd kept from Mrs. Garza was anything involving the elf. The ancient creature was taking great pains to keep himself a mystery, even to me. Hell, I didn't even know his name, or whether he *had* a name. Every time I thought about mentioning him to Mrs. Garza, something held me back. But, the elf aside, I'd opened myself to the old dame in a way I hadn't done with anyone in a long time, and the effort drained me in a way I'd never experienced. It would have been an easy thing to shut my eyes and give in to my fatigue. A ten-minute nap, I thought, would clear the remaining cobwebs from my head and set me straight.

I snapped my eyes open and sat up in my chair. "Does your nephew own that apartment in the Tanielu? Was Hunbatz living there rent-free?"

Mrs. Garza's smile was warm, and her eyes sympathetic. "You're tired, Mister Alexander Southerland. I don't think you slept last night. Let me get you more coffee. You must be hungry, too. I'm afraid I don't have much to offer. I don't entertain often. I can cut you a slice of curuba melon. Have you ever had it? It's delicious. Quite refreshing. You can wash up in the bathroom. Down the hall and to your right."

I'd never had curuba melon. In fact, I'd never heard of it. But my stomach was growling and I was ready to eat anything put in front of me. After a trip to the facilities, I came back to find a fresh cup of coffee on a TV tray in front of the easy chair. Mrs. Garza emerged from the kitchen with a pulpy red half-melon on a plate, which she set alongside the coffee.

"Save the coffee for when you've finished the curuba," Mrs. Garza advised. "The two flavors don't mix that well together, but the coffee makes for a real nice finisher." She went back into the kitchen and returned with the other half of the melon for herself.

Mrs. Garza watched with a hint of a smile as I spooned a tentative sample of the curuba. I was afraid the melon would be too sweet, but I was pleasantly surprised. A bit on the sour side, it had a rich, flowery flavor with a minty aftertaste. I relaxed and dug in.

A pleased cackle came from Mrs. Garza. "Careful, dear. It's a treat, but if you eat it too fast, you'll get a bellyache." She spooned a bite for herself and smiled as she swallowed. "There was a time when I practically lived on curuba. It's hard to find in this part of the world, but I know a place that sells it when it's in season."

I looked up at Mrs. Garza. "Where did you grow up?"

The old woman's expression turned crafty, and her eyes twinkled as she peered at me sidelong. "I lived in a little village you've never heard of down south in the Cutzyetelkeh Peninsula. But I've been around a bit since then."

I stared back at her. "I've been running into a lot of people from the south lately. Sonoma Deerling is from a village in Cutzyetelkeh."

Mrs. Garza smiled, and I rubbed my eyes as her face went out of focus. "Is that so?" Her voice blended with the music on the radio, as if it were a part of the song. "What a small world we live in, Mister Alexander Southerland. What a small world."

I tried to stand, but my legs had turned into noodles. I slid down the edge of the easy chair. The last thing I saw was the blades of the overhead fan turning slowly and steadily above my head.

Chapter Thirty-Two

The scent of wet grass filled my head, and I heard the splashing of raindrops on a thatched rooftop. I opened my eyes to see Ixquic's ivory face inches from my own, her dark lips parted slightly to reveal the tips of her pointed teeth. When she saw that I was awake, her pale gray eyes blinked once, and she smiled.

"I've been waiting for you, Mr. Southerland. Tonight, the blood moon rises. It will reach its peak at midnight and then begin to wane. When it does, the night is mine. I will make my sacrifice to Itzamna and receive his blessing." Her hands were as cold as ice as she placed them gently on my shoulders. "Give me the heart and liver of the Huay Chivo. It will be a fitting sacrifice to Itzamna. He will find favor with it and with me. Take the liver and heart from the Huay Chivo and offer them to me tonight when the full moon wanes. I will change the world, and you will find reward in the world that will emerge. You will enjoy health, long life, and the fruits of this earth. And that's just for starters."

Ixquic's voice was as soothing as the songs from Mrs. Garza's radio, and even more seductive. My own voice sounded harsh and unreasonable in comparison. "And if I don't?"

Ixquic's grip on my shoulder tightened, and ice entered my bones. "Then I will drain the life from your heart and liver and offer it to Itzamna. I will beg that he accepts your life's energy as an alternative to that of the Huay Chivo."

"How would he be satisfied with that?" I asked.

The gaze from Ixquic's pale gray eyes pierced my own. "I have tasted your energy. There is more to you than you know, Mr. Southerland. I tasted Cougar in you. Your life energy contains some of his." Her lips twisted into a scowl. "And there is something more. You have been tainted by one of the enemies of my twin sons. A piece of him lurks in you, a spark that will nourish Itzamna. It burned me when I tasted it, and it will give me no pleasure to approach it again. But it is potent. Taken together, the energy I take from Cougar and the spark left in you by one of this world's ancient oppressors, along with all your own life's energy, may be enough for me to receive the blessing I desire."

She released me. "But the heart and liver of the Huay Chivo would please Itzamna more. It's a simple decision: your own life, or the life of one who was a murdering beast even before he was transformed into a monster. The choice is yours."

I stared into her gray eyes. "The choice is mine? Does that mean you're done trying to force me?" I looked around the room, a wooden shack containing only the simple bed I was lying on and the wooden chair Ixquic was occupying. Outside, the gentle rain continued to fall. "Where's Hunbatz?" I asked. "Am I going to get a dart in the neck if I refuse to do what you want? Or a mouthful of fangs in my throat?"

Ixquic sighed. "What an imagination you have, Mr. Southerland. I know you've met him. He's rather a gentle fellow, and greatly wounded now. He is recuperating and preparing for tonight's ceremony. You judge him harshly and unfairly."

"I know he murdered his parents."

"An act of justice, and one of compassion for his sister. In any case, that's all behind him."

"His sister has other ideas."

Ixquic gave me a closed-mouth smile. "I'm unconcerned. She is irrelevant. Find the Huay Chivo. Cut out his liver. Cut out his heart. Your time is running short."

"Why should I do your dirty work?"

"Because you are the only one who can."

My vision blurred, and the room began to fade. "Wait!" I shouted, but it was too late. Darkness fell, and I fell with it.

***

I awoke in my own bed with my cellphone buzzing. I picked the phone off the end table next to my bed and saw Cozumel Hunbatz's number on the screen. It was five o'clock. Connect or dismiss the call?

I connected. "Yes?" I sounded like I'd just awakened from too little sleep.

"Mr. Southerland? I need to see you."

"Hello, Miss Hunbatz. I'll have to check my calendar." I pulled the phone away from my face and yawned.

"I need to see you right away. It's about my brother."

"I'm in the middle of something right now," I said. Right. Like trying to remember how I'd got to my bed.

"Did you just wake up? Wait. Are you... with somebody?"

"I'm disconnecting now, Miss Hunbatz."

"No, wait! Sorry. I need to see you. It's important."

"What's the hurry? Do you know where your brother is?"

"No, not for sure. But I've heard from him. He left me a voice message. He wants to meet me, but he says you've got to be there, too."

I sat up in the bed. "When does he want to meet?"

"As soon as possible."

"Well, call him back and tell him he'll have to wait. And see if you can find out where he is."

"He says he'll contact me when you're with me. And I can't call him back. I tried, but he wasn't using his own phone. I don't think he has one."

"Whose phone was he using?"

"The old lady's. The one with the gun."

That woke me up. "Mrs. Garza?"

"Right. Anyway, I tried to call back, but no one's answering. I think he might have hurt her." She sounded frantic.

"All right," I said. "Take your time and tell me what he told you."

"He told me to call you and to tell you to meet me outside my work. He must be around here somewhere watching me. Anyway, he says that when he knows you're with me, he'll contact me and tell me where to meet him. He said to hurry."

I stood up from the bed, sniffing the air, and noting for the first time that I was still wearing the clothes I'd been wearing that morning, including my shoes. They were rumpled, soaked with sweat, and smelled awful. "Okay. Stay where you are, and I'll be there as soon as I can. But I'm going to need a little time."

"Lord's balls! Why?"

"Well, for one thing, I need to take a shower and change my clothes. And, for another, I think I'm going to have to call a cab."

"I knew you were with someone. Get her into that cab and get over here. I'm still your client, and you've got work to do."

"The cab is for me. I'm not with anyone, and you're no longer my client."

"What?"

"You hired me to find your brother and bring you to him. I did. The job's done."

"But he got away!"

"Not my problem."

"The job's not done until I say it's done!"

"That's not how it goes, Miss Hunbatz. You need to read your contract. Point is, I did what you hired me to do. But I'll tell you what. I don't have to do this, but I'll make you an offer that's reasonable under the circumstances. If you're not satisfied with the results of my work, I'll keep your retainer and we'll call it even. Take it or leave it, but that's the best I can do."

"Lord's fucking balls! Just shut up and get over here."

She disconnected, leaving me staring into the screen of my cellphone. "That old Southerland charm," I muttered to myself. "You've still got it."

***

Whoever had sent me home had most likely left the beastmobile behind. I suspected I'd been carried through one of those portals that those nature spirits conjure up. I wondered who had done it. Had Mrs. Garza drugged my curuba? Was she working with Ixquic? I hoped not. I'd actually started to like her. But that could explain why she was providing Hunbatz with places to live.

After a quick shower and a change of clothes, I picked up my phone to call a cab. I had a message in my voicemail, and to my surprise it turned out to be from Stormclaw. His message, recorded while I was in the shower, told me he was in a car outside waiting to see me. I darted to the front window, and, sure enough, one of the Hatfield's black sedans was double-parked outside my office, blocking a lane of traffic.

"What the hell you doing here?" I asked after I'd settled into the sedan's passenger seat.

Stormclaw accelerated away from the cars parked along the curb. "I was dispatched to take you where you're going and drop you off."

"Dispatched? By the Hatfields? Why?"

"Beats me. I just go where I'm told."

I shot a glance at the troll. "How did the Hatfields even know I needed a ride?"

Stormclaw gave me the smallest of shrugs, indicating that I should already know he had no answer to my question.

"Do you know where you're taking me?" I asked.

"Nope. I figured you'd tell me."

I shook my head. "Take me to the Marina."

Stormclaw took the next right, which is not the street I would have chosen. When I looked at him, he muttered, "Short cut."

Somehow, it didn't surprise me that the professional wheelman knew the streets of Yerba City better than I did, even though I'd been living in the city for nearly a decade.

When Stormclaw pulled to a stop at a red light, I turned to him. "I didn't expect to see you today, but I'm glad you came by. I had a chat with Mrs. Garza this morning."

Stormclaw's glowing red eyes darted my way behind his shades, and a small grin appeared on his face.

"I'm not sure, but she could be in trouble. Either that, or she's causing some. We were talking, and she served me up some curuba melon. Not bad, by the way. First time I'd ever had any. After a few bites, I slipped into sleepytime. I don't know if the curuba was drugged, but it might have been. I didn't have no hangover afterward, though, so maybe it was something else that put me under. A spirit named Blood Moon, maybe. Of course, I might have been sapped, but I don't have any lumps on my noggin, so I don't think so. I woke up in my own bed, fully clothed. Later, Hunbatz, the mug we saw at those apartments, used the old lady's cellphone to call his sister, and no one picked up when his sister tried to call the number back."

The light turned green, and Stormclaw shot through the intersection. "Can't say I understand what you're telling me, but I'll be happy to pay a call on Mrs. Garza," he said. "Soon as I drop you off."

"You know where the Central Coast Drug Store is?"

"Yep."

"That's where I need to be."

"Ten minutes," Stormclaw said without hesitation. "At the most."

We got there in nine and a half, and, without another word, Stormclaw sped off as I was closing the door behind me.

Cozumel was waiting outside the store, and she came out to meet me in the parking lot. "That was no cab," she said.

"I've got friends in high places."

"Sure you do." She pointed off to her left. "I'm parked over there."

"Have you heard from your brother?"

"Not yet. I—"

Her phone sounded before she could finish her thought, and she tapped the "connect" button. She listened without speaking for a few moments and tapped out of the call.

"That was Duffy," she said. "He gave me an address. He wants us to walk. It's not far." She pointed. "Maybe a block and a half up that way. He says I have to leave my purse and my phone in the car."

I scanned the structures along the street, looking for signs of Hunbatz. I spotted a dark shape on the roof of a three-story bank building half a block away. I waved at it, and the figure ducked out of sight.

"Okay," I said. "Let's go."

After stopping off at Cozumel's car so she could deposit her purse, we headed in the direction her brother had told her to go. We caught sight of Duffy a few minutes later peering out at us from a delivery road behind a grocery store. He waited for us to come to him and led us deeper into the alleyway. I noted that he was noticeably smaller in stature than he'd been before, maybe half a foot shorter and several pounds lighter. Before he could say anything, I asked him, "Is Mrs. Garza all right?"

His brow furrowed beneath his thick head of hair. "Huh?"

Cozumel turned on him with a fierce expression. "You used her phone, and I couldn't reach her when I called back."

"Mrs. Garza is fine. She's a nice lady. She let me use her phone." Duffy held it up. "See? I don't have a phone. Mrs. Garza let me use hers."

"That's good, Duffy. We get the picture. And she's okay?"

Duffy nodded. "Mrs. Garza is fine."

"You're not upset with her for shooting you?" I asked.

Duffy frowned, and his voice was sharp when he spoke. "She didn't shoot me. It was an accident. Why are you asking me questions? Stop asking me stuff!"

Cozumel took a step toward him. "What do you want, Duffy? Why did you tell us to meet you here?"

The shapeshifter turned toward his sister. "I...." He turned toward me. "You're going to Bunker Park tonight. To the candlelight thing. She told me so."

"Who told you?" I asked. "Mrs. Garza?"

"No. Not Mrs. Garza, stupid. *She* told me. Ixquic."

I didn't waste any time trying to figure out how Ixquic knew about the candlelight vigil, or that I was planning on being there. Spirits had their ways of knowing things. I shrugged. "Okay. Sure, I'm going to be there."

Duffy nodded. "I know. She told me. She's going to be there, too. With the disciples."

I frowned. "The disciples? You mean the kids from the high school?"

"Yes. The disciples. They will be with her. Mr. Clearwater told me to tell you so that you would know."

"Will Jalen be there?" I asked.

Duffy seemed puzzled by the question. "Jalen? Who's Jalen?"

"One of the disciples," I said. "The son of the woman you murdered and butchered a few days ago after Ixquic tried to sacrifice me." Cozumel turned to stare at me, question marks in her eyes.

Duffy shook his head vigorously, as if trying to ward off a swarm of insects. "I didn't murder a woman. I don't know any woman. I don't know who Jalen is. I don't remember the discipleses names. I didn't murder anyone."

"Where did you and Ixquic go when you left me on that altar? Where did you go after she ate my elemental?"

Duffy's head continued to shake, and he grabbed at it with both hands to stop it. "I don't know! I don't know! Quit asking me questions!"

Cozumel took another step toward her brother and extended a hand. "Duffy. Duffy, listen to me."

Duffy turned to her. "I don't know what he is asking."

His sister leaned in and touched Duffy's arm above the elbow. "Duffy, do you remember when Ixquic was performing a sacrifice? When she was sacrificing Mr. Southerland?" She gestured toward me.

"No! I mean.... The sacrifice? To Itzamna?" Duffy looked at me, and it was as if he were recognizing me for the first time. "I shot you in the head," he said. "I tied you to the table. Ixquic told me to. She told me to make sure the disciples did what they were supposed to do. Mr. Clearwater says I have to do what Ixquic tells me to do." He grimaced. "Then the wind came in through the window. I was scared. I thought the wind would hurt Ixquic. But she hurt the wind, instead. She made it go away."

"That's right, Duffy." I kept my voice calm. "That's very good. Where did you go after Ixquic made the wind go away."

Duffy's brow furrowed again, making deep wrinkles. "We went through the tunnel. It came out on a street. With cars. I was scared, because it usually comes out in the jungle." His face broke into a grin. "I like the jungle. I like to climb the trees."

"You came out into the street? What happened when you came out into the street?" When Duffy didn't respond right away, I called his name and repeated the question.

"Hmm? Umm, let me see. We came out into the street. I watched the cars. Zooooom...." He balled his hand into a fist and moved it in front of him, imitating a car going past. "Zooooom...." He did the same with the other hand, moving it in the other direction. He laughed. "The cars were going fast. And then we went into the tunnel again and came out in the jungle. I like the jungle." He giggled. "I like the trees. Ixquic gave me fruit to eat."

It struck me that Duffy had lost more than some height and girth with the death of one of his monkeys. I'd hoped I could wring a confession out of the shapeshifter, but I was beginning to believe he hadn't killed Mrs. Novita after all. I thought I knew who had.

I stared at Duffy until he met my eyes, and I was sure I had his attention. "Duffy, think back to when you came out of the tunnel into the street. When you were watching the cars. Did you hear something then? Did you hear a whistle?"

Duffy stepped back as if he'd been punched. His mouth flew open, and his eyes darted this way and that. "A whistle?" he muttered. "What kind of whistle?"

I pursed my lips and whistled an imitation of the call of the lapa.

Duffy clapped his hands to his ears. "Stop! Don't do that! She'll hear!"

I stopped whistling and frowned. "Who'll hear? Ixquic?"

"Yes!"

"What does Ixquic have to do with that whistle?"

Duffy looked to the left and the right. He peered into the sky, as if expecting someone to fall from it. His eyes were frantic when he turned back to me. "Her demon makes that sound," he hissed in a stage whisper. "Her whistling demon."

I was puzzled. "What do you mean, *her* whistling demon?"

Duffy's eyes narrowed, and his lips curled into a snarl. "Stupid! She tells the whistling demon what to do. He does bad things for her. He whistles when he does them."

"Did you hear him whistle when you were on the street? When you were watching the cars?"

Again, Duffy tried to look everywhere at once. When he was convinced no one could hear, he waved me to come closer to him. I obliged and leaned in, turning my head a bit so that he could speak into my ear. Duffy cupped his mouth and pulled his face close to me. "Yes," he whispered. "I heard him whistle. That made her smile, because she wasn't hungry anymore. Then she opened the tunnel, and we went to the jungle."

Chapter Thirty-Three

Cozumel turned to stare at me. "What are you two talking about?"

"Your brother is telling me that the person who killed Mrs. Clara Novita, my late client, was possessed by a demon called the Whistler. I suspected that might be the case. For a while I thought maybe it was your brother who had been possessed."

Duffy stepped back from me. "No! Not me! Not me! I don't know who."

I nodded at him. "It's okay, Duffy. I don't think it was you anymore. But you heard the whistle while you and Ixquic were waiting in the street." I turned back to Cozumel. "That's when the Whistler killed Mrs. Novita. He did it because he serves Ixquic. That's something I didn't know until just now, but it explains a lot. Ixquic tried to sacrifice me to Itzamna, but she was hungry, and she was going to skim a little of my energy off the top to satisfy her hunger. It didn't work out, and she was forced to leave. She opened a portal to a place outside the home of one of her disciples, a kid named Jalen."

I looked over to Duffy. "Is Jalen possessed by the Whistler?"

Duffy shrugged. "I don't know. I told you, stupid. I don't know who Jalen is."

I sighed and turned back to Cozumel. "It doesn't matter. It has to be him. Jalen is just the kind of kid the Whistler would be attracted to. He grew up poor and hungry. His father was abusive, especially when he'd been drinking, which I'm told was often. That's the kind of kid the Whistler possesses. At some point, maybe even before he possessed Jalen, the Whistler began serving Ixquic, the spirit of the Waning Blood Moon, the spirit your brother serves. Under Ixquic's direction, the Whistler took control of Jalen and killed his mother, Clara Novita. Ixquic must have been near enough to feed on the life energy as it departed its host and satisfy her hunger."

Cozumel wrapped her arms around her chest, hugging herself. "So where is this Whistler now?"

"Still possessing Jalen, most likely, but Jalen is missing. The last time I saw him he was with someone who died the same way as his mother. It looks like the Whistler got him, too. I remember that Jalen was cold and hungry."

Cozumel shivered. "Lord's balls!" She turned on her brother. "These are the people you hang out with? They sound like your kind of people."

"No," Duffy protested. "I don't do bad things. I don't hang out with bad people."

"You killed your own parents!" Cozumel shouted.

I held up a hand. "Let's not start up with all that again."

Cozumel whirled on me. "He. Killed. My. Parents!" She slammed both fists into my chest with each word.

"He wasn't Daddy. He was a bad man. I had to protect you!" Duffy's eyes pleaded with his sister. "I saw what he did to you."

Cozumel turned on him. "Shut up, you fucking oaf! You don't know what you're talking about."

"I saw him!" Duffy shouted. "I saw you both! He was trying to do sex with you!"

Cozumel glared daggers at him. "Shut up! Shut your fucking mouth!"

"I heard noises and opened the door. I saw him doing bad things to you."

Cozumel's face was red as a beet. "Yeah? Did you see me objecting? You fucking idiot—I loved Daddy! I wanted it! And you killed him, you son of a bitch! You killed him! I never asked you to do that. I didn't *want* you to do that! You weren't protecting me, you retard! I wanted it!" She raised her fists and prepared to launch herself at her brother.

I pulled her back by her shoulders. "Stop it," I said. "I've had enough of both of you. The two of you can beat the tar out of each other later, but right now we have business to settle."

Cozumel turned and buried her fingers into my coat. "You're supposed to let me kill him. Hold him here. I have a gun in my car."

I grabbed her by the wrists. "No one is killing anyone."

"Then hold him while I call the police. You said you'd do that. I want to see the cops haul him away in handcuffs!"

I turned my head toward Duffy who was snarling at his sister and showing his teeth. "How about it, Hunbatz? You want to wait here while we call the cops? You're still wanted for questioning for your parents' death."

Duffy jerked his head in my direction, a growl coming from his throat. I pushed his sister from me and faced him.

"Mr. Clearwater wants you to protect me, Duffy."

Duffy's growl grew louder.

It was worth a try. "You sure you want to try me, Hunbatz? I don't have my back to you this time, and you're not as big as you used to be."

Duffy opened his mouth and let out a roar. The sound, surprisingly loud, echoed down the alley. I braced myself for an attack, but the shapeshifter turned and ran. With every step, a monkey leaped away until six monkeys were charging off in different directions.

I let them go, feeling relieved. I don't know what would have happened if Hunbatz had stood his ground, but I had no illusions. Despite my bravado, I'm pretty sure the shapeshifter would have beat me to a bloody pulp, especially if he had changed and come at me with twenty-four limbs and six mouthfuls of teeth.

Cozumel had a different assessment of the situation. "Don't just stand there—go get him! He's getting away!"

I looked her up and down. "Lady, you're nuts. I'm keeping your retainer, because I've earned it. I found your brother for you and brought the two of you together. Twice now, in fact. But we're quits. I'm not working for you anymore. Goodbye, Miss Hunbatz. Have a good life."

I turned and walked away, ignoring Cozumel's screams of protest.

**

I took a cab to the Redwood Towers and found the beastmobile in the parking lot where I'd left it that morning. I walked up to the third floor, but neither Hunbatz nor Mrs. Garza were in their apartments. I returned to the beastmobile, but before starting it up, I called Detective Kalama's personal cellphone.

Kalama answered just before the call could go to voicemail. "Whatcha got, gumshoe?"

"Is this a bad time?"

"Kai and I are in the middle of a TV show, but I set it to record, so go ahead."

"I think I know who killed Mrs. Novita and Randolph."

"Well? Are you going to tell me, or do I have to bring you in and sweat it out of you?"

"Are you familiar with the legend of El Silbón, the Whistler?" I asked.

"Doesn't ring any bells. Is it more interesting than the show I'm watching?"

"I don't know. What's the show about?"

"A handsome young LIA agent has been sent to bring in a Quscan terrorist, who turns out to be this beautiful doll. He arrests her in the middle of Angel City, where she's involved in a plot to blow up the city with a nuke. When her fellow bad guys find out the doll's been captured, they send out a team of thugs to ice her so she won't talk and give away their plan. The agent has to bring the doll safely back to the main LIA headquarters in Aztlan. They start out fighting and arguing, but then they fall in love after she realizes that her former friends are trying to kill her. We were in the middle of a car chase when you called. I'm guessing the agent will end up saving her, she'll defect to Tolanica, marry the agent, and go to work with the LIA as the agent's partner."

"How likely is it that a Quscan terrorist would be a beautiful young woman? And why would she fall in love with the man who captured her?"

"Don't ask stupid questions, gumshoe. How does *your* story go? Is there any romance in it?"

"Not much. Just a lot of death. Plus some cannibalism."

"Sounds lovely." Kalama sighed. "Okay, you better tell it. But be quick. I want to watch the bad guy's car flip into the air and explode."

By the time I finished telling Kalama the story of the Whistler, the sun was hanging low in the western sky.

Kalama didn't sound as impressed with the story as I thought she should. "So you think Jalen killed his mother?"

"While possessed," I clarified. "I don't think Jalen was aware he was doing it, so, really, it was the Whistler who murdered Mrs. Novita. And he was directed to do it by Ixquic, so Ixquic is our real killer."

"That's great, gumshoe. And what am I supposed to do about it—arrest the spirit of the Blood Moon?"

"If you could do it tonight, that would be great. She's coming after me sometime after midnight. She wants to finish sacrificing me to Itzamna."

"Itzamna?"

"The toothless one who brings nothing but good."

"Well, *that* sounds nice," Kalama said. "At least you'll be giving yourself up for a good cause."

"It's making me feel all warm and fuzzy," I said.

"I'll bet." Kalama sighed. "Southerland, anyone ever tell you that you were nothing but trouble? How are you still alive?"

"Good clean living, probably. And my natural good looks and charming personality."

"Right. Do you have a plan to get out of this?"

"Not exactly. But I've been told that I could save my life by finding out who killed Mrs. Novita. And I think I've done that. The problem is, Jalen's still missing, along with Sonoma. But I know where Sonoma is going to be tonight, and maybe Jalen will be there, too. I'm going to be there, and it looks like that's where Ixquic plans to offer me up as a sacrifice. I'm thinking that if some cops are there to arrest Jalen, then maybe we can all find a way to stop Ixquic from sticking a knife in me. Although, technically speaking, she doesn't use a knife. She doesn't need to. She just chants a few words and yanks the life out of her victim's heart and liver."

"Sounds efficient, and surprisingly clean for a sacrifice," Kalama noted.

"That may be, but I'd like to keep it from happening to me."

"Mmm. Yeah, I can see where you would. All right, gumshoe. Where and when is all this going to be happening? And am I going to have time to watch the end of this TV show first?"

"I thought you didn't like the show."

"I'm kind of caught up in it. The LIA agent and the terrorist are a cute couple."

***

By the time I parked the beastmobile in Gio's lot and headed back to my apartment, the sun had long set and the full moon was rising in a clear night sky. Later, I'd have to drive back across the city to Bunker Park, but I needed to get to my apartment first to grab a bite to eat and retrieve my thirty-eight from my office safe. I didn't pack iron often, but this was going to be one of those nights. I also wanted to have a chat with Chivo if he hadn't already left for the night.

The goat creature was just beginning to stir when I opened the door to the laundry room, and he nodded at me as I entered. Rising on his hind legs and forcing his lips into an unnatural curl, he spoke my name in a quivery, but discernible voice: "Alekksss."

"Are you hungry?" I asked.

Chivo reformed his lips. "Pl-leeeze," he said, using two separate bleats.

I scooped yonak into a dish, which I held in front of me for the moment. "I've been meaning to ask you something. Where do you go at night? What do you do?"

Chivo's snout opened, and his lips curled back into something that might have either been a smile or a prelude to an attack. He lifted the index finger of a humanlike hand. The mouth closed again and his lips twisted. "Luuuk-keeeng fffor mmmy hhhuuummm."

"Looking for your home? You mean Cutzyetelkeh?"

The red glow in Chivo's eyes glazed and grew dull. "Nnnoooo. Ssshee... baaal... buhh."

"Xibalba? The realm of the dead? That's your home?"

Chivo's goat head nodded. "Iiii aammm sssuunn uuvvv...." He drew in a breath. "Kisssn." The name came out of his snout as an explosive burst.

The son of Cizin. I wondered what that meant, to be the son of a spirit. Not a biological son, I assumed. I also had questions concerning his search for the realm of the dead. Did he want to die?

I ran a hand over my hair, wiping away some moisture. "See, it's just that you're becoming more sentient by the hour, and you're going to be staying here with me in my house. Well, not *my* house, technically. I'm just a tenant. But I've been renting this place for several years now, and I consider it my home. But you've got some law enforcement agencies looking for you. A very competent police detective knows you're here, and, as a favor to me, she's keeping her mouth shut about it as long as you aren't a problem. The point is, allowing you to stay here holds some risk for me." I held up a hand. "Not that I mind. It's not that. When it comes down to it, I guess you could say I'm happy to have you around, especially now that we can talk to each other. But at some point you're going to need to prove to me that you aren't causing any trouble in the neighborhood when you're out at night, looking for Xibalba. I don't want to be responsible for dead pets. Or home invasions. Or worse. You get what I'm trying to tell you?"

Chivo's lips stretched, and a hissing sound that might have been a laugh emerged from his snout. He waved his finger at me. "Not nowww," he said. "Laaaterrr."

I stared into his glowing red eyes without any ill effect. After a few moments, I took a deep breath through my nose and lowered the food dish to the floor. "Have it your way. For now. But let's talk about this sooner rather than later, all right?"

Chivo nodded. "Yessss. Sssooonnn." He lowered himself to the floor and began slurping up the yonak.

I watched the sentient goat beast eat for half a minute before speaking again. "I'm going out myself tonight, and there's a chance I won't be back."

Chivo lifted his snout out of his food dish and looked up at me. "Isshh-kik."

I nodded. "She wants me to give you up to her, but I'm not going to do that. So she'll come after me, instead. I've made some preparations, but I don't know how it's going to all shake out. Worse comes to worse, well, you'll be on your own." I smiled. "No more free yonak."

"Doohhn diiie."

"Good advice, especially coming from a son of death. Any ideas on how I can prevent it from happening?"

"KKKiilll errrr fffffirsss."

"Kill a spirit? I don't think I'm in her league."

Chivo repeated his laughing hiss. "Sss-leeeep. Wyyohhb."

"A *wayob*? Yes, Ixquic is a *wayob*. I know about that. She comes to people in their dreams. She comes to me every time I go to sleep. It's driving me nuts. That's why I've been staying awake as long as possible."

Chivo's lips curled. "Isss... Ish...." Obviously frustrated, he stopped trying to speak and looked over his shoulder at Siphon, who, as usual, was stationed under the partially open window. After a few moments, Siphon's voice emerged from the depths of the twisting funnel of air. "Ixquic's realm is dream. She is the first daughter of Cizin, whose realm is death. The realms of dream and death share the same space."

I turned to stare at the creature, who rose on his hind legs. Holding out his hands, he spread his fingers and brought them together in an interlocking grip.

"Are you saying that the realms of dream and death overlap?"

Chivo nodded and lowered himself back to his food dish.

I took a breath and held it, letting it go slowly. "All right. That's good to know, but I don't think it's going to be helpful. I'm going to be meeting her soon, and I don't think I'm going to be asleep when I do. Neither will she. Still, it's good to know that she's not all-powerful."

Chivo's lips stretched. "Nnnooohhh puh... puh'rrr ohhhverrr deddd."

I didn't quite catch that. No power over the dead? Or was he saying no power over death. And how would any of that help me? "Do you mean...."

I cut myself off. As I stared at Chivo, he stopped eating and stiffened. As I watched, the goat creature faded from view. Beneath the window, Siphon whirled fiercely. After a moment, the elemental zipped through the open window and vanished into the night.

Chapter Thirty-Four

My assumption was that Sonoma and the Children of Cizin had repeated their summoning ritual, and I wondered where they were getting all the chickens. Hurrying back to the beastmobile, I made my way to the Children's "temple" with all due haste.

When I got there, the place was quiet. I used my picks to break into the loft, but it was empty. After a quick look around, I concluded that no blood rituals had been performed there since the one I'd been a part of. The candlelight vigil for Mrs. Novita in Bunker Park was set to begin soon. Maybe the Children of Cizin had gone there early and performed their summoning ritual out in the open under the full moon. The park was only a few blocks away, and with everything that would be going on there that night I knew I'd have little chance of finding a better parking spot than the one I already had. The starry sky was clear, and the rising moon was bright. Clusters of revelers dressed in gaudy costumes and carrying coolers were walking in the direction of the park. I decided to follow suit.

Once I reached the park, the next trick was figuring out where Sonoma was holding her vigil. Bunker Park covered a great deal of ground, more than a thousand acres, and it was packed with different groups in roped off sections celebrating the full moon in their own ways. Some of the groups appeared to be covens of witches. They were up to serious business, glaring and scowling at anyone they didn't recognize. Most people took the hint and gave the covens a wide berth. In contrast, some groups consisted of young people intent on nothing more than having a good time. They pressed themselves into packs in front of live bands and danced to senses-shattering music blasting from amplifiers. I assumed the candlelight vigil would be held in a quiet section of the park, as far from the noisier gatherings as possible.

Bunker Park was a long rectangle running east to west, and, after wandering the area for a good half hour, I spotted the soft glow of candlelight under a grove of oak trees on the far southwest corner of the park. The crowds were relatively light there, and, remembering what Manaia had told me, I kept an eye out for wolves as I approached. When I didn't see any, I wondered whether I was in the right place. As I drew nearer to the burning candles, though, I spotted a familiar face. He turned and saw me, too.

"Southerland?"

"Hi, Tlalli. I'm glad I ran into you. I wasn't sure where you'd all be."

We shook hands, and Tlalli said, "Good to see you. I didn't know if you'd heard about the ceremony."

"Manaia told me about it. She also told me you were letting wolves loose to keep the spectators away."

Tlalli laughed. "Sounds like something she'd say. She's just screwing with you."

"No wolves?"

He snorted. "Of course not. She's so full of shit." He flicked his eyes up at me. "Hope you're not disappointed."

"I'm relieved. She told me I'd be in no danger, but I don't know how much I can trust her."

Tlalli's lip curled into a half smile. "You can't. Anyway, she's not here yet. She'll be coming later with Sonoma."

"Sonoma's not here?"

"Not yet. The cops are looking for her, and she doesn't want to make it easy for them. Not that the cops are likely to come into the park tonight. Have you ever been to the Buck Moon Festival?"

"Is that what this is?"

"Yep. This is the month the bucks grow their new antlers. A lot of covens celebrate the Buck Moon as a time of renewal and growth. A lot of hunters celebrate it as a preview of deer hunting season. And a lot of college students come out here to put antlers on their heads and dance naked in the moonlight. A little something for everyone. It gets pretty weird out here, especially after midnight."

I listened to the sounds of bands in the distance, the amplified music clashing as it rolled through the park. "I'm surprised I've never heard of it."

Tlalli's eyebrows arched. "Me, too. It's been going on for decades."

"I live a quiet life."

Tlalli laughed. "You and me both. This is only the second time I've been here for it. The first time was when I was dating Mandy. We went a little nuts. Let's just say we're not the same people anymore. We're all about quiet nights in front of the television these days."

"Is Mandy here?"

Tlalli looked back over his shoulder. "She's back there somewhere. Last I saw she was passing out candles. Most of the people here are from the Children, but not everyone. Clara wasn't a member of our group. She didn't even like us. We're really here for Sonoma."

"When did you say she'd be here?"

"Probably not until close to midnight. The Children will conduct a formal ceremony then. Nothing much. Just a quiet memorial service." He looked at me and held my eyes. "I'd offer you a candle, but something tells me you're not really here for the vigil. You want to see Sonoma, right?"

"I do," I admitted. "I have some questions for her regarding Mrs. Novita's death. Also the death of a man named Randolph. But mostly I want to know if she's found her son. Have you heard anything about that?"

Tlalli lowered his eyes and shook his head. "I haven't. He's still missing, as far as I know. I hope the kid's okay." His face brightened. "Hey, why don't you come back and let me introduce you to Mandy? I think I can rustle you up a drink."

"Okay if I take you up on that a little later? I want to take a look around."

Tlalli smiled. "Sure, go soak in the festival before it gets too wild." He checked his watch. "It's not quite ten thirty. Sonoma will be making her grand entrance in another hour or so. Have a good time until then."

If I'd wanted a good time, I'd have been at the Minotaur Lounge sitting in a quiet booth with a bottle of whiskey, but I didn't say that to Tlalli. Instead, I thanked him and told him I'd see him later.

I hadn't wanted to be rude, but while talking with Tlalli, I'd become aware of something that needed my attention. Someone was watching me.

I wandered aimlessly in the direction of the more crowded part of the park, making a show of observing the various groups and activities, before circling back into the thick oak grove. I made sure I was plainly visible until I faded into the darkness under the trees. I waited. Within moments, a figure passed carefully into the grove, following the path I'd taken. When the figure drew close, I stepped from behind a tree into her path. "You looking for me?" I asked.

The woman's scream drew no attention from the festival-goers, and only a sigh from me. "What are you doing, Miss Hunbatz? You could have just called me."

"My brother said Ixquic was coming here tonight. I'm hoping he'll be here, too." She opened her purse and pulled out a twenty-two gat. "You don't want to help me, so I'm going to take care of him myself."

"Put that thing away, Miss Hunbatz. You're not going to shoot your brother in the middle of Bunker Park in front of ten thousand witnesses."

Miss Hunbatz's eyes widened. "Who says I won't?" she hissed. "He's a mad dog, and I'm going to put him down!"

"And what if you do?" I asked. "It won't bring your parents back."

"Maybe not. But I'll give them the justice they deserve."

"By killing their son? Is that what they would want?"

Miss Hunbatz snarled. "Yes. That's *exactly* what they'd want. They hated what he'd become. Howler monkeys. Lord's fucking balls. Howler monkeys! He's not human—he's a fucking animal! And I'm going to take him out." She pointed the gun at me. "And you're not going to stop—"

I had the gat out of her hand before she could finish her speech. When she reached to try to take it back, I held her off with one hand while ejecting the magazine with the other, which, by the way, is not as easy as it sounds. This was the second time I'd disarmed her, and maybe this time she'd learn her lesson.

"Just stop, Miss Hunbatz. Leave this alone and move on with your life. You're no vigilante. You're an attractive dame, or you would be if you jumped off the revenge wagon. Sure, you're a little screwy, but who isn't these days? Go join the festival out there. Find someone to dance with. Kick up your heels and have a good time. Your parents are gone, and nothing is going to change that. Stop using them as an excuse to ruin your life."

I thought it was a nice speech, and the advice seemed sound enough. But if I thought it would provide Miss Hunbatz with a burst of life-changing enlightenment, I was fooling myself.

"Fuck you!" she shouted, ending my career as a guidance counselor before it got started. "Who the fuck do you think you are, you slimy beast-loving son of a bitch! You love monkeys so much? Why don't you go fuck one in the ass!"

She made an incoherent noise before turning on her heel and running out of the oak grove, leaving me with a half-open mouth and an empty gun. I let her go.

***

I stayed within the grove of oak trees as I made my way back to the west end of the park. I was hoping that Sonoma, knowing the police wanted her for questioning, would stay out of sight as long as possible before surreptitiously joining the candlelight vigil. I was surprised she planned to show up at all, despite assurances that the police typically avoided the park during the Buck Moon activities. My guess is that she would lurk in the darkness of the oak grove until it was time for the Children's midnight ceremony.

According to Manaia, the ceremony would be a tame one, unlike the summoning ritual I'd helped with. Thinking about that one reminded me of Chivo. Apparently, he had not been summoned by the Children of Cizin after all. I wondered what had happened to him.

I continued through the grove until I was a few dozen yards from the light of the candles. The cacophony of sounds from the crowded park played havoc with my elf-enhanced awareness, but I tried my best to focus on any sounds or movements within the grove. Keeping to the trees and stepping with care, I circled the site of the vigil, keeping the candlelight at my right hand. As I was moving away from the gathering, I spotted two flashlight beams and heard a pair of soft voices. I stopped out of range of the beams and listened.

I recognized Manaia's voice. "You sure you want to do this? You don't have to."

Sonoma answered, "It's for Clara."

Manaia sighed in the way people do when they've been debating all day and the same repeated points are receiving the same repeated answers. "I know. I thought I would try one last time."

"I'm not going to change my mind. If the cops come, I'll go with them quietly. I don't have anything to tell them. And maybe they've found Jalen."

"Maybe." Manaia didn't sound pleased with the prospect.

The two of them were drawing near, and I decided it was time to make my presence known. I stepped into the beams of their flashlights. "Good evening, ladies. Nice night."

I shaded my eyes as the twin beams lit up my face.

Sonoma spoke first. "Mr. Southerland? Is that you?"

I stayed where I was, trying not to look threatening. "Yes. Would you mind lowering your lights? Thanks. I was hoping I could ask you a couple of questions before you joined your group. Do you have a moment?"

Sonoma sighed. "I suppose. Not too long, though. I don't want to hold up the ceremony."

I turned to her companion. "Manaia, you can go ahead if you want. This will only take a minute."

"Nothin' doin', buster. I stay."

Sonoma turned to her. "It's okay, Manaia. I'm safe with Mr. Southerland."

Manaia looked like she was going to argue, and I didn't have time for it. "It's all right, Sonoma. Manaia can stay if she wants, and if it's jake with you."

Both women looked at me. "What do you want to know?" Sonoma asked.

"What can you tell me about Colton Randolph? What happened there?"

Sonoma let out a breath. "I don't know. I really don't. Jalen and Mr. Randolph were talking for a while, and then Randolph curled up on the floor to take a nap. I remember thinking I should get him a blanket. But I must have fallen asleep myself. I was very tired. And hungry. The next thing I remember, I was on my hands and knees vomiting on the sidewalk outside a closed pawn shop three blocks from the apartment. I was covered in blood, and I didn't know why. I didn't know what had happened. I must have walked in my sleep. Jalen wasn't with me, and I turned around to go get him, but when I got to the apartment, the police were there. I got away before they could see me." She looked at me, her eyes anxious. "Do you know where Jalen is? Did the police take him?"

"I don't know where he is. The police don't either, as far as I know. Did he kill Randolph?"

Sonoma gave her head a dismissive shake. "Of course not! Why would he?"

"Randolph was with the two of you. If you didn't do it, then—"

Sonoma cut me off. "Then someone else must have done it. Manaia told me the man had been murdered, but I don't know anything about it. She said Jalen got away, but no one knows where he is." She reached up and rubbed her eyes. "I'm hoping he'll come here tonight. If he doesn't, then I don't know what I'm going to do."

"Are you sure you don't know what happened?"

Sonoma's jaw set. "I told you—I was sleeping! Afterward... I don't know. I don't know how I got to where I woke up. I can't explain it."

My skin prickled from head to toe as the pieces clicked into place and realization struck me like a body blow to the solar plexus. "Of course! I—"

It was only after I'd felt a sharp sting that I became aware of dark shapes in the trees all around me. I reached up and plucked a thorn from my neck. My legs lost their strength. As I felt myself toppling, I was aware of Sonoma and Manaia sinking to the ground, as well. The last thing I saw before my consciousness took a hike was the blurred face of a howler monkey inches from my own, saliva dripping from the fangs extending from behind his curled lips.

Chapter Thirty-Five

When I woke, I was lying on a marble altar, naked, in the middle of a jungle clearing lit by a rosy glow from a pink full moon hanging directly overhead. Ixquic stood over me, chanting under her breath. I couldn't move a muscle, but I was aware of other figures around me. Six howler monkeys were perched in the surrounding trees. The school kids who made up Ixquic's following were gathered in a group to one side of the altar, cloaked, hooded, kneeling, and chanting the name 'Ixquic' in low voices over and over again in unison. Drops of blood dribbled from their hands to the grass-covered ground. Three of the hooded disciples stood apart from the others behind three unconscious shapes slumped on the jungle floor. The disciples were holding the heads of the figures up by their hair with one hand. With the other, each held a knife to the exposed throats of the slumped victims. I recognized the unconscious figures as Manaia, Tlalli, and Tyanna: water, earth, and fire. Ixquic was going for all four elements. Even under the circumstances, I couldn't help but admire the elegance of her work.

The chanting grew louder, and as it did, I saw the skin on the right side of my abdomen part. I felt no pain as I watched a brown wedge-shaped object rise from the opening. I'd never much cared for the liver and onions my mother served as often as three times a week when my father was out of work and times were tough, and I liked it even less when the main course was being lifted out of my own body. Without the onions. As I watched, my liver rose to a spot a foot above my bloodless wound and hovered motionless. The air around the brown mass began to sparkle as tiny bolts of energy shot from the organ. A tingling sensation prickled the back of my eyes and spread to the top of my head. My surroundings faded, and my vision narrowed until I saw nothing beyond my liver hanging over my body in the shimmering light.

My head ached. It was filled with cheese, the kind with the holes in it. Thinking was for the living, and I was stepping off that train at the next stop. But I wasn't there yet. I tried to form the sigil for Badass in my mind, and then remembered Badass was dead, consumed by the Blood Moon. My own ticket was punched for the land of the dead, I realized. Xibalba, or wherever. The last stop. The end of the line. The train was already slowing down. Thinking about Xibalba reminded me of Chivo telling me over interlocked fingers through the voice of Siphon that the realms of dream and death share the same space.

Dream! I was dreaming! I'd been wrong when I'd told Chivo that I wouldn't be sleeping when I met Ixquic again. The realization was a splash of cold water in my face, and my heart began to pound. Ixquic was a *wayob*, and she could influence me in my dreams, but the dream was mine, and I had control over it.

I focused my vision on my liver, floating over the hole in my abdomen. Reminding myself that I could manipulate my dream, I tried to will my liver back into my body.

It was no use. No matter how much I fought with both my mind and my flesh, I couldn't force my liver back to where it belonged. I tried to envision myself free and whole, but I remained motionless on the altar under the pale pink light of the Blood Moon. Ixquic's iron grip on my dream was too strong. My own hands were swollen lumps of wet clay, soft, numb, and useless.

The memory of Chivo came to me again, speaking in his own voice: "Nnnooohhh puh... puh'rrr ohhhverrr deddd."

A smile came to my lips. My dream, like all dreams, overlapped the realm of the dead. I called out with my mind, and a great funnel of dust and flying debris descended from a black rip in the moonlit sky. In my dream, Badass had become something more than a whirlwind; the elemental had gathered the night winds and grown into a living tornado. Lightning flashed inside the dark whirling vortex as it fell to the earth, and Ixquic let out a bloodcurdling screech as the violently swirling twister swept her off the ground and into its midst.

I woke with a start to discover that I was lying—fully clothed, I noted with relief—atop a wooden picnic table in Bunker Park in the black night, no more than a hundred yards from the candles softly glowing for Clara Novita. A cloud blotted out the moon, and Ixquic and Hunbatz were nowhere to be seen. Neither was Badass. Ixquic's disciples were on their feet, hoods down and wandering aimlessly. I searched with my magical awareness for Jalen, but he wasn't with them. The three punks standing over Manaia, Tlalli, and Tyanna held their knives loosely in their hands and stared at each other in confusion. Their would-be victims were conscious and stirring but bound hand and foot with zip ties.

With a groan, I pushed myself to a sitting position. My right side felt as if a slug from a forty-five had passed through it, taking vital chunks of me with it, and my legs were useless slabs of meat. I tried to rub some life into them with my numb hands. "Hey!" I shouted at the three punks. "Cut them loose. Now!"

They turned to stare at me, but didn't otherwise move.

"I mean it," I said in my sternest voice, but I must not have seemed all that threatening sitting on the edge of a picnic table massaging my upper legs.

The punk standing over Tyanna lowered his knife to her throat. "Stay away from me, old man, or I'll cut her," he shouted. The other two punks followed his lead and threatened Manaia and Tlalli with their blades.

Old man? What the hell? I glared at the punk. Old man, indeed. Why, I was only... twice his age? I groaned out loud at the thought and momentarily forgot about anything else.

Tyanna turned her head to look up at the punk above her. She opened her mouth, and a cavernous masculine voice—a voice from a nightmare—emerged: "Stand away, you piece of filth!"

With a vigorous shake of my head, I focused on my present predicament.

The punk's eyes widened when he heard the sepulchral voice, but he held his ground and pressed the edge of his knife closer to Tyanna's throat. "Shut up, you old hag!"

Tyanna opened her mouth again, and a jet of flame shot a dozen feet into the air, passing close enough to the punk to singe his eyebrows. He leaped backward, his knife falling to the ground, turned, and beat feet into the park at a mile a minute, followed closely by the entire group of Ixquic's disciples.

I slid off the table on wobbly legs and used the punk's knife to cut Tyanna and Tlalli free. They hurried over to join the vigil. As I was cutting the ties from Manaia, I asked her, "Have you seen Sonoma?"

Manaia shook her head. "In case you hadn't noticed, I've been a little out of it. What happened?"

"I'll explain later. I need to find her."

Manaia nodded toward the candlelight. "Maybe she's with the others at the vigil. I hope so. It looks like they're in the middle of the memorial ceremony."

I gazed in the direction of the ceremony but couldn't focus my awareness. The various activities throughout the park were in full swing, and my mind was still reeling from my dream experience. "I'll go check," I said.

I heard Manaia gasp and turned back to see Ixquic standing tall in the pale pink glow of a moon no longer obscured by clouds. The furious gleam in her eyes made my skin crawl. I didn't hesitate. I reached inside my shoulder holster for my gat and put three slugs into the raging spirit's chest from point-blank range.

I heard screams and sensed people running from the sounds of gunfire. The bullets didn't stop her, of course. You can shoot the moon, but you won't bring it down with lead.

Manaia reached for Ixquic but fell tumbling back as if she'd been shoved. Ixquic hadn't even turned in her direction.

"Go find Sonoma!" I shouted at Manaia, more to get her out of the way than anything else, and she hustled off toward the others.

Ixquic took a step toward me. As I backed away, I sent out a mental call and felt it connect. "Now," I said with my mind. "Hurry."

Ixquic took another step toward me. Something I couldn't see slammed against my chest and sent me to the deck in a heap. My gat flew out of my hand and sailed off into the night. Ixquic took another slow, deliberate step in my direction. I scrambled away, panic grabbing me by the throat and squeezing hard.

Ixquic leaned over me, and I couldn't move. She spoke, and her voice dripped with menace. "Idiot! Do you know what you've done? You're useless to me now as a gift to Itzamna. But I have time. The moon will rise full again soon enough. You, however, are out of time. You may be useless as a gift, but I hunger, and you are still useful as food."

I tried to think of a clever and brave retort but came up empty. So much for famous last words.

She leaned closer, and I could feel her cold breath brush my ear. "Your death will not be the painless one it would have been if you hadn't interfered with my sacrifice. The pain you will suffer now will taste sweet."

Ixquic stood, and Sonoma stood behind her. Beneath the panicked screams and the din from the festival, a faint whistle rose in pitch and volume, and then fell: the call of the lapa, sounding far off in the distance.

Which meant that El Silbón, the Whistler, was near at hand.

Ixquic stepped to one side, giving me a full view of Sonoma Deerling standing in the darkness behind her. As I watched, she changed. Her body fell in on itself, becoming thin and wiry. Her legs shortened, her arms lengthened, and claws the size of daggers stretched from her fingertips. Her face twisted into an expression of pure fury. Her nose and mouth extended into a ferret-like snout, and her lips parted to reveal two rows of pointed teeth.

The demon that had been Sonoma closed its snout. Its lips circled into an "o," and a series of whistles emerged, one slow drawn-out call following the other, each one sounding as if it were coming from somewhere far away.

I pushed myself back and rose to my feet on legs that were still shaky. I tried to find Sonoma in the monster in front of me, but the only trace I could detect was the tattoo of a passionfruit flower on its right arm. Trying to beat the demon to the punch, I launched a short left hook at its earhole. The demon moved like lightning. Catching my fist in its hand, it squeezed with strength that was more than human. I heard the popping of bones.

I let out a yelp and kicked at the side of the demon's knee. It was like kicking a tree trunk. The Whistler, still crushing my left hand, picked me off the turf and tossed me twenty yards through the air. I hit the ground like I'd fallen from a two-story building. The air whooshed out of my lungs, which refused to replace the supply I'd lost. Knowing I was overmatched, I looked up and groaned. The monster was coming for me, and I knew I wouldn't be able to do anything to stop it.

Suddenly, the demon lurched forward. A brown ball of fur and fury had buried its teeth in the Whistler's hip and was hanging from it. At first I thought it was one of Hunbatz's howler monkeys, but when a second one hit I saw that it was a dog with a broad chest, oversized jaws, close-set eyes, and short, stubby ears. The second dog closed its powerful jaws on the Whistler's hamstring and twisted just as the monster brushed the first dog off its hip. As the monster turned to swipe the second dog away, a third dog shot through the grass and sank its fangs into the back of the demon's ankle.

The Whistler screamed, not a whistle, but a high-pitched wail that sounded as if it were coming from a child. As it sank to one knee, batting at the dogs, a fourth dog arrived and leapt for the demon's throat. The Whistler found itself on its back, pulling dogs off its body and tossing them away, only for the dogs to scramble to their feet and resume their attacks. Finally, the Whistler rolled into a ball on the grass and let out loud piercing cries of pain and despair.

I caught a movement beyond the struggling figures and looked up to see Detective Kalama, Smokey at her shoulder, sprinting across the park with a squad of officers. When she drew near, she shouted, "That's enough, Blu." The four bulldogs ceased worrying at the slashed and bloody body of the demon and backed away from it. As I rose to my feet, the dogs stepped into each other, merged, and I found myself staring at Detective Blu, who was panting openmouthed and wiping saliva off his chin with a bare arm. An officer ran to him with a coat and a pair of sweats, and the detective slipped them on.

Kalama nodded at the demon, still rolled up in the fetal position on the grass and whimpering like a baby. "Cuff that thing," she commanded, and an officer carrying an unusually thick set of silver shackles moved to obey.

Before the officer could reach the body, it gave a violent shudder, and a gray mist rose from it into the air, leaving the unconscious form of Sonoma lying in the grass. Ixquic stood near her prone body, the spirit's ivory face shining in the darkness. I rubbed my good hand over my eyes. It seemed as if the moon spirit had been there all along, unnoticed. She drew in a breath, and the mist disappeared between her dark lips.

Ixquic glared at me, and she began to shine with a pale red glow. "You think these weak fools can protect you from me? My hunger burns. Your death will be excruciating."

Every officer in the area flashed iron. A hundred yards away, a crowd of people holding candles, their ceremony interrupted, peered at the glowing spirit of the Blood Moon, no doubt wondering at the presence of the police on the festival grounds. Further in the distance, the crowds had thinned, the covens, partiers, and oglers abandoning the park for safer and friendlier environs. Ixquic, smiling, swung her head slowly from one side to the other, letting her eyes drift over the faces of the officers. Perceiving no threat from any of them, she took a step in my direction.

A growl filled the air. Ixquic stopped, a look of annoyance on her face. She turned to face a large wolf with silver fur and liquid orange eyes. When she spoke to the wolf, her voice was sultry. "What is it, father? You wish this meal for yourself? Find another. This one is mine."

A clear voice came from the mouth of the wolf. "It's true, then. You infected my chosen with the demon who hungers. You have violated the envoy I sent to negotiate an agreement between the two of us. This is unacceptable."

Ixquic faced down the wolf. Her voice, when she spoke, dripped with venom. "Spare me your mock outrage, elder. When have you ever played by the rules? Even now you take the form of the gentle wolf. But I see you for who you are. Did you think I didn't know your favorite was back in your fold? Why do you bother trying to hide it? Lord Cadmael is with you now. Drop the disguise! Show me your true form!"

The wolf shook its head. "You violated my envoy. I cannot forgive you for that. There will be no agreement between us. I will not support you in your quest to receive the blessings of Itzamna."

Ixquic laughed. "Do you think I need you now? All I need is Lord Cadmael, and, thanks to you, he is now within my reach. Don't you see? Everything I've done has led to this moment. You have brought me my prize, and I am prepared to take it."

Ixquic didn't do anything I could detect, but the silver wolf shimmered with a light so bright I had to turn my head away. When I turned back again, the wolf was gone. In its place stood two figures: the Huay Chivo, standing on all fours, and a living corpse, at least seven-feet tall, with a cigarette dangling from a broad slit in its skull where a mouth would be.

Ixquic pointed a finger at the other spirit, now revealed as Cizin in his ancient form. "You speak to me of violation, yet you have taken back your chosen in violation of the conditions of your surrender to my sons. The bond between you and Cadmael is now broken. This creature belongs to me, and I will sacrifice his life to Itzamna, as I have promised." She opened her hand. "Give him to me. You cannot refuse. You have lost the right."

The air between the two unearthly spirits sizzled with energy. I stared, transfixed, along with Kalama and her officers. None of us moved. In the presence of such power, I'm not sure we could.

Sonoma lay at Ixquic's feet, her breathing shallow and erratic. Blood was leaking from the wounds she'd suffered from the dog attack, and I knew she needed immediate treatment. I wanted to take her to safety, but my feet were rooted to the ground.

I sent out a call for Cougar, but my spirit animal didn't respond. Still sitting this one out, I thought, not without anger.

Neither spirit moved, but Chivo stood on his hind legs and took a halting step toward Ixquic. Wind brushed my ear. I couldn't remember when Smokey had come to me, but the whirling funnel of air was perched on my shoulder. The elemental's voice, unconcerned by spirits and demons, sounded in my mind: "Hello, Alekkkssss. Howsss trickssss?"

I don't know how, but Smokey's voice broke the spell that had immobilized me. Maybe it was because the air elemental, who had been around since the formation of the earth's atmosphere, was older than the spirits of the Blood Moon and the Dead, who, if Kalama's husband, Kai, was correct, had taken shape as a result of the stories told by the elves to the first sentient humans. Maybe it was simply because the tiny creature was unawed by the confrontation of these terrible powers I couldn't begin to understand. In any case, when Smokey's voice entered my mind, I regained my ability to move.

"Thanks, Smokey," I muttered, rushing toward the wounded and unconscious Sonoma. As I crouched to lift her off the ground, Ixquic turned, an expression of surprise on her face. Her features twisted with fury when she saw what I was doing. Her eyes flashed as she raised her arm to sweep me away with a backhand slap that likely would have taken my head off.

"Don't do it!"

Ixquic froze in mid blow at the sound of the new voice and turned to find its source. I turned with her. Mrs. Garza stood a few yards away, the hunting rifle I'd seen mounted on her wall pointed at Ixquic.

Ixquic's lips spread into a smile that exposed the pointed tips of her teeth. "And what's this, then?" she asked, amused.

"Mrs. Garza! Don't!" I called. "Get back!"

"That's okay, champ," said a voice from behind me.

I whirled and gaped, astonished, at Stormclaw, fedora on his hairless head, red eyes glowing through his shades, and a flask of trollshine in his hand. "You go ahead and stand on back. I'll tend to the woman."

Ixquic whirled on the troll, exasperated. "What the everlasting *fuck*!"

"Southerland?" Kalama called to me. "What's going on here?"

I tore my gaze from Stormclaw. Cops were pointing their pieces at everyone, unsure who posed the most threat. Cizin puffed on his cigarette, while Chivo glanced back and forth staring at Stormclaw and Mrs. Garza. Was that a smile on his lips? I turned toward Kalama. "Beats me, Detective. But I think it's above our pay grades."

Ixquic stamped her foot, as if she'd been told she wouldn't be able to attend the party at the yacht club. "I am going to sacrifice all of you to Itzamna!"

"Sorry honey," Mrs. Garza said. "We don't accept your offering."

Ixquic whirled on her, and froze. "What did you say?"

Stormclaw, who had been kneeling next to Sonoma, stood. "We find your actions reckless. Your request for our blessing is denied."

Stormclaw stepped toward Mrs. Garza, who shuffled across the grass in his direction. When the two met, they merged into a single figure, the most ancient-looking man I'd ever seen. He was short and stooped almost double, propping himself up with a short staff. His back was hunched, his head nearly hairless except for a few long wiry strands sprouting out of his nose and ears. A ragged and filthy white robe failed to conceal arms and legs as thin as sticks. He peered at the rest of us with rheumy eyes, and his broad smile was toothless.

Ixquic's knees gave way, and she stumbled to keep her feet. "Itzamna," she breathed.

The night darkened. I looked up and watched a shadow creep over the face of the waning full moon.

Chapter Thirty-Six

"Well," croaked the ancient spirit. "Waning Blood Moon and the Lord of Xibalba. My, my, my. Don't just stand there gawking like empty-headed fools. Come over here. I'm displeased with you both. Very displeased. Quickly now, let's get this over with."

As Ixquic moved away, I bent down to check on Sonoma, who was sitting up and looking around her with a frown. "What happened?" she asked.

The odor of trollshine on her breath almost knocked me over. Drawing back a bit, I asked, "What's the last thing you remember?"

Sonoma looked up at me, her face twisted with confusion. She struggled to catch her breath. "Talking with you in the trees, I think. And then.... And then, I think I got stung in the neck by a wasp." She looked down at her bruised and slashed legs. "Have I been bleeding?"

"I suspect you're okay now," I assured her.

Kalama came over to join us, a pair of handcuffs in her hand. I gave the cuffs a pointed look before looking up at the detective. "Are those things necessary?"

Kalama ignored me. "Sonoma Deerling? You're wanted for questioning in the deaths of Clara Novita and Colton Randolph, and a whole lot of other things, besides. You're not under arrest at this time, but I recommend you get yourself a good lawyer."

Sonoma looked at me, a question in her eyes.

"It wasn't her," I told Kalama. "She didn't kill Mrs. Novita. It was the thing that possessed her."

Kalama stared at me.

"It was El Silbón," I said. "The Whistler."

Kalama shook her head. "We'll have to bring her in for questioning."

"I'll call Lubank. I'm sure he'll take Mrs. Deerling's case." I gave Sonoma what I hoped was a reassuring smile. "Go ahead and let them take you in," I told her. "Don't say anything until my lawyer gets there."

Sonoma rose to her feet, aided by two officers. Looking around, she asked, "Is Jalen here? Have you seen him?"

I shook my head. "He seems to have missed this show. Don't worry about him, though. I'm sure he'll turn up."

Manaia came running over then and pulled Sonoma into an embrace. Tears were in her eyes as she said, "Don't tell them nothing. You haven't done nothing wrong."

Kalama gave me a meaningful glance.

I reached for Manaia with my unbroken hand and gently pulled her away from Sonoma. "It'll be okay. She'll be represented by the best attorney in the city. But we have to let her go now."

Manaia looked like she wanted to protest, but Sonoma took her by the hand. "It's fine. We knew this would happen. It was only a matter of time."

Kalama put a hand on Sonoma's elbow and led her away without cuffing her. Most of the officers went with them, while a few headed toward the site of the candlelight vigil. Manaia watched Sonoma go, her eyes dry and her jaw tight. She turned to me with an angry glare before stomping off to join her friends at the vigil. I got the feeling she blamed me for everything that had happened. I guess I just had one of those faces.

Smokey floated in front of me, and, with a resigned sigh, I turned my attention away from the adaro. "Good job, tonight, Smokey," I said, and held out my good hand, palm up.

Smokey settled on my palm. "Smokey is happy to serve Alekkssss. Smokey thinks Detective Kalama is ssswellll."

I let out a chuckle. "Yeah, she's not a bad lady. For a cop." I looked up. The shadow that had been covering the moon was sliding off its face. "I'd better release you for the night, Smokey. Looks like I'm about to have company. Thanks again."

Smokey stretched itself and narrowed. The tiny elemental bent slightly at the waist, straightened, and shot into the night over the head of Stormclaw, who was leading Chivo by the hand in my direction.

"Southerland," Stormclaw drawled when he reached me.

"Lord's flaming balls, Stormclaw." I hesitated. "Or is it Itzamna?"

Stormclaw shrugged. "Does it matter?"

"Yes, it matters!"

The troll smiled. "I'm still Stormclaw. Itzamna is in there somewhere. He's in a lot of places, all over the world. Most of the time, I don't notice him. Sometimes, I do."

I stared at the troll for a few moments before shaking my head. "Is it all done?"

"Yep. The Blood Moon is going to behave. She won't invade your dreams anymore. She won't try to sacrifice you again, either."

I wiped perspiration off the side of my face. "That's a relief. And Cizin?"

"He'll go back to guiding the dead to Xibalba and staying out of politics. He'll be a wolf now, and not a smoking skull." Stormclaw nodded toward Chivo, who had been standing quietly at his side, his head bowed. "The Huay Chivo has been communing with Cizin during the night. That will stop. He will be given a new task soon, but, for now, Itzamna would appreciate it if you would continue to allow him to stay in your home."

I looked at Chivo. "That's jake with me."

Chivo didn't look up.

I frowned. "What's the matter with him?"

Stormclaw turned to look at Chivo. "He's fine. I think he's sulking. Itzamna has halted his cure at its current stage. If he behaves, his case may be reconsidered."

"When?" I asked.

Stormclaw shrugged. "This whole mess has left Itzamna tuckered out. It will likely be a while before he gets around to it."

Chivo's head slowly raised, and he fixed a glare on Stormclaw. The spikes along his spine straightened, and his long rat's tail swept slowly back and forth over the grass. Stormclaw removed his shades and stared back at Chivo, one set of glowing red eyes meeting the other. After a few seconds, the troll reached out and rapped one of Chivo's curved horns with the flat of his hand, knocking the goatlike creature off balance and breaking their staring contest.

"Trust me, beast man," Stormclaw told him. "You're better off without the death lord. Why do you think he summoned you tonight? He would have given you up to Blood Moon without a second thought if he hadn't found out she sent a demon to possess his envoy. Stay with Southerland. Watch over his home and keep your nose clean. And remember, Itzamna has his eye on you."

Chivo let out a bleat and nodded his head. He looked at me, shrugged, and lowered himself to all fours.

Stormclaw gave me a brief nod before turning and shuffling away.

***

My sleep was fitful that night, and not just because of the ache in my heavily taped up left hand. I spent all night tossing and turning, expecting Ixquic to drop in on my dreams. The spirit never showed up, but I was nonetheless restless with expectation, which I didn't think was fair at all. But that's the way the cookie crumbles.

In a reversal of habits, Chivo slept all night. When I checked in on him in the morning, he was curled up in his bed reading a book. I had no idea where he'd picked it up. It certainly wasn't one of mine. I had a bookcase filled with paperback thrillers, but I'd never owned an oversized tome with a tattered leather cover and a title embossed in stained gold leaf characters I didn't recognize.

He nodded a greeting at me and glanced up at Siphon, who, as usual, was pulling in cool fresh air from the open window. Siphon's trumpet-like voice transmitted Chivo's words: "After being barely conscious for half a millennium, I've quite a lot of catching up to do."

"Wait'll you discover the internet," I told him, but his concentration had returned to his reading. I closed the door and left him to it.

That evening, I was finishing up a bowl of canned beef stew and enjoying a cup of joe when I received a call on my cellphone. When I saw who it was, I toyed with letting the call go to voicemail before tapping the connect button just in the nick of time.

"What can I do for you, Miss Hunbatz."

Her voice was frantic. "Duffy is at my house." She gave me an address in Huaxiatown. "He says he's going to kill me unless you get over here right away!"

"Let me talk to him," I said.

I heard Duffy's voice in the distance. "Tell him to come right *now*!"

"He won't take the phone. He's got a blowgun."

"All right," I said. "I'm on my way. But tell him it's going to take me a half hour, at least."

"Hurry!" she said before disconnecting.

I stuffed my phone in my pocket and stared at the ceiling. I'd sincerely hoped never to hear from either of the Hunbatz twins again. Climbing to my feet, I gathered up my coat, hat, and gun, and stopped by the laundry room to tell Chivo I was going to be out for a bit. The room was freezing. Chivo ignored me, his eyes fixed on a page of his book while muttering something that sounded like an incantation. Hoping he wasn't trying to renew his contact with the Lord of Xibalba—or call up a demon—I closed the door as silently as possible and slipped away.

Twenty minutes later, shouts from the Hunbatz twins reached me from half a block away as I locked up the beastmobile and hustled my way to Cozumel's apartment. The screeching voices made it easy to find.

A group of middle-aged women stood outside a ground-floor apartment looking uneasy. One of them turned to me as I approached. "Are you the police?" she asked.

"No, but you should call them."

"We did," she said. "A half hour ago."

"All right, stand clear. I'll take it from here." I moved past the onlookers to the front door.

After knocking and shouting, "It's me, Southerland," I tested the doorknob and found it unlocked. "I'm coming in."

Cozumel's hands and feet were zip-tied to a kitchen chair in the middle of the living room, and blood trickled from a cut over her eye. Duffy stood a few feet away from her, holding a two-foot wooden blowgun in his outstretched hand as if it were a sword. Tears streaked down his cheeks into his thick bush of a beard. They both watched me as I stepped through the door.

I kept my voice steady. "What's going on here, Duffy?"

"She wants to kill me!" he wailed, pointing at his sister with his blowgun.

"I'm the one tied to a chair, you imbecile!" Cozumel fired back.

"Don't call me names, you slut!"

"Fuck you, moron!"

That was enough for me. "Shut up! Both of you. Cozumel, quit using those words with your brother. It's rude. Duffy, quit acting like an animal and untie your sister."

Duffy whirled on me. "I'm not an animal!"

"Prove it," I said. "Cut her loose."

Cozumel twisted her head in my direction. "*You* cut me loose. I don't want that retard anywhere near me."

I sighed. "You're not making this easy, Cozumel."

Her face reddened. "Whose side are you on!"

I raised my hands in a shrug. "I'm not on anyone's side. I'm just trying to keep you two from murdering each other."

Duffy glared at his sister. "If I turn her loose, she'll kill me."

"She's not going to kill you," I said. "Are you, Cozumel."

Cozumel's eyes narrowed. "Cut me loose and we'll find out."

Duffy's eyes widened. "See? See?"

I sighed and rubbed the bridge of my nose with my one good hand. "Duffy? What is it you want?"

Duffy's face twisted in confusion. "I... I..."

"He doesn't know what he wants," Cozumel said, scorn dripping from every word. "His 'goddess' is gone, and he doesn't know what to do without her."

I turned to Duffy. "Is that right, Duffy? Ixquic left you behind?"

Duffy's eyes teared up. "She's gone. She won't take me home."

"To your apartment?"

"No, stupid! To the jungle. The jungle is my home. I want to go back."

"What about Night Owl?"

Duffy's shoulders slumped. "Night Owl won't talk to me anymore."

That figured. Night Owl only helped those who could help him. I wondered if the police would be showing up soon. Or at all.

"I can send you to the jungle, Duffy. Would you like that?"

Duffy turned to me, eyes filled with hope. "Can you? Can you send me home?"

"I'll buy you a plane ticket. You can fly to the Borderland."

Duffy's face twisted. "No! I don't want to fly. I don't like to fly."

Cozumel lowered her head and shook it. "Fucking loser." I glared at her.

Duffy whirled to face her. "Shut up! I'm not a loser!" He lifted his blowgun, prepared to use it like a billy club.

Things were getting out of hand, or, to be more precise, even more out of hand. I stepped in before Duffy could club his sister and shoved him away from her with both hands, grimacing as pain shot through my left arm. "None of that, Duffy. Striking a woman with a blunt instrument while she's tied up isn't fair."

Cozumel's voice was laced with sarcasm. "Stupid little man. You hit me once, and, believe me, you've got nothing. That monkey we shot must have been the one with the balls. Go ahead. Hit me again, little man."

I stepped between them. "Enough!" I shouted. I turned to Cozumel. "Alkwat's flaming pecker, woman! Keep it up and I'm leaving. You hear me?" She gave me a look that would have curdled milk.

A siren sounded in the distance, and I let out a breath. It was about fucking time.

I turned to the brother. "You hear that, Duffy? The cops are coming. They want you for the murder of your parents. Let's cut your sister loose and get out of here. I'll find a way to get you to the Borderland. Promise. Okay, champ?"

Duffy's eyes widened and his lips twisted into a knot. "The police? I don't want the police."

"I don't want them either, champ. Come on. We need to leave now. The police will take care of your sister."

"You're not fuckin' leaving me for the cops, buster. There's a knife in the kitchen. Cut me loose."

"No time," I told her. "The cops don't want you for anything. They'll free you and you can tell them what happened." Turning back to Duffy, I said, "Come on, Duffy. Time to get out of here."

"Sure, run, you motherfuckin' monkey!" screamed Cozumel. "You won't get far. The cops will be watching the airport. They'll shoot you on sight like the crazy animal you are! And your precious Blood Moon won't do a thing to stop them. She doesn't want you anymore. You're a fuckin' loser, and you don't got no one!"

Duffy stepped back and lifted his blowgun. "I never fucked my mother! You fucked my daddy! You're bad! You're a daddy fucker!" With a deft motion, he plucked a thorn from his pocket and stuffed it into the mouthpiece of the blowgun.

"Don't do it, Duffy!" I shouted, reaching inside my coat for my gat.

"Get back!" Duffy shouted at me. "I'll kill you both!"

"Don't let him do it!" shrieked Cozumel.

Duffy drew in a breath and looked straight into my eyes. He raised the blowgun to his lips and pointed it at me.

I knew I'd never be able to close on him before he let me have it. I had no choice. I drew my gun. He puffed. I squeezed the trigger.

Epilogue

"It was well done, all things considered. It pleases me that you survived." The elf's sea-green eyes reflected the light of the moon setting over the water.

"Thanks," I said. "I'm happy about it, too. Life for us humans is brief enough as it is."

We stood, as usual, at the end of the Old Placid Point Pier under a starry sky, the sound of crashing waves filling the air. A brisk wind blew into my face, but the cold couldn't touch me in this dream that wasn't a dream.

"I'm still not clear about a few things," I said. "What was Ixquic up to? What was her game?"

The elf's grin deepened the wrinkles around his eyes. "Her *game*, as you put it. Indeed. Ixquic, the Waning Blood Moon, has long attempted to enlist the aid of her father, Cizin, the Lord of Xibalba, in her scheme to secure the blessings of Itzamna, the ruler of the sky. Itzamna perceives Ixquic as young and irresponsible. Cizin has ever been more highly regarded by the Lord of the Sky, and Ixquic desired her father to speak to Itzamna on her behalf. Cizin had little attention to give to his daughter, and he grew to loathe her after she brought the Dragon Lords Ketz-Alkwat and Manqu from Hell. But she was his daughter, and he agreed to let her speak to him through one of his chosen."

"Sonoma Deerling."

"Yes. The human acted as Cizin's envoy. But Cizin had also given this chosen another task: find the Huay Chivo, once known as Lord Cadmael."

"And she found him when she came to my office after she'd discovered her wife had hired me to find out where their son was going during the night."

The elf nodded. "She gave her blood to the Huay Chivo. I believe that awakened the spirit of hunger that had been lying dormant within her."

"The Whistler, right? That's the spirit of hunger? I thought it was a demon."

"A demon is nothing more than a spirit who means you harm," the elf said, shrugging. "One man's demon is another man's angel, and so the opposite. This particular spirit of hunger is Ixquic's creature. If she is using the spirit against you, then it can be called a demon. She sent the spirit to lie in secret within Cizin's envoy the first time they met. He was to be Ixquic's eyes and ears when the envoy returned to Cizin."

"The Whistler was Ixquic's spy? And Sonoma was unaware she was possessed?"

"That is correct."

"Huh. Spirits are worse than humans."

The elf's smile broadened. "Not worse, but certainly no better, since the spirits of this world were shaped by the minds of humans. And that would be a good thing to remember the next time you find yourself involved in the affairs of spirits."

I shuddered. The less I saw of spirits in the future, the better.

The elf turned his gaze to the moon over the ocean. "Ixquic learned from the hunger spirit that the Huay Chivo had been discovered. Her plans changed. Lord Cadmael was a person of enormous energies, a sorcerer who had proved himself a bulwark against Lords Ketz-Alkwat and Manqu for many years. She believed she no longer needed Cizin's help. She believed that Itzamna would accept her gift of Cadmael's potent energies and give her the blessings she sought in return. But she lacked the power to enter Cadmael's dreams. Even in his lesser form as the Huay Chivo he was too strong for her."

"She thought I'd be able to kill Chivo and take his heart and liver for her."

The elf nodded. "You and he had built a trust. She believed you could be persuaded to betray him in order to save your own life."

"Or tricked."

"In the end," the elf said, "she manipulated events so that Cizin would bring Cadmael within her reach. And within the reach of the spirit of hunger. The two of them together may very well have been able to subdue Cadmael in his lesser state."

"But the Whistler was ambushed by a pack of bulldogs. The way I hear it, he never had much luck with dogs, not since his grandfather chased him out of his village with a pack of them. Where is he now? I saw something leave Sonoma's body, and then Ixquic came and sucked it out of the air." The same way she'd taken Badass, I remembered.

"Then she may still have the hunger spirit."

That didn't sound good to me at all. "Could it be dead? I mean, do spirits die?"

The elf shrugged. "Of course. But death to a spirit is something different than death to a human. Or an elf."

"What about the death of an elemental?"

"Elementals are a type of spirit, and they die the death of a spirit. I could teach you about such things if you were younger. At its current stage of development, however, I fear your brain no longer has the flexibility to absorb such foundational knowledge without much reshaping and preparation. The process can be painful."

I shook my head. Maybe I'd see Badass again, and maybe I wouldn't. And if I did, would it still be the spirit I'd known? "Never mind," I told the elf. "I don't want to know."

***

I awakened to the sound of metal sliding into metal and the opening of my cell door.

"Wake up, bright eyes! Check out time. Alkwat's balls! Guard! Give my client something he can use to wipe that drool off his face. That's disgusting!"

I sat up in the bed and used the thin stained pillow to wipe my mouth. Turning my bleary eyes to Lubank, I asked, "Is that better? I didn't know you were so sensitive."

"Th'fuck!" The attorney looked me up and down with a disapproving snarl. "You look like you've been on a bender."

"I haven't had a drink in... I can't remember. The cops wouldn't let me have one while they were questioning me." I reached for my hat, which had fallen to the floor sometime during the morning.

"Yeah, well, you're a mess. What the fuck happened to your hand? Never mind, you can tell me later. Let's get out of here before they change their minds and charge you with murder."

I stopped. "Murder? Did he die?"

"Hunbatz? Yeah, he croaked on the operating table. But the dame spoke up for you. She said it was self-defense. The D.A. is jake with it. He told me to thank you for helping them wrap up a fourteen-year-old cold case. He's happy to have one less unsolved murder on their books."

"Gee. Maybe I should ask for a medal."

"You willing to settle for lunch? I'm starving!"

I looked at him. "Are you possessed by the spirit of hunger?"

"The spirit of.... Alkwat's balls, Southerland! Th'fuck you talking about."

I climbed to my feet, shaking off the remnants of some unremembered dream. "Never mind. Wait. You're springing for lunch?"

"Sure. I'll just add it to your bill. By the way, I had a visit from Anton Benning this morning. Seems that someone broke into the Peninsula Property Management office a couple of nights ago." He gave me a sidelong glance. "That's a Hatfield-owned business, in case you didn't know."

I stifled a yawn. "Is that right?"

"According to Benning, they caught the perp on their security tape. Funny thing, though. They seem to have misplaced the tape."

I perked up. "Really? That was careless of them."

Lubank nodded. "Sure was. Benning says the damage was minor, and nothing of value was taken, so they don't plan to report the break-in to the police. But they're performing an in-house investigation, just in case the intruder ran off with something valuable that they haven't noticed yet. If that were the case, then Benning thinks they'd be able to find the missing security tape and see that a friendly judge threw the book at the offender."

My heart sank. "Sounds like whoever broke in might owe Benning a favor or two."

"That's the way I read it, too," Lubank said. "Too bad for the poor bum, whoever he is. Personally, I'd rather do time than be in debt to the Hatfields."

I followed Lubank out of the cophouse, nominally free, my back breaking under the weight of a heavy debt.

Later, over a platter of curried shrimp and rice at a Huaxian diner, Lubank told me that the thorn from Duffy Hunbatz's blowgun had been dry: no toxins.

I swallowed. "Where'd they find it?"

Lubank put down his fork and sat back in his seat. "It was stuck in the wall. Your shot made him miss, but it didn't matter. It wouldn't have done anything to you except sting a little. The fuckin' thing was a blank."

I grimaced. "He knew it. He didn't want to hurt me. He wanted me to take him out."

Lubank nodded. "Yep. It was suicide all the way."

I let out a breath. "He didn't want the cops to do it. He wanted it to be me."

"Looks that way. I guess he liked you."

I put down my fork. "Or he wanted to punish me."

"I wouldn't feel too bad about it. He murdered his parents. He had his sister zip-tied to a chair. Guy like that, he's better off pushing up daisies."

I sighed. "I don't know. A lot of things pushed him to be what he turned out to be."

Lubank shrugged and picked up his fork. "We all get pushed. Some of us are better at pushing back."

Maybe so, I thought to myself. Maybe that's what he'd been doing since the day he'd discovered he was a shapeshifter. Pushing back at parents who tried to beat the "disease" out of him. Pushing back at a guiding spirit who made him do things he didn't want to do. Pushing back at a sister who wouldn't stop berating him even while tied to a chair. And, finally, on his own with no place to go, pushing back at a man he knew would push back a little harder so that he wouldn't have to take being pushed around anymore.

***

I was arranging the new furniture in my office when Cozumel Hunbatz arrived with a check in her hand.

"You did the job," she told me, sitting in a brand new customer's chair. "You did what I asked you to do."

"Keep it. I wasn't on the case anymore, remember? Your retainer is all you owed me."

She brushed away a lock of hair that had fallen across her cheek. "Take the dough. You earned it."

"I told you before, I'm not an assassin."

"It wasn't an assassination. He kidnapped me in my own home." She dropped the check on my desk and leaned forward, putting both elbows on my desktop and her chin in her hands. "He attacked you, and he probably would have killed me. You stopped him. It was noble of you."

The last thing I wanted to hear was how noble I was for pumping lead into a poor sap who wanted to die. On the other hand, my rent was coming due, and the new furniture hadn't been cheap.

"All right, Miss Hunbatz. But we're square. Next time you get in trouble, call the cops."

I reached for the check, and Miss Hunbatz dropped a gentle hand over mine, the one that was still taped up. She looked past my shoulder to the staircase leading up to my apartment. "Do you live upstairs?"

"Yes."

"Anyone up there?"

"No."

Her eyes found mine. "How 'bout you show me your stamp collection."

"I don't collect stamps," I said.

"That's okay." She rose from her chair and started for the staircase. "Neither do I."

The sex was mean, violent, and quick. When it was over, she rolled off me and slid her panties on under her skirt. After I'd walked her downstairs to the front door, she took me by the back of the head with both hands and kissed me hard. She stood on her tiptoes and brushed my ear with her lips. "Thanks for killing the son of a bitch," she hissed.

She hurried out the door without looking back.

***

When the next full moon rose, it ducked behind a thick layer of low-hanging clouds, embarrassed to show itself. A salty breeze pushed at the brim of my fedora on my eight-block walk to the Black Minotaur Lounge, where I planned to munch deep-fried calamari and put away a few beers before resuming my diet in the morning. I'd weighed in that morning at two-twenty-one and reasoned that if I put on another few pounds during the night, I'd be extra motivated to get serious about dropping back down to two-ten. The logic is sound. Trust me.

Tayanna had called me that afternoon to tell me that Sonoma Deerling had moved out of the city. Jalen was still missing, despite an intensive search by the YCPD. According to Tayanna, Sonoma believed her son was on his way back to Cutzyetelkeh, and she was determined to find him.

"She lost her job, you know," Tayanna told me. "The city wouldn't keep her on with all the legal troubles. They're not saying so out loud, but I think they're afraid of having their buses driven by someone who was possessed by a demon. They're afraid she might be susceptible to possession if the Whistler were to show up again."

"I'll bet Lubank could have forced the city to take her back," I said.

"Maybe. But it could be that with Clara gone and Jalen missing, Yerba City simply doesn't have anything to offer her anymore. Manaia tried to talk her into staying, but I think her attraction to Sonoma was more one-sided than she thought."

The district attorney had decided not to press charges, reasoning that Sonoma hadn't been in control of her actions. The law was a little murky when it came to crimes committed while possessed, but Lubank planted a story in the media hinting at some shady real estate deals involving the D.A.'s son and members of the Hatfield family, and the D.A. decided that the time wasn't ripe to take a stand on the controversial possession issue.

Tayanna went on to tell me that the Children of Cizin had elected her to be their new leader. "We were originally formed to find the Huay Chivo," she explained. "We don't have a purpose like that anymore, so we're going to be strictly a social club now. No more blood rituals. We'll still be wringing chicken necks for barbecues, though. Speaking of which, we're going to be hosting a mixer in a few weeks. Barbecued chicken, a live band, dancing.... I'll send you a formal invitation."

"Sounds like fun. Should I bring Chivo?"

Tayanna laughed. "Now wouldn't *that* be interesting. I'd pay good money to watch him shake a leg on the dance floor."

The mental image of the goat creature kicking up his heels with a dance partner was still bringing a smile to my lips as I made my way to the Minotaur. Chivo had been spending far too much time with his books lately. I'd found him a bookcase and a desk at a thrift store, and my laundry room was slowly being converted into the old sorcerer's private office. He hadn't seemed all that happy when I'd installed a new washer and dryer in the room, but I'd reminded him that he contributed nothing to the rent, so he'd have to accept a few inconveniences. I moved my weights up to my bedroom, though, and gave up on the idea of hanging a new heavy bag.

As I drew near to the Minotaur, my attention was drawn by a commotion up the street. A young man in an army jacket stood atop a wooden crate and harangued the gathering crowd with a speech denouncing the fighting in the Borderland. Both of his arms were intact, but he was using one to hold a crutch, which he leaned on for support. I scanned the area for a big, black sedan and found it nearby. The troll sitting behind the wheel wasn't Stormclaw.

A sudden gust of wind threatened to take my hat off my head, and I felt something brush against my mind, soft as a feather and quickly gone. Whatever it was stopped me in my tracks, and I tuned out the rabblerouser's speech.

Badass? I called up the elemental's sigil and sent out the call.

Nothing. No response. I tried again and again with the same result, fighting back a tear or two. Had I imagined it? Had it been another elemental, similar enough to remind me of Badass? I opened my mind to the world of elementals and searched among the wind currents. A few air spirits wandered by, but none of them were the one I was looking for. I took a deep breath and continued walking. Was Badass dead? Could the wind really die? Surely, I thought, it could only be stilled for a time. Or did it dissipate and reform itself into new swirls, gusts, and eddies? If that was the case, then Badass was still out there somewhere, still a part of the atmosphere, but scattered, redistributed, pieces of the old Badass combined with other gusts of wind and reshaped into new elementals. Not gone, then, but transformed into something both familiar and new.

Stupid ideas, maybe, but I took comfort in them. The elf could tell me whether they held any water. The old elf, one of the ancient teachers of humankind.... Yeah, he'd be able to tell me a thing or two about life and death and the creation and dissolution of spirits. All I had to do was ask him. I chuckled to myself, knowing I never would. Knowing that, sometimes, believing is more satisfying than knowing. Ahead of me, the sign over the Black Minotaur Lounge spilled its neon light into the street and over the crowd listening to the would-be revolutionary's rants. I pulled the brim of my hat down over my forehead and pushed my way against the breeze toward the door.

The End

Thank You!

Thank you for reading *The Blood Moon Feeds on My Dreams: A Noir Urban Fantasy Novel*. If you enjoyed it, I hope that you will consider writing a review—even a short one—on Amazon, Goodreads, or your favorite book site. Publishing is still driven by word of mouth, and every single voice helps. I'm working hard to bring Alex Southerland back, and knowing that readers might be interested in hearing more about his adventures in Yerba City will certainly speed up the process!

Acknowledgements

I had a lot of help with this one. First and foremost, as always, I want to thank Rita, my co-creator, co-editor, sounding board, best friend, wife, partner, inspiration, and hero. We wrote another one, pal!

A big thank you to my parents, Bill and Carolyn, for being there for me, and to my sisters, Teri and Karen, two of the best beta readers around. The encouragement I get from my family is *HUGE*, and I deeply appreciate it.

I want to thank Elaine, who has a supernatural ability to spot typos, no matter how hard they try to hide from her eagle eyes.

My thanks once again to Assaph Mehr, author of the fantastic *Stories of Togas, Daggers, and Magic* series, for his thorough review of my manuscript. If you like the Southerland books, you can thank Assaph, who, after reading my first one, convinced me that it could be the beginning of a series.

A special thank you to Karim and Andrea for their inspiration and encouragement. Andrea is from a rural region in Venezuela, where they tell an old tale about a specter called El Silbón. I hope she'll forgive me for the artistic license I took with her excellent rendition of the story.

A big tip of the fedora to Duffy Weber, who never fails to kill it with his production and narration of my audiobooks. Incidentally, I used his name without permission in this book, and I hope he doesn't sue. Any resemblance between the real Duffy and my Duffy Hunbatz character—other than the fact that both occasionally hang by their toes from tree branches—is coincidental.

I thank anyone who ever gave me the slightest bit of encouragement or support. I've received a lot of great advice, and, if I didn't take it, that's my fault, not yours.

Finally, a big thank you to anyone and everyone who has read my books and taken the time to rate or review them. Every review—good or bad—helps me in the end. Readers have an abundance of choices, and I appreciate every one of you who chose to read something I wrote. It's been a great ride, and I can't wait for you to see what's coming next!

About the Author

My parents raised me right. Any mistakes I made were my own. Hopefully, I learned from them.

I earned a doctorate in medieval European history at the University of California Santa Barbara. Go Gauchos! I taught world history at a couple of colleges before settling into a private college prep high school in Monterey. After I retired, I began to write an urban fantasy series featuring hardboiled private eye Alexander Southerland as he cruises through the mean streets of Yerba City and interacts with trolls, femme fatales, shapeshifters, witches, and corrupt city officials.

I am happily married to my wife, Rita. The two of us can be found most days pounding the pavement in our running shoes. We both love living in Monterey, California, with its foggy mornings, ocean breezes, and year-round mild temperatures. Rita listens to all of my ideas and reads all of my work. Her advice is beyond value. In return, I make her coffee and tea whenever she wants it. It's a pretty sweet deal. We have two cats now, Cinderella and her new pal Prince. Both of them are happy to stay indoors. Cinderella continues to demand that we tell her how pretty she is, especially since we brought an interloper into the fold. Prince is excitable and loves to play for hours at a time until he drops from exhaustion.

Printed in Great Britain
by Amazon